TREACHERIES OF THE SPACE MARINES

Edited by
Christian Dunn

BLACK LIBRARY

A BLACK LIBRARY PUBLICATION

First published in Great Britain in 2012 by
Black Library,
Games Workshop Ltd.,
Willow Road, Nottingham,
NG7 2WS, UK.

10 9 8 7 6 5 4 3 2 1

Cover illustration by Hardy Fowler.

A CIP record for this book is available from the British Library.

UK ISBN: 978 1 84970 211 9
US ISBN: 978 1 84970 212 6

See Black Library on the internet at
www.blacklibrary.com

Find out more about Games Workshop
and the world of Warhammer 40,000 at
www.games-workshop.com

Printed and bound by CPI Group (UK) Ltd, Croydon, CR0 4YY

It is the 41st millennium. For more than a hundred centuries the Emperor has sat immobile on the Golden Throne of Earth. He is the master of mankind by the will of the gods, and master of a million worlds by the might of his inexhaustible armies. He is a rotting carcass writhing invisibly with power from the Dark Age of Technology. He is the Carrion Lord of the Imperium for whom a thousand souls are sacrificed every day, so that he may never truly die.

Yet even in his deathless state, the Emperor continues his eternal vigilance. Mighty battlefleets cross the daemon-infested miasma of the warp, the only route between distant stars, their way lit by the Astronomican, the psychic manifestation of the Emperor's will. Vast armies give battle in His name on uncounted worlds. Greatest amongst his soldiers are the Adeptus Astartes, the Space Marines, bio-engineered super-warriors. Their comrades in arms are legion: the Imperial Guard and countless planetary defence forces, the ever-vigilant Inquisition and the tech-priests of the Adeptus Mechanicus to name only a few. But for all their multitudes, they are barely enough to hold off the ever-present threat from aliens, heretics, mutants - and worse.

To be a man in such times is to be one amongst untold billions. It is to live in the cruellest and most bloody regime imaginable. These are the tales of those times. Forget the power of technology and science, for so much has been forgotten, never to be re-learned. Forget the promise of progress and understanding, for in the grim dark future there is only war. There is no peace amongst the stars, only an eternity of carnage and slaughter, and the laughter of thirsting gods.

CONTENTS

THE MASTERS, BIDDING

by Matthew Farrer

IN THE DAYS between the third and final Waaagh! Ung-skar and the wars that the Imperium was to name the Greyblood Tribulations, Chengrel of the Iron War-riors greeted four visitors in his fortress home among the wrecked worlds of the Mitre Gulf.

It was an outlandish procession that came from the landing craft which had touched down at his outer walls. Chengrel watched it with surly suspicion, for all that he had invited these visitors himself. The paths were lit up with the riotous clamour of the Emperor's Children and the more regal but equally dazzling livery of the Thousand Sons. The Night Lords cloaked their armour and kept their silence, but the Word Bearers hoisted their banners proudly and lifted their voices in discordant songs of worship. Chengrel glowered at them all as they converged on the meeting-square he had built, exchanging taunts and boasts.

They had landed in a great ring of fortifications that Chengrel had erected on the world he had claimed, a place designed to flaunt his power. In a half-circle around the eastern walls he had built stone ziggurats capped with platforms for the landers, and broad fields in which his visitors could set their pavilions. In the centre of the ring were the ruins of an old Imperial settlement, and in these ruins was the meeting-square beneath a canopy of wiry and blighted trees, just large enough for Chengrel to confer with only his most distinguished guests. There was a surrounding wall and an arch for his guests to file through, and a stone platform upon which Chengrel himself could stand and address them.

Chengrel had made his own home out of a crashed orkish raider-ship, which had ploughed into the world's surface during the fiercest fighting of the Waaagh! years before. He had hollowed out the great mound of hull, sunk pits into the rock beneath it, and filled the space with barracks, forges and batteries. The ramming-prow was rebuilt into a high-crowned gate and processional down which Chengrel could lead his warriors when he wished to hunt, or to go forth to war.

It was when Chengrel first picked over the wreck of this ship that he had found an unusual prize. In a net of fine diamond-fibre were a full dozen stones, fist-sized, gently curved almost like eggs, impossibly hard, so smooth they were almost slick to the touch, and such a deep and lustrous red that they almost seemed to burn. Chengrel knew full well what he had found, although not how they had come to be there. Had the eldar really allowed so many soulstones to fall into the hands of the orks? Or had the stones already been torn from their dead owners' baubles that caught a greenskin's eye when their original collector had become a trophy in their own turn? No matter. Although Chengrel himself had little direct use for the stones, he knew many others valued them as precious indeed, and so he sent out his heralds.

For four responses. That gnawed at his pride. Certainly, Chengrel had not expected every one of his summons to be answered. Some of his heralds had been unable to find their recipients amongst the churn of the Eye of Terror or along the perpetual trails of war that the Traitor Legions blazed. Others had returned with rebuffs, and some had not returned at all. But still, no more than four. Was there some plot afoot among the other Legions to defame him and isolate him? What enemies were moving against him?

So thinking, he went down from his fortress to greet his guests.

MASTER CHENGREL WAS an Iron Warrior of old, who had earned his scars and his honours at the walls of the Imperial Palace during the last fearful days of the Horus Heresy. Millennia of fighting the Long War had taken its toll on his body, stripping the flesh and then breaking the steel which replaced it. Now Chengrel's remains floated in a thick flesh-syrup within a great four-legged Dreadnought built to his personal design. His face, miraculously untouched by war but bloated and puffy like a baby's, peered out at the world through a hemisphere of armoured glass built onto the hulk's front, with eyes that writhed as though their sockets were packed with maggots.

What those eyes now saw was the four emissaries striding into the square, each seeking to outdo the others in the arrogance and power of their bearing. Chengrel had set out a half-circle of iron chairs for his guests, adorned with sullenly glowing gems and angular scrollwork, and now each wordlessly paid their respects to their host and took their seats.

On the far left sat Hodir of the Night Lords, dressed in worn and pitted battle armour over which he had thrown a cloak of shining black feathers. Every so often, luminous blue-white trails would crawl and sizzle from the cloak and worm their way over the surfaces of his warplate. At each hip was a braided leather rope to which the scalps of his enemies were fixed with wire, each rope trailing far behind him as he walked. As he sat he drew them in, coiling them about his feet and stroking the scalps as though they were pets.

To his right, second in the arc, was Emmesh-Aiye of the Emperor's Children, a notorious reaver and architect of degeneracies. Emmesh-Aiye's skin was pallid and wrinkled, the mark of the neural mites with which he had infested himself on some trackless death world to ensure the constant, agonising stimulation of his nerves. He was armoured in a breastplate of dazzlingly polished silver, studded all down its length with barbed hooks and metal burrs of exquisite fineness and elegance, and he wore his tongue stretched from his mouth, drawn down and pinned over these spikes, so that he could toss his head and relish the sensation of the tender meat being torn.

Third was the Word Bearer Drachmus, who placed in front of his seat a brass bowl of smouldering ash that was his personal talisman. This ash was made from the burning bones of Imperial Adeptus Astartes whom he had defeated but who refused to turn their loyalties to the Ruinous Powers he served; worked so that they would burn forever in the bowl and never be consumed. Atop the left pauldron of Drachmus's ancient and dark red plate rode a tiny gargoyle whose belly was all bright clockwork and engines, but whose limbs and head were daemon-flesh. The creature grasped one of the great steel horns on his helm and whispered passages from the works of Lorgar in a tiny, scratching voice.

The fourth in the arc, sitting at Chengrel's right, was Khrove of the Thousand Sons, who had arrived alone declaring himself the envoy of the several sorcerer-lords to whom Chengrel had sent heralds. Khrove was dressed in the baroque custom of his Legion, his armour and cloak worked with lustrous blue and gold, adorned with a rich azure surcoat whose hem shimmered with all the colours the eye could describe and with the indescribable hues of the warp. In one arm he cradled a tall adamantine staff, inlaid with threads of psycho-reactive crystal and topped with a great darkened sapphire.

Chengrel's head bobbed in its little curved window as he looked from one to the other, his displeasure unabated. He resolved to make it known from the first who was the master of masters here, and addressed the other legionaries with the following.

'Resolve upon my words, my blood-cousins and fellow champions of the Legions! You attend here upon Chengrel, birthed a child of long-razed Olympia and wrought a blood-child of great Perturabo, mighty among all the primarchs! Named Iron Warrior in the Great Crusade of old and named Traitor when our Legion-fathers rose up to make an eternal corpse of the one who named himself Emperor, in punishment for his vanity and his faithlessness! Made outcast when our Legion was forced from the ramparts of Terra, and made master on unconquerable Medrengard when my warsmith saluted my prowess before Perturabo's gates and in sight of my company!

'It is I who claim this world and make this fortress of it, and I who recovered these caged souls before you,' for the lustrous stones were set at Chengrel's feet, flanked by two of Chengrel's most trusted Terminator guard. 'And although I shall dispose of these stones to whichever of you offers the greatest tribute in exchange, you must acquit yourselves in another way.' The grate of his voice from his speakers mixed with the creak of metal and the hiss of pistons as his tank shifted on its stout legs.

'I am no beast-thrall or petty hetman such as think themselves grand for raising up a rabble in the Eye of Terror or on some decaying colony world,' he told them. 'And I shall treat with none who are not my peers. For your bids you shall present not only your material offerings, but an accounting. You shall tell, on the honour of your Legions, of a feat of arms and generalship, showing yourself most deserving of this prize.

'And consider now the evidence of my goodwill and

favour, for before you begin your bids I shall furnish you with an account of myself, by which you shall know my power and my worth.'

In this way Chengrel of the Iron Warriors began his tale.

'ACCURSED ARE THE sons of Dorn, who call themselves the Imperial Fists! Accursed are the sons of Guilliman, who call themselves the Ultramarines!

'Do you recall the face of Dorn? His vanity and his intransigence? His petulance? His worming sycophancy?

'Do you recall the face of Guilliman? His arrogance and his presumption? His treachery? His cowardice?

'What soothing balm it was to see those faces at the Iron Cage! Dorn's cries in the trenches, Guilliman's dismay when he saw what we had made of his weakling brother. These were memories I took care to harden against the passage of time and to return to over and again. By the day of my ascension to my own command, when I watched a cohort of Iron Warriors raise their fists above their heads and shout their loyalty to me, I knew my first endeavour would be to once again see the sign of the Fist and the sign of the Omega brought low together.

'Heggoru! This was the world I chose for my purpose. Slow-boiling Heggoru with its shifting lands of slick, grey rock and the rich red cauldrons of its oceans under sulphur skies. I had passed close by there in Crusade – and you, any of you, did your fleets take you into the galactic south-west? No answer? No matter. At Heggoru, we heard, the Imperial Fists had celebrated the world's compliance with a ring of great works around the polar coast. Towering hive-cities, thrusting high above the heat-haze of the land, linked one to the next with bullet-rails and laser nets that flickered in the cloudy dusks.

'The Imperial Fists had crowned Heggoru, so they said, given it a regal coronet to celebrate its accession to our Human Imperium. We laughed to hear that, until we saw that Perturabo did not laugh, but looked at the picts through hooded eyes and then turned his back upon them. From then on we only spoke of "yellow-crowned Heggoru" in soft and bitter tones.

'Much later, too long and strange a time of warp-faring for me to know the years, the name came to my ears again, as I roamed that tract of space brooding upon how best the Crusade's work could be unworked again. The warp was thick with the babble of Imperial astropaths, and when my own seers plucked the connections between their minds we found the hailing codes of the Ultramarines, the strutting and preening heirs of the strutting and preening Guilliman. They boasted of an Ultramarine's triumph, doubtless unearned. Bloodshed had come to Heggoru in the form of reaving xenos whose nests the Ultramarines had purged. What water-blooded things the Thirteenth have become, to boast of this as a mighty victory! But boast they did, and when I led my loyal Iron Warriors back to Heggoru their words still burned in my mind.

'Their words burned, so we burned the cities to match them. We re-crowned Heggoru in the rich yellow of flame, not the spiritless yellow of the Seventh's banners. We showed the defenders of the Dorn-built cities who was the more steeped in siegecraft. Our lance and battery strikes tore the atmosphere until it boiled, scrubbing whole flights of their attack craft out of the skies, forcing their defence silos to try to track us through superheated clouds and radiation static while we bombarded them with precision. Twenty days we jousted with their cannons from orbit, the sum of the numbers of Guilliman's and Dorn's Legions, and on the twenty-first we took to our landers to bring the little mortals their doom with our own hands.

'I was not as you see me, not then. I strode to war in Terminator array, badged in adamantium and black and yellow. I rode with my assault pioneers in the first flight of storm-torpedoes, spearing through the skin of Roeghym Hive, whose voids had crumbled to us. The upper hive had been sloped to deflect just such an entry, layered and honeycombed to rob a storm-torp of its momentum and trap it in a maze of half-collapsed cells. But those we left behind in the Imperium are stupid, my brothers, and they forget. The defences had been quarried hollow, leached of their strength by complacent generations. Ah, the glorious clamour of a storm-torpedo's passage into an enemy bastion! There are moments in a siege more satisfying, but few more exhilarating.

'Once we were in among them they forgot any fortitude they had known, and fled from us. I had vowed that I would spend my shells only in true combat, and so instead slew with my power fist and the raking-spikes of my armour, painting my arm in blood to the shoulder. The blood and dust from our bombardment made a red-grey slurry on my fist, which stained the golden aquila from the temple spire when I crushed it in my claws.'

Chengrel's head twitched and bobbed in its fluid as the memories of the slaughter excited him more and more.

'What worth now, the pride of Dorn? Had he made something that could stand against us? He had not! Roeghym was our breach and into it we poured. The Emperor's flocks were panic-blind, and only one of the neighbouring hives thought to destroy its bullet-rail links in time. To reward them, my artisans built blast-carriages that rode out along the rails faster than sound, wrecking themselves where the rails had been severed and flinging plasma charges into the flanks of Tolmea Hive. Along the other line to Behremvalt Hive went the hive's own cars, wrapped in cunning armour fashioned by my metalworkers and warpsmiths, filled with warriors I had handpicked to present my greetings. Cold-armoured, cold-eyed siege teams, adept in crippling a hive's vital systems or weakening its adamantium and carbon-foam bones. And, the fire to their frost, hot-blooded berserkers, brothers who had forsworn their loyalty to the Throne of Gold and pledged it to the Throne of Skulls.

'No one who has not built a fortress can truly understand what it is to destroy one. A fortress falls the way a warrior falls, and every fortress's death is unique. Every tine in Heggoru's coronet died its own death.

'Tolmea died like a warrior before an enemy's guns, its side caved by the plasma charges like a breastplate breached by a bolt-round. For two days it staggered in a death agony and sagged over the crater in its side as a man might double over a death-wound, and then the peak and shoulder fell in upon the foundations, crumpling in that obeisance to dying that we have all seen on the battlefield. The pall from the collapse still shrouded its ruin as we took our leave from Heggoru.

'Behremvalt was stung by our troop trains like an unwitting scout stung by death world vermin. My warriors were the infection, the venom. The berserkers roared through its halls like a fever in the veins, wetting the toothed chains of their weapons so deeply that they may still drip with Behremvalt blood today. My own Iron Warriors were a subtler poison, stopping the organs and nerves: they crippled the power and data lines, the air and water purifiers, the climate controllers, and left Behremvalt's corpse dark and still.

'Massoga Hive perished like a trooper whose foot has kicked a mine. A seismic bombardment cracked its geothermal core and the shockwave of magma that burst up through its foundations toppled the hive, lit up the night and choked the sky. Dekachel Hive bled out, its populace streaming out onto the hot gravel of the wastelands as we wounded the upper levels. Kailenga Hive died a coward's death, paralysed by the sight of true war, torn between trying to evacuate itself, fight or surrender. The indecision robbed it of sinew and made it prey for us. Dauphiel Hive, weakened the most by the xenos purging, died a death worthy of respect, the death of a wounded veteran who will not allow his wound to humble him.

'It ended in madness, at Attegal Hive, with all the

rest of Dorn's coronet left behind us in ruin. My berserkers still rode their rage, as though their fury was a furnace and the endless bodies they scythed through just fuel to stoke it. Some had drowned so deep in bloodlust that they chased fleeing refugees away into the wastes and could not be recalled, but the rest put the sacking of Dauphiel at their backs and lunged across the wastes. When they exhausted the fuel in their own transports, they pillaged the refugee columns for trucks or gravel-crawlers; when they had burned out the engines of their new steeds, they tore them apart in pique and rushed on, on foot. They had run loose in bloody delirium through half of Attegal before we caught up and saw their handiwork.

'We found Khorne's sigil hacked into the rockcrete walls with chainblades, or scrawled in the blood slicks that ran in the roadways. We heard the guttural prayers they had set the hive's address systems to repeating, beneath squeals and crackles as the power of the name surpassed the fragile vox-circuits' tolerances. We heard them screaming the name of their god over the scream of chain-teeth biting bone.

'Now their brass-shod master's gaze fell on them, counting the skulls they littered in their wake for him, and as Attegal Hive became a slaughtering-pen he made his favour known. Some berserkers seemed to be running through water, leaving ripples and wakes behind them. Others cast too many shadows, which reared and thrashed with a life of their own. The smoky breeze carried howls and snatches of shrieking laughter that came from no human throat. Gash-marks and bloodstains began to scar the walls where there were none to make them. The daemons of Khorne were making themselves manifest.

'In silence my brothers and I left the charnel-floor to the berserkers and climbed through the hive. We witnessed screeds etching themselves into its walls, blasphemies bursting from the vox-horns, faces forming in the clouds beyond the window-walls. The trees in the arboreta had turned blood-red and sprouted thorns like fangs, and their boughs thrashed in time with the heart-drums of the daemons below them.

'Standing at the pinnacle of Attegal Hive I proclaimed our task complete. We cast down the golden aquila that had spread its wings atop the final tine of Heggoru's coronet, and in its place raised our own marker, a single upright girder decked in adamantium and yellow and black as our own armour was, splashed with blood from Khorne's killing-house below us.

'The hives of Heggoru burned! The legacy of Dorn was trampled and cast down!

'The verminous Imperials of Heggoru perished! The labours of the children of Guilliman were in vain!

'And so I show to you the trophies of my victory!'

Into the amphitheatre clattered a procession of Defilers, each bearing the wrecked remains of a golden Imperial aquila high on its hull like a diadem.

'The eagles from each spire-tip that fell into Heggoru's stinking clouds! The prize from my finest conquest! Iron within! Iron without!' The two Terminators guarding the bag of stones took up the Iron Warriors' mantra at Chengrel's shout, and a moment later it began to issue from the speech-horns of the Defilers themselves in counterpoint to their tread. The whole meeting-square filled and rang with the noise.

WHEN THE MONSTROUS parade had passed, Chengrel declared the first day of the gathering to be over, and bade all his guests depart to muse upon his tale and decide for themselves if they had any to match it. Then, satisfied that he had the measure of this meagre assembly, Chengrel returned to his citadel where he withdrew his bloated head deep into his tank and had his chamber shrouded in darkness.

Emmesh-Aiye hurried away to his barbed and scarred cutter-craft – he craved raw sensation after so long with little but words for his senses to batten on. Khrove was behind him on the trail to the landing-camps, but made no effort to enter the shining, pyramidal lander that hung over his ziggurat. Instead he drew his feet up under him, hanging unsupported in the air, and a moment later the ground beneath him creaked and erupted into a great thicket of thorned tendrils formed of strange stuff that seemed at once metallic and gem-like. They enclosed him and hid him from view.

Drachmus the Word Bearer and Hodir the Night Lord went walking more slowly back through the ruins, their cadres filing behind them and studiously ignoring one another.

'How do you consider our host, then?', asked Drachmus after an interval long enough for his little homunculus to have recited the *Four Thousand and Eighty-Second Epistle of Lorgar* in its entirety.

'Old,' Hodir replied thoughtfully, 'Clever. Fortunate.' He looked behind him. 'Well-guarded.'

'Fortunate,' Drachmus replied with equal care. 'Fortunate, indeed. And one whose fortunes will bear watching. Perhaps we are of one mind here?' Hodir was generous enough to concede this with an inclining of his dark-helmed head. 'Well then,' Drachmus went on, 'we shall hear more of this convocation soon.' He did not bow or salute, but made a deliberate step away to show the conversation was at an end. Hodir did likewise, weaving his feet so as not to crush his ropes of scalps, and the two parted to return to their camps.

SEVENTEEN HOURS PASSED before a klaxon sounded from Chengrel's fortress, the blaring followed by a quartet of household serfs, who scattered out through the ruins and to the landing-pads with the message that the master would soon be ready for the new day's audience.

Khrove was the first to return, appearing from his nest of vines as it unravelled and striding alone to the meeting-square to take his seat. After a few moments footsteps sounded behind him, and over them came the voice of Drachmus's daemon-homunculus droning through the opening stanzas of *Meditations on Two Transcendences*. It was one of Lorgar's more pedestrian works, and the papery little monotone did nothing to capture what nuances it did have. Hodir took his seat, settling silently into the same posture he had had for the previous audience. The addition of two silver armatures mounted on his armour's backpack, which now kept his scalp-ropes suspended in a cat's cradle above his head, was the only sign he had moved at all.

Emmesh-Aiye was the last to join them. He still wore his silver breastplate, although his tongue had been unpinned from it and rearranged on a different sequence of hooks. Across his shoulders was a mantle of glass links, deliberately crude in make so that they grated against one another with a sound to put the teeth on edge. Maddening as the sound was to those around him, it clearly soothed Emmesh-Aiye, whose amplified hearing craved input in this relative quiet.

Chengrel broke that quiet for them, his tank-hulk walking into the enclosure with a heavy tread and taking up position on his stone platform.

'I have granted you ample time to prepare yourselves,' he boomed. 'Now we shall see what you bring me in return. Look to your own accounts. Hodir! Night Lord! Master Hodir, son of the fallen Curze! You shall speak first. Begin.'

If Hodir took offence at the curt instruction, he gave no sign of it. Instead, he stood and walked towards Chengrel with something in his hand.

Instantly, one of the Iron Warrior's bodyguards came forth, something in a shape that might once have been an armoured Space Marine but which was now a hunched and creaking thing. Its legs were fused together and it moved on a rolling tank-track that had replaced its feet, although this track was made of thick muscle and its treads were bone claws. Its arms ended in bundles of gun-barrels and its face, sprouting directly from its neck between clusters of thick steel horns, was a leering mask made of tarnished ceramite. A meaty tongue flopped through the mask's mouth-slit and tasted the air.

'I intend no violence to your master, and none to

you,' Hodir told it, 'but since you are studying me for him, then examine this.' He held out the thing he was carrying: a triangle of white and yellow cloth, obviously cut from a larger piece, embroidered with a complex design. As the green-black tongue lapped the air near it, Hodir turned it over to show that it had been sewn, back-to-back, with a triangle of human skin.

'Skin only recently stripped,' Hodir declared. 'Can you sense that?' The bodyguard, uncertain of its reply, swivelled on its squelching, clicking tread-foot and looked up at Chengrel. 'Fresh to confirm that we do have him, and that he's still alive and healthy. He was when I set out to visit you, anyhow. From there on you must take us on faith.'

'You give me riddles,' replied Chengrel amid the thrum of his speakers. 'Give me an offering and an accounting, or be sent back to tell your Legion of my disappointment with their envoy.'

Hodir did bristle at that, drawing himself up and letting the others see that his free hand had made a fist. But he kept his temper and turned so he addressed both Chengrel and the other Traitor Marines.

'If I am to recount something for my bid,' he said, pointedly not using Chengrel's word offering, 'then my account and my bid go together. Here.' He held up the sewn flap of skin and cloth again. 'I will explain what it is, how we came by it, and what it is worth. To all of you.'

Hodir of the Night Lords began his tale.

'THE TATTOO ON this skin,' declared Hodir, 'is a Navigator crest, the sign of the House of Drunnai. A House of no particular glory. I had not heard of them before the man who yielded us his skin told us his name. Vivyre Drunnai. A young one, but a skilled one. How skilled, you shall see.

'Vivyre Drunnai is not the bid, but he is part of it.

'Now. There is a warp-vortex northward of the Tembine Drifts in the galactic north-west that pierces down through the galactic plane. It boiled there when the Crusade first mapped the borders of what they now call Obscuras, and it boils there still. The violence of the funnel-current is fed by the storms radiating out from the Eye below and north-east of it. Shipmasters driven by haste or hubris sometimes catch the edge of the tide and let it fling them towards Cypra Mundi, but it is a turbulent, dangerous passage. Its lower reaches, I am told, have never been charted, and who is to say if there is any end to it? Perhaps it plummets out of our galaxy and continues forever down into the gulfs. Drift too close into the funnel of the storm and you will be dragged in and dragged apart. There is no surviving it.

'The vortex is not the prize, but it is part of it.

'There is a place where the vortex bends through an angle from the push of a counter-tide, and there the storm's cohesion breaks. That is the Jaw, where a storm-whirl juts out like a greenskin's chin. It throws out blast-fronts that are felt sectors away, vortices that spin for a hundred light years before they exhaust themselves. It makes storm-stitched patterns that wriggle and swim and fight to come to life. And it disgorges ships. The Molianis Reach in real space out beyond the Jaw is a hulks' graveyard like few others. The storm drags ships from their courses and plunges them through who knows what depths, and the gravity well of Molianis's great blue star is where so many of them are dragged back again. A trail of wrecks, parsecs long, strung out and drifting.

'The ships' graveyard is not the prize, but it is part of it.

'The Imperium sits with their back to it! They are so sure that this great ships' graveyard is a graveyard indeed, and no threat to them. They have built a fortress at the far end of the stream of wreckage. A magnificent thing, truth be told, tier on tier of gun decks, lance mounts, deep-gauge auspex arrays. It trails free-floating fortifications behind it, communications boosters, munitions depots, shipyards and repair docks. Squadrons of warships fuss around it. The scale of the place has grown. They are colonising other moonlets nearby so the fortress crews can expand. Who knows? Perhaps Molianis might one day house a world's worth of colonists.

'The fortress is not the prize, but it is part of it.

'The Imperials are sure that the stream of warp-wreck emerges from the storm broken beyond all chance of threat. Fitful patrols through the graveyard sweep the hulks with auspex, and they mutter on the vox about quarantine checks, wrecks to be sterilised of genestealers and ransacked. Beyond Molianis there are thickly-infested orkish enclaves, and so the Imperium's attentions turn that way. The goal is to place an Imperial eye between the greenskins and the graveyard, to make sure that no salvage can fall into orkish hands and into their war machine.

'The Imperium's unguarded flank is not the prize, but a part of it.'

While he spoke, Hodir had been walking slowly to

and fro beneath the window in Chengrel's tank-hulk, while the Iron Warrior looked down at him with an expression intended to show benevolent indulgence. Now he faced the other bidders, again holding up his token of stitched skin and cloth.

'We went raiding, my Night Lords and I, in the Greater Tembine Drift, which stretches out across the north-eastern quadrant like a shoulder blade. Ships striking out from the rich worlds of the Lesser Tembine Drift and pushing up through the unsettled layer between them can expect a long and tranquil voyage, coasting on the gentle outward pressure of the drift-tide towards the far northern marches of the Ultima Segmentum. Such was the voyage our prey had in mind when they ignited their drives at Isith.

'It was a supply convoy, heavy and slow like fattened cett-cows, plodding towards the reaches with materiel from the Mechanicus forges. Fusion-formed alloys, tailored reactant blocks for plasma furnaces, biological stock, weapons, machines. We heard tell that the cargo was on its way to a string of new colonial hives. We had other intentions for it.

'You need not hear the details of how we struck and what we took. All of us know the ways of these things. You can imagine the ambush and the boarding. We had three of the four ships by the time they reached the Isith jump-zones, plucked them where the Imperial flotillas could not defend them. The convoy's lead ship was the *Hymn of Phelinde*, and I marked her as my prey and my prize. We harried her with weapon-bursts and vox-taunts. We collected vox-signals from the taking of the other craft, boosted them and beamed them into the *Hymn of Phelinde*, to let them hear how they die, those who fight the Night Lords, and when they did not surrender we opened our own engines and bore down on them, skewering their hull with lance-cuts and flying assault boats into the wounds, driving the crew into their suits, ready for the fighting.

'To a Night Lord, shipboard survival suits are a weapon in themselves. They blinker the sight, with their little goggle insets or their narrow visors, so the prey's imagination fills their blocked peripheral vision with monsters almost the equal of the monsters we are. They blur the hearing and fill it with scratches and garbling echoes to taunt tight-strung nerves. In those lucky enough to have vox-circuits, they open themselves to our whispers and screams should we find and break their transmission band, and we always, always do. They surround the limbs with heavy wrappings, burdening movements, concentrating the sense in each prey's mind that they are cut off, alone, their companions now unfamiliar shapes on the other side of a visor.

'To a Night Lord, each of these things is like a slender stiletto, planted in the enemy before we even lay hand to them.

'We breached some sections of the *Hymn* to space. In others we pumped dusts and toxins into the airflows, or bled superheated gas from the plasma pipes to send firestorms through whole decks, then walked through flames and chemical smoke to cut apart repair teams. We let word of us travel up the ship, always leaving one prey alive long enough to scream a warning into a speaking-horn or flee to spread panic in person. We cut the lighting to whole decks, then left those decks to panic while we showed ourselves in compartments that had thought themselves uninvaded. Then we made those levels erupt in cries or fall silent forever, so that as we worked our way towards the bridge we were fighting enemies tormented almost to madness by their own fear. This is our way, and if you, my fellows, have fought alongside us then you will know it for yourselves.

'The only way this prey-boat could think to fight back was to spite us of our prize, and drag us into the immaterium to die with them. The ship began to shake around us, and we heard the alarms in the corridors and the prayers and weeping of those who knew what they meant. We had not wrecked the warp engines, not when there would be salvage to be had there, and the captain had given the order to breach.

'We had little time. We had broken through in a calm current, but soon the fear and the violence would echo, cohere and turn in on us. Geller field systems are tenuous things even on an undamaged craft. We had to move swiftly.

'Now we became true predators, dealing out quick butchery in place of slow terror. By the time we had scoured the crew-decks and mustered at the base of the bridge tower, hot shadows were moving in the *Hymn of Phelinde*'s warp-wake, and as we brushed aside the last surviving crew we could all feel the ship shudder and our thoughts twist as conscious force began to grip the Geller field and crush.

'There were none left living among the bridge crew. By the time we reached them some had turned on the others. Fear? An attempt to mutiny and make for real space again? Warp-phantoms colouring their thoughts? No matter. But then we found that the captain had ceded control of the helm directly to the Navigator roost. Our steersman now was Vivyre Drunnai. And Drunnai's order was to plunge the ship into that vortex that leads to the Jaw, to be torn apart down to its adamantine bones and its plasma heart.

'And now the battle for the *Hymn of Phelinde*, and for our own lives, began in earnest.

'Engineering servitors had welded the shutter-doors to the final sanctum that held the captain's and Navigator's eyries, the welds new enough to still glow in our infrared as we broke through. All the while the vortex tides tore at the Geller field like a butcher trying to flay a carcass with too blunt a knife. We could feel the hottest humours of the immaterium trying to boil into our thoughts.

'Three servitors were still there, sealed in with instructions to try and fight us. Two had had their welding torches broken so that we could not commandeer them, and those two assaulted us with rivet-drivers that scarred our armour with red-hot plugs of alloyed steel.' Hodir turned now, dipping one shoulder to show chips and scoring along one rim of his pauldron. 'The third rushed at us with its torch still ignited and Gyaz, who aspired to lead my Second Claw and is boastful and eager, stepped forwards to show how he could cut it down. Then we heard the ultrasonic whine of its power pack and understood its purpose; it was overcharged and about to explode, and so Gyaz shot it apart instead.

'In the captain's roost all light was extinguished, as though he thought darkness might discomfit us. But we could see the smashed holotank, the displays and consoles slagged by the servitors' torches, and we knew then how desperate we had made this man for him to mutilate his most sacred sanctum like this. He intended to take away all hope we had of breaking back through into the materium.

'The captain himself was a dim shape behind the glassaic of his support cocoon. "Kill me now if you must, traitors," he told us through the brass horns that clustered at the corners of the room, "or let the warp take me as it will take you. And let mine be the last loyal life you murder before you yourselves stand before Him for your final, immortal rebuke."

'With that he abandoned his threats and turned to prayers, which began to distort and be intertwined with more profane voices and more obscene words as warp influences trickled through the failing Geller field and began to alter the ship. But we realised that not all the screaming in the vox-horns was the work of… outside. No intruder from the warp would ever have cried out an Imperial prayer, or plead for the captain to show mercy and rescind his order. The voice was Vivyre's, losing his mind to fear as he saw before him a fate that Navigators must understand more keenly than any of us.

'The captain roared back, his voice shaking the horns, and even with only those mechanisms to give him speech rather than his own throat and tongue, even as the ship's gravity began to fail and light and sound to distort, we could hear the note of command in that voice that must have propelled his crew to take up arms against us even in their terror. He shouted into the storm, telling the Navigator to obey his captain and his Emperor, lay down his life and soul and deny the traitors to the last.

'Ulsh breached his cocoon and killed him then. "Traitor" has never been a label he has cared for.

'Now the guidance of the ship fell solely to Drunnai, and I knew I would perish there. Navigator's commands must pass through the captain's own systems to be turned into intricate orders to the helm and crew, manipulating all the ship's systems in concert. What little direct control a Navigator normally wields could not prepare him for this. We were as good as adrift, at the mercy of the vortex.

'So I thought. So we all thought. But here is a lesson all Night Lords know: terror transforms. And when Drunnai thought himself lost, his terror ousted all conscious thought. He could not bring himself to abandon his soul to the warp.

'And so we rode the vortex down. How? I do not know how. I am no Navigator, nor a seer,' and here Hodir gave an inclination of his helm towards Khrove, who returned the politeness in kind. 'But I have seen warriors lent a genius by terror. Who amongst you has not seen it, friend or enemy, terror fuelling their prowess until it burns them out entire? Navigator Drunnai, who had steered us into a suicide plunge against orders he had never wished to hear, now broke those orders and fought for his life against the storm.

'I remember moments of calm when the ship spun in its length so fast that the failing gravity was overwhelmed and we skidded and crashed against the walls. Uzchel, our best demolisher whose chainfists had cut our way from the bridge, was thrown into the dead captain's cocoon and vented his fury on the corpse and its systems.

'I remember the times when the vortex stripped the field away from us, and Drunnai would shriek with panic to match the shrieking of the ship's hull. The shrieks, too, of whatever was grasping the hulk of the ship. Cries of pain at contact with matter, perhaps, or of pleasure at having this new strange thing to play with. Perhaps they were born of no emotion any of us could understand. Perhaps some were even from survivors elsewhere on the ship, meeting the fate from which Drunnai was fleeing. At these times the whole ship would lash back and forth like a crotalid's tail.

'I remember seeing the controls come to life again. The slag of the instrument panels began to writhe and rearrange itself, and a ghostly form of the holotank lit up over the wreck of the original. They lit up and showed us our own faces, and faces we had murdered and faces we had fought with, and turned them into faces such as no human has ever worn. Electricity leapt between the craters in the instrument panels, the arcs rising up and taking on shapes I cannot describe, for they have left only pock-holes in my memory. I remember that the sound of the engines, the great deep note that permeates every starship, never ceased, but it faltered and choked, and sometimes became a rhythmic sound like a living heartbeat, and sometimes like laughter. Uzchel said he heard whispers in it, and when he tried to talk back to them whatever those whispers told him in reply made him howl and swing his chainfists at empty space in front of him.

'The form of the ship began to soften and stretch around us. The captain's remains flowed and blended, the debris they lay in bubbled and shifted. Parts of it turned to emerald, parts to blood and parts to light.

The whole chamber stretched and narrowed. The deck under our feet suddenly darkened with corrosion and spat little puffs of dust, but as we looked back through the door we saw the antechamber's walls turn to ribbed bone, gasp and rattle with some manner of life, then fossilise in seconds and become stone. Dancing lights cackled and chased each other around our heads. Gyaz shot a bolt-shell at one, and it turned from the chase and enveloped him for no more than a second. When it pitched him to the deck and departed, he thrashed on the floor and told us that it had dragged him into itself and toyed with him for thirteen years.

'How long all this lasted I do not know. I can tell you that four months passed by the sidereal calendars between us breaching warp at Isith and overhearing our first Imperial transmissions at Molianis, but to most of us that plummet down the vortex seemed to take only days. But we all know the fickleness of the warp and time.' The other legionaries made small motions to indicate their assent.

'Finally, however, the vortex gave us up. After a final, wrenching convulsion, the ship began a steady turning that we realised was a drift through real space. The decks and bulkheads ceased to change, leaving the chamber in its strange, angle-less shape. Beyond it we could see the stone ribs of the remade antechamber walls lit by dim starlight. Cautiously, we left the captain's sanctum to see what was left of our prize.

'The warp had remade the *Hymn of Phelinde* beyond any recognition. Her whole form was drawn out and scattered as though something in the warp had pegged her out on a dissecting table. The hull had opened up to space, in some places looking torn open, in some places simply gone, as though melted or dissolved or stretched until it had parted. In some places it had even grown. A ridge of excrescences had pushed out of the hull along the port side that aped the shape of the bridge tower, even growing vestigial windows. Vanes and turrets had been shorn off or had sunk back into the surrounding hull to form strange, organic-looking shapes. The plasma engines had finally fallen silent, and we could see the tail of the ship cold, with no reactor heat or drive plume. In the plasteel of the decking was a set of neat footprints, of bare feet the size of a child's, sunk into the metal the way they will sink into wet sand. They meandered into the bridge and ended there. We never learned what made them.

'But when we turned out attention back the other way we realised that Vivyre Drunnai yet lived. The seals and provitae systems of the Navigator's roost are intended to allow it to function while sealed off unto itself, so that any warp intrusion there might be checked before it can spread to the rest of the ship. Here they had worked in reverse, protecting him from the efforts of the warp to render the *Hymn* down to nothing.

'As we walked back through the wreckage towards the roost we could hear Drunnai mewling on the vox, trying to hail the crew. His systems must have been wrecked by the transit, and his eyes out to the rest of the ship were blind. He did not know that we were the only ones he shared the hulk with now. He called for his captain and his retainers. He pleaded for status reports and sustenance. At times he even seemed unsure whether the ship was still in the warp – I think his senses were still ringing from the storm in the Jaw.

'I think he realised what company the storm had left him with when we began trying to break into the roost. The roost was an easy thing to see now. It had largely withstood the warp erosion, but the hull and decking around it had been reduced almost to lacework. We linked the vox and auto-sensor systems in our armour under the guidance of Hotesh, our signal-smith. These roosts are built with defences and wards, but not against the kind of attack we were mounting now, and not against invaders of our skill. Soon we had control of the internal cogitators of the roost, cut off Drunnai's vox-link and began to use the roost's more powerful systems to spy out our location.

'The sensors of our own armour had registered whipcracks of noise and flickers in our visors, which we dismissed as the after-effects of the tumult from the voyage. But coupled into the Navigator bubble we were able to decipher what they were. We were listening to a cascade of military-strength auspex pings: a stream of them, all tumbled over one another, some from mere light minutes away, others far older and fainter, sounded by ships prowling the other side of the system. The Molianis system.

'With a brilliance born of terror and reflexes strung with the raw instinct to survive, Vivyre Drunnai found a skein of warp-flow down through the vortex from the Tembine Drift into the warp storm of the Jaw. A needle's eye that leads into a blind and undefended flank of a prime Imperial military system.

'The Night Lords will ride on Molianis again.

'And that is the prize. This is what I am empowered to

offer you, Brother Chengrel. Take this crest as a token of alliance. What Drunnai did once, he will do again. Send your finest warriors to ride back down the vortex and through the Jaw with us, or honour us by leading the force yourself. Let us come upon the Imperial sentries whose eyes are all turned outwards, and fall upon them, become their red-eyed nightmares.

'If you wish simply to wound the Imperium, then wound it we shall. If you wish the fortresses of Molianis as your prize then claim them, my Legion has no plans for them. If you wish a share of the plunder when the system is ours, then you shall return to your own fastness with great riches indeed.

'That is the account and the bid of the Night Lords. What say you?'

HODIR FINISHED HIS tale standing directly before Chengrel's tank, with his token upraised. The bodyguard's tongue had once again slipped out and twitched in the direction of the skin. The other three Traitor legionaries sat and studied the embroidery again, allowing their host to be the first one to speak. After a long silence, he did.

'My warsmith imparted good words to me,' he said. 'He told me "there are none among us more cunning than a Night Lord with the opportunity of murder put before him". You understand why I recall those words now.' Hodir made a gesture of assent. 'You had all the makings of an offering that would honour the Night Haunter's memory, Hodir,' Chengrel went on, 'and perhaps, with my own tale to inspire you, you will be able to leave this place and do so.'

The other three, experienced in reading hints of

posture and movement through bulky armour, saw the anger rise in Hodir. They watched as he folded the token with exaggerated care and clipped it at his waist, and they saw how his hands clenched the instant he was not consciously controlling them. Chengrel, not seeing this or not caring, talked on.

'In exchange for your offering, Chengrel of the Iron Warriors gives his salute to your cunning and your audacity. But let my fortress and my account be an instruction to you. You must learn ambition, Hodir. A legionary with ambition befitting his stature would have come to me not begging for alliance, but piling trophies before me. The heads of the Naval captains and commissars, their caps nailed to their skulls, a barge-hold full of materiel looted from their vessels. From Navy vessels, mark you, Hodir. Warships. I would not have accepted an offering of your scroungings from a graveyard of hulks, or some fat and plodding supply convoy.

'So this is your account? Chasing a handful of cargo haulers and being pulled into a storm you had no intention to enter? This is the tale that will have me think your warband great among the Night Lords? You belie your own pretensions to greatness. But still,' and there was a slow burbling as Chengrel made what passed for a sigh, 'if the offerings of these others are more meagre still then I may yet confer the prize upon you.'

As the echoes of his voice died away, the enhanced hearing of the others, Emmesh-Aiye's most of all, detected a small, rhythmic, metallic noise. It was the mechanised joints in Hodir's armour. They were sounding as he rocked almost imperceptibly back and forth, one hand now openly gripping the hilt of the power knife slung at his left hip.

'When the Night Lords return to Molianis,' said Hodir in a voice plainly shaking with the strain of controlling his anger, 'I do not think we will enlist the forces of Master Chengrel as our allies.' For a moment he seemed to have more to say, but instead he walked stiffly to his seat, placed himself upon it and would say no more.

'DRACHMUS!' BOOMED Chengrel as his bodyguard lurched back into the shadows by his tank. 'Drachmus of the Word Bearers! Your Legion has written its history with distinction. I have no doubt that you have a magnificent tribute and majestic tale to bid for my prize. Speak, Drachmus, and stake your claim.'

For a few moments Drachmus still sat, staring down into the bowl of cinders on his lap and listening to the imp on his shoulder declaiming the *Liturgy of Vilemost Blessing*. Finally he seemed to see something in the ashes that pleased him. He placed the bowl carefully on the flagstones and walked to the centre of the half-circle. His gargoyle lowered its head and dropped its voice to a whisper, but never stopped speaking as Drachmus raised his own voice over it.

'Lorgar tells us in the eighth chapter of the *Admonition to the Belocrine Crusade* that "they are contemptible who seek an abdication of the self in subjugation to the transcendent", and now you shall hear how I and my brothers gave exegesis to his words through bold action, through spiritual strength and through the war we brought to the world of Aechol Tertia.

'How wretched was the furthest world in the Aechol

cluster when we came upon it! Tertia had been a world of humanity since ages before our memory, paying tribute to the Great Crusade and its self-proclaimed Emperor. But the shadow of the Imperium waned over the millennia, the grip of the dead faith of the aquila began to slip. Aechol became fickle. One of its worlds fell to the lure of the four-armed marauders heralding the hive-fleets, and only then did the Imperium show a face in the system to stamp out the infection. But they won no love from Aechol by it, and before long Aechol Tertia was in open secession to seek shelter in the fold of yet more xenos – the ambitious and striving tau, who seek not to expunge other races but to subjugate and regiment them under the "Greater Good" in whose name they claim to rule.

'But Lorgar tells us in the *Varigon Encyclical* that "the strong hand cannot be directed by the clouded eye" and as you shall see the eyes of the tau are clouded indeed. Their viceroys promised a just and firm rule of Aechol rather than the capricious and neglectful Imperium, but having taken the reins at Aechol the creatures could not hold them.

'The tau do not understand the warp-touch in the way that humans can. They cannot feel the currents of the god-sea and respond to it, can never share our relationship to the primal. And thus blind, they knew not how to govern once a new generation began to grow on the world they had "freed" for themselves to rule. The children grew. Their children grew. The numbers of psykers grew. And the tau would not understand what was happening. They scoffed at the Imperial traditions as witch-myths peddled by Imperial confessors, to foment anger and weaken the flock for more effective control. And so the warp-touch spilled out upon Aechol Tertia.

'Lorgar tells us in the *Sixty-Four Primary Meditations* that "the gifts of the god-sea must never slip the traces of understanding" and when we saw the fate of Aechol we gave praise to the primarch's words. Here was a world caught between two masters, slipping free of the xenos leash, but not yet back beneath the shadow of the aquila. A world ready for a deeper, grander, truly godly allegiance.

'When we overflew the broad land that rode high against the planet's polar circle like a pauldron on a shoulder, we found the frost-dusted shingle plains crisscrossed with railtracks and pocked with mass-driver silos. When Aechol had been in its prime, the tau had loaded shells full of Aechol's silica sands and rich biocultures, and blasted them into orbit for their freighters to snare and drag back to their own heart worlds. After the tau quit the system, bands of humans came fleeing from the bloodshed further south and turned the stripped silo compounds into refuges. Some still held out, some were abandoned, some had become home to psyker-children and become charnel houses or worse.

'Two of Aechol's continents straddled the equator. The first was a jagged, dislocated thing split by two tectonic seams, knuckled with mountains and restless with earthquake and lava. The humans here were base creatures of no dignity who scavenged the rubble of tau-built cities. In the winters they formed great caravans, travelling to sell their salvage to the surviving cities along the temperate coast. The scavengers prized their psyker-children highly, and willingly took the risks of raising them in order to make them weapons against their rivals.

'The second equatorial continent was low and flat, and stippled with seas and forests where survivors lived and warred. A belief had sprung up there that the psyker resurgence had come upon the world because the tau had fled it, not the reverse, and so they had turned the old tau sandmining rigs in the shallow inland seas into holy places. Here they would congregate according to ceremonial calendars, ritually hang those they suspected of psykerhood, and perform acts of worship to abandoned tau artefacts, pleading for their old xenos masters to return and deliver them. Between the great lakes the rest of the old citizens had taken their loyalty in the other direction, hailing the emergent psykers as their saviours, reaching back for old scraps of memory of the Imperial faith to weave fanciful stories of saints and angels around the mad and possessed creatures whom they made their kings and prophets.

'It was the last continent, and among its serried islands and basalt reefs, where madness had truly incarnated. Here was where the tau had laid down their quarantine camps for what they thought was madness and rebellion, exiling here the first psykers to arise among their subjects as they strove to stay ascendant. By the time we landed there, the black cliffs and lichen groves had become playgrounds to the warp-touched at their maddest and most free. When we stepped from our lander we were greeted by a flayed torso and head that walked towards us on spider-legs made of lightning, calling our names. Behind it crawled a thing made of four human bodies that wriggled along on a tangle of limbs and turned the ground it passed over to bleeding flesh.

'But Lorgar tells us in the second book of the *Tractatus Entropia* that "to some Powers it is given to us to be pupils; to some we are destined to be soldiers, but to others we know ourselves to be their masters, and over some we must understand that we are stewards". So I had sermonised to my brothers before we landed, to resolve them upon our mission. We were here as stewards, as builders and marshals and generals, and the folk of Aechol Tertia, awoken to the grandeur of Chaos, were to us as children now, as pupils given us to guide.

'We sought them out, these wild ones who ran in packs or covens or roamed alone. They were feral, even the potent ones, wild and untrained, and we contained them and brought them to heel, showed them the meaning and the glory of their natures. Others were insane, or given over wholly to something that had entered them as their untrained gifts blazed into the immaterium. We found places where distance and dimension had been mauled and folded in the wake of some calamitous possession that had consumed its host utterly. We found stretches of land burned sterile by warp-fire, or torn up as though by monstrous hands or claws, although we never found any possessed whose forms matched those marks.

'Some we broke to the lash, some we bound with wards and scriptures. Some could not be made subjects, and then with prayers and absolutions we broke the flesh vessel and let the pure essence dissipate back into the warp. Some we harnessed to occult engines or bound into metal beasts of war. And when that land was ours we moved north again.

'On the continent of seas we came as both conquerors and liberators. We subjugated the tribes with might and with zeal and inspiration. Assembled in great throngs along the shores, they watched while we stormed the old tau rigs and slaughtered their enemies there. After that they did not trudge before us as serfs, but marched joyously in our train as acolytes, begging any Word Bearer they saw to teach them, or bless them, or pray over them, for as Lorgar tells us in the *Four Entreaties to Kyush-Beghan*, "it is the breaking of dead loyalties that leads to transfiguration and rapture". We put them to work rebuilding the rig-cities as fortresses, temples and armouries. Then we moved on anew.

'We voyaged to the shore of the great fractured continent and its cities. No great hives these, but sprawls full of violent slums, the compounds of vicious and arrogant nobles, and towers or pits where the raw psykers would congregate and fight or brood. To each city we announced our presence, declared that we were there to teach them a more potent faith than the leprous lies of the Imperium or the bloodless wittering of the tau's "Greater Good". Some cities embraced us and saw us in to preach and teach. Some did not recognise us for what we were and fought, and we sent the smoke of their burning into the sky as a beacon to the faithful.

'We rode out into the volcanic plains at the end of the winter, and by the turning of the summer every scavenger clan was mustered behind a Word Bearers banner and their chieftains pledged to us. When the next winter in turn came we did not allow them to flee to the temperate coasts, no – now we made them prove themselves to us. They raised a chain of shrine-cities across the heart of the continent, then mustered for war and raiding across the sea to the north, doing battle in the bitter winds and bringing Tertia's final continent into our grip.

'We could make the people of Aechol march for twenty-four hours without rest, fight like daemons with autogun or blade or simply their fingers and teeth, and send up a shouted sacrament to the Four Powers in beautiful unison from an assembly that might number ten or ten thousand. Every chieftain could recite the titles of all the works of Lorgar and repeat scriptures on spiritual leadership, fealty, zeal and hatred of the Imperium. Every ordinary subject on Aechol could bow down and say the correct blessings and oaths when a Word Bearer passed them by, and by now every psyker had been bound over to service in the great congregation of Chaos, or had laid down their life in disobedience. We had found Aechol the home to a worthless rabble, and made of it a congregation befitting any temple from Milarro to the palace of the primarch himself.

'Now we remade this world. Every city was rebuilt around its shrine, and we put the forges on our own war-hulk to work to turn out what was needed: weapons, wargear, everything from devotional icons to brands with which to etch the proverbs of Lorgar upon our new soldiers' flesh.

'For we knew what was coming. Our omen-setters had seen an eagle's wings spread across the stars, and been haunted by visions of kneeling before a shrine to the Four Ruins that remade itself into a golden throne amid screams and the crashing of hammers. We knew that the Imperium was on its way.

'And they broke! Broke, my brothers! The aquila's claw broke upon the rock we had made! A flotilla of warships, two great transports of the Imperial Guard, a clarion-craft bonded to the Ecclesiarchal sisterhood, and they could not sway Aechol Tertia from our teaching! Their soldiers disgorged onto the surface in their millions, sure of easy conquest, but we harried them on the frost plains, we savaged them with ambushes and raids as they tried to overthrow the temple-forts beneath the volcanoes, we made them pay a hundred lives for every las-bolt and siege shell they fired at the rig-cities that yet stand in the inland seas!

'The Sisterhood spread out with the Imperial vanguard, to make Aechol buckle once again to Throne and eagle, but now our congregation showed us what they had learned. They marched with their own banners held high, the Eightfold Arrow and the icons of the four greatest behemoths of the god-sea. The Imperials shed blood on the frost, burned our tanks beneath the ash clouds, even felled brother Bearers of the Word in our fortresses... But they could not make our congregants doubt their loyalty. They could not sow treachery among our flock.

'The Guard fought until our counter-attacks rolled them back, exhausted them and crushed them. The Sisters preached and burned until the Aecholi turned on them in flames of rage and destroyed them. They even brought inquisitors, two learned old fools with great retinues whose boasts, we were told, were that they could loosen the hold of Chaos on the most dedicated minds. And both their heads swung by their hair from the front of my Land Raider as we paraded in triumph down the length of the volcanic plains! All their learning and all their violence. And not a single word of treachery could they sow. Aechol Tertia remains a bastion of the Eight Blessings of Chaos, loyal to the true faith to this very day.

'This is what faith can achieve, Master Chengrel! This is the power that worship brings! Does Lorgar not pay tribute to it in the _Pentadict_, and the _Book of Lorgar_, and the _Codex de Barathra_? And so in celebration of what blessings we may earn through worship, here do I present my offer. But say the word, and from my craft up above us I shall bring you an endless scroll, warp-charged, that will hang in the air about you and present you with the words of any and every scripture of Lorgar, moulded to your thoughts and situation, for you to be enlightened and strengthened. With it I offer sixty-four Flesh Prayers, the eyeless and limbless bodies of the enemies of Chaos, now with their minds stripped and left only with the ability to howl out prayers and psalms to Chaos. They are all strong, all will cry out their prayers many times before they perish, and between them they recite every major supplication and blessing from our body of doctrines. Also do I pledge to you four orbital shrine-spires, to be wrought by the finest artisans of my congregation. Each shall be a personal retreat for your worship and meditation, each dedicated to one of the four Powers who are the chief manifestations of that ultimate and divine Ruin to which we all owe fealty. They shall be consecrated in your presence and set in motion about this world, that you and your warband may always know that the gods of the warp watch over you.

'How say you, Chengrel Iron Warrior? Do you accept our price?'

CHENGREL'S FACE HAD distorted in an expression that after a moment became recognisable as concentration. His eyes had drifted closed, and his toothless mouth worked. After a moment he opened his eyes and spoke.

'You speak with great care of your... missionary efforts, and the state of the world before you arrived there. But when you come to the meat and bone of the matter, Drachmus, to the iron of the matter, you leap over it with little care. Is all your story about preaching? About listening to this rabble say their lessons? Have you no pride in how you met the Imperial assault?'

'The war was magnificent,' declared Drachmus in reply, as his little daemon scuttled up behind him, clambered up his back and resumed its perch on his shoulder, whispering all the while. 'But the war was the proof of our work, not the work itself. I have spoken to you of the spreading and marshalling of faith, Master Chengrel. The true faith that our primarchs and ancestors battled the Emperor himself to uphold. Is this not the great work, as Lorgar tells us?'

'It is not, Drachmus!' snarled Chengrel, his tank creaking forwards as he spoke. 'It is not! The great work is not to prate of this verse and that psalm, and these prayers and those books! Shake the dust of Colchis from your feet, Drachmus, and remember yourself! Remember your Legion and your legacy! Does the shaming of your primarch mean nothing to you? Are you so soft-hearted that you set aside your grudge so easily? I set nothing aside, Drachmus. I do not value the scriptures and scrolls you offer me. They will not win you my prize, and your account, which could have had me hail you a true brother, does not earn my respect. You may be seated.'

Drachmus turned to look at each of the other guests in turn, but none would give any word or any sign of their thoughts. The Word Bearer walked to his seat, picked up his bowl of smouldering bone and stared into the smoke from it as he stood with his back to Chengrel's tank.

'I withdraw,' declared Chengrel when it became apparent that Drachmus was not going to turn around. 'Emmesh-Aiye of the blood of Fulgrim. Khrove, scion of Magnus. Consider what you have heard from your brothers and resolve, each of you, to tell a tale worthy of your Legions' names.'

Once again Chengrel's tank backed away from the little assembly and stalked off, and after a few moments the other four Chaos Space Marines made their impassive way back to their landing-camps to let the night end and the next day of bidding begin.

'So. Neither of us, it appears,' observed Drachmus to Hodir. Once again, the two found themselves walking away from the meeting together, with Emmesh-Aiye loping rapidly ahead of them in his clinking glass cloak and Khrove, solitary and inscrutable, hanging behind.

'None of us at all,' growled Hodir in reply. 'It seems to me that so-called Master Chengrel has made up his mind that his prize will not change hands at all, whether or not he has done so consciously.'

'Chengrel's strength must be formidable, to entitle him to such a prize, let alone to this demeanour,' said Drachmus. Everything in his tone made the statement a question.

'To parade such a prize in front of armed visitors would require great… confidence that one had such strength,' Hodir replied.

The two walked on a little further, each turning to look at the terrain about them and back at Chengrel's palace. Each examined the other's marching retinue. Each knew the other was doing the same. Each knew that the other was appraising their followers as potential opponents as well as potential allies. Neither bothered to comment on the fact.

They came to a halt at the top of a little rise from which they could see their landing-ziggurats and pavilions. Emmesh-Aiye was a dot scrambling up his ziggurat's steps to the open hatch of his cutter.

'Do Lorgar's scriptures have much to say on being ready for the necessity to strike?' Hodir asked.

'Indeed,' Drachmus chuckled. 'I can think of over a hundred passages.'

'I thought so.'

At that moment Khrove overtook them, moving up the road, in haughty strides but somehow seeming to glide along even faster than the movement of his legs warranted.

'Have you a bid ready, then, Lord Khrove?' asked Hodir as it became clear that the Thousand Son was about to simply pass them by.

'A bid and an account, as have we all,' Khrove answered him.

'We were discussing our host's humours,' said Drachmus. 'We have contingencies ready if matters go astray.'

'As have we all,' said Khrove again, and with a perfunctory salute with his staff was on his way. The other two Legion contingents parted a moment later and went their own ways.

'THESE REPORTS I hear do not move me to admiration,' Chengrel declared to his sullen guests the following afternoon. 'Under the Warmaster's banner we lanced the hide of the false Imperium from Cadia to Calth and back again. How is it that the Legions send such little lost lambs to me now? Emmesh-Aiye of the Legion of Fulgrim, I know that you have special reason to desire what I offer. Come before me and prove it.'

This day Emmesh-Aiye had not come alone. Pinned to his flesh were two long cords of woven skin, and tethered by collars to these cords were two crippled and naked followers, twin brother and sister, both Emmesh-Aiye's slaves of many years.

Emmesh-Aiye had blinded the boy and deafened the girl, and then had cut off their arms at the shoulders. In this way they were always aware of one another, but unable to converse or embrace. Sometimes their master allowed them to sit together, clumsily trying to comfort each other with their cut and scarred bodies unable to embrace, Emmesh-Aiye giggling and trilling with excitement over the misery he was inflicting.

Unable to shape words with his mutilated tongue, Emmesh-Aiye would grunt and yelp and clash his distended fingers in a cacophony that he had carefully and brutally trained the boy to interpret. Now strutting in the centre of the meeting-square, Emmesh-Aiye began to warble and clap. At each pause in his antics the boy-twin spoke while the girl, unable to hear her brother's words, looked up at Chengrel or around the chamber at the others.

'Emmesh-Aiye, whose words I speak, speaks his gratitude,' said the master through the voice of his slave. 'Emmesh-Aiye, whose will and instrument I am so pleased to be, speaks welcome and companionship to his fellow devotees and servants of the Powers of the Wellspring.' Hodir and Khrove exchanged a look at that, and Chengrel's expression turned stony, but Drachmus nodded and stirred the smoking ashes in his bowl.

'Emmesh-Aiye presents himself for your admiration as the brave, the elegant, the exquisite master in the train of Slaanesh. Emmesh-Aiye shall present his offering and his account, certain that both shall delight even as our service to the Great Ruin delights us all. Emmesh-Aiye now speaks to his fellow masters direct, and bids my voice to speak just as his own as he recounts a tale of his deeds.'

In such a fashion, laced with both vanity and strangeness, did Emmesh-Aiye begin his tale.

'IT IS EVIDENT that there is no higher calling than of delight,' went the boy-twin's words, 'and there is no higher delight than subjugation at the feet of Slaanesh, who bestows riches of excess that this cold and rule-bound universe cannot match. What better account to present than that of a liberation from drudgery and the elevation into rapture? Is this not the most perfect refinement of the concept of victory?

'We all know, we of the Nine Legions, of the one Legion among us who have turned their back on delight. Who have not only allowed the life of the senses to slip through their fingers but who have opened their hand and let it fall into the dust.' Emmesh-Aiye's gestures aped his words, slowly uncurling the six joints in each of his six fingers. 'You, Khrove, subject of the Great Conspirator, may vouch for this! These are your enemies as they are mine. The devotees of Nurgle. And here is what I won from them.

'My court and I were dancing our celebration of the ruin of the maiden world Ethuaraine when word came to me that Typhus, that bitter little soul, was mustering his plague fleet for some great work. The news pricked my wits, woke me to possibilities. What a conquest! What a victory to lay at the feet of the Ecstatic Prince! What new doors might be opened to my consciousness in reward!

'My sweet daemon-consorts slid their barbs into my senses and cast visions into my eyes and words into my ears. They showed me Typhus's contention with some mighty Imperial preacher, who had led a great host of his faithful to claim a world whose own faith was already claimed elsewhere. They showed me Typhus raising his tattered banner in the fray, the confrontation that drove the Imperial invaders back, and the tiny clutch of eggs under the preacher's skin, undetected among the sting-welts from Typhus's unhallowed Destroyer swarm, incubating in him even as their parent swarm lived in Typhus's own flesh. Soon the upstart swarm had made a hollow wreck of the upstart missionary's body but yet had not taken his life, and now Typhus was preparing to follow the failed crusade back home, wither the man's hive down around him and take him away with them, reborn into an endless life of servitude to despair.

'How repugnant a fate! How bountiful my Thirsting Mistress's generosity that allowed me to make him mine instead! Truly I am the instrument of magnificence!

'My visions showed me the *Terminus Est* leading Typhus's fleet out of its anchorage, and we flew like darts to remain ahead of them. We found his doomed preacher before he did, and we went to work.

'The man had ordered himself into seclusion, you see. He had ordered the reclusiam at the summit of his temple to be sealed, with himself and the handful of survivors of his failed crusade inside. He understood he had brought contagion back from the dark places, and he had it in his mind to bow down before the aquila in prayer until his Emperor rewarded his passion by burning the swarm out of his flesh. But his Emperor's ear seemed deaf to him, and when the swarm hatched anew his cries for his gold-enthroned god were drowned out by the cries of his congregation devoured around him.

'But his true salvation was on its way, by my hand.

'I brewed a delicious psyker-scent that we breathed into the blooms that lined the temple roads. Now the fragrance coaxed the pilgrims' spirits out of the drab grey rut of the Emperor's footsteps. My courtiers sent whispers floating about the penitents so that their scourges and brands inflamed their senses rather than punishing them.' Emmesh-Aiye no longer strutted, but hunched over and padded about as if creeping among shadows. The clinking of his armoured feet against the flagstones counterpointed the rustle of the bright-coloured rags that dragged from his ankles. A drop of pinkish-white fluid, formed in one of the gouges in his tongue, ran down it to the pierced and dangling tip, and splatted to the ground.

'Oh, none were wise to us, for we were cunning ghosts wrapped in clever warp-weaves,' he went on in the voice of his slave, 'but the mangy hounds who herd the cud-chewing Imperial mob could see that mob becoming unruly, and tried to lash and harangue them into renewed obedience. Useless! Fruitless! The fire was spreading. We had opened minds, and now we opened bodies, letting the herd see their hounds picked apart and spread out beneath the hot purple-white sun. They began to rejoice as they felt their senses brightening, and raced to outdo one another in fresh ways to flood their nerve-endings. Now we showed ourselves, my courtiers and I, and danced among them on blood-slicked roads as the spires lit up and then burned down around us.

'Finally, as the very shape of the stones and the colour of the sky began to change, and the breezes and flowers themselves began to dance and sing and murder, Typhus's plague fleet arrived.'

Here, at the memory of the joke he had played, Emmesh-Aiye was consumed by fits of laughter that doubled him over and shook him to his knees. Both his slaves instantly knelt to mimic him, but Emmesh-Aiye paid them no heed. His mutated larynx gave out squeals so shrill that the blind boy-slave moaned in pain to hear them, and guffaws so deep that for a few moments Chengrel was sure he could feel the inhuman racket buzzing through his life-support syrup and into the remains of his organs. Finally the fits passed and the Traitor Marine collected himself.

'When the *Terminus Est* appeared in the night sky,' he said, 'it dimmed the stars around it with its presence, its bleak aura glowing like a chilly canker sore over our heads, eating the life out of the space around it to draw the rest of the fleet through. Skeletal hulks, whose crews brooded in decks rotted open and sealed shut again with hull plates flayed from vessels they preyed upon, drives burning hot like killing fevers.

'And oh, my brothers and companions, it was a killing fever that came upon Typhus when he saw what had become of his conquest! He led his reeking and downtrodden column down to the doctrinopolis where we ran and slit our skins and laughed aloud. He planted his boots on the great road that led to the doctrinopolis spire and spoke in a voice like a bone-rasp, that clouded and cracked the road he stood upon, which had been dusty flagstones and was now brightly-coloured glass.

'There was no grandeur to the rage of Typhus. He did not brandish his blade up to the sky or call down vengeance in a thunderous voice. But in that sick-roughened tone he demanded who had brought this insult against him. I answered his call, dancing upon the chiming, scented glass of the road in front of him. He hissed his rebukes of me, struck with his blade at me, sent fat and dripping creatures of his swarm through the air to sting and lash at me. I capered away from him, eluding him, drawing him on.

'As Typhus gave chase, drooling mucus from his

armour-seams, his host began to make war with us. And faltered! Failed! For we had made this place so wholly ours that when the thralls of Nurgle tried to mar it, it changed them instead! Our new city brought tingling to their long-dead nerves and thawed the rime over their hearts. The foot soldiers, the ones with no Mark from their master but only the marks of their weary servitude to him, cried and spasmed as our delirium woke their senses in ways they had never known. Typhus had brought daemons whose bodies were made from the purest dream of rot given form in the Wellspring, but my own master's most exquisite beasts and fiends came to meet them, and when they found that the enemy would not dance with them they took pity on such creatures as were made unable to feel delight, and unravelled them.

'As for Typhus himself, vengeance had put blinkers on his eyes and all he could see was myself, his enemy, dancing ever backwards.' Emmesh-Aiye's distended fingers whipped and whistled in the air, sometimes conducting the mad daemon-chorus that saturated his memories and sometimes re-enacting his duel against the champion of Nurgle. Above him Chengrel's face twisted in distaste, but Hodir, of all the onlookers the most accomplished in bladework, noted what was concealed in the buffoonery of Emmesh-Aiye's movements: the speed and poise, the deft nuances to his parries, the lightning shifts of balance and angle on his ripostes. Hodir grew thoughtful, his hand once again drifting to his knife-hilt.

'I tempted him and baited him, oh, and I drew him on into our city. In the great crossroads, beneath the cathedral, its buttresses meeting a half-mile over our heads, we fenced together – he silent, I laughing my delight as my combat-glands flushed ever-stranger liquors through my veins. Finally Typhus's rage pushed him into speech.

'"You dare?" he demanded of me. "This city and this world and all its prizes were mine, in the name of Grandfather-Beyond-The-Eye. They were mine that they should be his. Who are you to dare denying us what is ours? Have you no concept of what you contend against?"

'"Contend?" I asked, for this was long ago and my face and tongue had not yet been remade as you see them. "No contention here, only joy! No words of harsh contumely here, only the clear and endless song of nerves and dreams flayed bare!" And I spread my arms wide, inviting Typhus to turn his senses outwards and behold the blessing we had made. But he only saw me as inviting him to assault me anew.

'"Why do you tolerate this treatment from this grandfather of yours?" I asked him as we duelled again. "Your grandfather (if such you must call him, for surely your primarch's sire is your grandfather) has laid this reeking cloak upon your body and soul and called it good! Your grandfather's curse is not the plague or rot, it is numbness, sloth, eroding your passions and senses into drab despair or plodding servitude! Who would inflict such a thing on you is not your friend, Master Typhus. Let me show you! Let me turn you outwards again! Exchange your grandfather's sulking stagnation for my mistress's blazing raptures!"

'But Typhus, he would not be swayed, such was the draught of bitterness that he had swallowed to the dregs so long ago. "Grandfather?" he retorted, and swung his scythe with fresh strength and fury. "That broken toy in its palace on Terra is no grandfather of mine. His blood was water-weak, and his sons took on his weaknesses. Look at you!" and he matched the words to a twist of blade that came exquisitely close to opening me. "They tried to become conquerors and never understood what conquest truly means. True conquest is not defeat. True conquest is despair. True conquest is taking not only the life but the will to live. I will mortify the desires of my enemies to live, rot their souls into despair, and ride that despair into dominion. But you, you prancing puppet," and with that he stepped back, presenting his blade en garde, and looked me up and down, "Fulgrim's little whelps never did understand, for all that they bragged about how they would open the doors of their own minds and understand all. The soil of Chemos grew nothing but poppinjays."

'At that I laughed again. "Misguidance upon misguidance," I told him, as I watched the little creatures hatching from his hive and swarming into the air only to scatter senseless about his feet as our perfumes reached them. "I am no child of Chemos. Isstvan and Tallarn and Terra and even lost Skalathrax were memories by the time the Emperor's Children called me into their ranks. And conquest? Of what value is conquest? What cares the gleeful mind for conquest when the ecstatic awaits? You think that taking away that grey little missionary's faith has made him another conquest for you? Let me show you what we have proven on him! Let me show you what he is with the chains of mortal sense taken from him!"

'And with that I sang a command in a voice that shattered all the glass flagstones underneath us, and Typhus looked up to see two Raptors from my court's militia, carrying their passenger down from the Cathedral spire. His hair, which had hung to his waist and been matted with pus and sweat in his seclusion-cell, had been washed, perfumed and braided, and each braid was knotted about one of the Raptors' wrists. Their claws gripped his shoulders.

'And Typhus beheld that this man, this preacher and crusader, set so high in the Ecclesiarchy, was not his prize now but ours. He saw the marks, heard the delicate warp-keening that wreathed the man's twitching body, smelt, even over his own supernatural plague-reek; the warp-musk that the preacher's flesh had begun to sweat. And he saw what had become of that first infection, the eggs that his swarm had planted whose blossoming had brought his plans and mine into motion.

'The destroyer hatchlings in the preacher-man's flesh had nearly claimed him for Nurgle's embrace, but we had worked too much of Slaanesh's wiles on him for that to last. In the preacher's body the Nurgle swarm was transfigured. Clouds of brilliantly-hued mites swarmed about his face, so small they could have been coloured smoke. Spiders pushed their way out through the flesh and then clung to it with their bright red and gold legs, holding the wound apart so the meat beneath could be stirred by the air. Elegant worms in magnificent clashing hues wriggled under his skin and hatched forth to spit sparks and perfumes at one another. The preacher's eyes were gone, but his face was pulled in a grin of delight, not the scowl of despair.

'This final humiliation Typhus could not bear. He hawked a battle-curse from his inflamed throat and lunged forwards, intent on wrecking the evidence of his defeat, but the Raptors opened the throats of their engines and bore the man away. He roared with his psyk-voice, calling the foul breath of his grandfather to wither us, and sent his Destroyer swarm to devour the preacher afresh, but our Prince's touch was on that place too firmly. His swarm scattered to the ground, insensible and already mutating, and his warp-call was choked off as our mistress's songs pressed in upon him.

'I laughed at him, and laughed some more, and he chased me into the middle of my host. There he rasped and roared and laid about him, until he began to see the faces of his own soldiers around him. Some were overcome by what we had shown them, dancing in among us. Those who had fought that liberation were paraded in pieces, heads and limbs tossed and juggled and kicked underfoot. And in amongst this I presented myself again, ready to duel Typhus until the duel ended one of us. But Typhus stared at me a long moment, and then in the sickly inrushing light-burst of a teleporter he was gone. Within the hour, I was to hear the word of my seers that the *Terminus Est* had left orbit and was forging its way to a jump zone. Where the tiresome brute went after seeing our wonders, I do not know.'

Emmesh-Aiye's words tapered off, and he stood slumped on Chengrel's little stone stage as though his theatrics had exhausted him. He let his eyes close for a moment, then stalked back towards his seat, head down, yanking hard on the collars of his slaves and making them stumble behind him. He dropped into his seat with a clatter of armour and ornamental fetishes, and sat there silent.

'We thought something from that tale would be your bid here, brother,' said Khrove, after it became apparent that Emmesh-Aiye did not plan to speak further. 'You have presented your account, but what is your payment to be? Pardon my impatience, but our host must hear it before I speak.'

But they never heard what Emmesh-Aiye planned to offer for the stones, for at that moment Chengrel stamped the adamantium feet of his hulk against the flagstones and thundered the anger that had been building in him while the Slaaneshi had given his account.

'No!' he roared. 'No more! I forbid it! I shall not hear it!' The hulk's motors groaned as it tilted back and forth, and there was a great crack as one of its rear legs broke a flagstone in two. 'You think this some sort of noble account? You think this is a tale befitting one of the Legiones Astartes? You think this should win anything but my contempt?' The girl-slave had shrunk behind Emmesh-Aiye, staring at Chengrel wide-eyed; the boy could not see him but wept quietly at the pain that Chengrel's shouts brought on his hearing.

'No more! No more of this treachery! Count yourself blessed by your so-called Prince, Emmesh-Aiye, that I do not crush you upon this spot and have your carcass flung into the corpse-marshes! How can you brag of this? Have you any conception of how low you have brought yourself?'

Chengrel's fury had set the scraps of his body to twitching, and his unanchored head had floated through a fifty-degree turn. A minute, then another, passed by while he gradually manoeuvred his head around to face the front again. The occasional burbling growl of frustration came through his speakers.

'And so what of the preacher?' Drachmus asked, turning to Emmesh-Aiye while Chengrel was otherwise occupied. 'You have neglected the crucial message of your tale. Which of the Powers kept their claim upon him? Or did he return to the shadow of the aquila? Brother?'

Emmesh-Aiye did not raise his head but made a low buzzing with his breath that the boy-slave was able to interpret.

'It is barely in my memory. The manner in which my court acquired him was the marvel and the story, so what cared we for what became of him after that? We may have sold him on some border-world in the Wellspring, I think. What of it?'

Drachmus was about to reply when Chengrel cut them off again.

'No! Be silent! I'll have no more treachery discussed. Speak to him no more, Drachmus, so that his shame does not shame you.'

At that Drachmus rose from his chair, his little familiar keeping its balance on his shoulder with practised ease.

'My remark was addressed to fellow master of a fellow Legion, sir,' he declared. 'Your own labours have kept you here in this… quieter place for quite a time, Brother Chengrel, and perhaps you have not heard of Emmesh-Aiye of the Emperor's Children and his infamous Wandering Court. The reaving of the fleet of Craftworld Rhosh'aeth? The seizing of the

Thanemost Clock from its Mechanicus keepers, and the holding of it against the vengeance of the Storm Wardens Space Marines? The Epideurgic Crusade through the Segmentum Pacificus? I show respect to you as a witness to the Horus Heresy and the birth of our Long War, but I pay the respect to Emmesh-Aiye that his service to the Fourfold Ruin commands.'

Drachmus's tone made the rebuke in his final words clear, but Chengrel paid no heed to it.

'Respect?' he boomed. 'Of course you show me respect. Am I not mighty? You saw my fortress. You heard the account of my wars. And when you…' And there Chengrel caught himself as something about Drachmus's words struck home.

'Explain to me, Drachmus Word Bearer. You said you paid me respect as one who had borne arms while the Corpse-Emperor was still just the False Emperor. Explain why you remarked upon it, when it is that war, and the hate that burns from it, that defines all of us here?'

'My memories of Horus's war have been taught to me,' Drachmus said, making no attempt to conceal the surprise in his words. 'I was born into a people chosen by Lorgar to carry copies of his writings into exile when he could not be sure how far or deep the persecution of his true faith would run. I was born into the seventy-third generation, in the two hundred and fourth year of our exile after we had been hounded from our home on Kelhyte, twelve hundred years after the end of the Heresy. Omens led us to a Word Bearers barge and the fleet gave up its young as aspirants in gratitude.'

Chengrel's eyes pulsed and blinked as he pondered

this, before he directed his gaze at Hodir.

'You?' he asked.

'The Te'Oran Scouring,' Hodir answered. 'The Night Lords tox-bombed the cities, then sabotaged the shelters one by one so we all had to fight for places in the last one. When there was only one shelter left they stormed it, took a hundred youngsters and left the rest to choke. I was one of the hundred. Thirty-seventh millennium, Imperial reckoning.'

'And you?' Chengrel snarled at Emmesh-Aiye. Without opening his eyes the latter nudged his boy-slave with the side of his foot.

'The lineage of my master, Emmesh-Aiye, I shall present for brevity,' the slave said. 'He knows not where he was born or how. His memories begin in the great cages towed behind the procession of the daemon prince Avrasheil, journeying to war. He remembers a great war and a great dying beneath the gaze of many-armed Fulgrim and being remade by Fabius Manflayer. He was given commission into the Emperor's Children warband of Chardra Bloodwine in the eighth millennium after the so-called Heresy.'

Once again there was silence in the little circle of legionaries. Chengrel glowered at his guests. Hodir and Khrove sat motionless. Drachmus picked up little pinches of ash between his fingers and let them drop back into the bowl, studying the patterns they made in the air as they fell and settled. The glow from them burnished his faceplate, for dusk was falling now and the meeting-place was shrouded in gloom. Emmesh-Aiye fidgeted and stroked his lacerated tongue. Finally Chengrel gave another growl through his speakers.

'Khrove,' he said, 'Khrove of the Thousand Sons.

Scion of Magnus. Son of... But are you truly a son of Prospero? Or are you, like these others, a stripling latecomer? But speak your piece, speak your piece. If your account is glorious then it may even sweeten my disposition enough to hear the bid from this so-called Emperor's Child.'

Slow and quiet, Khrove walked into the middle of the circle and stood a few moments. Then he let out a cry and smote the flagstones with the heel of his staff, and instantly was wrapped in hissing flames of pink and blue, bright enough that Emmesh-Aiye's girl-slave squeezed her eyes shut from the pain of it. Khrove struck again and flames fell from his body, flowing out to become a billowing ground-mist and lifting Khrove into the air on a pedestal of coloured fire. He pointed down with his staff, and wherever he pointed into the roiling colours underneath him they began to twist and churn.

With no preamble other than this extravagant show of sorcery, Khrove of the Thousand Sons began his tale.

'NO,' HE SAID, with a nod to Chengrel. 'No, I was not among the first of our Legions as you, venerable Master Chengrel, were. I never saw the face of the living Emperor. I have never set eyes upon Terra or foot upon Prospero. I was raised among the mendicant logicians of Prekae Magna, travelling the roads between the Universitariate city-hubs, working to find mathematical patterns in the phrasing of Imperial scriptures and offering these insights to young scholars and labourers in exchange for alms. When we crossed paths with travellers around the space ports we would exchange tracts and treatises with them, and that was how my family came into possession of more esoteric works, passed to us in secret with whispers of truths that the most eminent scholars knew but would not teach to any save their own favourites and sycophants. We applied our calculus to these new texts and were steeped in wondrous and terrible revelations, insights that came so easily that it was like picking up treasure from the ground after a lifetime of battling to pry open locked vaults.'

As Khrove spoke, the mist and fire below him swam up into a little tableaux of light that acted out the scenes he was describing.

'We counted ourselves students only, always seeking understanding, but while we pursued our studies we were being studied in turn. These disciplines were stoking the light of my own dormant gift, and when they perceived me the Thousand Sons acted.

'This was not the true Legion of Magnus, ignorant as I was of that when they appeared among us. For all their dread bearing and proud demeanour, these were lackeys of Ahriman the Librarian, the meddling exile whom Magnus had barely spared from death. They took me away without a word. This was just after the breaking of the forty-first millennium.

'My proper education began, built on the foundations the secret tracts had laid. I learned to master passion and delusion and dominate the Ocean with will and intellect alone. Thirsting for knowledge I began to elaborate upon my masters' principles in my own ways, every waking moment ablaze with insights and possibilities.

'Ahriman did not remain my master. One of the

roving magisters of the core of the Thousand Sons intercepted us in the galactic north-east. I took no part in their battle, but sensed it waged with weapons and wills across the nameless world where Ahriman had landed in search of I still know not what. They were driven from that rock before their search was successful, and I was taken as a trophy into the court of Magnus the Red.

'And now the doors of learning were truly thrown open to me. I laboured for the sorcerer Abhenac on deriving the seven syllables of the seven true names of the Nurgle prince Phoettre Rotchoke, and then he released me into the service of Sulabhey the Arch-Invoker, who set me to work refining the principles by which his warding and summoning sigils were formed. My labours added such puissance to his own that he named me first among his adepts, and taught me the Third and Fifth Concatenations by which we could counter direct the eight fundamental immaterial temperaments. In contest with Xerdion of Nine Towers he had me create and enact a ritual by which the warp-radiance from a human psyker, as defined in the works of Carrackon the Elder, was matched in three secondary nuances of character to the tempest-flashes observed in the epistles of Ghell. Xerdion acknowledged the adepts of Sulabhey to be the better after my success, and when I used elements of this ritual to bind and discognate the daemon Herakdol, I was once again brought before Magnus and dressed in the livery of an aspirant mage.'

In the glowing mist beneath him, Khrove's fire-puppets made gestures and wrote signs that caused the air to groan and spark.

'Now I was taught warfare. My gifts and spells were honed to a martial edge, and I mastered the baser, more physical weapons of the Legiones Astartes. I could loose an unerring fusillade from a bolter, fence with a chainsword, command one of the Legion's ancient vehicles, march to battle with one of my battle-brothers or one hundred of them and know what was expected of me with never a question or order needed. I rewrote my soldiers' doctrines with the incandescent skills of the mage.

'At every step, I was tested. I remember a battle of one hundred and sixty-two hours, beneath a sky crowded with silver towers, against two hetmen of Magnus. One plucked up stones and bones from the plain and hurled them at us upon tendrils of thought laced with scarlet sparks. The other unlaced the safe fabric of space and distance and sent crawling, crackling runes to uncouple our minds from our senses. I alone remained master of thought and limb, commanding the others in the fray. When the test was done and the towers spoke to one another in the voices of their masters, they acclaimed me, declared me no longer aspirant but adept, and gave me those others who had survived as the core of my first coven.

'I was brought wargear, the hollow armour of a Legion brother long dead. I reshaped it alongside the Legion's finest forge-magi, engraving it with warp work so that it blazed with living etheric fire where once had been the simple energies of its reactor pack. When I donned the armour I was plucked from the foundry floor, to hang in a cell of folded space while the armourers assaulted the defences I had made. They tested my forge-work, my spell-carvings, the connections from my spirit into the armour's anima, the predatory instinctual spirit-weaves, just short of minds, that I had patterned into each tooth of my chainsword and each round loaded into the magazine of my pistol. Such was their power that the simple attention of their minds scorched my body and soul, but though they picked apart my designs from every angle in four dimensions they could find nothing that displeased them, and I walked from the Seeing Mount to begin my studies with...'

But here Khrove, like Emmesh-Aiye before him, was cut off by his host's fury.

'Be silent, Khrove! Be silent! Be silent, Thousand Son!' for Khrove was still attempting to speak. When the sorcerer realised that Chengrel would brook no further speech, he shrugged and allowed himself to sink back to the ground. His ghostly pantomime collapsed back into glowing fog, which whipped around Khrove's ankles, stirred the writhing hem of his surcoat, and was gone.

This time Chengrel's tank made no movement, but behind it in the shadows came the tread of metal on stone.

'No more, Khrove,' he repeated. 'No more from any of you. Go from here. Be among your fellows. You shall hear from me in the daylight.' Chengrel wheeled his tank about, moving it deceptively fast on its stubby legs. The two Terminators carrying the bag of stones were already departing.

Emmesh-Aiye sat with his head down and made no move to leave. Drachmus had leaned towards

Hodir as if to speak, but the latter turned his back on the rest of the assembly and got to his feet. Khrove, however, kept his position in the centre of the stone circle. He said, quietly:

'I have not finished speaking, sir.'

The other three turned and looked at him, but Khrove continued to stare after Chengrel and his retinue. Out in the dark, the sound of armoured tread stopped. Emmesh-Aiye closed his lips around his stretched tongue to slick them; Hodir and Drachmus exchanged a look and then moved quickly and purposefully out to Khrove's flanks.

There was silence for a moment.

'My account is not done,' Khrove said. 'I understood that we would treat with one another here as equals, in comradeship and respect. I trusted that we would each present our bid to you, and even these accounts you saw fit to demand of us, and be heard. I came here ready to graciously acclaim any of these others whose bids I believed to surpass mine, and to leave with no other prize than their fellowship, and yours. But I am denied. You have not heard my account or what I offer as my bid. Master Emmesh-Aiye has likewise been refused full hearing. You are a poor host, Master Chengrel. My fellows and I deserve more respect than you show us.'

Away in the shadows a moving light appeared. It was the window on the front of Chengrel's tank, coming into view as he wheeled around, the green-white glow from inside the tank brightening as he stampeded back towards them.

'Respect?' he roared. 'Respect for you, you worthless, bloodless little inbreed? You disgrace to the gene of

Magnus? Had you any understanding of respect you would be prostrate on the flagstones now, begging my forgiveness!'

A bank of bolters cresting Chengrel's tank-hulk rattled through sixty degrees of elevation and barked a salvo into the interlaced boughs overhead.

'This is base betrayal!' he shouted over the crashing of burning debris around them. 'I sent out more than a hundred heralds, and this is the respect shown me? Four such weaklings? We are Legiones Astartes! We strode out in fire and blood to be humanity's living gods of war! And we wage the Long War to split the galaxy asunder and remake it, to make the Imperium weep for the day they failed us!'

A Defiler had stamped into view on each side of Chengrel's tank, and shapes moved on all sides of the lamp-lit circle of paving.

'But now I see treachery indeed!' Chengrel went on. 'A pack of scatterbrained infants who do not understand the task their gene-seed brings with it! I expected accounts of blows struck against the Imperials, worlds burned, lords and generals cast down, revenge on the Legions who would not march with us into righteous rebellion. Accounts of you fulfilling the purpose for which your primarchs' genes were placed into your misbegotten and ungrateful bodies. And what did I hear?

'From you, Hodir, I hear that the children of Curze are so dissipated that you brag of being able to pluck some fat supply convoy and must beg for my help assaulting an Imperial fortress. Drachmus, you tell me how your Word Bearers barely managed to hold the line against Imperial invasion. Khrove, your Legion of all of them must have a grudge burning white-hot against the Emperor, but instead, as if the burning of Prospero meant nothing to you, you yap about tempest-flashes and concatenations and fundamental temperaments. Tell me of the tempest-flashes you inflicted on our erstwhile brothers in war! Tell me of how these "concatenations" helped you to bring even a single Imperial life to an end! You cannot! You betray your heritage and waste yourself!

'And from you, Emmesh-Aiye.' Chengrel was no longer shouting, but his voice was blistered with contempt. 'What possessed you to be anything other than ashamed? Crushing an Imperial city for no other reason than to thwart another Legion? Thwart a brother as great as Typhus? Where is your pride? Have the shallow glamours of your patron blinded you to the fact that if we all turn on one another so, there will be none left to strike at the Golden Throne? How may we weld ourselves together again into a force to raze Terra with such as you in our ranks?

'And you demand to know why I will not hear your bids, Khrove? Do you understand now? Do you understand why I will allow none of you this prize, until your Legions can send me champions who prove that the fires that Horus kindled in us all still burn hot? Tell those Thousand Sons you claim to speak for that their ambassador is a poor specimen indeed.'

If he had intended to say more then it was lost. For a moment it seemed as if some terrible weapon had detonated in front of Chengrel's tank, for the space on the flagstones was filled with blue-white blaze. When the light passed Khrove once again hung in the air, suspended off the ground in sizzling cobwebs of lightning. His staff pointed straight between Chengrel's eyes.

'And what of you, then?' he demanded. 'Mighty Chengrel, revered Iron Warrior? Great Chengrel, acclaimed by his warsmith? Chengrel, who once managed to sack some Imperial hives at the head of an army and fleet, and whose greatest accomplishment since then has been to build a hideaway in a sector so gutted by war that he would be safely beyond challenge in a sackcloth tent?'

At this Chengrel let out a bellow and his bolters coughed out a bright cluster of shots. An arm's length from Khrove the shells tumbled in the air and scattered away from a sparkling rune that had not been there a split second before.

'What are you, Chengrel?' Khrove went on, as though nothing had happened. The lightning had spread to form an arch that framed him. 'You set yourself up over us, sneer at our histories. You brag that you had fought in Horus's lunge for power, as if that were some badge of greatness. You who marched in the rank and file ten thousand years ago! Praised for your prowess by your warsmith on Medrengard itself, you say? Were you one half, were you one third of what you boast of being, your praises would have been born in the throat of Perturabo himself, not some vassal outside his gates. And if you are such a magnificent beast of war, Chengrel, why must you style yourself with titles like "Master"? After a hundred centuries to prove your worth, why are you not a warsmith yourself?'

'Bring him to me!' roared Chengrel in reply, as weapon armatures unfolded from the sides of his tank and two rotary cannons began scouring the ground and throwing up dust and rock chips. A Defiler scrambled past him on its cluster of metal legs and sent a belch of yellow flame towards where Khrove hung, and without looking down the Thousand Son caught the blast and stilled it in mid-air as though he had imprisoned it in a picture of itself. A moment later the flame, now a glowing cobalt blue shot through with scarlet and emerald, reversed its motion, reversing back into the Defiler's flame-tank, which exploded in a ruinous fireball.

'Traitors, all of you!' screamed Chengrel through the din. 'The Long War is not done while the Emperor sits on that throne on Terra! And all we have left is fops and cowards who will not do what it takes to settle the account!' Even as he crashed forwards, bolters and cannons tracking, the left cannon mount fell silent. Hodir had glided forwards with perfect calm, slipped between two hulking thralls whose senses were full of flame and gunshots, and gutted the cannon's mechanism with a single precise jab of his power knife. Now he spun to defend himself as the grunting thralls closed in.

'Us?' cried Khrove as a burst from Chengrel's other cannon drove Drachmus back from his other flank, the little daemon scrambling for a grip but continuing its monologues with not a syllable out of place. 'Are you so stunted, Chengrel? So trapped? Leave your so-called Long War to the elders, all eaten up with spite, who cannot drag themselves out of a rut of ten thousand years! Think of all that Chaos offers you. Think of the power and grandeur. Think of what you have built already, and what you could achieve if you let the Great Ocean pour through you and push wide your understanding. Think of what awaits you if you would just shrug off your dreary little feud and strike out to explore! You are the traitor, Chengrel! Traitor to the potential our forefathers saw in us when they turned their backs on the Emperor and led us out into the void! Think on that, Chengrel, and learn shame!'

A shocking storm of gunfire erupted on the left flank. Drachmus's Word Bearers, waiting in the dusk, were hammering Chengrel's followers with bolts and cannonades. On the right, a pack of household thralls hacked at Hodir with power rams and combat blades, to find a moment later that they had shredded an empty cloak. Next instant the creature holding the cloak pitched over dead, a smoking hole in its forehead from where Hodir's power knife had punched through its skull. As the corpse fell, Hodir lifted a pistol in his other hand and shot the thrall overseer through the throat.

Chengrel's dorsal bolters blazed again, and once more Khrove undid the salvo with a gesture. This time the shells began to dance in front of him, leaving trails of sky-blue light that formed strange letters in the air. Chengrel snarled in anger, and the snarl emerged from his speakers as a squeal of static that detonated the bolt shells. The concussions did not harm Khrove, but sent him skittering back through the air. Fire and lightning spread like a second cloak about his shoulders.

'The Long War gives us meaning!' Chengrel shouted as he stormed forwards. 'The War is our purpose! Our primarchs swore it so! How dare you turn away from the pacts that they made before Horus and each other! Traitor! I name you traitor!' He would have said more, but now the chassis of his tank crashed through the sigils that Khrove had left hanging in the air and shivered them apart. As they cracked, the space around them seemed to crack too, and suddenly Chengrel was surrounded by dazzling spectres of light that cohered into harder, physical forms. Squat blocks of pink-glowing flesh split by chanting mouths swarmed about the tank's legs, cackling and clawing at the joints. Beaked and toothed things with skirted mushroom-stems for bodies bounded in circles around Chengrel and his Defilers like children about a bonfire, breathing streams of coruscating light that crawled across their enemies' metal skins. Darker shapes screamed about the Defiler's turret, leaving furrows in its armour.

'Soulless, substanceless little remnant of a man,' sneered Khrove, with blue and silver light now blazing from every seam of his armour. A rippling disc of silver-white metal manifested beneath his feet and he stepped down from mid-air to stand on it. 'The war is as good as won, and we are the victors! We who understand! The Imperium means as little to us as the tawdry ambitions of those who cannot bear to stop making war on it. The only losers in your precious Long War are those who are unable to let it go. You and your Imperium deserve one another.'

Next to Chengrel the Defiler's cannon boomed, but there was no seeing where the machine-beast's shot had gone. A second later one of the capering pink daemons vaulted up its side and rammed a grotesque arm straight through its turret-plates and into its innards.

'And yet you swagger in front of us demanding

that we prove ourselves your equals?' Khrove went on, scattering from his hand a sizzling radiance that pierced Chengrel's followers like quills. 'It is no small satisfaction to me that I could not do so. What true heir to the primarchs would wish to lower themselves to equality with such as you?'

The obscenities that burst from Chengrel then were too foul and fast to comprehend, for his speakers could not keep pace with his rage. A streaking missile from Drachmus's followers shattered his remaining cannon before it could fire. Chengrel's vision swam with red and black as feedback from the hit lanced into him, but all his attention remained on the incandescent figure of Khrove in front of him. He fired his bolters again and again, and although many of the shells vanished in the sorcerer's aura of flame, some had been warp-worked by Chengrel's smiths and crashed home against the ancient blue armour. Chengrel's roar as Khrove lurched back through the air was one of feral satisfaction.

WHILE THIS MELEE blazed at the meeting-space a second contest, smaller but no less fierce, had begun on the road back to Chengrel's palace. The two Iron Warriors Terminators were marching onwards with the soulstones when the auto-senses of the rearmost registered movement and heat in overgrown ruins that should have been empty. Straight away he lashed the ruins with double combi-bolter shots, beginning in an ancient Legiones Astartes suppression pattern, then abruptly switching to a semi-random drill designed to catch a target who might have learned the same fire pattern.

Walking backwards, gun still nosing the night, the Iron Warrior watched tracking overlays and hit readouts. They showed plumes of rock dust, splintered vegetation, a little cloud of atomised sap where a bolt had punched through the bole of a twisted tree. But both he and his armour systems knew, from bitter lessons begun on Isstvan, the look and sound of a bolt-shell hitting Space Marine war plate, and there had been no evidence of that.

Then a melta-blast slagged the plasteel-bound frame of the combi-bolter, and an eye-blink later the white-hot wreck of the weapon was blown apart by the shells still in the magazine. Startled but not frightened, the Iron Warrior shook weapon fragments off his gauntlet as his companion's reaper cannon sent a salvo at the source of the blast. The two warriors had just enough time to close together before a quick-lunging figure raked a chainblade across the leader's faceplate, precisely exploiting a weak spot in the Terminator suit's range of movement that made it hard to twitch the head aside from an attack on that one vector. The Iron Warrior's eye-lens was damaged and his vision jittery with feedback, but instinct took over. There were three ways an enemy could dodge after that lunge. Two were back to safety, but the third carried forwards and would allow a grab at the bag of stones on the way clear. Without looking he swept the bladed barrel of the reaper through that space and was rewarded with the sound of splintering armour and a cry of fury.

But now more Night Lords were joining the fray. The meltagunner shot a blast into the leader's faceplate that destroyed several sensory inputs and overwhelmed the others for whole seconds. That was long enough for Hodir's power knife to begin hacking at the arm whose gauntleted fist still held the bag.

A terse bark of battle-cant between the two Terminators communicated Hodir's position, and the Night Lord realised how long he was taking, and what a mistake that was, when the muzzle of the reaper cannon clanked into the pit of his left arm. Even in the split second between contact and firing he was twisting away, presenting the Iron Warrior with a curved armour surface for the shells to carom off. But that could not save him completely and the triple shot spun him four metres away with an ugly crater in his armour.

The Iron Warrior holding the stones felt another blast of heat that failed to injure him, but damaged enough of the fine componentry in his arm that the limb locked stiff; from behind him came the crack and flare of a thunder hammer, and he heard the curse as his companion went down on one knee. He twisted so that the bag of stones would be carried away from the Night Lords on that side, but now pain sizzled in his fingertips and he snarled in frustration as he felt the bag being snatched away. Then there was only the two of them, part-crippled, firing a hail of shells into the dark where the Night Lords had vanished.

HODIR GAVE A liquid, agonised cough as his fractured rib-carapace ground and his lungs worked to expel the blood already half-clotted in them. But meanwhile his thoughts danced with what power he could purchase now that the prize was out of the clutches of the pompous Iron Warrior fool.

Strange and avaricious dreams filled him, such as he had not remembered having before. These dreams, Hodir realised, did not even seem to be his own. The dance of his own thoughts was alien to him. At that moment his brother Night Lords let him drop to his knees on the ground.

Hodir looked around and saw that his band of reavers had stumbled to a halt. Some were readying weapons, but clumsily, with none of the fast and lethal cohesion born of so many thousands of battles. One or two of them were even making little jerking motions as though resisting some mad call to dance, gasping and crying into the vox.

With the ethereal song of Slaanesh trilling from his distended lips, Emmesh-Aiye sauntered into the group. His two slaves still trailed behind him, but behind them in turn came an extravagant parade cloaked in pastel light and scented steam. Hodir had faced their like before, but there was no preparation or readiness that could protect him from the savage ache of desire that flashed from his skull to his heels. He wanted to move with their beautiful rhythms, laugh like them, be like them, and these desires barely faltered when he saw them take the head of one of his warriors and drop it to the ground in a shower of blood and laughter.

But still, his pistol kicked and the creature who was reaching for the bag of stones shrieked and rippled. For a moment it was something whose features took all those strange desires and wrenched them back on themselves, and then it shrieked as Hodir's power knife opened it from throat to belly. That damage was more than its will to stay corporeal could override, and the daemonette shivered into nothing.

The thing's destruction managed a moment of ugly counterpoint to the blanket of hypnotic noise, and the Night Lords, whose minds had needed only the slightest opportunity, seized on the change and fought. Now suddenly the Slaaneshi cavalcade had to contend with resistance: curved claws and barb-tipped tongues clashed with blades, hammers, and desperate, point-blank bolter shots.

But Emmesh-Aiye would not be denied his prize. Shivering from the resonance of the sonic discharges in his bones, Hodir shivered anew as Emmesh-Aiye's finger-quills slid into his arm. His hand went warm, then numb, and Emmesh-Aiye plucked the bag from his fingers. Hodir saw the ruby light from the stones kindle in the Slaaneshi's own eyes, and then he brought his power knife up and jammed it into Emmesh-Aiye's hip.

The man convulsed, the wounds in his pinned tongue opening into weeping holes, and his red-reflecting eyes stared into Hodir's face for a moment. Then he backhanded the injured Night Lord to the ground and scampered lopsidedly away from the fight, doubled over the bag of stones he held to his belly with his slaves dragged along behind.

THE MISTRUSTFUL CHENGREL had ordered his troops to prepare a killing-ground for his guests even before they had landed, and now his warriors prepared their positions at the landing-camps. These were Iron Warriors combat engineers, crafty and capable. They threw open carefully concealed foxholes and enfilades, and used scatter munitions to lay down instant fields of krak mines and webs of memory-wire strong enough to entangle even power-armoured legs. Shadow-quiet, they moved in amongst their new trenchworks, their fire-lanes already planned and directed, ready for master Chengrel's fleeing guests.

But of course their enemies were Space Marines too. Each point the Iron Warriors had chosen to fortify had been anticipated by the Night Lords, and the first team found themselves dealing with ambushes of diabolical precision and cohesion. Newly opened foxholes were already trapped; Iron Warriors simply vanished on the way to their positions; odd bursts of interference interrupted the vox-chatter no matter which band the Iron Warriors used, just enough to muddle their commands and make their attempts at organisation worse than useless.

The attempt to cut off Drachmus's retreat did better, but when Drachmus left Chengrel and Khrove to one another's mercies and struck out for his ship, he had more warriors with him. In time to his gargoyle's recitation of the Spiral Catechism he marched towards his landing-camp with his bowl of burning ashes held high and his banner-bearer behind him. The Iron Warriors in his way almost laughed at the crude approach, but caught themselves; Drachmus was making himself so visible for a reason. They realised that reason barely in time to mount a fight against an expert Word Bearers pincer assault with Drachmus at its hinge.

On the far flank the Iron Warriors around Emmesh-Aiye's battered little cutter was bogged down in a hellish firefight against the ship's guards, Noise Marine artillerists who fought with percussive rumbles that could shake armour and bone apart, and shrieks to rupture flesh from cellular membranes on up. Into the middle of this came Emmesh-Aiye himself, his daemonic retinue left behind to finish the fight against Hodir's elite, dancing through the Iron Warriors line. He chirruped laughter as one armoured figure after another fell to his warp-screams and the venom of his finger-quills, and when the last scrap of resistance was desperately falling back he could control himself no longer. He leapt and cut capers on the blasted ground, scoring his slaves' skin with the spines and hooks of his breastplate, and leaving the welts and wounds slicked with the secretions of his tongue.

That was how Khrove found him. The sorcerer had fought Chengrel to a standstill; the warding and working of the tank, and the sheer brute force of the will driving it, had been enough to blunt most of the assaults Khrove had cared to throw, and the fury of Chengrel's assaults did not allow him time to prepare deeper and more potent measures. Finally, Khrove had redirected one of his attack calculi through a false logical form, outflanking Chengrel's wards and hitting home. The forelegs of Chengrel's tank turned from metal to an elegant blue crystal that instantly shattered under the tank's weight. As Chengrel howled his fury into the dirt, Khrove had turned his back without further ado.

He did not hail Emmesh-Aiye, or curse him either. Khrove had had enough of words, and so he threw his staff down like a javelin into a spot not far from where Emmesh-Aiye danced. Suddenly Emmesh-Aiye found that he was mired in something that seemed to be at once tarry liquid and clinging dust, and after a moment found that he had sunk from his ankles to his thighs. Seeing Khrove standing on his disc up above, he launched a savage witch-howl that might have stripped armour and flesh from the sorcerer's body had he not dismissed it with a gesture.

Now Emmesh-Aiye was up to his waist and screaming with anger. He held the bag of soulstones up to keep it from becoming submerged and, like Hodir before him, felt it being plucked from his hand. What had taken it not even his senses could discern, but as he sank up to his chest he saw Khrove hang the stones from his belt.

Now, casting about desperately for leverage or footing, Emmesh-Aiye saw his slaves. Like him, they were trapped and sinking, but they had leaned together and put their heads on one another's shoulders. Each careworn face now carried a small, sweet smile, for they had realised that soon they would finally be free of their misery, and would go into oblivion together.

That stung Emmesh-Aiye more than the loss of the stones. That he could not prevent his slave-twins from dying happy suddenly seemed the most profound of defeats, and he groaned and wept and tried to lunge at them as the ground finally took all three of them under. A moment later they were gone and Khrove looked about him.

Doubtless there were ambushes around his lander too, but they did not matter. Khrove had descended from his ship by more direct means, and the blocky, golden craft in his camp was nothing more than a diversion. Now it buckled and faded as Khrove dissolved the knots of force that bound it together.

The sun was starting to rise, and Khrove could see

the great ring of fortifications take shape in the dawn. Here and there was a bark and twitch of motion as the last of the brawl among the Word Bearers, Iron Warriors and Night Lords played out. Emmesh-Aiye's retinue were not to be seen, having tumbled back into their craft in a panic when they saw their master die, or melted back into the warp.

Khrove's left hand dropped to the bag of soulstones at his belt, and his right extended. After a moment his staff flew up out of the ground and into his grip. There seemed no good reason to stay longer. The sorcerer murmured a word, followed it with another, and departed for his ship in a soft thunderclap of displaced air and a flowering burst of light.

In the time between the ravages of the final Waaagh! Ungskar and the beginning of the Greyblood Tribulations, Chengrel of the Iron Warriors built himself a fortress home upon Burjan's World in the Mitre Gulf. He dwells there still, although his lordly demeanour is not quite what it was and many of his Iron Warriors have now departed from his service.

Chengrel has spent much time combing the ruins of Burjan's World for another prize like the one that was stolen from him, for he is convinced that with it he can once again purchase power and allies. When he floats in a circle inside his tank-hulk so that his head nestles in the scraps of what was his body, he still broods on revenge; but now rather than revenge on the Golden Throne he plots it on the legionaries who came to visit him after that long-ago summons, and who betrayed him so bitterly and so foolishly.

Khrove of the Thousand Sons would be amused

by that, should he ever learn of it. If he and master Chengrel should ever meet again, doubtless he will point the irony out.

THE CARRION ANTHEM

by David Annandale

HE WAS THINKING bitter thoughts about glory. He couldn't help it. As he took his seat in the governor's private box overlooking the stage, Corvus Parthamen was surrounded by glory that was not his. The luxury of the box, a riot of crimson leather and velvet laced with gold and platinum thread, was a tribute, in the form of excess, to the honour of Governor Elpidius. That didn't trouble Corvus. The box represented a soft, false glory, a renown that came with the title, not the deeds or the man. Then there was the stage, to which all sight lines led. It was a prone monolith, carved from a single massive obsidian slab. It was an altar on which one could sacrifice gods, but instead it abased itself beneath the feet of the artist. It was stone magnificence, and tonight it paid tribute to Corvus's brother. That didn't trouble Corvus, either. He didn't understand what Gurges did, but he recognised that his twin did, at least, work for his laurels. Art was a form of deed, Corvus supposed.

What bothered him were the walls. Windowless, rising two hundred metres to meet in the distant vault of the ceiling, they were draped with immense tapestries. These were hand-woven tributes to Imperial victories. Kieldar. The Planus Steppes. Ichar IV. On and on and on. Warriors of legend, both ancient and contemporary, towered above Corvus. They were meant to inspire, to draw the eye as the spirit soared, moved by the majesty of the tribute paid by the music. The works of art in this monumental space – stone, image and sound – were supposed to entwine to the further glory of the Emperor and his legions.

But lately, the current of worship had reversed. Now the tapestry colossi, frozen in their moments of triumphant battle, were also bowing before the glory of Gurges, and that was wrong. That was what made Corvus dig his fingers in hard enough to mar the leather of his armrests.

The governor's wife, Lady Ahala, turned to him, her multiple necklaces rattling together. 'It's nice to see you, colonel,' she said. 'You must be so proud.'

Proud of what? he wanted to say. Proud of his home world's contributions to the Imperial crusades? That was a joke. Ligeta was a joke. Of the hundred tapestries here in the Performance Hall of the Imperial Palace of Culture, not one portrayed a Ligetan hero. Deep in the Segmentum Pacificus, far from the front lines of any contest, Ligeta was untouched by war beyond the usual tithe of citizens bequeathed to the Imperial Guard. Many of its sons had fought and fallen on

distant soil, but how many had distinguished themselves to the point that they might be remembered
and celebrated? None.

Proud of what? Of his own war effort? That he
commanded Ligeta's defence regiment? That only made
him part of the Ligetan joke. Officers who were posted
back to their home worlds developed reputations,
especially when those home worlds were pampered,
decadent backwaters. The awful thing was that he
couldn't even ask himself what he'd done wrong. He
knew the answer. *Nothing*. He'd done everything right.
He'd made all the right friends, served under all the
right officers, bowed and scraped in all the right places
at all the right times. He had done his duty on the
battlefield, too. No one could say otherwise. But there
had been no desperate charges, no last-man-standing
defences. The Ligetan regiments were called upon to
maintain supply lines, garrison captured territory,
and mop up the token resistance of those who were
defeated but hadn't quite come to terms with the fact.
They were not summoned when the need was urgent.

The injustice made him seethe. He knew his worth,
and that of his fellows. They fought and died with the
best, when given the chance. Not every mop-up had
been routine. Not every territory had been easily paci-
fied. Ligetans knew how to fight, and they had plenty
to prove.

Only no one ever saw. No one thought to look,
because everyone knew Ligeta's reputation. It was the
planet of the dilettante and the artist. The planet of the
song.

Proud of *that*?

Yes, that was exactly what Ahala meant. Proud of the

music, proud of the song. Proud of Gurges. Ligeta's civilian population rejoiced in the planet's reputation. They saw no shame or weakness in it. They used the same logic as Corvus's superiors, who thought they had rewarded his political loyalty by sending him home. Who wouldn't want a pleasant command, far from the filth of a Chaos-infested hive-world? Who wouldn't want to be near Gurges Parthamen, maker not of song, but of *The* Song?

Yes, Corvus thought, Gurges had done a good thing there. Over a decade ago, now. The Song was a hymn to the glory of the Emperor. Hardly unusual. But *Regeat, Imperator* was rare. It was the product of the special alchemy that, every so often, fused formal magnificence with populist appeal. The tune was magisterial enough to be blasted from a Titan's combat horn, simple enough to be whistled by the lowliest trooper and catchy enough that, once heard, it was never forgotten. It kept up morale on a thousand besieged worlds, and fired up the valour of millions of troops charging to the rescue. Corvus had every right, every *duty*, to be proud of his brother's accomplishment. It was a work of genius.

So he'd been told. He would have to be satisfied with the word of others. Corvus had amusia. He was as deaf to music as Gurges was attuned to it. His twin's work left him cold. He heard a clearer melody line in the squealing of a greenskin pinned beneath a Dreadnought's foot.

To Lady Ahala, Corvus said, 'I couldn't be more proud.'

'Do you know what he's offering us tonight?' Elpidius asked. He settled his soft bulk more comfortably.

'I don't.'

'Really?' Ahala sounded surprised. 'But you're his twin.'

'We haven't seen each other for the best part of a year.'

Elpidius frowned. 'I didn't think you'd been away.'

Corvus fought back a humiliated wince. 'Gurges was the one off-planet,' he said. Searching the stars for inspiration, or some other pampered nonsense. Corvus didn't know and didn't care.

Hanging from the vault of the hall were hundreds of glow-globes patterned into a celestial map of the Imperium. Now they faded, silencing the white noise of tens of thousands of conversations. Darkness embraced the audience, and only the stage was illuminated. From the wings came the choir. The singers wore black uniforms as razor-creased as any officer's ceremonial garb. They marched in in their hundreds, until they filled the back half of the stage. They faced the audience. At first, Corvus thought they were wearing silver helmets, but then they reached up and pulled down the masks. Featureless, eyeless, the masks covered the top half of each man's face.

'How are they going to see him conduct?' Elpidius wondered.

Ahala giggled with excitement. 'That's nothing,' she whispered. She placed a confiding hand on Corvus's arm. 'I've heard that there haven't been any rehearsals. Not even the choir knows what is going to be performed.'

Corvus blinked. 'What?'

'Isn't it exciting?' She turned back to the stage, happy and placid before the prospect of the impossible.

The light continued to fade until there was only a narrow beam front and centre, a bare pinprick on the frozen night of stone. The silence was as thick and heavy as the stage. It was broken by the solemn, slow *clop* of boot heels. His pace steady as a ritual, as if he were awed by his own arrival, Gurges Parthamen, Emperor's bard and Ligeta's favourite son, walked into the light. He wore the same black uniform as the musicians, but no mask. Instead...

'What's wrong with his face?' Ahala asked.

Corvus leaned forwards. Something cold scuttled through his gut. His twin's face was his own: the same severe planes, narrow chin and grey eyes, even the same cropped black hair. But now Corvus stared at a warped mirror. Gurges was wearing an appliance that flashed like gold but, even from this distance, displayed the unforgiving angles and rigidity of adamantium. It circled his head like a laurel wreath. At his face, it extended needle-thin claws that pierced his eyelids, pinning them open. Gurges gazed at his audience with a manic, implacable stare that was equal parts absolute knowledge and terminal fanaticism. His eyes were as much prisoners as those of his choir, but where the singers saw nothing, he saw too much, and revelled in the punishment. His smile was a peeling back of lips. His skin was too thin, his skull too close to the surface. When he spoke, Corvus heard the hollow sound of wind over rusted pipes. Insects rustled at the frayed corners of reality.

'Fellow Ligetans,' Gurges began. 'Before we begin, it would be positively heretical of me not to say something about the role of the patron of the arts. The life of a musician is a difficult one. Because we do not produce a tangible product, there are many who regard us as superfluous, a pointless luxury the Imperium could happily do without. This fact makes those who value us even more important. Patrons are the blessed few who know the artist really can make a difference.'

He paused for a moment. If he was expecting applause, he did not receive it; the knowledge and ice in his rigid gaze stilled the audience. Unperturbed, he carried on. 'I have, over the course of my musical life, been privileged to have worked with more than my share of generous, committed, sensitive patrons. It is thanks to them that my music has been heard at all.' He lowered his head, as if overcome by modesty.

Corvus would have snorted at the conceit of the gesture, but he was too tense. He dreaded the words that might come from his brother's rictus face.

Gurges looked up, and now his eyes seemed to glow with a light the colour of dust and ash. 'Yes,' he said, 'the generous patron is to be cherished. But even more precious, even more miraculous, even more worthy of celebration, is the patron who *inspires*. The patron who opens the door to new vistas of creation, and pushes the artist through. I stand before you as the servant of one such patron. I know that my humble tribute to the Emperor is held in high regard, but I can now see what a poor counterfeit of the truth that effort is. Tonight, so will you. I cannot tell you what my patron has unveiled for me. But I can *show* you.'

The composer's last words slithered out over the hall like a death rattle. Gurges turned to face the choir. He raised his arms. The singers remained unmoving. The last light went out. A terrible, far-too-late certainty hit Corvus; he must stop this.

Then Gurges began to sing.

For almost a minute, Corvus felt relief. No daemon burst from his brother's mouth. His pulse slowed. He had fallen for the theatrics of a first-rate showman, that was all. The song didn't sound any different to him than any other of Gurges's efforts. It was another succession of notes, each as meaningless as the next. Then he noticed that he was wrong. He wasn't hearing a simple succession. Even his thick ears could tell that Gurges was singing two notes at once. Then three. Then four. The song became impossible. Somehow still singing, Gurges drew a breath, and though Corvus heard no real change in the music, the breath seemed to mark the end of the refrain.

It also marked the end of peace, because now the choir began to sing. To a man, they joined in, melding with Gurges's voice. The song became a roar. The darkness began to withdraw as a glow spread across the stage. It seeped from the singers. It poured like radiation fog into the seating. It was a colour that made Corvus wince. It was a kind of green, if green could scream. It pulsed like taut flesh.

It grinned like Chaos.

Corvus leapt to his feet. So did the rest of the audience. For a crazy moment of hope, he thought of ordering the assembled people to fall upon the singers and silence them. But they weren't rising, like him, in alarm. They were at one with the music, and they joined their voices to its glory, and their souls to its power. The roar became a wave. The glow filled the hall, and it showed Corvus nothing he wanted to see. Beside him, the governor and his wife stood motionless, their faces contorted with ecstasy. They sang as if the song were their birthright. They sang to bring down the sky. Their heads were thrown back, their jaws as wide as a snake's, and their throats twitched and spasmed with the effort to produce inhuman chords. Corvus grabbed Elpidius by the shoulders and tried to shake him. The governor's frame was rigid and grounded to the core of Ligeta. Corvus might have been wrestling with a pillar. But the man wasn't cold like stone. He was burning up. His eyes were glassy. Corvus checked his pulse. Its rhythm was violent, rapid, irregular. Corvus yanked his hands away. They felt slick with disease. Something that lived in the song scrabbled at his mind like fingernails on plastek, but couldn't find a purchase.

He opened the flap of his shoulder holster and pulled out his laspistol. He leaned over the railing of the box, and sighted on his brother's head. He felt no hesitation. He felt only necessity. He pulled the trigger.

Gurges fell, the top of his skull seared away. The song didn't care. It roared on, its joy unabated. Corvus fired six more times, each shot dropping a member of the choir. Finally, he stopped. The song wasn't a spell and it wasn't a mechanism. It was a plague, and killing individual vectors was worse than useless. It stole precious time from action that might make a difference.

He ran from the box. In the vestibule, the ushers were now part of the choir, and the song pursued Corvus as he clattered down the marble steps to the mezzanine and thence to the ground floor. The foyer, as cavernous as the Performance Hall, led to the Great Gallery of Art. Its vaulted length stretched a full kilometre to the exit of the palace. Floor-to-ceiling glassaics of the primarchs gazed down on heroic bronzes. Warriors beyond counting trampled the Imperium's enemies, smashing them into fragmented agony that sank into the pedestals. But the gallery was no longer a celebration of art and glory. It was a throat, and it howled the song after him. Though melody was a stranger to him, still he could feel the force of the music, intangible yet pushing him with the violence of a hurricane's breath. The light was at his heels, flooding the throat with its mocking bile.

He burst from the grand doorway onto the plaza. He stumbled to a halt, horrified.

The concert had been broadcast.

Palestrina, Ligeta's capital and a city of thirty million, screamed. It convulsed.

The late-evening glow of the city was stained with the Chaos non-light. In the plaza, in the streets, in the windows of Palestrina's delicate and coruscating towers, the people stood and sang their demise. The roads had become a nightmare of twisted, flaming wreckage as drivers, possessed by art, slammed into each other. Victims of collisions, not quite dead, sang instead of screaming their last. Everywhere, the choir chanted to the sky, and the sky answered with flame and thunder. To the west, between the towers, the horizon strobed and rumbled as fireballs bloomed. He was looking at the space port, Corvus realised, and seeing the destruction caused by every landing and departing ship suddenly losing all guidance.

There was a deafening roar overhead, and a cargo transport came in low and mad. Its engines burning blue, it ploughed into the side of a tower a few blocks away. The ship exploded, filling the sky with the light and sound of its death. Corvus ducked as pieces of shrapnel the size of meteors arced down, gouging impact craters into street and stone and flesh. The tower collapsed with lazy majesty, falling against its neighbours and spreading a domino celebration of destruction. Dust billowed up in a choking, racing cloud. It rushed over Corvus, hiding the sight of the dying city, but the chant went on.

He coughed, gagging as grit filled his throat and lungs. He staggered, but started moving again. Though visibility was down to a few metres, and his eyes watered and stung, he felt that he could see clearly again. It was as if, by veiling the death of the city from his gaze, the dust had broken a spell. Palestrina was lost, but that didn't absolve him of his duty to the Emperor. Only his own death could do that. As long as he drew breath, his duty was to fight for Ligeta, and save what he could.

He had to find somewhere the song had not reached, find men who had not heard and been infected by the plague. Then he could mount a defence, perhaps even a counter-attack, even if that were nothing more than a scorched-earth purge. There would be glory in that. But first, a chance to regroup. First, a sanctuary. He had hopes that he knew where to go.

He felt his way around the grey limbo of the plaza, a hand over his mouth, trying not to cough up his lungs. It took him the best part of an hour to reach the far side of the Palace of Culture. By that time, the worst of the dust had settled and the building's intervening bulk further screened him. He could breathe again. His movements picked up speed and purpose. He needed a vehicle, one he could manoeuvre through the tangled chaos of the streets. Half a kilometre down from the plaza, he found what he wanted. A civilian was straddling his idling bike. He had been caught by the song just before pulling away. Corvus tried to push him off, but he was as rigid and locked down as the governor had been. Corvus shot him. As he hauled the corpse away from the bike, he told himself that the man had already been dead. If Corvus hadn't granted him mercy, something else would have. A spreading fire. Falling debris. If nothing violent had happened, then...

Corvus stared at the singing pedestrians, and thought through the implications of what he was seeing. Nothing, he was sure, could free the victims once the song took hold. So they would stand where they were struck and sing, and do nothing else. They wouldn't sleep. They wouldn't eat. They wouldn't drink. Corvus saw the end result, and he also saw the first glimmer of salvation. With a renewed sense of mission, he climbed on the bike and drove off.

It was an hour from dawn by the time he left the city behind. Beyond the hills of Palestrina, he picked up even more speed as he hit the parched mud flats. Once fertile, the land here had had its water table drained by the city's thirst. At the horizon, the shadow of the Goreck Mesa blocked the stars. At the base of its bulk, he saw pinpricks of light. Those glimmers were his destination and his hope.

The ground rose again as he reached the base. He approached the main gate, and he heard no singing. Before him, the wall was an adamantium shield fifty metres high – a sloping, pleated curtain of strength. A giant aquila was engraved every ten metres along the wall's two-kilometre length. Beyond the wall, he heard the growl of promethium engines, the report of firing ranges, the march of boots. The sounds of discipline. Discipline that was visible from the moment he arrived. If the sentries were surprised to see him, dusty and exhausted, arriving on a civilian vehicle instead of in his staff transport, they showed no sign. They saluted, sharp as machines, and opened the gate for him. He passed through into Fort Goreck and the promise of salvation.

On the other side of the wall was a zone free of art and music. A weight lifted from Corvus's shoulders as he watched the pistoning, drumming rhythm of the military muscle. Strength perfected, and yet, by the Throne, it had been almost lost too. A request had come the day before from Jeronim Tarrant, the base's captain. Given the momentous, planet-wide event that was a new composition by Gurges Parthamen, would the colonel authorise a break in the drills, long enough for the men to sit down and listen to the vox-cast of the concert? Corvus had not just rejected the request out of hand, he had forbidden any form of reception and transmission of the performance. He wanted soldiers, he had informed Jeronim. If he wanted dilettantes, he could find plenty in the boxes of the Palace of Culture.

On his way to the concert, he had wondered about his motives in issuing that order. Jealousy? Was he really that petty? He knew now that he wasn't, and that he'd been right. The purpose of a base such as this was to keep the Guard in a state of perpetual, instant readiness, because peace might become war in the passing of a second.

As it had now.

He crossed the parade field, making for the squat command tower at the rear of the base, where it nestled against the basalt wall of the mesa. He had barely dismounted the bike when Jeronim came pounding out of the tower. He was pale, borderline frantic, but remembered to salute. Discipline, Corvus thought. It had saved them so far. It would see them through to victory.

'Sir,' Jeronim said. 'Do you know what's going on? Are we under attack? We can't get through to anyone.'

'Yes, we are at war,' Corvus answered. He strode briskly to the door. 'No one in this base has been in contact with anyone outside it for the last ten hours?'

Jeronim shook his head. 'No, sir. Nothing that makes sense. Anyone transmitting is just sending what sounds like music–'

Corvus cut him off. 'You listened?'

'Only a couple of seconds. When we found the nonsense everywhere, we shut down the sound. No one was sending anything coherent. Not even the *Scythe of Judgement*.'

So the Ligetan flagship had fallen. He wasn't surprised, but Corvus discovered that he could still feel dismay. The fact that the base had survived the transmissions told him something. The infection didn't take hold right away. He remembered that the choir and the audience hadn't responded until Gurges had completed a full refrain. The song's message had to be complete, it seemed, before it could sink in.

'What actions have you taken?' he asked Jeronim as they headed up the staircase to the command centre.

'We've been sending out requests for acknowledgement on all frequencies. I've placed the base on heightened alert. And since we haven't been hearing from anyone, I sent out a distress call.'

'Fine,' Corvus said. For whatever good that call will do, he thought. By the time the message was received and aid arrived, weeks or months could have elapsed. By that time, the battle for the soul of Ligeta would have been won or lost. The singers would have starved to death, and either there would be someone left to pick up the pieces, or there wouldn't be.

The communications officer looked up from the auspex as Corvus and Jeronim walked into the centre. 'Colonel,' he saluted. 'A capital ship has just transitioned into our system.'

'Really?' That was fast. Improbably fast.

'It's hailing us,' the master vox-operator announced.

Corvus lunged across the room and yanked the head-phones from the operator's skull. 'All messages to be received as text only until further notice,' he ordered. 'No exceptions. Am I clear?'

The operator nodded.

'Acknowledge them,' Corvus went on. 'Request identification.'

The soldier did so. Corvus moved to the plastek window and looked out over the base while he waited. There were five thousand men here. The position was elevated, easily defensible. He had the tools. He just had to work out how to fight.

'Message received, colonel.'

Corvus turned to the vox-operator. His voice sounded all wrong, like that of a man who had suddenly been confronted with the futility of his existence. He was staring at the data-slate before him. His face was grey.

'Read it,' Corvus said, and braced himself.

'Greetings, Imperials. This is the *Terminus Est*.'

TYPHUS ENTERED THE strategium as the ship emerged into the real space of the Ligetan system.

'Multiple contacts, lord,' the bridge attendant reported.

Of course there were. The Imperium would hardly leave Ligeta without a defending fleet. Typhus moved his bulk towards the main oculus. They were already close enough to see the swarm of Imperial cruisers and defence satellites. 'How many are on attack trajectories?' Typhus asked. He knew the answer, but he wanted the satisfaction of hearing it.

The officer looked twice at his hololithic display, as if he doubted the reports he was receiving. 'None,' he said after a moment.

'And how many are targeting us?'

Another brief silence. 'None.'

Typhus rumbled and buzzed his pleasure. The insects that were his parasites and his identity fluttered and scrabbled with excitement. His armour rippled with their movement. He allowed himself a moment to revel in the experience, in the glorious and terrible paradox of his existence. Disease was an endless source of awe in its marriage of death and unrestrained life. It was his delight to spread the gospel of this paradox, the lesson of decay. Before him, the oculus showed how well the lesson was being learned. 'Bring us in close,' he commanded.

'At once, lord.' The bridge attendant was obedient, but was a slow learner himself. He was still thinking in terms of a normal combat situation, never mind that the Imperial fleet's lack of response to the appearance of a Chaos capital ship was far from normal. 'We are acquiring targets,' he reported.

'No need, no need,' Typhus said. 'See for yourselves. All of you.'

His officers looked up, and Typhus had an audience for the spectacle he had arranged. As the *Terminus Est* closed in on the glowing green-and-brown globe of Ligeta, the enemy ships gathered size and definition. Their distress became clear, too. Some were drifting, nothing more now than adamantium tombs. Others had their engines running, but there was no order to their movements. The ships, Typhus knew, were performing the last commands their crews had given them, and there would be no others to come.

'Hail the Imperials,' he ordered. 'Open all frequencies.'

The strategium was bathed in the music of disease. Across multiple channels came the same noise, a unified chaos of millions upon millions of throats singing in a single choir. The melody was a simple, sustained, multi-note chord of doom. It became the accompaniment to the view outside the *Terminus Est*, and now the movement of the fleet was the slow ballet of entropy and defeat. Typhus watched two cruisers follow their unalterable routes until they collided. One exploded, its fireball the expanding bloom of a poisonous flower. The other plunged towards Ligeta's atmosphere, bringing with it the terrible gift of its weapons payload and shattered reactor.

Typhus thought about its landfall, and his insects writhed in anticipation.

He also thought about the simplicity of the lesson, how pure it was, and how devastating its purity made it. Did the happenstance that had brought Gurges Parthamen into his grasp taint that purity, or was that flotsam of luck an essential piece of the composition's beauty? The composer on a self-indulgent voyage, getting caught in a localised warp storm, winding up in a near-collision with the *Terminus Est*; how could those elements be anything other than absolute contingency? His triumph could so easily have never even been an idea. Then again, that man, his ambition that made him so easily corruptible, the confluence of events that granted Typhus this perfect inspiration – they were so improbable, they could not possibly be chance. They had been threaded together by destiny.

Flies howled through the strategium as Typhus tasted the paradox and found it to his liking. Chaos and fate, one and the same.

Perhaps Gurges had thought so, too. He had put up no resistance to being infected with the new plague. Typhus was particularly proud of it. The parasitic warp worm laid its eggs in the bloodstream and attacked the brain. It spread itself from mind to mind by the transmission of its idea, and the idea travelled on a sound – a special sound, a song that was an incantation that thinned the walls between reality and the immaterium, and taught itself to all who had ears to hear.

'My lord, we are being hailed,' said the attendant.

Typhus laughed, delighted, and the boils on the deck quivered in sympathy. 'Send them our greeting,' he ordered.

NOW HE HAD an enemy. Now he could fight.

Corvus rejected despair. He rejected the odds. There

was an enemy, and duty demanded combat. There was nothing else.

Corvus stood at the reviewing stand on the parade grounds, and, speakers turning his voice into Fort Goreck's voice, he addressed the assembled thousands. He explained the situation. He described the plague and its means of contagion. Then he laid down the rules. One was paramount. 'Music,' he thundered, 'is a disease. It will destroy us if it finds the smallest chink in our armour. We must be free of it, and guard against it. Anyone who so much as whistles will be executed on the spot.' He felt enormous satisfaction as he gave that order. He didn't worry about why.

LESS THAN A day after his arrival, Typhus witnessed the apotheosis of his art. The entire planet was one voice. The anthem, the pestilence; the anthem that *was* pestilence, had become the sum total of existence on Ligeta. Its population lived for a single purpose. The purity was electrifying.

Or it would have been, but for one single flaw. There was that redoubt. He had thought it would succumb by itself, but it hadn't. It was still sending out desperate pleas to whatever Imperials might hear. Though Typhus could amuse himself with the thought that this one pustule of order confirmed the beauty of corruption, he also knew the truth. Over the course of the next few days, the song would begin a ragged diminuendo as its singers died. If he didn't act, his symphony would be incomplete, spoiled by one false note.

It was time to act.

* * *

THE ATTACK CAME on the evening of the second day. Corvus was walking the parapet when he saw the sky darken. A deep, unending thunder began, and the clouds birthed a terrible rain. The drop-pods came first, plummeting with the finality of black judgement. They made landfall on the level ground a couple of kilometres from the base. They left streaks in the air, black, vertical contrails that didn't dissipate. Instead, they grew wider, broke up into fragments, and began to whirl. Corvus ran to the nearest guard tower, grabbed a marksman's sniper rifle and peered through its telescopic sight. He could see the movement in the writhing clouds more clearly. It looked like insects. Faintly, impossibly, weaving in and out of the thunder of the pods and the landing craft that now followed on, Corvus heard an insidious buzz.

The darkness flowed from the sky. It was the black of absence and grief, of putrefaction and despair, and of unnameable desire. Its touch infected the air of the landing zone, then rippled out towards the base. It was a different disease, one Corvus had no possible defence against. Though no tendrils of the blackness itself reached this far, Corvus felt something arrive over the wall. The quality of the evening light changed. It turned brittle and sour. He sensed something vital becoming too thin, and something wrong start to smile.

All around him, Fort Goreck's warning klaxons sounded the call to arms. The din was enormous, and he was surprised and disturbed that he could hear the buzzing of the Chaos swarms at all. That told him how sick the real world was becoming, and how hard he would have to fight for it.

The drop-pods opened, their venomous petals falling back to disgorge the monsters within. Corvus had never felt comfortable around Space Marines, his Ligetan inferiority complex made exponentially worse by their superhuman power and perfection. But he would have given anything to have one beside him now as he saw the nightmare versions of them mustering in the near distance. Their armour had long since ceased to be simple ceramite. It was darkness that was iron, and iron that was disease. They assembled into rows and then stood motionless, weapons at the ready. Only they weren't entirely still. Their outlines writhed.

Landing craft poured out corrupted infantry in ever greater numbers. At length, the sky spat out a leviathan that looked to Corvus like a Goliath-class transport, only so distorted it seemed more like a terrible whale. Its hull was covered with symbols that tore at Corvus's eyes with obscenities. Around it coiled things that might have been tendrils or tentacles. Its loading bay opened like a maw, and it vomited hordes of troops and vehicles onto the blackening soil of Ligeta.

The legions of plague gathered before Corvus, and he knew there was no hope of fighting them.

But still he would. *Down to the last man*. Though there might be no chance of survival, there would, he now realised with a stir of joy, be the hope of glory in a heroic last stand.

Night fell, and the forces of the *Terminus Est* grew in numbers and strength. The host was now far larger than was needed to storm Fort Goreck, walls or no, commanding heights or no. But the dark soldiers didn't attack. They stood, massed and in the open.

Once disembarked, they did nothing. Heavy artillery rumbled out of the transport and then stopped, barrels aimed at the sky, full of threat but silent. The rumble of arrivals stopped. A clammy quiet covered the land.

Corvus had returned to the command centre. He could watch just as well from there, and the low buzzing was less noticeable on this side of the plastek.

'What are they waiting for?' Jeronim muttered.

The quiet was broken by the distant roar of engines. Corvus raised a pair of magnoculars. Three Rhinos were moving to the fore. There were rows of rectangular shapes on the top of the Rhinos. They were horned metal, moulded into the shape of screaming daemons. Loudspeakers, Corvus realised.

Dirge Casters.

If the Rhinos broadcast their song, Fort Goreck would fall without a shot being fired.

Corvus slammed a fist against the alarm trigger. The klaxons whooped over the base. 'Do not turn these off until I give the order,' he told the officers. Still not loud enough, he thought. He turned to the master vox. He shoved the operator aside and flipped the switches for the public address system. He grabbed the mic and ran over to the speaker above the doorway to the command centre. He jammed the mic into the speaker. Feedback pierced his skull, mauled his hearing and sought to obliterate all thought. He gasped from the pain, and staggered under the weight of the sound.

The men around him were covering their ears and weaving around as if drunk. Corvus struggled against the blast of the sound and shook the officers. 'Now!'

he screamed. 'We attack now! Launch the Chimeras and take out those vehicles!'

He would have given his soul for a battery of battle cannons, so he could take out the Rhinos from within the safety of the noise shield he had just erected. But this would have to do. He didn't think about how little he might gain in destroying a few speakers. He saw the chance to fight the opponent.

He saw the chance for glory.

He took charge of the squads that followed behind the Chimeras. He saw the pain of the men's faces as the eternal feedback wore at them. He saw the effort it took them to focus on the simple task of readying their weapons. He understood, and hoped that they understood the necessity of his actions, and saw the heroism of their struggle for the Emperor. Gurges had been a fool, Corvus thought. What *he* did now was worthy of song.

The gates opened, and the Chimeras surged forwards. The Rhinos had stopped halfway between their own forces and the wall, easily within the broadcast range of the Dirge Casters. The song was inaudible. Corvus felt his lips pull back in a snarl of triumph as he held his laspistol and chainsword high and led the charge. The courage of the Imperium burst from the confines of the wall. Corvus yelled as he pounded behind the clanking, roaring Chimeras. The feedback whine faded as they left the base behind, but the vehicles had their own din, and Corvus still could hear no trace of the song.

Then something spoke with the voice of ending. The sound was enormous, a deep, compound thunder. It was the Chaos artillery, all guns opening up simultaneously, firing a single, monumental barrage. The lower slope of Fort Goreck's rise exploded, earth geysering skywards. A giant made of noise and air picked Corvus up and threw him. The world tumbled end over end, a hurricane of dirt and rocks and fire. He slammed into the ground and writhed, a pinned insect, as his flattened lungs fought to pull in a breath. When the air came, it was claws and gravel in his chest. His head rang like a struck bell.

When his eyes and ears cleared, he saw the wreckage of the Chimeras and the rout of his charge. The vehicles had taken the worst of the hits, and were shattered, smoking ruins of twisted metal. Pieces of men were scattered over the slope: an arm still clutching a lasgun, a torso that ended at the lower jaw, organs without bodies, bodies without organs. But there were survivors, and as the enemy's guns fell silent, the song washed over the field. Men picked themselves up, and froze as the refrain caught them. A minute after the barrage, Corvus was the only man left with a will of his own. He picked up his weapons and stumbled back up the slope towards the wall. As he ran, he thought he could hear laughter slither through the ranks of the Chaos force.

The gates opened just enough to let him back inside. The feedback blotted out the song, but wrapped itself around his brain like razor wire. He had lost his cap, and his uniform was in tatters. Still, he straightened his posture as he walked back through the stunned troops. Halfway across the grounds, a conscript confronted him. The man's eyes were watering from the hours of mind-destroying feedback and his nose was bleeding. 'Let us go,' he pleaded. 'Let us fight. We'll resist as long as we can.'

Corvus pushed him back. 'Are you mad?' he shouted over the whine. 'Do you know what would happen to you?'

The trooper nodded. 'I was on the wall. I saw.'

'Well then?'

'They look happy when they sing. At least that death isn't pointless torture.'

Corvus raised his pistol and shot the man through the eye. He turned in a full circle, glaring at his witnesses, making sure they understood the lesson. Then he stalked back to the command centre.

A NIGHT AND a day of the endless electronic wail. Then another night of watching with nerves scraped raw. Corvus plugged his ears with cloth, but the feedback stabbed its way through the pathetic barrier. His jaw worked, his cheek muscles twitched, and he saw the same strain in the taut, clenched faces of his men. The Rhinos came no closer, and there were no other enemy troop movements. Fort Goreck was besieged by absolute stillness, and that would be enough.

The third day of the siege was a hell of sleeplessness and claustrophobic rage. Five Guardsmen attempted to desert. Corvus had them flogged, then shot.

As the sun set, Corvus could see the end coming. There would be no holding out. The shield he had erected was torture, and madness would tear the base apart. The only thing left was a final, glorious charge that would deny the enemy the kind of triumph that they clearly desired. But how to make that attack if the troops would succumb to the anthem before they even reached the front lines?

Corvus covered his ears with his hands, trying to block the whine, to dampen it just enough so that he could think. Silence would have been the greatest gift the Emperor could bestow upon him.

Instead, he was granted the next greatest: inspiration.

The medicae centre was on the ground floor of the command block. Corvus found the medic, and explained what was required. The man blanched and refused. Corvus ordered him to do as he said. Still the medic protested. Corvus put his laspistol to the man's head, and that was convincing enough. Just.

The process took all night. At least, for the most part, the men didn't resist being rendered deaf. Some seemed almost relieved to be free of the feedback whine. Most submitted to the procedure with slack faces and dead looks. They had become creatures of stoic despair, held together and animated by the habits of discipline. Corvus watched yet another patient, blood pouring from his ears, contort on a gurney. At least, he thought, he was giving the soldiers back their pride for the endgame.

There wasn't time to inoculate the entire base contingent against the anthem, so Corvus settled on the best, most experienced squads. That would be enough. They were Imperial Guard, and they would give the traitor forces something to think about.

MORNING CAME QUICKLY, and though one more enemy gunship had landed during the night, the enemy's disposition otherwise remained unchanged. His eyes rough as sand from sleeplessness, Corvus inspected his assembled force. The soldiers looked like the walking dead, unworthy of the glory they were about to find. He would give it to them anyway, Corvus thought, and they could thank him in the Emperor's light.

He glanced at the rest of the troops. He would be abandoning them to their fate. He shrugged. They were doomed regardless, and at least he had enforced loyalty up to the last. He could go to his grave knowing that he had permitted no defection to Chaos.

He had done his duty.

He had earned his glory.

'Open the gates,' he roared, and wished he could hear the strength of his shout over the shriek of the feedback. The sentries couldn't hear him either, but his gesture was clear, and the wall of Fort Goreck opened for the last time.

THERE ARE SONGS that have been written about the final charge of Colonel Corvus Parthamen. But they are not sung in the mess halls of the Imperial Guard, and they are not stirring battle hymns. They are mocking, obscene doggerel, and they are snarled, rather than sung, with venomous humour, in the corridors of dark ships that ply the warp like sharks. A few men of the Imperium do hear it, in their terminal moments, as their positions are overrun by the hordes of Chaos. They do not appreciate it any more than Corvus would have.

The charge was a rout. The men ran into las-fire and bolter shells. They were blown to pieces by cannon barrage. They were shredded by chainswords and pulped by armoured fists. Still, they made it further down the hill than even Corvus could have hoped. A coherent force actually hit the Chaos front lines and did some damage before being annihilated. Their actions might have seemed like glorious heroism born of nothing-to-lose desperation. But the fact that not a single man took cover – that not one did anything but run straight ahead, weapon firing indiscriminately – revealed the truth. They were running to their deaths, and were glad of the relief.

Corvus was the last. It took him a moment to notice that he was alone, what with the joy of battle and the ecstasy of being free of the whine. He was still running forwards, running to his glory, but he wondered now why there didn't seem to be any shots aimed at him. Or why the squad of Chaos Space Marines ahead parted to let him pass. He faltered, and then he saw who was waiting for him.

The monster was huge, clad in what had once been Terminator armour, but was now a buzzing, festering exoskeleton. Flies swarmed from the funnels above his shoulders and the lesions in the corrupted ceramite. His single-horned helmet transformed the being's final human traces into the purely daemonic. His grip on his giant scythe was relaxed.

Corvus saw just how powerful disease-made flesh could be. He charged anyway, draining his laspistol, then pulling his chainsword. He swung at the Herald of Nurgle. Typhus whipped the Manreaper around. The movement was as rapid as it was casual and contemptuous. He hit Corvus with the shaft and shattered his hip. Corvus collapsed in the dirt. He bit down on his scream as Typhus loomed over him.

'Kill me,' Corvus spat. 'But know that I fought you to the end. I have my own victory.'

Typhus made a sound that was the rumble of giant hives. Corvus realised he had just heard laughter. 'Kill you?' Typhus asked. His voice was deep. It was smooth as a deliquescent corpse. 'I haven't come to kill you. I have come to teach you my anthem.'

Through his pain, Corvus managed his own laugh. 'I will never sing it.'

'Really? But you have already. You believe you serve order and light, but, like your carrion Emperor, everything you do blasts hope and rushes towards entropy. Look what you did to your men. You have served me well, my son. You and your brother, both.'

Corvus fought against the epiphany, but it burst over his consciousness with sickly green light. The truth took him, and infected him. He saw his actions, he saw their consequences, and he saw whose glory he had truly been serving. As the pattern took shape for him, so did a sound. He heard the anthem, and he heard its music. There was melody there, and he was part of it. Surrender flooded his system, and the triumphant shape of Typhus filled his dying vision. Corvus's jaw snapped open. His throat contorted with ecstatic agony, and he became one with Ligeta's final choir.

LIBERATOR

by Jonathan Green

It should be noted that desertion amongst the ranks of the honoured Adeptus Astartes is extremely uncommon. However, much as it pains me to write this, neither is it entirely unheard of. Those who have studied the works of Belteshazzar D'Aubigny and Master Filius Victor will speak in hushed whispers of the dark days of the Great Heresy, but, much as I hate to put this to the record, this has not been the only occasion when brother has turned upon brother and the very architects of the glorious Imperium of Man have sought to undo the great work of past noble deeds, and tear down that which they once fought so hard to establish.

It has been calculated that there is one Space Marine for each of the million worlds of the Imperium, and that that number, though small, is sufficient to protect humanity from the foul schemes of the alien, heretics and the powers of the warp. But if even only one of those brothers should turn from the light of the Emperor's Truth and fall upon his fellows like a thing run mad, how can it be enough?

So I say to you, whether you be a student of the ordos, a ranked interrogator or a Lord Militant of His Imperial Majesty's Blessed Inquisition, be ever watchful of the primarchs' get, the proud warriors of the Adeptus Astartes, for only the Emperor Himself is infallible.

From the treatise *Quis Custodiet Ipsos Angeles Mortes?*
by Gideon Lorr, Inquisitor, Ordo Hereticus

HE HAS ALWAYS known this day would come, one day.

The skies of Constantinium are the colour of raw meat, the clouds crimson as fresh blood or hot iron, painted by the fires raging in the old Ecclesiarchy Quarter of Cirtus city. The Great Cathedral, re-consecrated to Constantinus the Liberator – a glorious edifice to one man's over-reaching ambition, the size of an entire city sector – is ablaze.

The raw-meat sky is streaked black by the trails left by falling drop-pods, descending Thunderhawk gunships and ground-to-air heavy ordnance fire. The atmosphere is thick with the smell of the burning promethium refineries and the cloying scent of death.

He turns to the Iconoclast at his side, one of his honour guard. The warrior's gold-edged armour is scuffed and scarred from the battles he has had to endure of late. In some places the battle plate is so badly marked that faint glimmers of blue and white can be seen beneath the gold and red-black, an echo of a memory of what the warrior had once been; of whom he had once served.

'Brother Maimon,' he says, addressing the Iconoclast, 'tell me, who is it that comes against us now with sword and flame, with hammer and bolter.'

The Iconoclast studies the incoming craft, the esoteric systems of his helmet visor locking on to the falling, swooping landing craft. Targeting reticules focus on the Chapter markings cast upon the vehicles' atmospheric entry-heated hull plates, magnifying the badges and Adeptus Astartes insignia. The Iconoclast sees gunmetal-grey cross-crosslets against a black shield.

The Liberator himself goes bare-headed, as he has done ever since the glorious day when he earned that honorific and liberated Nova Terra, as the planet was known then; when the people gazed upon the face of their saviour and knew him for the mighty avenging angel he was – the avenging angel he still is.

'Iron Knights, my lord,' Iconoclast Maimon replies, his voice a rumbling growl.

'Iron Knights?' The Liberator laughs. 'Well, let us see how their iron might fares against the armour of faithfulness.'

He takes in the shattered walls of the bastion behind him with a weary glance. After thirteen years of fighting the Imperium, his defiance and his contempt for the ailing Empire of Mankind is all he has left.

The moment he broke his vows of brotherhood and obedience, he had known, somewhere deep inside of himself, that this day would come. If he had not launched his pogrom against the other worlds of the Viridis subsector, perhaps it might not have come as soon, but it would still have come. It had been as inevitable as the wrath of the False Emperor.

He turns from the breach blasted through the ferrocrete walls of the bastion – a rift one hundred metres high, its heat-fused lips like dribbled black wax – and gazes across the lower slopes of his citadel stronghold.

Much of Cirtus is ablaze now. The metropolis looks like it did all those years ago when he first liberated this world, only on that occasion it was he who had put its populace to the sword and set its streets alight. His gaze is slowly drawn back to the silhouette of the Great Cathedral, backlit by the firestorm engulfing that region of the city.

The stern features of the golden edifice that stands before the broken basilica seem to shift in the flickering light of the flames. One minute the cyclopean effigy is smiling upon the people of Cirtus, the next it is a furious deity of rage, its face a mask of hatred at the hubris of the invaders, that they should dare deny him that which was his by right, that which he had fought so long and so hard to win. That which he had finally won through great personal sacrifice – the greatest anyone on Constantinium had ever had to make.

Within the canyon streets of the tenement habs, within the tekannibal-haunted industrial quarter, within the shattered ruins of the grand arena, the fighting is at its most intense.

The battle-lust burns in his blood. He yearns for combat. The stink of fyceline and cordite has him panting for action once more. Despite the risks that such an action would bring with it, he wishes to be there in the thick of things himself. After all, it is the manner in which he has conducted his entire reign;

it is how he raised a battle force that – at its height – conquered entire star systems in his name, plunging the worlds of the Viridis subsector into a new Age of Darkness.

In the armies of the Imperium he had been a mere sergeant. But free of the shackles of duty he had risen to become as a god. Worlds shook at the tread of his armoured feet. Entire dynasties were toppled at mere mention of his name.

It is then that he sees them for the first time, making for the breach, emerging from the clouds of drifting smoke, giving voice to their mewling battle-cries, declaring their subjugation to the Golden Throne: a gaggle of soldiers in black and grey fatigues and ashen flak armour, lasguns held low, bayonets fixed, not a heavy weapon between them.

He would laugh if it wasn't so insulting that these insects thought they could challenge him, here on his world, coming at him like children, armed with wooden swords and shields.

He does not need to give the command; those who follow him know what is expected of them. It is but one thing.

The Zealous who fight in his name, making the invaders pay for every metre they advance in blood. The Enlightened, who have witnessed first-hand the fate of those who would challenge this dominion. The Iconoclasts – once his brethren, now his bodyguard – who helped shape this world, and the fate of a dozen others like it. Just one thing, that is all he asks; the one thing that was denied him in a former life.

Loyalty.

He leads the charge himself, striding down the

scree of shattered walls and through the smoke, resplendent in his gold-chased, blood-black armour, the unutterable names of a thousand unspeakable things picked out in sigils and runes that seem to glow and smoke with molten heat.

At his back march his personal bodyguard – his Iconoclasts – Maimon and Pius, the most loyal of all his devotees, their armour red-black and gold like his, the eight-pointed star raised from the ceramite of their left shoulder pads where once was displayed an altogether different insignia.

Behind them come Kabaiel, also known as the Skull-taker, and Gha'gur Nor the Slythian, once of the warband of Ghorgoth the Oppressor, now Herald of Constantinus, the most faithful of the Enlightened, *Foe-smiter* held reverently in his gauntleted fists.

Zipping las-bolts *spang* from ceramite plate that has withstood the slavering attentions of ravenous daemon-blades and even the excoriating blades of a degenerate Helbrute, some years before. His honour guard do not even break stride.

Five demi-gods against ten times as many Guardsmen; demi-gods who made the star-realm of Man what it was, and who could tear it down and remould it just as easily. The invaders would be as wheat before the reaper's scythe.

The weapon in his hand hums with unnatural life. It is an instrument of destruction, a crackling golden blade set within an ebon hilt. It is a weapon that, in his hands, has taken the heads of his enemies by the score. It is a slayer of champions, a killer of kings. It has had other names in ages past, but it answers to only one name now: *Ruin*.

The first Guardsman dies with a plaintive prayer to the God-Emperor on his bloody lips. It doesn't stop *Ruin* cleaving him in twain from crown to groin.

Then the Iconoclasts are upon the Guardsman pack and the broken ground runs red with the blood of mortals.

The Liberator's humming blade opens flak armour as readily as it cleaves flesh from bone and boils blood.

Something much larger than a man comes at him then, a sweating abhuman ogryn; but it falls like the rest of them, *Ruin* stuck in the brute's chest, the sword's energy field cooking the mutant's enlarged heart with its sun-hot coruscating discharge.

He carries out the killings with clinical precision. No berserker battle-cries for him, no chanting to the gods of the warp. There is no need. What he achieves with his blade is his sacrament to the Powers that be, writ in the blood of those who would dare come against him.

Then there is no more killing to be done, the broken ground awash with the vital fluids of the Imperial Guardsmen, steaming offal declaring the Powers' approval, intestines spilling from opened bellies to form shapes pleasing to the true masters of the universe.

He feels the boom of the great golden statue's destruction as well as hearing it. His old eyes find the cathedral precinct, wherein once lay the Place of Testing, and he sees the cyclopean effigy topple from view behind the smoky ruins of the worker habs with the slow inevitably of a cliff-face sliding into the sea. The cheering tumult that comes after is almost as loud as the Shadowsword volcano cannon blast that has toppled the statue.

'They would liberate this world from me, would they?' he purrs, his stony expression softening at last as a cruel smile curls his lips. 'Well let them try.'

THE PERSONAL TRANSPORT of Dvar Ghorgoth, Scourge of Worlds, rumbles to a halt before the broken gates that once marked the limits of an Ecclesiarchy compound, but which now forms the entrance to the arena.

The arena has no particular name, it needs none. It is enough that it is the place to which they are called by their dark gods, champions and their warbands by their dozens, to test themselves against the upstart emperor of this beleaguered backwater world.

Ghorgoth emerges from his transport then, heralded by the screams of slave-psykers and bound and blinded priests, as skull-faced cherubic-things goad the damned with crackling agonisers. One of the black-winged cherubs detaches itself from the rest of the flock, following the Packmaster with jerky fluttering movements.

The place of battle is adorned with the heraldry of scores of petty tyrants and upstart kings, whose warrior bands now swear fealty to another.

Icons of blood-quenched iron loom above the packed stands of the coliseum alongside tattered banners of weathered human hide. A thousand renegades, loyal to the Powers and sworn to follow the lord of this world, in whose name it has been remade, watch Ghorgoth as he enters the arena. Some watch in cold silence, others jeering and baying like beasts for his blood, all of them the spoils of a hundred previous gladiatorial contests.

The Packmaster is resplendent in his scrimshawed battle plate. Even under skies choked with the smoke of a thousand bone-fires, the bony ridges and overlapping calcified plates give him the appearance of a simulacrum of death, a golem of ancient bone. It is as if the remains of one of those funerary pyres have risen from the ash and embers to be revenged upon he who liberated the unbelievers from the shackles of their misguided dogma. In his hands the Dvar holds the chainaxe *Interfector*.

Gha'gur Nor has heard it said that Dvar Ghorgoth had once been loyal to the False Emperor, just as the lord of this world had been once; before he broke his own vows of brotherhood, along with the rest of the Calix Chapter, following the Massacre of Ravenscar.

Gha'gur Nor had not known Ghorgoth then, of course. He had been recruited later, after the Calix Chapter became the Screaming Skulls, taken from his tribe during a raid on the planet he later learned was called Lithos VI, and implanted with cursed seed said to have been procured from the Apothecary Errant of the Emperor's Children himself in exchange for a thousand human slaves.

Gha'gur Nor marches out of the Rhino along with the rest of the Oppressor's elite. Their battle plate bears little resemblance to the Dvar's ornate scrimshaw. Some wear the armour of conquered victims, or that scavenged during raids on worlds where mighty battles had once taken place. Others combine plate artificed by the heretek-magi of the Auretian Schism with relics that perhaps date back even as far as the

Dark Age of Technology. There are those who still wear pieces of the vulgar armour they once brought with them from their primitive home worlds. But they all wear the mark of the Dvar upon their left auto-reactive shoulder guards, in mockery of a practice that dates back to the days when the Screaming Skulls had still been the Calix Chapter. The mark they all wear now is the eight-pointed star with a halved human skull set at its centre.

Gha'gur Nor surveys the serried rows of cultists and vassal lords who have already sworn fealty to the Liberator of Constantinium.

The effigy of a golden demi-god, thirty metres high – fashioned from the melted down idols and icons of the False Faith promoted by Imperial Terra – gazes down upon them all, but its burnished gaze weighs particularly heavily upon those who come to test their mettle against the master of this world. The giant's head is bowed, its hands resting upon the hilt of a mighty sword, ready to pass judgement on all who come before it.

Gha'gur Nor had heard the rumours of what happens here. Under the giant's golden gaze, only the most worthy champions received the honour of engaging in their own trial by combat against the master of Constantinium. The prize they fight for is a worthy reward indeed. The winner claims all that the vanquished possesses – his warriors, his wargear, his battlefleets and even those worlds that pay him fealty.

But Gha'gur Nor also knows that the master of Constantinium has not lost a battle yet. Some said that the Liberator had been marked out by the Powers, but then which champion of the warp had not received such a boon from the true gods of the galaxy?

In the shadow of the great idol, a figure – a giant of a man – sits upon a throne of black metal and burnished gold, a cloak of snowtusk fur draped about the broad shoulders of his ensorcelled armour. His head is bare, the lines of a dozen duelling scars visible on a face that is an alabaster echo of the edifice staring down at everything taking place within the arena. So the Liberator himself gazes down upon the Oppressor and his retinue with invidious intent.

The Lord of Constantinium rises to his feet and a hush descends over the bloodthirsty throng without ever a word being spoken. Gha'gur Nor cannot help but be impressed.

The Liberator speaks then, his voice echoing from the shattered walls of the once-cathedral. 'Who is it that comes seeking death and disgrace?'

The Dvar comes to a halt, his retinue forming up behind him, a wall of ceramite, steel and scrimshaw. His personal arms – the skull set within the star – displayed upon the banner-pole that rises from his own ornate armour, snaps in the wind that sends eddies of dust dancing across the amphitheatre. The cherub beats the air at Ghorgoth's shoulder.

Gha'gur Nor feels the atmosphere palpably thicken about him. He has never heard a man, demi-god or otherwise, speak to the Packmaster like that and live a moment longer.

At a nod from the Dvar, the malformed, crow-winged servitor flies up to the balcony where the Liberator sits and clears its throat.

'My lord's name is spoken of in hushed whispers on a dozen worlds. At his behest war-fleets that rival those seen during the days of the Great Uprising strike out across the stars. Civilisations fall and worlds burn at his merest displeasure. He is the ravager of a hundred worlds, victor of a thousand battles. He is Dvar Ghorgoth the Oppressor, flayer of worlds and Packmaster of the Screaming Skulls.'

The Dvar thumbs the activation rune of his axe and with a shrill shriek the gore-stained fangs of tyranids and carnosaurs set within its adamantium links, eat up the air.

The proud words of the Dvar's herald fade to wind-hushed echoes and are replaced by the hollow sound of clapping gauntleted hands.

'Proud words,' the giant in red-black and gold armour says. 'But does Dvar Ghorgoth, also known as Oppressor and Packmaster, not know that a warrior is not judged here upon his rhetoric but by the strength of his sword-arm?'

'Then I hereby issue my challenge!' Ghorgoth roars, silencing his herald before the thing can even attempt a response. 'I challenge you, Constantinus, sometimes called Liberator, sometimes Oathbreaker, to a duel.'

A gasp passes like a breeze through the gathered throng of cultists. Some call for the Dvar's head whilst defending their lord's reputation, calling down vituperative curses upon the Screaming Skulls.

'Fight me, in single combat, if you dare!'

'The question, Dvar,' the giant in gold-chased power armour rumbles as he descends the steps from the balcony to the arena floor, one hand on the pommel of the sword sheathed in the ornately tooled scabbard hanging at his side, 'is do *you* dare?'

Gha'gur Nor watches with intent interest as the

giant strides across the ash and sand of the Place of Testing towards the Packmaster. He really is a giant; but it is not just his physical stature that makes him appear enormous. It is his bearing, the way he carries himself; the air of supreme self-confidence that hangs about him like his mantle of snowtusk fur.

'But understand this, Oppressor,' Constantinus the Liberator declares as he unsheathes his golden sword, the spectators within the coliseum hanging on every word of their lord's proclamation. 'To the victor, the spoils. The war-host of the other.'

Ghorgoth hefts the whirling chainaxe in both hands, revving the whirling teeth with a squeeze of a bone-encrusted gauntlet as he strides forth to meet his opponent.

'His men, fighting machines, unholy relics, slaves, battleships and all worlds that are his dominion.'

'Enough talk!' the Packmaster roars. The duellists are almost upon each other. 'Shut up and fight!'

'So be it,' the Liberator says, and Gha'gur Nor feels something he has not felt in a long time. He feels fear.

He cannot tear his eyes away. His fate, and that of the Screaming Skulls, rests upon the outcome of this one battle.

With that the two champions bring their weapons to bear, axe and sword clashing; the whirling teeth of one kicking sparks from the humming blade of the other.

Gen-hanced muscles bunch and tense, power armour servo-motors grind in protest. Face to face, eyes as hard as adamantium drill bits boring into the bone-ringed eye sockets of the Packmaster's skull-helm, the Liberator makes one last utterance as battle is joined; 'To the death! And pray that the denizens of the warp do not make too much of a meal of devouring your damned soul.'

THE MASS OF humanity gathered before the broken steps of the Great Cathedral of Cirtus City, looks, to Brother Maimon's mind, like a grotesque monster; some spawn of the outer darkness, one body with a thousand gurning faces. It is a beast that has grown fat and bloated and hideous, feeding, driven by its own greed, a hunger that has become insatiable.

The mob wants a change to the established order. The people want to take the place of those who were once their betters and who are now nothing more than burning bonfires of xenos-tainted flesh. The people want to rule where once they were ruled. They want power.

There is only one way to tame such a beast, that Brother Maimon knows of, and that is to break its spirit, to make it fear you. Respect takes time; it must be earned, and it can be a fickle beast too. Fear, however, is instantaneous. Fear is constant. Fear can be forever, if you want it to be.

The power-hungry crowd fills the plaza, the rioters gathered now within the precinct of the Great Cathedral. The city has burned at their hand. Thousands have died, innocent and guilty together, going to their deaths side by side.

Constantinus stands before the beast now. He is as still as a statue, the coldly impassive expression on his face as constant as if it were cast in steel as he regards the monster. The monster he made.

This world's erstwhile rulers deserved to die. They

had given themselves over body and soul to the other, the unclean, the unnatural; to the alien. The sergeant had acted swiftly, cutting off the head of that gene-stealing brood before the cult's taint could become too deeply rooted within the general populace of Nova Terra. But that same populace had not seen with the same clarity of thought as the Sons of Guilliman had.

Enraged by the summary execution of their leaders perpetrated by Constantinus and his battle-brothers, the masses had risen up in revolt. The Space Marines had freed the ungrateful horde from corruption, alien rule and, ultimately the insatiable appetite of the Devourer of Worlds, only for the throng to turn on their saviours in their thousands.

Maimon knows that was the moment when everything had changed. Sons of Guilliman had died for this world, fighting to stem the alien tide in the Emperor's name, and every single one of those Sons had been worth more than the entire numberless, treacherous horde put together.

It was said that there was one Space Marine to fight for each of the million worlds that made up the Imperium, to save mankind from the forces of the alien, heretics and the corrupting powers of the warp. It was also said that one Space Marine for each world is enough for the task in hand. Yet two dozen battle-brothers of the Fourth Company of the Sons of Guilliman have sacrificed themselves for this world, this Nova Terra, only for those who had remained behind to battle the tyranid threat – unremembered and unrewarded – to now have to suffer this final dishonour.

That had been the final disgrace, the final injurious slight that had pushed Sergeant Constantinus beyond the brink. It was more than any mortal man, or immortal Adeptus Astartes, should ever have to endure. If the scum of Cirtus city wanted rebellion, to see their world burn, Squad Constantinus would light the fire for them.

But the revolt that spawned the beast, and the sergeant's actions that followed, could only ever have led to one outcome. That was why Constantinus and his battle-brothers stand before the mob now, Sons of Guilliman no longer, ready to break the beast. The sergeant will demonstrate to the mob who is the mightier, who is possessed of the stronger will, who it is that will dominate whom.

There are those who had already sworn themselves to the sergeant, having seen what Constantinus and his brethren have wrought within the city sectors – Guardsmen who have seen their fellow soldiers die to save Nova Terra from the tyranids, looters, rioters, the dispossessed, former servants of the Ecclesiarchy, members of the Adeptus Arbites stationed on this world. They appreciate what the sergeant and his men have done, what they have been forced to do and why. They follow Constantinus now, and even go so far as to call him Liberator.

Those faithful to him are gathered about his feet, upon the broken steps of the cathedral, their weapons – guns, knives, and anything else they have been able to lay their hands on – displayed in a crude show of might. Behind Constantinus stands Maimon and his brothers, Pius and Hector, who came to this world with the sergeant and who have helped shape it beyond all recognition. They sweep the throng of humanity before them – the panting beast – with boltgun and flamer, armoured incarnations of war and wrath, vengeance and retribution.

Constantinus appears regal in his quartered power armour and snowtusk cloak. In his right hand he grips the ebon hilt of his power sword, the tip of the blade resting against the fractured rockcrete at his feet. For the time being he keeps his left hand behind his back, the trophy he hides there held just as tightly in its gauntleted grasp.

Then Constantinus speaks and the beast learns of the sacrifices its new master has made, how what they have lost cannot compare to what he has given up, in their name; how he has forsworn all he once held true and noble and honourable having seen the Imperial Truth for the lie it really is.

In his very next breath he decries the Emperor and his minions, Constantinus's loyal brethren echoing his words like a mantra, Maimon feeling a part of himself die forever as he does so.

The crowd chant and cheer in response to the sergeant's rhetoric. They are Sons of the false prophet Guilliman no longer, he tells the frenzied mob, for they have been betrayed by those they once called 'brother'. He has gazed upon the true face of the false God-Emperor of Mankind, he tells them, and fathomed the true nature of the universe. He has torn down the false idols raised within the Great Cathedral, he and his fellow Iconoclasts, and just as he has freed his battle-brothers from the shackles of their misguided faith, so shall he liberate all the peoples of this forsaken world.

It is then, and only then, that he reveals his trophy, holding it high so that the gathered masses may see that what he has told them is the truth and nothing less.

Brother Maimon regards Antenor's severed head with cold detachment. Antenor had been disloyal. He had paid the price for that disloyalty, and rightly so, as had the rest. For that was all Constantinus the Iconoclast, Constantinus the Liberator asked of any of them. All he desired was their devotion. Their trust. Their loyalty.

THE CITY OF Cirtus burns, its fine avenues awash with blood and thick with rioting mobs. In the outlying districts of the industrial quarter a firestorm consumes the templum-manufactories where certain cult elements made a futile last stand in a vain attempt to resist the wrath of the Emperor, meted out by his finest warriors in violent fashion.

The labyrinth of the mercantile district has been purged with bolter and flamer, and tactically detonated thermic charges. Every metre has been won in hard-fought battle, but now not a single hybrid or purestrain 'stealer remains alive.

The purging of Cirtus city has not been without its cost. Where ten quit Nova Terra's volcanic plateau regions – having cleansed the basalt caverns that lie there with flamer, sword and boltgun – eight now reconvene within a shattered plaza in the skeletal charcoal shadows of the palaces of the nobility.

It was the city's ruling aristocracy who were the first to face the full force of the Emperor's divine retribution, for it was they who had broken faith with

Him, giving themselves over to the xenos contagion. The taint riddled the families of the planet's ruling classes. But, driven by their sergeant's righteous fervour, Squad Constantinus had acted swiftly, hunting down the infected, rooting out the evil and eradicating any sign of the cult's bloodline. Now they are dead, all of them, and the threat the insidious alien infection posed is no more.

That is where the purging of Cirtus city should have ended.

If only that had been the case, Brother Antenor thinks as Squad Constantinus reunites at the centre of the rubble-strewn plaza, the weapons in their hands still hot from the battles they have fought, befouled with blood and viscera and in serious need of holy cleansing and reconsecration.

Antenor, with Brother Cain at his side, climbs the slope of broken rubble on the northern side of the plaza. Brother Maimon enters from the east, via a shattered colonnade, Brother Hector sweeping the ruined alcoves with his flamer. Brothers Diomed and Palamedes join them, emerging from the shadows that have collected beneath a cracked Imperial eagle. It turns out the sergeant has been waiting for them all along, hidden in plain sight beneath an ornamental archway, its stuccoed plaster façade riddled with bullet holes. A bowed and bloodied Brother Pius skulks behind him.

Antenor hears the crackle of flames in the distance, as entire city sectors are consumed, along with the cries of looters and madmen running riot through the mercantile zones and once proud avenues of Cirtus city.

The eight stand together, reunited once more. But as the sergeant scrutinises his battle-brothers, Antenor feels uneasy – as if there has been a sudden drop in atmospheric pressure, or some unknowable sleeping psyker-sense is trying to pass on a warning, a traitorous thought worming its way into his subconscious and worrying at his surface thoughts. Antenor cannot help thinking that they have never been less united, as if their bonds of brotherhood have never been less certain. Less binding.

Using his free hand, the sergeant deactivates the mag-locks securing his helmet to the neck-ring of his power armour, removes it, and clamps it instead to his side. In the other, he still grips his power sword tightly.

Constantinus fixes each of them in turn then with his granite-hard gaze. But when the stare, as unrelenting as an orbital bombardment, lingers on him, Antenor sees something else in the sergeant's eyes: a fire he has not seen before. The sergeant has always been possessed of an ardent righteousness, a proud desire to see that no wrong-doer goes unpunished, but this is something else. Antenor's throat feels suddenly dry.

The sergeant's blood is up, that is clear, but his spirit is no longer fired by a righteous desire to see the will of the Emperor done but by the hungry fires of untrammelled rage and thirsty blood-lust.

'Well met, my Sons,' the sergeant says, a cruel smile on his lips. His argent and azure quartered battle plate has become a uniform black and red, scorched by the fires he has marched through in order to see the city purged of those he has declared heretics, and doused in the blood and bodily fluids of the same, which even now steam from the energised blade of his active power sword. 'How goes our campaign?'

'It goes well, brother-sergeant,' Brother Maimon replies, with rather too much gusto for Antenor's liking. 'These ungrateful heretic scum will not forget the toll their transgressions against us have exacted. Those that still live.'

'Excellent, excellent. I myself have purged half a dozen city sectors with fire, bolter and sword, with Brother Pius at my side,' the sergeant announces proudly.

'Such is the price of treachery,' exalts Pius, sounding like some pontiff quoting scripture from his mobile pulpit.

'And what of the rest of you? What do you have to report, Brother Antenor? Brother Palamedes? How goes your holy work?'

'It grieves me to hear you call what we have done here holy work, brother-sergeant,' Antenor says with a heavy heart, knowing that such words, once said, can never be unspoken.

'How so?' Constantinus's voice is a guttural growl, the sound made by a cornered carnodon or an angry grox.

'Because what you have decreed is against all the teachings of the holy *Codex* and flies in the face of the oaths we swore when we became Sons of Guilliman.'

'We all swore oaths of moment when we first arrived on this Emperor-forsaken world,' Constantinus declares, his own words coming louder now, and venom-edged, 'and that moment lasted for three long years. I swore to liberate this world from the grip of the Great Devourer, as did you, Brother Antenor, as did we all. Have you forgotten that?'

'No, brother-sergeant, I have not forgotten, and thanks to our tireless upholding of those oaths the tyranid menace has been expunged from Nova Terra.'

'Yes, but only to be replaced by the taint of heresy!' Constantinus roars. 'The people of this world are no better than the worms that even now feast upon the flesh of our dead brethren, noble Sons like Brother Ignatius and Brother Lucian. These whoreson wretches have no appreciation of who has saved them from a fate beyond damnation. We are the guardians of mankind and yet mankind does not deserve us. The people of Nova Terra owe us a debt that can never be repaid. But worse than that, we free them from the threat of alien tyranny and they rebel. So it is up to us to educate them, so that they understand fully the error of their ways.'

'We are done here, Constantinus. The cult is vanquished, the last of the tyranid broods eradicated. We should leave Nova Terra and set out upon a penitent crusade, in acknowledgement of our own transgressions, and seek the Emperor's absolution for the crimes we have committed here in His name.'

'Absolution? I am absolved every time I bathe in the blood of heretics and traitors,' the sergeant snarls, not once breaking eye contact with Brother Antenor.

The implication is shocking. 'And would you include me, one of your battle-brothers, under that banner?'

'That depends on what you decide to do next. *Brother*.' Never has the word 'brother' seemed so lacking in implied brotherhood. 'After all, as the holy *Codex* teaches, actions speak louder than words.'

'So be it,' Antenor says, inhaling deeply. 'I am a loyal son of the primarch, and Roboute Guilliman would surely turn his face from the atrocities we have committed against the people of this world. I ask our father-primarch and the Emperor Himself for forgiveness. And, as a consequence, I must renounce my place within Squad Constantinus.'

'What?' the sergeant laughs. 'You cannot! The only way you will leave my command is when our masters see fit to promote you – if our masters ever see fit to call us back to the Cyclades at all – or when one of us dies.'

It is with an even heavier heart that Antenor utters the next three doom-laden words: 'So be it.'

'So be it?' The expression on Constantinus's face says more than words ever could. 'And do you speak for you alone or are there others here who feel as you do?' The sergeant challenges the others with his granite gaze.

'Never!' Maimon declares. 'I would follow you into the Eye of Terror itself, my lord!'

'And you might yet,' Antenor warns the other.

'How dare you?' Maimon roars, his boltgun finding a new target.

'No! Brother Antenor is right,' Diomed says, his tone as hard and as cold as marble. 'We have broken our vows to the Chapter. We must repent and atone for our sins.'

'And we live or die in brotherhood,' Pius announces, quoting scripture himself now. 'Brother-sergeant, I pledge my bolter to your service, always.'

'What say you, Brother Hector?' Constantinus growls. 'Where do you stand?'

'I stand with you, of course, brother-sergeant. The bond of brotherhood is what makes us what we are. Without our fellow battle-brothers we are nothing.'

'Well said, brother!' Pius proclaims.

'What of you, Brother Palamedes? We fought together at the walls of Burranax and against the upstart tau on Numenor Six. Where do your loyalties lie?'

'First and foremost I am loyal to the Golden Throne, then to the greatest of all his sons, Roboute Guilliman, and then to my Chapter. When my sergeant's commands are contrary to the credos of the greater authority, then he is my commander no longer.'

Palamedes, ever the orator, has put the case as clearly as any of them.

'Fine words,' Constantinus retorts, 'but what are your fine words worth when your Chapter abandons you, and through no wrongdoing on your part?'

'We do not know that that is the case,' Palamedes states plainly.

'I fought long and hard to save this world from the Great Devourer and then for another three years – unrewarded and unremembered – at my Chapter's behest to save it again. I do not ask for reward, only to be remembered. I ask for no more. I deserve nothing less.'

'You?' The sergeant's choice of words bothers Antenor. Words have power. Such power can be all too easily abused. 'We have all shed our life's blood for Nova Terra.'

'Nova Terra?' the sergeant snarls. 'I have shed so much blood for this world, seen so many battle-brothers under my command die for this world, it would be better if it were called Constantinium.'

'You jest, surely?'

'Constantinium, Antenor! In honour of the fallen brothers of Squad Constantinus!'

Antenor scans the plaza again. The brothers have grouped together, as the debate has raged, each according to the troths they have made or the vows they have broken. Only Brother Cain, the newest recruit to join Tactical Squad Constantinus, stands apart from the rest.

'Brother Cain, it is time you revealed to us your heart and mind,' the sergeant says, pointing a ceramite-armoured finger at the young Space Marine. 'Come, join me.'

'Much as it pains me to say so,' Cain replies with a faltering voice, 'I cannot.'

'You *cannot*?'

'I walked with Brother Antenor through the streets of the city as it burned and saw the evils we have perpetrated – not in the Emperor's name but in the name of vengeance and bloody-minded obstinacy.'

The last eight Sons of Guilliman upon this strife-torn world face each other across the fragmented square, the smoking ruins of the palaces of the nobility rising like blackened fingers pointing to the skies in silent accusation behind the wild-eyed sergeant.

'Then we have reached an impasse. Brothers,' Constantinus says, addressing only those who stand with him still. 'The traitors have revealed their true colours. Once again we find ourselves confronted by treachery upon this hell-world, treachery that must be excised like a suppurating canker.'

'Do not do this,' Antenor warns, as Palamedes, Cain

and Diomed line up alongside him. 'If you cross this line there will be no going back.'

'There has been no going back since the moment you broke faith with your sergeant!' Pius rages.

'You crossed that line long ago,' Constantinus growls. 'Traitor.'

In that moment, the universe turns and nothing will ever be the same again.

'Brothers!' Constantinus booms. 'The enemy has revealed itself. The traitors have broken faith with those of us dedicated to the work that is still to be completed here. So I say to you, brothers, suffer not a traitor to live!'

Boltguns are primed, Brother Hector's flamer blazes, and Constantinus's blade hums with lethal power.

'Sons of Guilliman!' Antenor shouts, his unwavering gaze locked upon the errant sergeant, his finger tightening about the trigger of his own thrice-blessed boltgun. 'Remember, Cirtus city! Remember Nova Terra!'

With that battle is joined.

THE CAVERNS THRUM with the cacophonous clamour of battle, the rattle of bolter-fire, the sharp crack of frag grenades and the alien screams of the tyranids. Even the earth and rock cry out, shifting beneath them, protrusions cracking and crashing to the ground such is the savagery of the close quarters fighting now consuming the lava tunnels.

'Brood-nest clear!' Brother Ignatius's voice crackles over the vox. It is only through their helm-comms that any Space Marine of Squad Constantinus can hear any other speak. The distortion is the result of geomagnetic interference, according to Hector's auspex scans, but it doesn't stop them doing their job.

'In the Emperor's name, fire in the hole!' comes Brother Pius's voice.

At his battle-brother's warning, Brother Lucian drops into a crouch, one gauntleted hand upon the winged U raised from his breastplate, closing his eyes momentarily and offering up a prayer to Father Guilliman, once again asking the primarch to watch over their endeavours as they pursue their holy mission on Nova Terra.

Another seismic boom rocks the caves, shaking the crust of the planet. The torrent of flame comes moments later, licking at the grieves and shoulder guards of his blue and white battle plate, while Lucian intones the Prayer of Protection over and over.

The fires recede and Lucian rises to his feet again, his prayer-inscribed boltgun in hand, the vituperative words of his furious prayer still on his lips and an undying anger in his heart.

Something is burning within the extinct volcanic vent. Something that screams in pain and fury. Dancing shadows leap and caper across the walls, backlit by the flickering flames.

Pius has shaken another nest of the hibernating xenos from their bio-stasis slumber. They are angry, like fire-wasps – their hive disturbed by a dozy grox – and they are coming.

But Lucian and his brothers are ready for them.

Ridged, elongated skulls and fiercely taloned forelimbs throw leaping shades across the pitted walls of the lava tube tunnels. The retreating fires reflect from obsidian scales and in the lidless black pearl orbs of their alien eyes.

Chittering and screeching, the genestealers come at them. The four Space Marines form into a line of unyielding armour across the width of the magma-carved passageway: Brother Cain, like Lucian, with boltgun in hand; Brother Pius, his bolter loose in one hand, fingering the trigger-pin of a frag grenade in the other; Ignatius, the snout of his charging plasma cannon aimed at the core of the approaching brood.

'In Guilliman's name, fire at will!' Lucian bellows over the screeching cries of the xenos.

The clatter of bolter-fire ricochets from the basalt walls, accompanied by the crack of carapace exoskeletons being smashed open and the concussive boom of the detonating mass-reactive shells.

Lucian's marksmanship is remarkable even among the Adeptus Astartes. No shot is wasted – bolter-rounds entering through eye sockets, exploding alien hearts and severing spinal columns; every hit a kill shot.

Pius is more measured and restrained, loosing off very deliberate shots into the throng. The genestealers fall, lower limbs fracturing, tumbling into the path of others. Those creatures behind that don't react in time are sent sprawling.

Brother Cain, the newest member of the squad and not long out of the Chapter's Scout Company, is nonetheless the veteran of countless battles since elements of the Fourth Company came to the aid of Nova Terra. Happenstance and necessity have made him an accomplished tyranid hunter.

Then there is Brother Ignatius. He and Lucian were

promoted to Squad Constantinus together, on the eve of the Laskarr Landings. While the others might look up to Lucian – seeing him as Constantinus's natural successor, should the unthinkable happen – just as Lucian himself holds his sergeant in high esteem, it is Ignatius who has been afforded the honour of carrying a revered relic of the Chapter into battle.

With xenos bodies creating a bottleneck within the lava tunnel, Brother Pius hurls his frag grenade into the seething, shrieking mass. In the time it takes Lucian to whisper 'the Emperor protects', the grenade detonates.

A wave of concussive force flings 'stealer body parts at the Space Marines, hooves, skull ridges and limb pieces clattering against their besmirched battle plate.

Ignatius gasps.

Lucian looks.

A razor-sharp shard of chitin is embedded in his right thigh.

'Guilliman's bones!' Ignatius curses, checking the plasma cannon's charge. It is not yet ready. He curses again.

As the smoke and dust clear, and once his helm's HUD has recovered from the shock-flash of the grenade's detonation, Lucian sees the second wave of 'stealers advancing along the tunnel into the kill zone.

A purestrain leaps its fallen brood-kin, its powerful spring carrying it clear of their guns. It lands on top of Brother Cain, its claws scoring marks in his battle plate. His boltgun useless at close quarters, Cain lets the weapon fall to the ground, at the same time taking his combat knife from its sheath with his right hand as his left closes around the creature's snout.

Cain puts the edge of the knife to the creature's throat as the genestealer writhes within his grasp. The first cut takes off the end of the creature's muzzle and its darting purple-black tongue. It gives a hideous wail as Cain repositions the blade and tries again. Space Marine and genestealer fall to the floor.

Brother Cain kicks the bucking monster from him, as violent, convulsive death throes take control of its body, his knife buried up to its hilt in the knot of ganglia and cerebral tissue that passes for the 'stealer's brain.

Lucian observes all this at the periphery of his vision as he looses off a shot that blasts out the back of another purestrain's skull.

'Suffer not the unclean to live,' Pius intones, 'and uphold the honour of the Emperor!'

It has been regularly remarked upon by the brothers of Squad Constantinus that it can surely only be a matter of time before Pius is called to join the elite echelons of the Chapter's Chaplains. He punctuates his vituperative mantra now with bursts of fire from his boltgun.

'Thank the primarch!' Ignatius's voice booms over the comm-net. Lucian recognises the high-pitched hum emanating from the relic weapon in his battle-brother's hands.

The plasma cannon fires and the melee is bathed in light as intense as that at the heart of a star. Tyranids die in their droves. Armoured carapaces crack, soft tissue sizzles and alien ichor boils in the heat blast.

The glow suffusing the cannon's power coils fade to a dull ultramarine, the weapon's energised plasma reserves expended again.

'Good shooting, Brother Ignatius,' Lucian says, picking off the surviving 'stealers with controlled bursts of bolter-fire.

'The primarch is beneficent.'

'None can resist the ardent fires of the Emperor's holy wrath,' Brother Pius chips in.

'Nor the blast from a fully energised plasma cannon,' adds Brother Cain.

The burning thing comes at them then. It is huge, its chitinous carapace the same glossy black as the 'stealers, its underbelly the same anaemic white.

Lucian is unsure whether this particular specimen is a 'stealer, like the others – mutated to gigantic size by the unknowable workings of alien hyper-evolution, to fill a void left by the departure of the tyranid splinter fleet three years before – or whether it is some other, as yet unidentified xeno-form. But what is clear is that it is on fire and it is coming straight for them.

It is so vast it practically fills the lava tunnel. It pounds towards them on crushing hooves, huge scything talon-arms slicing the air before it. It gives voice to a hideous shriek, a sound that seems horribly high-pitched for something so large, so monstrous.

Ignatius prepares to face the monster's barrelling charge with his plasma cannon, but it is still recharging after the last sun-burst blast that took out the bulk of the genestealer brood.

'Guilliman's oath!' Lucian hears Ignatius cry before a burning bladed limb – more razor-sharp chitinous sword than organic appendage – descends with startling speed, leaving a smoking trail in the air behind it as it slices open the battle-brother's power armour from shoulder guard to tasset.

Ignatius falls, his body bifurcated. The plasma cannon hits the floor of the cavern-tunnel with a dull thud. Rage boils within Brother Lucian.

'As one! As all!' Lucian screams, turning his boltgun on the beast.

With any other 'stealer every discharged bolter round would have been a kill-shot. Against this brute beast the mass-reactive shells detonate against chitinous hide leaving nothing more than lunar crater pock-marks on the surface of its obsidian armour.

'Guilliman's teeth!' Pius rails against the hideous truth they are all confronted with now.

Another malformed limb lashes out, this one like some lumpen, chitinous wrecking ball, trailing smoke and plasma flames. The force of the impact launches Lucian back down the passageway, his head hitting the curved basalt wall hard.

His helmet absorbs the worst of the blow, but his vision blurs for a moment nonetheless. In that moment he sees a figure in blue and white, its gleaming armour under-lit a ruddy orange, bound up the monster's back. The coruscating power sword in its hand flashing once as the armoured figure vaults over the tyranid's head, the humming blade singing as it slices through chitin, ligaments, bone and oesophageal tubes.

The somersaulting figure, a cloak of snowtusk spread out behind it, lands on the floor of the tunnel, the basalt cracking under the avenging angel's ceramite boots. A moment later, the tyranid's head hits the floor in a welter of oozing ichor.

The over-grown brood-beast continues to claw the air, one spasming strike dealing Pius a grievous wound even through his chestplate. Then the carcass topples to the ground as well, the yellow-white pus that passes for the creature's blood pumping from its severed neck, the persistent plasma fires fading at last, the decapitated body still twitching with muscle-spasms for several seconds afterwards.

Sergeant Constantinus rises to his full impressive height, the cloak settling behind him. He regards Brothers Lucian, Pius, Cain and the savagely slaughtered Ignatius, the faceplate of his helm betraying no emotion.

'Brother-sergeant!' Lucian exclaims in unalloyed delight, shaking his head clear and getting to his feet again. 'Thank the primarch!'

'Well met, Brother Lucian.' The survivors of the assault gather round their sergeant like delighted children at the arrival of a favourite uncle. 'Brother Pius. Brother Cain.'

'Brother Ignatius–' Lucian begins.

'Will be remembered, and his name added to the roll of the honoured dead who have given their lives for this world, for a great many of the hated xenos met their end at his hands, unable to match his might or vengeful wrath.'

The remainder of Squad Constantinus join them then, following Constantinus up from the deeper tunnels.

'Brother Hector,' the sergeant says, addressing another of the warriors joining them now, and who is holding his left hand with care – Lucian can see savage bite marks in the ceramite gauntlet – 'what says your auspex's machine-spirit?'

The Space Marine consults the scanner held in his

other hand. It is a moment before he answers.

'The caves are clear, Sergeant Constantinus.'

'You are sure?'

'Yes, brother-sergeant, I have recalibrated and rescanned twice to be certain.'

'Then the Emperor be praised. Our work here is done.'

The sense of relief and joy is palpable.

'Let us take up the body of our fallen battle-brother and return to the *Ardent Fire*, that we may preserve his gene-seed and signal our Chapter that Nova Terra is free of the xenos at last.'

'Brother-sergeant,' Brother Palamedes interrupts. 'I have been monitoring a number of Adeptus Arbites transmissions over the Imperial vox-net. The signal is degraded but the implication I believe is clear.'

'What is it, brother?' asks the sergeant. 'What are you trying to tell us?'

'The nests in these volcanic plateaus were not the only place where 'stealer broods went to ground after the splinter fleet was repelled from the shores of Nova Terra.'

The atmosphere of joy in the air evaporates in an instant.

'Brother,' Constantinus says, his voice a sinister guttural growl, 'be clear. What are you trying to tell us? Do you speak of' – he hesitates – 'cult activity?'

'I fear so, brother-sergeant,' Palamedes confirms, his remorseful tone giving the impression that he is confessing to some terrible transgression of his own.

'Then this world is not yet free of its xenos taint,' Sergeant Constantinus says darkly, 'and our work here is not yet done.'

Suddenly raising his power sword high, he makes a new oath of moment in a voice that booms like an orbital assault.

'I shall not rest until this world is free!'

TWISTING HIS WRIST, Fauchard brings the chainsword back around, the jagged adamantium teeth quickly chewing through the neck of another maniacal cultist. But where one blasphemer falls, beneath the shattered vault of the Great Cathedral of Cirtus city, there are a dozen more ready to take its place.

Many of the deranged devotees come at them armed with nothing more than dull-edged knives and the insane belief that somehow they have a hope of prevailing against the Iron Knights.

The cultists possess little in the way of armour either, or even clothing of any sort. Their filthy robes hang like rags about them, what little flesh that clothes their near skeletal frames is covered with all manner of blasphemous symbols. Some have been tattooed on, some are unhealed scars cut with the point of a knife or a ragged fingernail. The glyphs make even Fauchard sick to the pit of his stomach if he looks upon them for too long.

The flagellants scream blasphemies to their unspeakable masters as they come at the Space Marines – wave after rushing wave of them – but the armour of their unshakeable, unholy faith does nothing to save them from Fauchard's blade or the Emperor-inspired wrath of his brother knights.

From out of the pack emerges a bald man, flayed skin peeled back from the top of his head to expose the glistening skull beneath, the blood-wet bone incised with the star-rune of the arch-enemy.

Fauchard plunges his sword into the man's stomach. The cultist gasps, the foul invocation that was on his lips cut off in that instant. But the wildness in the man's stare remains, while a delighted, shark-like smile twists his face into a grotesque grimace.

The cultist grabs hold of the chainsword and gives a sharp tug. Dark blood gushes from his mouth as the man convulses and pulls himself up the blade. Now with only the hilt protruding from his belly, the fanatic reaches up to claw at Fauchard's helmet with broken, bloodied fingernails, the same insane smile still etched on his face.

The Iron Knight raises his bolt pistol and explodes the lunatic's skull with a single round. Shaking the limp corpse from his chainblade, he turns to meet the charge of the next insane idiot desirous of a hasty death.

Not five metres away, Brother Adnot takes a cultist's head in his hands and wrenches it from the woman's shoulders, the arterial spray of blood that follows send a shower of red mist down upon their gunmetal-grey battle plate, the blasphemer's unholy blood baptising them all.

There is a flash of steel to Fauchard's right and Brother Nihel takes down a mewling, conjoined thing with one stroke of his treasured relic blade.

Brother Urs gives a bestial bellow and barrels past, the huge Space Marine crashing into the cultist pack, sending the suicidal servants of the Ruinous Powers tumbling to the ground, crushing their skulls under his armoured feet.

Another burst of bolter-fire and another body

performs its own *danse macabre* before falling to the ground, suddenly eerily still. Then there is no more killing to be done, and the broken ground is awash with the blood of the blasphemers.

Sergeant Fauchard regards the twisted, pulverised and bludgeoned bodies for a moment, finding himself wondering once again how anyone could choose such a life – and such a death: bodies daubed with unholy sigils, flesh already rotting, minds and souls sick with corruption – over a life of service to the Emperor and the Imperium.

He doesn't know what's worse: that such weak-minded mortals can sink to such levels of depravity, or that the thing they revere as lord of this world was once like the sergeant and those battle-brothers under his command – one of the Emperor's finest, an inheritor of the genetic legacy of the highly revered Primarch Guilliman. A loyal Space Marine.

The so-called Liberator must have known, as soon as he broke faith with his vows of brotherhood, turned his back on his devotion to the Emperor, and renounced the sacred trust that had been placed in him by his Chapter Master, that this day would come.

'Brothers,' Fauchard announces, the squad gathering together again, forming a ring around their sergeant. 'Let us swear an oath of moment, to reaffirm the vows we made on coming to this hell-world, that we shall not rest until the traitor's head adorns the battlements of his own citadel. Swear it now!'

'We so swear!' the Iron Knights bellow in furious affirmation of their sergeant's words.

'The Iconoclast's blasphemous idol has been toppled, and after thirteen long years of fighting his forces are in rout. Now this once great cathedral has been purged of his profane acolytes too. It is now only a matter of time before the Emperor guides us to the place where we shall meet with the arch-traitor himself in battle. With his death, we shall reclaim this world for the Emperor. This I so swear!'

The knights' antiphonal response reverberates from the broken pillars of the once mighty edifice like the roar of a Thunderhawk's engines. 'So we all swear!'

'Vigilance! Valour! Vengeance!' Fauchard roars, his brethren quick to echo the battle-cry of their Chapter. 'Let us be ever watchful for signs of treachery and be ruthless in our prosecution of those who would willingly turn from the Emperor's light, as we exact His divine retribution upon them.'

Fauchard thrusts his chainsword high into the sky then, its tip appearing to scrape the hell-storm clouds of blood and smoke that shroud the ruined city.

'For I shall not rest until this world is liberated from the traitor's tyrannical rule. This I swear!'

*A case in point is the dark tale of Constantinus –
sometimes called the Oathbreaker, sometimes called the
Iconoclast – renegade battle-brother of the noble Sons of
Guilliman...*

*Having renamed the world Constantinium, the renegade
sergeant plunged his newly conquered domain into an age
of anarchy, darkness and blood sacrifice. Not content with
having consecrated one world to the Ruinous Powers, the
traitor embarked upon a campaign of savage slaughter, a
terrifying pogrom that engulfed planet after planet, system
after system, until within the space of ten short years, the
entire Viridis Sector owed him fealty.*

It took a unified force of three Space Marine Chapters, twelve Imperial Guard foundings, an entire battlefleet and agents of both the Officio Assassinorum and the mighty Ordos Hereticus to finally recapture the planet. Even then the bloodshed only ended with the death of the traitor Constantinus himself.

Even now, some three hundred years after the end of his tyrannical reign, it is said that cult-gangs of rebels still hold out in the volcanic plateaus, having made their lair within the labyrinthine lava tunnels found in that region. It is from these hidden cave systems that the rebels carry out guerrilla raids against the Emperor-fearing folk of Nova Terra. It is within those haunted caverns that they continue to make sacrifices to their blasphemous gods in the name of Constantinus the Liberator – a name that will forever be a stain upon the reputation of the noble Sons of Guilliman.

From the treatise *Quis Custodiet Ipsos Angeles Mortes?*
by Gideon Lorr, Inquisitor, Ordo Hereticus

THE LONG WAR

by Andy Hoare

FERROUS IRONCLAW, WARSMITH of the Iron Warriors Traitor Legion, snarled in bitter derision as the smoke parted to reveal the battlefield across which his grand company would assault the enemy fortress. He barely noticed the sharp crunch of scattered bones beneath his tread, or the hot wind, which carried the stench of propellant, death and the rank fear of the lackeys of the Emperor who cowered behind the towering walls barely a kilometre ahead.

'In the name of Perturabo,' Ironclaw growled into the vox-pickup mounted in his Terminator armour's collar, his voice a blasphemous fusion of the machine and the organic, 'unleash the fires of damnation.'

There was a brief pause during which stray autocannon rounds whipped in across the battlefield to burst ineffectually against the Iron Warriors' fieldworks. Muzzle flares blinked along the length of the curtain wall, individual las-rounds whip-cracking overhead, their energy all but dissipated by the dense particulates obscuring much of the killing ground.

Then, a deep tremor grumbled through the cratered, bone-wreathed ground, and the warsmith's mouth twisted at one corner as something like anticipation bloomed inside him. The tremor grew to a roar, and in an instant the air was split by a sonic boom that made even the nearby Traitor Marines pause in awe.

A barrage of super-heavy munitions thundered through the tortured skies of Bellum Colonia, parting thick banks of black smoke and scattering the debris littering the ground below with their turbulent wake. Ironclaw had paid his apostate Mechanicus allies handsomely for their aid in breaching the Bastion Primus, scouring an entire subsector for the price the fallen tech-priests had demanded in return for fielding their terrible siege engines. The soul-foundries of their daemon forge-world would blaze for decades to come as a result.

Seconds later, the barrage struck. The Bastion Primus had been constructed in millennia long passed by the finest of the Imperium's siege masons, yet no stronghold in the entire galaxy was beyond the capability of the Iron Warriors to breach. None except one – a flash of contempt seared through Ironclaw's mind – but that would come, one day, at the conclusion of the Long War.

Nucleonic fires burst into being as the warheads obliterated themselves upon striking the invisible void shields thrown up to protect the bastion. But Ferrous Ironclaw knew the science of siegecraft as others

A veteran of countless breaching operations, the warsmith had concentrated his barrage in such a way as to bring the fabric of the walls crashing down to form a ramp, up which his forces could climb. Even as the Iron Warriors pressed on, the ground beneath them rearing up this new, artificial rise, the daemon-engines raced forwards in their eagerness to tear apart the soft meat cringing beyond the rubble.

'Warsmith,' one of Ironclaw's Chosen barked a clipped warning. ''Ware the breach.'

Slowing his advance up the uneven base of the rise, the warsmith glanced towards its smoke-wreathed summit. His lip curled in derision, baring iron teeth sharper than any predator's as a ripple of las-fire erupted from hidden firing positions amongst the tumbled masonry. Evidently, the defenders had rushed their second line forwards to defend the undefendable. The warsmith's expression turned to savage eagerness as the lust to rush the breach all but consumed him. But the Iron Warriors were no mindless berserkers ready to throw themselves carelessly down the gullet of death. They wielded their fury artfully, as a weapon of precision, overwhelming their foe with clinical slaughter.

'*Ka, ib norag,*' the warsmith growled, the air around him visibly rippling as the word of power left his mouth. A moment later, the ground beneath his feet shook and great chunks of debris dislodged themselves from further up the ramp, crashing down before being swallowed in the drifting banks of smoke. The reek of burning souls assailed the warsmith's nostrils, and three dark forms reared up behind him. Without turning, he gestured with one of his lightning claw-gauntleted hands and the three Defilers prowled forwards. Within seconds, the weight of fire had doubled and then tripled as the defenders at the summit saw their doom clawing its way upwards towards their position. Each of the engines was constructed like some huge, mechanical spider, the weapons mounted on the sides of their turrets spitting death as vast, scorpion-like foreclaws flexed in anticipation of the ruin they would soon exact upon the soft flesh of their enemies.

'How like the taking of the Lazurite Citadel,' Ironclaw mused aloud as the three daemon-engines crawled ever upwards, hundreds of las-rounds snapping through the air to strike harmlessly against their armoured hides.

'My lord?' the nearest of Ironclaw's Chosen answered, his features obscured by the impassive mask of his Terminator armour.

Ironclaw's deeply lined eyes narrowed as he regarded the Chosen, dredging through countless years of memories. No, this warrior had not been present during the Tallarn campaign, so he had not witnessed the final battles against the fractured remnants of the loyalist armies, nor had he been present when the gleaming domes of the Lazurite Citadel had been shattered.

'It matters not,' the warsmith snarled. 'All that matters is the destruction of these walls. Muster the warriors. We advance, for the glory of Perturabo.'

As the Iron Warriors began their ascent of the breach, the weight of fire pouring from the defenders' positions at the summit grew steadily more intense. The

Defilers took the brunt of it, and while they could easily shrug off the blizzard of lasgun-fire, the defenders wasted no time in bringing forwards heavier weaponry. As the Defilers clambered claw over mechanical claw towards their position, the defenders opened fire with lascannons and missile launchers. The first shot, a warhead fired in haste and panic, corkscrewed through the smoke-wreathed air, its machine-spirit improperly appeased, to explode against the jagged masonry of the breach's interior edge. The second shot was from a lascannon, the bright beam lancing downwards and missing the lead daemon-engine by no more than a metre. Enraged by this affront, the infernal will that animated the war machine sent it surging forwards so fast that the second shot aimed towards it went awry, though it struck another engine a glancing blow to its turret.

The weapons blister mounted on the Defiler's turret's side exploded in a hail of sparks and razor-sharp shrapnel, the daemon-engine rearing up upon its spider-like mechanical legs and unleashing a metallic howl of rage. The weight of fire raining down from the summit faltered as the defenders cowered before such daemonic fury; then Ironclaw caught the sound of a voice bellowing for order and the fire returned to its former rate.

'Mine…' the warsmith growled, striding forwards. Using his lightning claws to aid his ascent, Ironclaw hauled himself up the rubble-strewn breach, the wounded Defiler so close behind that its massive claws and legs churned up the ruined ground about him, its hull looming ominously overhead. Now, the Defiler's body was cratered from repeated strikes, lascannon-rounds and krak missile warheads streaking about it. Another blinding beam lanced out and this time the firer's aim was true, striking the Defiler just beneath the mantlet of its main gun. The beast shuddered as the lascannon-round punched out its rear deck.

Knowing his protector was slain, Ironclaw redoubled his rate of ascent until he was at the very van of the force storming the breach. Behind him, the mortally wounded Defiler thrashed and spasmed as the daemon within shrieked its pain and fury into the air. With its armour compromised the daemon was free of its arcane fetters, but it was apparent the fell thing craved not release but the blood of its foe. Unable to animate its machine-prison, the daemon had lost its ability to slay its enemies and its frustrated rage was a terrible thing to witness. The creature howled as its essence leached through the wound in its former prison, and the defenders flinched before the abominable spectacle. Inured to the taint of the warp, the warsmith gritted his teeth as he attained the plateau where the defenders waited, their faces blanched with shock and their eyes alight with terror.

'Address!' Ironclaw heard the voice again. It was a voice used to command. It was a voice used to being obeyed.

Savouring the moment, the warsmith waited, activating his lightning claws and flexing the weapon-tipped mechatendrils that writhed at his back. Arcing energies played up and down the gleaming lengths of the wickedly serrated claws, their power field humming threateningly.

'Address!' the voice bawled again, and the sound

of several meaty impacts reached Ironclaw's ears. He took a step towards the shouts and a shape emerged from amidst the shattered blocks of masonry.

It was an Imperial Guardsman, a veteran of numerous campaigns, judging by the scar tissue visible beneath the layer of grime and soot that coated his face. As the man pulled himself erect he gunned the motor of a chainsword held loosely at his side. Almost pitiable, the warsmith mused, until his eye was drawn to more figures stirring from the gaps between the fallen blocks behind their leader. His eyes narrowed as he snarled. Perhaps there was a challenge here after all, he thought, though still it would scarcely test one of his skill and experience.

'Blessed be the martyr,' the man said, his eyes blazing with defiance. 'For he shall live eternal by the Emperor's side.'

A twin flare of bitter derision and long forgotten memory flashed through the warsmith's consciousness. For a moment, he was standing at the gates of the Crescent City, the hosts of Tallarn arrayed upon the blasted wastes before their erstwhile capital. The Caliphar was mortally wounded and his doomed armies had mustered in one last act of defiance against the Warmaster's forces. The ruler's vat-grown champion, a berserker-dervish of fearsome repute, had stepped alone through the city gates to confront them. That champion had said something very similar. The man was a fool, but he had died well, Ironclaw conceded.

'The codes of my Legion demand I offer you one opportunity to quit this wall,' the warsmith addressed the enemy leader, paraphrasing his primarch. He knew the man would not do so, and in truth he cared little either way. This lone defender was utterly insignificant, no matter how many of his men joined him in their futile defence.

'Be gone, Emperor-hating *bastard*,' the man barked. Perhaps there would be some sport here after all, the warsmith thought. 'Be gone, for with my last drop of blood I shall–'

Anger flaring in his bitter heart, the warsmith brought one of the metallic tentacles waving at his back sharply about. The melta-discharger mounted at the mechatendril's tip blazed searing orange and the bold Imperial Guard leader was atomised in an instant. One moment the man had stood defiant at the summit of the breach, the next his body had been seared to angry cinders drifting upon the irradiated wind.

A metallic growl rumbling deep in his chest, Ferrous Ironclaw swept his baleful glare across the mass of defenders arrayed against him. He knew nothing but contempt for these worthless scraps of human flesh, their flak jackets bearing the same two-headed eagle device he himself had once marched to war under. How little they knew of the deeds that had been done in the name of that sigil. How little they deserved to bear it. How little they deserved to even *live*…

Baring his metallic teeth in a feral leer, the warsmith spread his serrated lightning claws wide. Unleashing a war cry that was at once a blurt of soul-shattering scrap code and a howl of primordial rage, he started forwards, his Chosen advancing in his wake.

The slaughter that ensued was over in seconds, the blood of the Imperial Guard defenders anointing the rune-encrusted Terminator armour of the warsmith and his retinue as an offering to the Ruinous Powers. Scenting spilled viscera, the daemon-engines surged up the rubble slope with such haste that their claws and tracks dislodged mighty chunks of rubble, and brought more loose debris tumbling from the ragged edges of the shattered walls on either side. Another wave of defenders rose up from positions further back, the breach echoing to their cries of misplaced piety. Las-rounds whipped through the air, and soon the throaty roar of a battery of heavy bolters was added to the deafening cacophony of battle.

Rounds splitting the air about him, Ironclaw gloried in the anarchy of war. Standing upon the rubble of a fallen wall, the heat of battle stinging the flesh of his face as the stink of burned flesh filled his nostrils – here was where he was created to be.

Precise bursts of disciplined bolter-fire rang out as more of the warsmith's squads advanced. Soon the last of the fleeing defenders were gunned down and the breach belonged to the Iron Warriors.

Turning his back upon the last of the slaughter, the warsmith looked down the length of the rubble slope. A pack of Maulerfiend daemon-engines had paused by the wreck of the fallen Defiler like carnivores gathering to pick over the remains of some larger predator further up the food chain than they. Then the pack was overcome by their impatience to be through the breach, each engine clambering up the loose rubble slope, their hunger to share in the killing obvious.

After the Maulerfiends came more of the warsmith's Iron Warriors, their formation impeccable even as they negotiated the rough and uneven terrain. In their wake came a group of Mutilators, each a hulking mountain of armour and muscle, a former Chosen whose body had been warped beyond all recognition by the glory of Chaos. The air was thick with the stink of propellant and burned fuel, and it visibly shimmered with the proximity of the warp. Beyond a lumbering Dreadnought that had just begun its ascent, the drifting smoke obscured the remainder of Ironclaw's army; as well as the forces of the other factions that had allied themselves to him.

One of those factions was making its presence known even as the warsmith turned back, just in time to catch sight of a banner borne aloft by a bold, if suicidal, Imperial Guard trooper. The view beyond the summit was still obscured by the clouds of dust thrown up when the walls collapsed, but it was clear that the defenders were intent upon mounting a counter-attack.

Good, thought Ferrous Ironclaw, let them come. Let them come on in endless waves like they did on Corinar when we breached the Shriving Wall and cast down the Lucid Tower. Let them bellow their defiance even as we scythe them down as we did upon the plains of crimson marble.

For an instant, Ironclaw's vision wavered as nigh overwhelming memories of past battles impressed themselves upon his consciousness. In his mind he was striding from his drop-pod onto the flatlands of Tallarn's primary continent, the once-verdant pastures reduced to bubbling slag by the life-eater virus his primarch had unleashed upon that world. The ground at his feet was thick with the viscous slime that had once been an entire planet's biomass. So voracious was the primarch's curse upon Tallarn that even the world's native bacteria had been destroyed. Without them, the rendered-down stuff of life would take years to disintegrate. The stink of so much organic matter reduced to slurry assailed the warsmith's nostrils, the false reality threatening to overwhelm his senses entirely.

Then a hard round *spanged* hard from his left shoulder, his armour's auto-reactive systems countering the impact with a hiss of hydraulics. The sundered plains of Tallarn melted away in an instant and he was back on Bellum Colonia, in the very gullet of the breach in the walls of the Bastion Primus. A second shot whipped past his face, its stinging wake bringing him fully back to the here and now.

Someone had dared fire upon him.

Someone would die.

The smoke parted as the counter-attacking defenders rushed headlong towards the Iron Warriors. This time, there must have been an entire company, and every Guardsman had his bayonet fixed to the barrel of his lasgun and was bellowing a prayer to the hated Emperor of Mankind. Squad after squad emerged from the roiling dust and smoke, throwing themselves into the defence of the breach.

'Hold!' Ironclaw bellowed, firing his serrated gauntlets to full power as his Terminator armour-clad Chosen formed up beside him. The air filled with oaths the defenders would have denounced as blasphemy had they not been shouting their own so loud they could hear nothing else. More Iron Warriors took position at their warsmith's back, and the daemon-engines prowled behind them, barely restrained by their master's command.

Only one of Ironclaw's allies had not yet made itself known, and therein lay the reason for his order to hold. The moment to unleash this ally was now.

A shadow as dark as the abyss passed over the Iron Warriors, the smoke at their backs parting as dark waters swell at the unseen passing of an oceanic predator. Ironclaw fixed his enemy with a baleful glare, a cruel leer twisting his war-torn features. Having cast the warsmith's gathered host in night, the shadow crept forwards towards the oncoming Imperial Guardsmen. As it passed over their front ranks, Ironclaw saw the first of them falter as their wrathful gaze was torn from the object of their hatred to the vast shape resolving itself in the breach.

The front rank stumbled as the Guardsmen took in the shocking enormity of the war machine looming into view. Men fell, and others trampled over them before coming to a desperate halt, their eyes wide with stark terror.

Then, it gave voice to its own war cry.

The Traitor Titan's war horn blared forth such a blasphemous, atonal dirge that men's hearts froze at the sheer horror of it. The noise was in part the wailing of a gargantuan klaxon, but that was by far the lesser part. The worst of it was the voice of the god-machine venting its rage upon the souls of man, singing the doom of the Imperium and ten thousand years of hatred for the withered carrion god seated upon its throne. All of this men knew even as their eardrums burst and they collapsed to their knees, hands clasped to their heads to shut out the infernal sound.

Ironclaw raised one taloned arm high as he watched the proudly borne banner waver, its custodian stumbling upon the bodies of fallen comrades, his gaze fixed wide-eyed upon the form in the breach.

The Titan was, as the name suggested, a vast war machine. Vaguely humanoid in form it towered dozens of metres into the tortured skies. One of its arms was a colossal power fist, with which the god-machine grasped the ragged edge of the breached wall to steady itself as it began its ascent of the rubble slope. The other was a laser weapon able to unleash such fearsome power that it could, in theory, pluck a warship from low orbit, should the Ruinous Powers confer their blessings upon the weapons-moderati. Beneath a metres-thick carapace, on which was mounted a pair of multiple-missile launcher pods, glowered the head that served as the machine's cockpit, its eyes aglow with warp-spawned furnace fire.

The god-machine hauled itself forwards, uncaring of the rain of debris dislodged from the shattered wall as it gripped the side. Though not one of the warsmith's warriors showed an iota of fear, the counter-attacking Imperial Guard were by now paralysed by the awesome sight.

The warsmith clenched his taloned hands, the air ringing as the serrated blades scissored shut.

The god-machine heard, and the god-machine obeyed.

The multiple-missile launchers on the Titan's carapace erupted into fire, dozens of guided munitions closing on their target within the blink of an eye. The summit of the breach was transformed into a vision of hell, men and masonry swallowed up in the raging infernal fires. The overpressure propelled jagged shrapnel outwards in a tidal wave of death that shredded those defenders not consumed by the fires, razor fragments scything through the air and ricocheting from the dull metal armour of nearby Iron Warriors.

Even before the fires had fully receded, Ferrous Ironclaw saw that the defenders had been slain to a man. Nothing but scattered fragments of charred flesh and the stink of flash-cooked meat remained of the hundred and more men.

The breach was taken. Now the Bastion Primus must fall.

WITHIN THE HOUR, the Iron Warriors had marched down the reverse slope of the breach, howling daemon-engines pressing forwards as the warsmith's squads consolidated their victory. The Titan strode onwards, hauling itself up and through the breach using its colossal power fist before taking position on the other side, Rhino and Land Raider armoured vehicles passing under its vast bulk as it stood overwatch.

Beyond the breach, the interior of the Bastion Primus was a mass of structures crammed together seemingly at random. As was common in such fortifications, an open space separated the wall from the city proper, a space in which the defenders could muster a response to an attack such as the Iron Warriors had undertaken. As Ironclaw led his warriors out and onto the rockcrete expanse, he knew that such a response would surely be launched at any moment, and he scanned the tall buildings beyond for any sign of it developing.

The buildings were constructed from a pale sandstone far weaker than the black masonry of the curtain wall, and barely any of them were untouched by the hand of war. Most bore signs of the thunderous preparatory bombardment the Iron Warriors had launched before their final assault, the once finely wrought statues of saints and martyrs covering their surfaces now pock-marked and burned. Others had almost entirely collapsed, leaving little but blackened skeletal remains. Centuries of experience of war told Ferrous that a ruined cityscape was far harder to take than an intact one, for the defenders could move through it by unpredictable routes, fire upon an attacker from every cracked wall and launch devastating, if suicidal, ambushes from the least expected quarter. Scanning the line of ruins, the warsmith caught sight of just such a defending force, a mass of figures appearing from the rubble.

A blurt of scrap-code told the warsmith of the Titan's eagerness to lay waste to this second wave of defenders, but Ironclaw's sub-vocalised growl silenced it. He was master here, and even the god-machine towering overhead would acknowledge that fact.

A second burst of feedback-laced machine code told Ironclaw that the mighty war machine would heed his will, if reluctantly. Satisfied that the Titan would hold its fire, the warsmith studied the killing ground between the breach and the mass of buildings.

The far side of the open space was now swarming with figures, a line several hundred metres wide advancing in such tight formation that it presented a mass of flesh. But the warsmith was blessed with the acute senses of his Legiones Astartes heritage, refined to preternatural sharpness by the gifts of the Ruinous Powers. He soon saw that the wave of defenders represented no disciplined counter-attack by well-prepared Imperial Guardsmen. Indeed, at least one in three of the figures carried no weapon and few wore a complete set of body armour.

'*Convicts*,' the warsmith sneered, his voice laced with hate. 'They dare send penal troops against me…'

The air filled with the pounding of feet and a roar of maddened savagery as the penal legionnaires advanced into the open space. But the warsmith knew that 'advanced' was the wrong term. No, these wild-eyed scum were not advancing, they were being herded. Each wore about his neck a thick collar containing an explosive charge. At the first sign of cowardice the overseers would detonate a select few of these and make a grisly example the remainder could not fail to appreciate. In addition to the collars, the warsmith knew that it was likely that the convict-troopers were pumped up on frenzon or some other combat stimm, administered by implanted dispensers and controlled by those same overseers. In all probability, the penal legionnaires were in the grip of a chem-fuelled rage that would render them immune to pain and devoid of all sense of self-preservation.

A small part of Ironclaw approved of such tactics, for the Traitor Legions often fielded such auxiliary cannon fodder in a similar fashion. There was no shortage of lesser men driven to give their lives in the service of the warp, and the same was true of those fighting in the name of the Emperor. But another part of the warsmith knew the real reason the convicts were being herded forwards to their obvious doom.

'God-machine,' Ironclaw said into the vox. The Titan's bale-eyed features turned in his direction, seeking out its master in the mass of tiny beings at its feet.

Following the line of buildings to the extreme left and right flanks, Ironclaw said, 'Our enemies believe us fools to be so easily distracted by such an obvious target. The flanks,' he ordered. 'Open the unseeing eye.'

The Titan's war horn sounded, deep and booming, its bass tone alone so violent it seemed as if it would bring the entire city crashing down. Even as the first, apocalyptic blast faded, a second, even louder one brought debris toppling down from already weakened towers.

Following its master's order, the god-machine engaged its full array of sensors, from conventional augurs to sorcerous etheric inductors. The machine's princeps, a once-celebrated hero of the Imperium long ago reduced to a drooling shell animated by the divine power of Chaos, imbibed the full range of sensor feedback and in an instant located what the warsmith suspected must be nearby.

'Imperial armoured battlegroup,' the princeps' voice gurgled over the vox. 'Descending at battle speed from the south.'

At last, thought the warsmith. An enemy worthy of my attentions.

'Constituting?' Ironclaw replied.

The princeps did not answer straight away, the god-machine's systems, an unclean hybrid of silicon and cranial matter, working to refine the signal stream flooding in from its sensors.

'Three super-heavies…' the phlegmy voice bubbled over the vox. 'A dozen battle tanks. Numerous lighter vehicles.'

The warsmith was thrilled that three super-heavy tanks might be about to join the battle, but he could hardly miss the disappointment in the princeps' voice. Clearly, the god-machine desired to match its power against one of its erstwhile brothers in the Titan Legions. Ironclaw could well understand such a desire, though he had little time or inclination for empathy. With countless frenzon-driven penal legionnaires screaming across the open ground, and the real threat pushing in from the south behind the cover of the ruined city, he had very little time at all.

In the span of time most men take to decide to flee, the warsmith formulated his response, as he had in so many equally pressing battlefield situations throughout his long tenure as commander of an Iron Warriors grand company. Memories of the Triumphal Gate at Argent Rex smashed asunder surged to the forefront of his mind, but he repressed them savagely lest his senses became dulled on the glut of past glory.

'Iron Warriors!' the warsmith bellowed, his voice amplified over the roar of the oncoming horde and the thrumming systems of the Titan at his back by his numerous machine augments. 'Forward by squads, wipe them out! Stain the ground crimson as we did upon the moons of Lemuria!'

At their warsmith's order, the squad leaders led their warriors forwards to meet the onrushing horde, their advance implacable as their bolters spat mass-reactive death in disciplined staccato bursts. Yet, Ironclaw had more orders to give.

'God-machine,' he addressed the Titan, its weapons already tracking towards the as yet unseen armoured battlegroup. 'Target the intact building with the statue of Saint Arxades upon its façade. Sustained beam, but only upon my express order, understood?'

The Titan's only response was a grating howl of feedback as its torso rotated with the titanic grinding of vast gear wheels. Its turbo laser levelled upon the target building, but as ordered, the princeps held his fire.

Before the warsmith could proceed, a warning bark from one of his nearby Chosen brought his attentions back to the open ground. The Iron Warriors were pressing forwards, and those penal troopers equipped with ranged weapons were returning fire. Their aim was so badly awry they could only have been dosed with a lethal amount of frenzon, making it clear that the legionnaires' overlords held no expectation of them surviving. But then, Ironclaw knew, that was not the point.

In the final moments before the two opposing masses of troops crashed together, the warsmith barked a series of clipped orders. So well disciplined were his warriors that the force reacted as if it were an extension of his own body, each squad a limb, each of their weapons his own.

At the centre, boltguns spat a continuous stream of fire, each shot aimed and deliberate, though the enemy were so densely packed that the Traitor Marines could scarcely miss. As the range closed still further, the Iron Warriors stowed boltguns and drew weapons more suited to the butchery of close combat. Chainswords screamed as their motors were gunned in eager readiness to cleave the flesh of the enemy, while bolt pistols barked well-aimed shots that sent severed limbs arcing through the blood-misted air.

In amongst the ranks of the Iron Warriors strode other elements of Ironclaw's command. Hulking Obliterators, each half as tall again as a Chosen Terminator and twice as broad, formed walking gun-phalanxes, unleashing a devastating torrent of fire, gunning down dozens with each blast of the weapons that grew from their twisted metal flesh. A pack of howling Possessed, each once an Iron Warrior and now the vessel for a fell daemon of the warp, were the first to plunge headlong into the melee, their distended, claw-tipped limbs thrashing about so violently that each was soon wading through a flood of gore and viscera.

With a savage grin, Ironclaw braced himself to receive the convicts' charge. An instant later the torrent of bodies broke upon his line, and the battle was truly joined.

The press was so great that individual enemies seemed to melt into a screaming, surging mass of limbs. Lasguns wielded as clubs thudded against his armour while stray shots whip-cracked all around. Within seconds the warsmith was covered with grasping foes, his Terminator-armoured form taking on the appearance of a hulking prehistoric predator assailed by numerous lesser creatures, each hanging from an ironclad limb as they clawed for some weak point in his armour.

They would find none, for the only exposed part of the warsmith's body was his face, and despite appearances, even that was protected. The bone of his skull had long ago been transmogrified to ceramite and his tendons replaced with unbreakable plasteel cabling. The bodies of the penal legionnaires were not so fortunate, however.

With a machine-flesh nerve impulse, the warsmith activated the generators in his matched lightning claws, the serrated blades spitting arcs of searing light. Flexing the blades once, he lashed out in a wide arc, and in a second everybody within a three hundred-and-sixty-degree arc was eviscerated. Even before the spilled guts of the dozen and more foes he had struck down had hit the rockcrete ground, the warsmith brought the metallic tentacles that were his mechatendrils whipping about. One was tipped by a flared flamer nozzle burning with its baleful blue pilot light.

The mechatendril lashed about and its weapon-tip vomited a searing blast of alchemical fire. A circle of foes still wider than those the warsmith had eviscerated was transformed into a wall of flaming bodies, a hideous screech erupting all about. Only those legionnaires clinging tightly to the warsmith's Terminator armour had avoided death, their fellow convicts scattered and burned in a wide circle about him.

A desperate trooper, his face alight with frenzon-induced bloodlust, hauled himself onto Ironclaw's massive shoulder as another wrapped his body about the warsmith's leg. Twisted and blackened limbs grasped upwards from the body-strewn ground, the combat stimms driving the fallen to fight on through what should have been unbearable pain and mortal wounding.

A claw grasped for the warsmith's face, the fingers spread wide like an animal's talons. Even before he could react, a thumb dug into his eye socket up to the knuckle in a vain effort to blind him.

A metallic growl surging from his throat, the warsmith bared his sharpened metal teeth and plunged them savagely through the wrist of the hand seeking to extract his eyeball. Blood spurted across his vision as the wrist was entirely cut in two, the hand remaining in place until the warsmith shook his head, dislodging the thumb from his eye socket and clearing the blood from his vision. Thanks to his Legiones Astartes heritage and the numerous blessings of the warp, the trauma barely made an impact on the warsmith's eyesight.

His attacker was equally unmoved by the ruin done upon his own body. The man was so dosed up on frenzon that he was barely slowed by the loss of his hand. Even now, he was attempting to bring his other hand to bear as the assailant clinging to Ironclaw's back grasped down towards his bare head.

'Enough,' the warsmith growled, lashing out with both lightning claws with such fearsome speed that the legionnaire had no chance to see his death coming. The steaming chunks of his ruined body splattered across the ground.

The attacker upon the warsmith's back was lifted high by a pair of snaking mechatendrils, one coiled about his neck, the other around a foot. With a brutal thought-impulse, Ironclaw tore the man in two and cast his still-thrashing remains into the surging crowd.

Now the two forces were merged into a chaotic, seething ocean of death and rage. Each Iron Warrior fought his own war against any enemy who dared approach within his reach, and certainly, none cowered from doing so. The legionnaires numbered in the hundreds and they were utterly fearless. Men fought on even with limbs torn away by screaming chainswords, and refused to die even when mass-reactive bolt-rounds exploded their guts across the ground. Ironclaw's perceptions shifted to that timeless state of mind only attainable in the boiling cauldron of battle, where blood sung and the powers of the warp gibbered and writhed but a thought away.

Ever had it been thus, since the earliest days of Ironclaw's existence. Even before the bitter days of the Great Betrayal, he had mastered every form of death. He had fought across a hundred warzones before the Warmaster had mustered at Isstvan, from frozen wastes to boiling death world jungles. He had fought beneath the ammonia seas of Ixacta Luminus and across the anti-grav extractor platforms in the upper atmosphere of Newton Prime. But always, in moments such as this when his steel-lined veins sang with the glory of battle, he was back at Tallarn, fighting across the oozing remains of that once-verdant world. Whatever enemy he was facing, that enemy was the Tallarns. Whatever general commanded them was always the Caliphar of the Crescent City, and his champion was always that whirling cyber-berserker who had been so blessed as to die at the hands of the mighty, proud IVth Legion.

But ever were the foe too little of a challenge for one who had bestridden the battlefields of the galaxy for countless centuries. There was only one foe Ironclaw truly felt honoured to confront…

An ordnance shell thundered overhead and the warsmith's consciousness snapped back to the murderous reality of his surroundings. The enemy piled up at his feet were not the forces of the Caliphar, nor that other, hated foe. They were the penal cannon fodder of the defenders of the Bastion Primus, and they were on the verge of achieving what their brutal overseers had meant of them.

'God-machine!' Ferrous Ironclaw bellowed, his machine-augmented voice carrying over the raucous clamour of war. 'Now!'

The Titan made no answer to its master's order – not a vocalised one, at least. Instead, it braced its massive limbs and opened wide its plasma couplings. The power of a captive sun cascaded through its conduits to feed the turbo laser mounted at its left shoulder.

Forewarned of the impending blast, the Iron Warriors engaged protective armour systems, for to do otherwise would have left even such mighty warriors blinded. The penal legionnaires were not so fortunate, however, and as the air turned white, hundreds of them suffered their optic nerves burned to ash. Hair and clothing flash-ignited as the laser blast lanced overhead in a continuous stream, accompanied by a sound as of a star screaming in rage.

The object of the Titan's wrath was the building the warsmith had indicated, but its true target lay beyond the shattered mass of statue-decked masonry. The lead super-heavy, its commander hoping to approach the Iron Warriors under cover and to catch them mired in the open killing ground, was about to crash through the ruin. The turbo laser blast obliterated what remained of the building, passing through its atomised fabric with no appreciable loss of power, and lanced into the frontal armour of the oversized tank behind it.

Incredibly, the tank's glacis withstood the searing beam for several seconds before the armour turned to molten lava and the beam punched through the turret and into the engine deck beyond. The tank's plasma reactor was obliterated and the roiling energies contained within set free in an instant.

The resulting explosion left nothing whatsoever of the target, the ground torn into a ragged black crater several metres deep. The blast crippled the second super-heavy, its frontal armour torn to shreds and its crew flash-boiled alive at their stations. The third was raked by a pressure wave that rocked its titanic mass back on its suspension and buckled its main cannon. Of the other, lighter armoured vehicles that followed in the wake of the super-heavies, nothing but smoking wrecks remained.

The area between the walls and the city proper was indeed the killing ground it was designed to be, but not for the attackers. The defenders were in utter disarray. The penal legion, herded forwards to mire the Iron Warriors in the open so that the armoured battlegroup might gun them down, was all but dead, the turbo laser blast fired scant metres overhead having seared the meat from the bones of hundreds of combat-stimmed troopers. Of those that remained, it appeared that bitter reality was slowly asserting itself as the frenzon washed away. Though most were blinded by the laser burst, the survivors were stumbling away through the human wreckage strewn across the open ground, finally more scared of the invaders than of their cruel overseers.

Burning debris scything down all about him, Ferrous Ironclaw was suddenly aware that night was closing in. The city was now alight with raging fire touched off by the turbo laser blast, the roiling clouds overhead underlit flickering orange like some mad remembrancer's vision of damnation. Shattered buildings were silhouetted black against sheets of fire dozens of metres tall, the figures of fleeing defenders darting across them intermittently.

'And now begins the true battle,' Ironclaw snarled, blood rising in expectation of what was to come. The breaching of the walls had been performed according to principles of military science long ago perfected by the Iron Warriors and their genius primarch; the next phase would be something altogether different.

An air of tense expectation descended upon the Iron Warriors. Each of them was smeared in gore and dirt, their normally shining armour dulled by war. Visored helms scanned the flame-wreathed ruins and weapons tracked slowly back and forth. Time slowed as the warp pressed in about them, the eyes of its unknowable denizens turned towards these ultimate betrayers of all they had been created to be. Such destruction had been wrought this day that the soul-thirsty beings of the empyrean were even now watching with that curious mixture of cruel approval and rank jealousy.

Sensing the pent-up fire burning in the soul of each of his warriors, Ferrous Ironclaw bared his teeth in a feral leer, the blood of his last attacker smeared across his features. The pressure of the warp increased exponentially, until it could be resisted no longer. The

Iron Warriors were no longer assaulting the Bastion Primus, and neither were their foes the defence forces of Bellum Colonia. Now, each and every one of the Traitor Marines believed with utter conviction that he was closing on the inner fortress of the Caliphar, the Crescent City burning around them.

Even as reality stretched to breaking point, the warsmith gave the signal. As one, the entire force started forwards. The mighty god-machine strode across the killing ground in but three steps, a vast mechanical foot passing directly over the warsmith's retinue in its eagerness. Dreadnoughts and Defilers pounded the rockcrete to dust as they surged forwards, smashing aside the ruins as they surrendered to the fury within. Forgefiends and Maulerfiends, the daemon-engines bound to the Iron Warriors' service by unspeakable pacts, now sought to claim what was rightfully theirs, their daemonic preysight latching on to the flaring soul-light of their foes.

But most terrible of all were the Iron Warriors themselves. Each of these veterans of the Long War was a brutal tyrant, a slayer of worlds, a champion of the Ruinous Powers and the doom of mankind. They bestrode the burning city like gods of war, their ceramite tread crushing rubble, their power-armoured shoulders crashing through tottering walls, and their relentless bolter-fire gunning down any enemy they encountered amongst the ruins.

The warsmith gloried in the song of war, but he and his warriors were far from mindless berserkers and their foe far from defenceless weaklings. The Iron Warriors wielded their bloodlust as a coldly precise weapon, focusing it, rendering it down to an incandescent core. The warriors of other Legions had long ago surrendered all self-control, the bloody World Eaters being the most infamous, but the warsmith would never allow his warriors to do so. Others of his Legion had answered the call of the Blood God, burning brightly, yet all too briefly as they drowned entire worlds in blood. Ferrous Ironclaw had vowed to wage the *Long* War, and would never surrender himself to such short-lived and shortsighted victories.

As the carnage ground on and the weaker of the bastion's defenders were ruthlessly culled, the stronger, more experienced of their number mustered near the city's centre to mount what must surely be their final stand. Whoever was in command of the defenders, the warsmith was forced to give him due credit, for after the initial slaughter the defenders mounted a series of well-coordinated counter-attacks. Venting their pent-up bloodlust in their typically cold fashion, the Iron Warriors were by necessity forced to spread out through the shattered, burning city and so became prone to envelopment by any sufficiently organised foe.

The warsmith had anticipated this, of course, and ensured that each of his sub-commands was formed into a smaller version of the overall force, well able to defend itself against a range of enemies. Individual squads were accompanied by Dreadnoughts, Obliterators, Predator tanks or, where they could be controlled, the fearsome daemon-engines. These small, concentrated, all-arms groupings were able to take on many times their own number, and to deal with any type of enemy that dared oppose them.

Soon, a score of bitter, close-quarter battles were

raging amongst the ruins, each every bit as bloody as the slaughter beyond the breach. These confrontations came down to combat blades and knives, grenades and pistols. Where before the penal legionnaires had come on in a frenzied horde, now the defenders were drilled Imperial Guardsmen, determined to repel the brutal besiegers or to fall defending the bastion. They knew the city well, and used sewers and service conduits to move about unseen and to launch a series of coordinated ambushes.

By the time the warsmith and his retinue were closing on the central citadel, his force was separated into a dozen sub-commands. None had avoided casualties, and none had expected to. One of Ironclaw's own Chosen, a veteran of the Siege of Terra, had been slain when an enemy gunship had strafed the street the retinue was crossing. It was not the gunship's fire that had struck the warrior down, however, but a cruel twist of fortune – or perhaps the fickle judgement of the Ruinous Powers, punishment for some unknown failing. The warrior had unleashed a fearsome torrent from his autocannon as he turned in the centre of the street he was crossing. The gunship's cockpit had disintegrated in a hail of micro detonations, and bereft of control the vessel had upended, veered about and come smashing to the ground. That veteran of the Long War had been struck down and consumed by the explosion, his Terminator armour, a suit as old as he, unable to protect him from the impact and resulting explosion. In what amounted to a powerful portent, the warrior's armour had survived almost unscarred, while the body within had been burned to ash.

As the warsmith finally laid eyes upon the citadel,

reports of the night's battles came flooding in. Over a dozen Iron Warriors were unaccounted for, while one of the Dreadnoughts had been lost when an air defence battery had been turned upon it. Two more Defilers had been struck down, each overeager and incautious as the lust for battle overcame the daemon-things within them.

For the defenders, however, the butcher's bill was many times higher, and the battle was not even concluded. Indeed, the siege of the Bastion Primus was yet to enter its final, climactic phase.

The warsmith had no way of calculating the precise casualties his force had inflicted, and no real desire to do so. All that mattered was that the raw stuff of reality was even now being twisted and stretched out of all recognition by the pressure of the warp as it crowded inwards. Were the slaughter to continue to engulf the entire planet of Bellum Colonia, were the Iron Warriors to slay and brutalise its entire population, then perhaps the thin skein that separated reality from the Sea of Souls might be breached, like the walls of this very bastion. Then, the denizens of the warp would come swarming through, and in all likelihood a full-scale daemonic incursion would ensue. Bellum Colonia would become a daemon world, a half-light realm ruled over by the immortal servants of the Ruinous Powers.

But that would not be, for Ferrous Ironclaw had no interest in the world of Bellum Colonia. He cared only for its central strongpoint, the lynchpin in its defences. The Bastion Primus.

The citadel at the heart of the bastion soared overhead, its bulk black and glinting with the flickering reflections of the fires that consumed the city all about. The sky behind was lightening with a grey false dawn, and the warsmith vowed there and then that not a single defender would see the *true* dawn rise. He vowed that the citadel would be cast down, one block at a time if necessary, each torn asunder by his taloned hands. The Caliphar, wounded unto death and bleeding into his silken sheets, would soon be slain, and there was nothing that the pitiful forces of Terra could do to save him…

With a snarl, the warsmith stalked before the rearing citadel, barely noticing the wall he ploughed straight through, nor the shower of debris scattered in his wake. His Chosen at his back, he walked into the open, his baleful glare fixed on the citadel's armoured portal.

'*Ghar nhag*,' the warsmith spoke a word of binding into his vox. A sound as of a furnace opening wide to vent its infernal heat sounded from nearby. '*Lor!*'

A ruin to the warsmith's left exploded in dust and scattered rubble as a mechanical form powered forwards on mighty-pistoned forearms, followed a moment later by three more. Though smaller than the spider-form Defilers, these particular daemon-engines were far more suited to what Ironclaw had in mind for the citadel. The lead engine was a mass of pistons and flailing mechanical tentacles, its central mass a heavily armoured shell. Its forelegs were far larger than those at its rear, lending it a vaguely simian gait, its glowering head low between its massively armoured shoulders. Those following behind were of a similar type, though no two were armed identically. It was clear that here was the work of the most blasphemously skilled of daemon-engineers.

Imagining the Caliphar that doomed city stark with terror upon his deathbed, Ferrous Ironclaw gestured towards the citadel with a taloned hand.

The daemon-engines surged forwards to obey.

The first powered across the open space before the citadel, the tower's weapons batteries opening up, hundreds of rounds churning up the ground and ricocheting from its armoured bulk in a hail of dirty sparks. Ten metres from the base of the tower the mechanical nightmare bent almost double, its piston-driven limbs tense and coiled, before propelling itself with unimaginable force at the wall.

The impact was staggering, the daemon-engine's foreclaws digging into the citadel's armoured hide to lend it purchase. The creature hauled itself up the wall, its animalistic head sweeping back and forth as if hunting some unseen prey. The head shot suddenly about, its glowing eyes narrowing as it caught some trace of its prey. It withdrew an arm, stretched it back and pistoned it hard into the wall; the entire structure trembling under the force. It seemed to listen, as if deciphering the seismic echo or sniffing out the souls of stunned defenders.

Then a searing fire guttered to life as clusters of melta-weapons mounted on its limbs unleashed the power of a sun. The roar of the weapons' concentrated fire searing through the citadel's outer armour was nigh deafening to those on the outside; it must have rendered those within entirely senseless.

But before the daemon-engine on the wall could complete its task, the warsmith gestured a second time, and another engine ploughed forwards. Clearly akin to the first, this one had a trio of wide-mouthed cannons mounted to its fore where the other sported forearms and head. It put the warsmith in mind of the ancient legends of the Grekans, where three-headed hell-dogs had guarded the gates to the underworld. But this infernal engine would not be guarding anything. Rather, it would do the opposite.

As one, all three of the engine's weapons projected a blast of concentrated warp-stuff directly at the citadel's armoured portal. The fusillade was accompanied by an atonal roar that could only be the wailing of the damned as they writhed in eternal torment in the deepest, darkest reaches of the warp. Ironclaw's ears rang with the glorious outburst, while any mortal who had not dedicated his soul to the Ruinous Powers must surely have been driven utterly insane by the merest hint of that infernal cacophony.

The armoured portal, a five-metre-tall gateway designed to withstand massed melta-cannon fire, turned to seething liquid metal under the relentless, otherworldly blast. Spurred on by the spectacle, the other daemon-engines joined the assault, throwing themselves at the walls as had the first or unleashing their own abominable weapons.

No man-made structure could hope to stand against such concentrated wrath.

The defenders' fire died off as those within were shaken and stunned by the terrible attack. Ironclaw could taste their terror, nigh see it coiling upwards as the warp closed ever tighter inwards. Truly, the eyes of unknowable beings were being turned upon the bastion this day, just as the warsmith had hoped.

'*Kharak!*' Ironclaw bellowed another word of

command, even his augmented voice barely carrying over the relentless clamour of the daemon-engines' assault. The Forgefiend concentrating upon breaching the armoured portal resisted the order for a few seconds, before silencing its weapon with undisguised reluctance. Ironclaw bared his metallic teeth at the daemon-engine and it backed off a step or two, cowed by the being bound as its master.

'Muster the warriors,' the warsmith ordered the nearest of his Chosen. 'The end draws near.'

As the Chosen relayed his master's order to gather the grand company before the bastion, Ferrous Ironclaw crossed the open space before the portal, the defenders' gunfire now silenced.

The portal writhed with unknowable energies, and waves of baleful power radiated from its surface. Looking upon it, Ironclaw saw the twisted faces of the damned rise and sink amongst the energies, and he gloried in the sheer blasphemy of the spectacle.

The roar of an engine and the grinding of huge tracks caused the warsmith to turn in time to see one of his grand company's Land Raiders smash through an already ruined structure before coming to a halt and lowering its forward assault ramp. As the warriors transported within dismounted, more armoured vehicles closed in on the gathering, and soon scores of ironclad Traitor Marines mustered to begin the final assault.

So effective had the primarch's virus-bombing of Tallarn been that his own warriors had been forced to wage war from the confines of their armoured machines for long weeks, only able to dismount for limited periods lest even their Legiones Astartes bodies be overwhelmed by the contagion still ravaging the planet. The defenders of Tallarn had been unable to fight outside of their own armoured vehicles at all. Now, they cringed within their shelters or beneath the last of their domed cities, their ruler wounded unto death and the primarch himself preparing their final doom.

'Warriors of Iron!' Ferrous Ironclaw addressed his grand company, a hundred and more grim-faced helms fixed expressionlessly upon him. 'The gods themselves watch our deeds this day, and our foe cowers upon his deathbed. This place is ours, and so too shall be our enemy's head before the day is out!'

A chorus of war-cries swept the ranks, but the warsmith held up one talon for silence.

'But our work here is not yet done,' said Ironclaw as the warriors fell silent. 'Only when our *real* foe deigns to enter the fray shall we truly prove ourselves worthy, in the name of the primarch.'

A bitter tension descended upon the warriors of the grand company, for each and every one of the warsmith's followers knew well the foe he spoke of. The thought of that most hated of enemies served only to fuel the already raging fires of war within each, their eagerness to face him once more a palpable thing.

Turning his back on his warriors, the warsmith faced the armoured portal, its surface still writhing with warp-spawned energies. The Caliphar of Tallarn cringed within; he was certain of it. The primarch would be pleased to receive the head of that foe, and in delivering it, Ironclaw knew that the Iron Warriors' true enemy must surely come.

Firing his lightning claws and girding himself to

the charge, the warsmith bellowed the war cry of his Legion as his warriors followed in his wake.

'Iron within!' he cried, his serrated claws scything through the armoured portal and sending gobbets of liquefied matter arcing in all directions.

'Iron without!' the warsmith's warriors replied as the grand company plunged headlong into the tunnels of the citadel.

The slaughter that ensued made the fall of the city appear no more than an appetiser at a feast of godless carnage.

FERROUS IRONCLAW'S TWIN hearts pounded deep within his Terminator-armoured chest as he stepped through the wrecked hatch and into the chamber at the heart of the Caliphar's palace. The warsmith was covered head to foot in the blood of his foes; for the last hour he and his warriors had fought the defenders hand-to-hand, face-to-face. Though none of the Caliphar's elite palace guard were the equal of a Traitor Marine, they had fought with all the ferocity and zeal they were famed for, and to a man had died well, if messily.

Debris crunching under his tread, the warsmith entered the Caliphar's inner sanctum and glanced balefully around. It was a large chamber, the walls hung with flickering pict-slates and looped with guttering cabling. The lumens had failed, the power now intermittent thanks to the devastation the Iron Warriors had wrought upon the infrastructure of the Crescent City. The only light illuminating the inner sanctum was the flickering of the screens, which every now and then locked on to a feed of the burning city before being consumed by churning static once more.

A sharp detonation sent a shower of sparks arcing across the chamber, snapping the warsmith's attention to the clustered command terminals at its heart. His blood-flecked lips splitting in a feral leer, his metallic teeth glinting in the bright static of the nearby pict-slates, he stepped forwards, his gaze now locked upon the figure at the heart of the chamber.

'Traitor...' the man slumped across the master command lectern spat through lacerated lips.

The warsmith's vision swam as he regarded his foe, his grey military uniform soaked in his own blood and caked with dust. Was this the Caliphar...?

'You'll pay,' the man coughed, the last of strength clearly ebbing away. 'Truly is it said that the wages of sin are–'

'Spare me your decrepit sermon,' said the warsmith, coming to stand before the broken figure. 'I come for your head.'

'Then take it, abomination!' the dying man spat, a trickle of blood running down his chin.

Ferrous felt the bow-wave of onrushing fate even as death loomed through the warp, a thousand potential events converging into a cold, bitter singularity. He moved to the left as fast as his hulking Terminator armour would allow, just as a shadow emerged from the darkness at his back.

'Kill it!' the Caliphar shrieked as loud as his ruined lungs could manage. 'Kill the traitor before he dooms us all!'

The Caliphar's champion was little more than a blur, his genhanced body a scything whirlwind of death.

With a thought, Ironclaw's serrated lightning blades spat into actinic life and he lashed out, one claw cleaving the air where the cyber-dervish had whirled but a fraction of a second before.

The champion dived back into the shadows before reappearing an instant later somewhere to the right, a pair of matched power scimitars scything out of the darkness in a vicious attempt to cleave the warsmith's head from his shoulders. Ironclaw snapped his head about sharply, yet still the tip of one blade parted the skin across his left cheek, the wound so clean and precise he barely felt it.

'I swore to my primarch I would present him with the head of the Caliphar of the Crescent City,' the warsmith bellowed as the whirling figure dashed to one side, nothing of it but shadow and steel visible. 'And that I shall do!'

Now the warsmith plunged headlong into that storm of blades. It was clearly the last thing the Caliphar's champion had expected him to do, and the rhythm of the enemy's swordplay changed drastically. One moment it was poised and deadly, the next desperate and clumsy. Sparks flew as the scimitars cut into the warsmith's armour, great tears rent in its fabric. Even as the eyes of the Ruinous Powers turned fully upon him, the pressure of the warp so great it threatened to crush reality to a pulp, the warsmith drew back his lightning claws and brought them together in a titanic sweep.

Where the two sets of fist-mounted, serrated blades converged, the body of the champion was cut into a dozen and more chunks of meat.

Silence fell upon the ruined chamber as the

unrecognisable human ruin collapsed at the warsmith's feet.

'It doesn't matter,' he heard the Caliphar whisper behind him, and he turned, flexing his lightning claws as he prepared to decapitate his enemy and deliver his head to the primarch. 'None of this matters...'

The warsmith stepped before the command lectern as the Caliphar raised his head with what must surely be the last of his strength.

'You think yourself the victor in this war,' the Caliphar said, his voice now barely audible. 'You've lost...'

With a last effort, the Caliphar of the Crescent City pushed his broken body upwards and off the command lectern, revealing a glowing pict-slate smeared with his own blood. Then he collapsed, his shattered legs unable to support his own weight, and lay before the warsmith, his face a mask a defiance.

His eyes narrowing, the warsmith approached the lectern, ignoring the man bleeding out at his feet. The screen showed a strategic plot of the region, and a mass of glowing runes had recently appeared in the upper atmosphere, directly above the fortress.

'You see, traitor,' the Caliphar breathed as his death rattle sounded deep in his lungs. 'You really have lost...'

'Fool,' Ferrous Ironclaw replied as the runes upon the pict-slate resolved themselves into solid icons rapidly descending through sub-orbital space. Each rune was a symbol, a clenched black fist within a circle, the hated Chapter sigil of the Iron Warriors' true foe.

The Imperial Fists.

'No,' the warsmith growled.

'I have won…'

THRONE OF LIES

by Aaron Dembski-Bowden

The *Covenant of Blood* tore through the warp, splitting the secret tides like a spear of stained cobalt and flawed gold. Its engines struggled, breathing white fire into the ever-shifting Sea of Souls. Pulsing like arrhythmic hearts, the thrusters laboured to propel the ship onwards. Its passage was a graceless dive, slipping through boiling waves of thrashing psychic energy.

Tormented fields of kinetic force shielded the craft from the warp's elemental rage, but the storm's force was merciless. Reaching out from the hurricane, the claws of vast creatures raked across the shields, each impact hammering the vessel farther from its course.

In a sealed chamber at the ship's prow, a lone figure knelt in silent repose. Her human eyes were closed, yet she was far from blind. Her secret eye, the eye she hid from the world beneath sweat-stained bandanas and uncomfortable helms, looked out into the void. The ship's hull was no barrier, and the crackling shields no obstacle. Her secret sight pierced them with effortless ease, and she stared into the storm beyond.

Like oil on water, the seas outside roiled in a sickening riot of colour. A beacon of light usually pierced the chaos – a lifeline of ephemeral radiance splitting the swirling murk. All she had to do was follow it.

There was no beacon this time. No radiant lifeline. The crackle of the shields buckling under pressure was all that illuminated the storm outside.

The tides rolled against the ship in jagged, unpredictable waves, too fast for human response. By the time she saw a flood of migraine-bright energy spilling towards her, the shields were already repelling it. They sparked with pained fire as they sent the assaulting wave back into the psychic filth from whence it came.

The *Covenant of Blood* trembled again, its engines giving a piteous whine as the tremor ran through the ship's plasteel bones. It couldn't take much more of this. The kneeling woman took a deep breath, and refocused.

Her lapse of attention had not gone unnoticed. The voice, when it came, was an insidious whisper breaching her heart, not her ears. Each word resonated, echo-faint, through her blood.

Centuries of conquering the void. Centuries of laying claim to the stars. The dance of hunter and

hunted, predator and prey. You, Navigator, will be my end. The death of glory. The pain of failure.

The ship was threatening her again. She didn't take that as a good sign, and hissed a single word through clenched teeth.

'Silence.'

She swore that, somewhere on the edge of imagination, she sensed its laughter.

Above all else, she loathed the crude poetry of the ship's primal intelligence. The machine-spirit at the warship's core was a bestial, dominant consciousness. It had resisted its new Navigator for weeks now. She was beginning to fear she would never rise as its master.

The claws of the neverborn tear at my hull-skin, promising to bleed my innards to the void, it whispered. **You are damnation. You are the bearer of blame. You will cast us into oblivion, Octavia.**

She bit back a reply, keeping her mouth as closed as her human eyes. Her third eye stared unblinking, seeing nothing but the storm raging outside.

No. No, there was something more now. Something else sailed the Sea of Souls, more suggestion and shadow than form and flesh. She pulsed a warning at once.

+Something beneath us, something vast. *Evade at once.*+

Octavia sent the command with all her strength, a desperate plea to the ship's pilots. At the speed of thought, she felt the response flash through the interface cables binding her to the throne of brass and bone. A dead voice, the tone of a lobotomised servitor at the ship's helm.

'Compliance.'

The *Covenant of Blood* shuddered now, its burning engines forcing it to climb through the psychic syrup of un-space. The predator, the vast presence beneath them, stirred in the etheric fog. She felt it thrash, and saw a shadow the size of a sun ripple in the storm. It drew closer.

+It's chasing us.+

'Acknowledged,' the servitor replied.

+Go faster. Go much, *much* faster.+

'Compliance.'

The vast presence broke through the lashing waves of psychic mist, unaffected by their density. She was reminded, for an awful moment, of a vast shark pushing through the open ocean, dead-eyed and forever hungry.

+We have to break from the warp. We can't outrun this.+

This time, the answer was rich with emotion, none of it pleasant. It was deep, low, and tainted with inhuman resonance.

'How far are we from the Torias system?'

+Hours. Days. *I don't know*, my lord. But we're dead in minutes if we don't break from the warp.+

'Unacceptable,' growled the Exalted, master of the *Covenant of Blood*.

+Do you feel the way the *Covenant* is shaking? A psychic shadow made of black mist and hatred is reaching out to swallow us. I am the Navigator, my lord. I am dragging this ship from the Sea of Souls, no matter what you say.+

'Very well,' said the Exalted reluctantly. 'All stations, brace for re-entry to the void. And Octavia?'

+Yes, my lord?+

'You would do well to show me more respect when Talos is not aboard.'

She bared her teeth in a grin, feeling her heartbeat quicken at the threat.

+If you say so, Exalted One.+

THE HUNTRESS MOVED through the chamber, one of many in the cavernous palace, clad in a stolen crimson gown and someone else's skin. Her name, for the last two hours, had been Kalista Larhaven. This was even confirmed by the numeric identity code tattooed onto the flesh of her right wrist.

The true Kalista Larhaven, the original owner of both the name and the exquisite dress, was now folded with graceless, boneless ease into a thermo-ventilation shaft. There she lay, silent in death, an unknown martyr to a lost cause. She had her own hopes, dreams, joys and needs – all of which had ended in the shallow thrust of an envenomed blade. It had taken longer to hide the courtesan's body than it had to end her life.

The huntress passed a flock of acolyte clerics. They shuffled along the carpeted floor, chanting in heretical murmurs. The first of them bore an incense orb on a corroded chain, the bronze sphere seething with coils of thin, sugary mist. This priest greeted the courtesan by name, and the huntress smiled with the dead whore's lips.

'Do you go to attend upon the master?'

The huntress answered with wicked eyes and an indulgent smile.

'I wish you well, Kalista,' the priest replied. 'Go in peace.'

The huntress offered a graceful curtsey, subtly submissive, moving as one born to a life of giving pleasure. The true Kalista had moved this way. The huntress had watched it, gauged it, captured the essence of it – all in a handful of heartbeats.

As she walked away, she felt the eager eyes of the whispering priests following her movements. She exaggerated the swing of her hips, favouring them with a last glance over her bare shoulder. She read the hunger in their dark eyes, and much better, the idiotic conviction. Let them go about their business without knowing the truth: that the girl they desired was already dead, packed into a tube close to the thermal exchange processors elsewhere in the palace.

The heat would accelerate the process of decay, so the true Kalista would become a quick victim to the bacteria that always laid claim to a human body in the hours after it drew its last breath.

But the huntress was unconcerned. She would be gone by the time any discoveries were made, her duty done and her escape a source of infinite grief for the people of this worthless planet.

Before she had become Kalista Larhaven, the huntress had worn the skin of a nameless maidservant for almost an hour, using the shape to reach the lower levels and move through the slave tunnels. Before that, she had been a trader in the palace's vast court-yards, licensed to sell holy relics to pilgrims. Before that, a pilgrim herself, wearing the ragged clothes of a vagabond: a wandering beggar in search of spiritual enlightenment.

The huntress had been on the world of Torias Secundus for a single day and a single night. Even as she drew close to completing her mission, she lamented the time spent so far. She was above this assignment. She knew it, her sisters knew it, and her superiors knew it. This was punishment – a punishment for the failures of the past.

Undeserved, perhaps. Yet duty was duty. She had to obey.

She moved on through the palace, passing chanting acolytes, scurrying clerks and raucous packs of intoxicated nobles. The halls were growing busy as noon approached, for with the coming of noon came the High Priest's long-awaited speech.

The woman who was not Kalista blended into the crowds, passing with smiles and feminine curtseys. Her irritation never showed on lips of rose-red, nor in eyes of ice-blue. The fact remained, though – this skin would not get her to the High Priest's side at the right moment. Time was a vicious factor. If killing him was the only goal, he would be dead from a sniper's kiss already, long before taking to the podiums later today and addressing the people of the city.

But no. His death had to be choreographed along exact lines, played out like a performance for all to see.

The huntress sensed she was reaching the end of this skin's lifespan. Already, the chambers through which she moved were the domains of the chosen elite, with clothing becoming increasingly ostentatious and more expensive. The apparent courtesan graced her way through the carnival of colours, her stolen eyes flicking in predatory need.

Noblewoman to noblewoman, priestess to priestess, courtesan to courtesan.

None of them suited. None would allow her to finish what she had begun.

She needed another skin. Soon.

THE DOOR TO the Navigator's chambers ground open on rough hydraulics. Nothing on this ship worked right. Octavia checked that her pistol was holstered at her hip, and left through the only portal leading out of her room. Her attendants, whom she despised as much as she loathed the ship itself, bustled around her, imploring her to return to her chambers.

She wanted to shoot them. She really, *really* wanted to shoot them. The most normal of them couldn't pass as a human even in poor lighting. It looked at her, smiling with too many teeth, clasping its hands together as if in prayer.

'Mistress,' it hissed. 'Return to chambers, mistress. For safety. For protection. Mistress must not be harmed. Mistress must not bleed.'

She shivered under its beseeching touch. Hands that possessed too many fingers stroked her clothes, and worse, her bare skin.

'Don't touch me,' she snapped.

'Forgive me, mistress. A thousand apologies, most sincere.'

'Get out of my way, please.'

'Please return, mistress,' it pleaded. 'Do not walk dark places of ship. Stay, for safety.'

She drew her pistol, sending the creatures scurrying back.

'Get out of my way. *Now*.'

'Someone comes, mistress. Another soul draws near.'

She stared into the blackened corridor outside her chamber, lit by weak illumination globes that did nothing to defeat the darkness. The figure emerging from the gloom wore a jacket of old leather, and carried two heavy pistols at his hips. A hacking blade – the kind of weapon one might find in the hands of a jungle world primitive – was strapped to his shin.

Half of his face glinted in the reflected light. Augmetic facial features, the most obvious of which was a red eye lens, were of expensive and rare craftsmanship. The human side of his face twisted in a crooked smile.

Octavia returned it.

'Septimus,' she said.

'Octavia. Forgive me for pointing out the obvious, but that was the roughest ride through the Sea of Souls I've ever had to suffer through.'

'The ship still hates me,' she scowled. 'Why are you here? Keeping me company?'

'Something like that. Let's go inside.'

She hesitated, but complied. Once they were back in her chamber, she ensured the door was locked. Anything to keep her annoying attendants away.

Octavia could, if one was being generous, be considered beautiful. But beauty needs light and warmth to bloom, and these were both denied to the young Navigator. Her skin was the unhealthy pale of unclean marble, marking her as a member of the crew aboard the lightless battleship, the *Covenant of Blood*. Her eyes were losing all colour as her pupils grew accustomed to remaining forever dilated. Her hair, once a tumbling fall of healthy dark locks, was a ragged mess held into false order by a ponytail.

She looked across to Septimus, who was absently picking his way through piles of discarded clothes and old food cartons.

'Look at this mess. You are a filthy creature.'

'Nice to see you too. To what do I owe the pleasure?'

'You know why I'm here.' He paused. 'Talk of your attitude is beginning to spread. You're making the crew uneasy. They worry you're going to enrage the Legion because you can't follow orders.'

'So, let them worry.'

Septimus sighed. '*Asath Jirath Sor-sarassan.*'

'Speak Gothic, damn it. None of that whispery Nostraman, thank you. I know you were swearing. I'm not a fool.'

'If the crew worries, they might take matters into their own hands. They'd kill you without a second thought.'

'They need me. Everyone needs me. Without me, the ship has no Navigator.'

'Maybe,' said Septimus slowly. 'But no one wants tension with the Legion. Things are always on the edge, but when someone starts to breed difficulties? The crew has lynched troublemakers before. Dozens of times.'

'They wouldn't try that with me.'

He laughed bitterly. 'No? If they thought it would please the Legion, they'd hang you from a gantry in the engineering deck, or beat you to death and flush your body from an airlock. You need to tread with care. Talos is off the ship. When First Claw isn't on board, be cautious in how you deal with the Legion and the crew.'

'Don't give me this crap,' Octavia snapped. 'I was

under more strain than you can even imagine. For Throne's sake, the Geller field was dying. The ship was moments from falling apart.'

Septimus shook his head. 'Sometimes, you still forget where you are. Your talent spares you the worst treatment, but you're still a slave. Remember that. Delusions of equality will get you killed.'

'You're as bad as those things that try to keep me sealed in here. I've survived three weeks without Talos watching over me. A few more hours won't make any difference'.

She paused for a moment before changing the subject. 'Any word from the surface?'

'Nothing yet. As soon as they vox confirmation, I'll bring them back on board. It's close to noon in the capital city. The High Priest will be speaking soon. Won't be long now.'

'I don't suppose you know what they're actually doing down there?'

Septimus shrugged.

'What they always do. They're hunting.'

AT THE HEART of Toriana, capital city of the world below, the masses waited for their leader. The plaza of the Primus Palace was flooded with an ocean of humanity – ninety thousand men, women and children. Each family had been carefully selected by the government's Departmento Culturum and marched to the gathering by armed enforcers.

Above the sea of cheering faces, an ornate balcony jutted from the palace's side. Ten figures stood in motionless silence, enduring the crowd's roars, with rifles clutched over armoured chestplates. Faceless black visors and carapace armour the colour of old blood marked these soldiers as the Red Sentinels, elite guard of the High Priest himself. The back-mounted power packs carried by each one hummed with suppressed tension, bonded to the ammunition sockets of their hellguns via thick, segmented cables.

The Sentinel leader kept up a constant stream of muttered words into the vox-network, checking on the position of his sniper teams situated on nearby rooftops. All was in readiness. Should trouble arise from the crowd, the Sentinels and the enforcers on the streets had enough firepower to paint the marble floors red and reduce the plaza to a charnel house.

The air itself thrummed as a Valkyrie gunship hovered overhead, its adamantium hull turned amber by the midday sun, and its cannons seeking targets in the windows of adjacent buildings. Satisfied, it moved away on growling engines, bathing the Red Sentinels below in a heated wind of thruster wash.

The Red Sentinel captain spoke a final order into the vox, and the massive double doors behind him opened. At the first sight of the robed figure walking onto the balcony, the crowd erupted in praising cheers.

High Priest Cyrus was the wrong side of middle age, and his fine encarmine robes looked painted onto his porcine form. Jowls shook as he raised fat hands to the sky.

'My people!' he proclaimed.

The High Priest, once Imperial Governor of this world, licked his lips as he bathed in the cheers rising to meet him. His was a solemn duty; to herald in a world free of Imperial taxation and tithe. A world under his rule, aided by the council of cardinals, known collectively as the Benevolence.

'My people, hear my words!' he continued. 'We stand at the dawn of a new age of peace and prosperity! No more shall we hurl our faith and fortunes into the furnace of Imperial slavery. No more shall our world suffer alone, ignored by the Imperium of Man. No more shall we struggle through famine and civil war, led into folly by self-serving ministers appointed by distant Terra.'

Cyrus paused, waiting until the cheers died down before he continued. 'This is the age of the Benevolence! The new faith! The Benevolence encircles us all, in hope and trust. Faith in one another! Faith in other worlds that have thrown off the same shackles! Shoulder to shoulder, we stand defiant against the oppression of the past!'

The crowd roared, as Cyrus had known it would. Already, they were chanting his name as their saviour, their saint.

'Brothers and sisters, sons and daughters! We are free, united far from the reach of the hated False Emperor! I... I...'

He never finished the sentence. The fat man staggered, gripping the balcony's railing. The Red Sentinels moved as one, their rifles up and panning for threats. The cheering from the crowd was drowned in confusion.

The huntress smiled as she watched. The timing had been perfect; the venom delivered the very moment this false prophet dared to decry the God-Emperor. The crowd had seen it. The hololithic image feeds had recorded it, so the whole planet had witnessed it.

Now they knew the price of blasphemy and secession.

The digital weapon concealed on her gauntlet was only good for a single shot, one sliver-dart, rich with neurotoxin. The targeting laser was flashless, and easily powerful enough to pierce the heretic's silk robes. She'd fired it right into his spine, and none of the Red Sentinels were any the wiser.

The High Priest tumbled forwards and he pitched over the balcony's edge. He didn't scream as he fell, for he was already dead.

The huntress smiled behind her faceless visor, moving with the other Red Sentinels, feigning panic and anger to mirror theirs. She disliked the bulky armour they wore, but the skin was a necessary one. The Sentinel she'd killed to acquire it had put up a reasonable fight – for an unaugmented human, at least.

The huntress made a show of scanning for enemy targets on balconies of adjacent buildings, relishing the panicked voices jabbering over the vox. In a matter of minutes, she would be able to leave this wretched gathering and make her way back through the city, in readiness to abandon this world forever.

She was already making her way to the double doors when the sun fell dark, and heavy engines whined behind her. The huntress turned, her eyes narrowed, her heart starting to beat faster.

Five shapes dropped from the sky. Armoured in massive suits of power armour, they thudded down onto the balcony. Flame and smoke retched from the thrust generators on their backs, and helms with painted skulls for faces watched her with unerring focus. Not the other Red Sentinels. Just her. These warriors had been waiting on the roof, knowing she would make her move.

Each of the figures raised a bolter clutched in dark gauntlets.

'Assassin of the Callidus Temple,' intoned one, his voice a growl through his helmet's vox-caster. '*We have come for you.*'

There was no thought of fighting. The huntress turned and ran, preternatural agility blurring her form like quicksilver. Sentinel armour rained from her as she sprinted back through the palace, discarded as fast as she was able.

She heard them giving chase. The clanging thuds of ceramite boots on mosaic floors. The coughing bursts of jump packs breathing fire, propelling the warriors down the halls faster than the huntress could run. Bystanders, innocent or otherwise, cried out as her pursuers cut down anyone in their way.

She heard the throaty crashing of bolters, and weaved across the detonating ground where shells hit home. She leapt as she ran, knowing they were targeting her legs, seeking to bring her down by an explosive shell to the back of the knee.

One shell impacted on the huntress's calf, but spun aside, deflected by her synthetic skin armour. Another exploded against the wall by her shoulder, sending chalky debris clattering over her face. Still, she ran.

When a shell finally struck home, it took her in the meat of the thigh. Despite years of pain resistance training and narcotic compounds introduced into her bloodstream to deaden her nerves, the agony was unrivalled. The huntress howled as she went down, her thigh reduced to nothing more than a ruin of hanging flesh and muscle stripped from the blood-stained, broken bone.

Spitting curses, she clawed herself forwards, vicious even in futility. She had enough of a lead to drag herself to her feet, and round the next corner in an awkward, limping run.

Her flight to safety lasted mere seconds. As she rounded the corner, shoving her way through a milling crowd of servants, two immense, dark forms brought her to the ground. Her muscles stung with chemical enhancement, straining against the armoured warriors pinning her to the floor. She went to draw her blade from her thigh sheath, only to scream in frustrated rage when she realised the scabbard and blade had been torn from her body when the exploding shell struck her leg. She yelled fresh curses as her reaching forearm was smashed under the boot of another trai-torous warrior.

She writhed under their oppressive strength, los-ing control in her anger, not even realising her face was flowing into the visages of a dozen women she'd killed in the last two days. From above, she heard the leader of the warriors speak while his men held her down.

'My name is Talos of the Night Lords Legion. And you are coming with me.'

THE HUNTRESS OPENED her eyes, feeling them ripe with stinging tears. The first thing to grace her senses was pain, jagged and unfamiliar in its intensity. Every-thing below her spine ached with sickening pulses in time to her heartbeat.

Immediately, training took over from disoriented

instinct. She had to learn her whereabouts, then escape. Nothing else mattered. Her vision focused, resolving the blurred gloom into a semblance of clarity.

The chamber was intentionally dark, kept that way by low-burning wall globes. With no furnishings beyond the table she lay upon, it had all the charm of a prison cell. The huntress tried to rise, but her limbs wouldn't answer. She could barely even raise her head.

She became aware, at last, of rasping breath, with the teeth-aching rumble of active power armour.

'Do not try to rise.' The voice was the same rasping growl as before. 'Your legs have been amputated, as have your arms below the elbows. You are conscious only because of chemical pain-inhibitors flushed into your bloodstream.'

The armoured figure came into view, stalking to the edge of the table. Its face was a battered war helm, the visage painted bone-white to resemble a human skull, and a rune from a filthy, forgotten language etched into its forehead. Across its breastplate, an Imperial eagle was ruined by ritual scarring, the holy aquila symbol no doubt profaned by the heretic warrior that wore it.

'You will not escape this chamber,' said the figure – Talos, she guessed. 'You will never return to your temple. There is no fate for you beyond the walls of this cell, and so I grant you a choice, assassin. Tell us what we wish to know, and earn yourself a quick death, or tell us after we have subjected you to several hours of excruciation.'

The huntress spoke through blood-flecked lips, her

voice a ghost of its former strength.

'I will die before speaking secrets to a heretic.'

Even through the vox-crackle, the reply was tinged with amusement. 'Everyone says that.'

'Pain… pain is nothing to me,' said the huntress.

'Pain is nothing to you when what remains of your body is flooded with inhibitor narcotics,' replied Talos. 'The interface nodes implanted along your spinal cord will change your perception of pain soon enough.'

'I am Jezharra,' she said defiantly, 'daughter of the Callidus. You will get nothing from me, fallen one. Nothing but curses heaped upon your worthless life.'

Talos laughed.

'Stronger souls than yours have cracked in our claws, assassin. No one resists. Do not make me do this.'

'How did you know I would come?'

'I saw it,' he said. 'I am a prophet of the Eighth Legion. In moments of affliction, I can see along the path of a future yet to come.'

'Sorcery,' spat Jezharra. 'Black magic.'

'Perhaps. But it worked, did it not?'

'You think yourself cunning for arranging that ambush? For luring a daughter of the Callidus to this backwater world, and baiting the trap with a cult's high priest?'

'Cunning enough to have you here, at my mercy, with your arms and legs severed by my brothers' chainblades.'

'My death is meaningless,' Jezharra sighed. 'My life was lived in service to the Golden Throne, so do what you will. Agony will never twist me into a traitor.'

'Then you have chosen,' said Talos. 'These are your

final moments of sanity, released from pain. Enjoy them while you can.'

'I am Jezharra, daughter of the Callidus. My mind is inviolate, my soul unbroken. I am Jezharra, daughter of the Callidus...'

The huntress grinned as she chanted the words. The warrior turned, addressing another presence in the room, a figure the bound assassin couldn't see.

'So be it. Excruciate her.'

JEZHARRA, THE HUNTRESS, resisted for seventeen days. It was by far the longest any human had lasted under the Legion's interrogation. When she broke at last, little remained of the woman she'd been, let alone the consummate killer.

She wheezed secrets from split lips, the words forming vapour in the chamber's freezing air. Once she had said all she needed to say, she lay slack in her restraints, trying to summon the strength to beg for death.

'The... Uriah System.'

'*Where* in the Uriah System?' asked Talos patiently.

'Uriah... is a dying star. Temple is... on the planet... farthest from it. Three. Uriah... Three.'

'What of the defences?' pressed Talos.

'Nothing in orbit. Nothing permanent. Local... local battlefleet patrols nearby.'

'And on the surface?'

'It... it is done,' breathed the dying huntress. 'Kill me...'

'What defences are on the surface of Uriah Three?' repeated Talos.

'Nothing... Just my sisters. Fifty... fifty daughters of Callidus. A lone fortress-temple... in the mountains.'

'Coordinates?'

'Please…'

'The coordinates, assassin,' insisted Talos. 'Then I will end this.'

'Twenty-six degrees… Eighteen… forty-four… point fifty-six. The heart of the tundra. Seventy degrees… Twenty-three, forty-nine point sixty-eight.'

'Is the temple shielded against orbital attack?'

'Yes,' she whispered.

'And the hololithic recording is there?'

'I… I saw it myself.'

'Very well,' said Talos.

The warrior drew a golden blade. Its craftsmanship was exquisite, forged in an age of inspiration long-forgotten by the Imperium. On a ship of ancient relics, this was by far the most revered. The Night Lord stepped closer to the husk on the apothecarion table.

'Jezharra…'

The warrior let the assassin's name hang in the air. With his free hand, he disengaged the seals of his helm, pulling the death-mask off with a serpentine hiss of venting air pressure. The assassin's eyes were gone, taken from her in the interrogation, but she sensed what he had done in the way his voice changed.

'Thank you,' he said softly.

She spat at him before she died – one final act of defiance. In a way, it was hard not to admire her. But Talos's blade fell, embedding itself in the table as the assassin's head rolled free.

The warrior stood in the stinking chamber for an indeterminate number of heartbeats, before replacing his war helm. His vision drowned in the red wash

'Why has the fleet gathered? What's so vital about one world out on the Rim?'

'If I knew, I'd tell you. I've never seen this many Legion ships in one place before. If I wasn't seeing it with my own eyes, I'd never believe it could happen.'

He moved to the bank of viewscreens adorning an entire wall. His gloved fingertip tapped ship after ship, each one a different class and size.

'These are supply ships. Promethium tankers, mostly. These look to be slave ships… Imperial Guard troop carriers, taken by the Night Lords over the years. These are Legion warships. There, the *Hunter's Premonition*. That's *Excoriator*, sister ship to the *Covenant of Blood*. This, here, is the *Serpent of the Black Sea*, one of the Legion's flagships from centuries ago. It was supposed to be lost in the Hades Veil. The Legion battleships alone could carry… ten, maybe twelve thousand Space Marines.'

'I didn't know they had that many warriors,' said Octavia, her voice tinged with worry.

'No records show how many there are. I doubt even the Exalted knows. These are just the ships close enough to answer the call, but even so, outside of the Warmaster's crusades, this is a gathering of rare significance.'

Septimus fell silent as he watched the warships shedding landing craft like a herd of beasts shaking off their fleas. Pods streaked planetwards, trailing tails of flame, each one a meteor burning through the atmosphere. Following them in majestic, arcing dives, gunships and heavy landers swooped through the cloud cover, their hulls gleaming orange with the heat of atmospheric entry.

Octavia came over to him, staring into the views-creens, unable to fixate upon a single image. It was all too much to take in.

'They're not sending any human craft down,' she noted. 'No slaves. No cultists.'

'It's fifty degrees below zero on the surface of Uriah Three. Even colder at night. Only legionaries can survive outside of shelter in those conditions.'

'How many of them are making planetfall?'

Septimus answered slowly. 'I believe... it looks like all of them.'

THE DROP-POD THREW up a torrent of snow and rock as it pounded into the earth. The edges of its dark hull glowed with fierce heat, its ceramite skin hissing and steaming in the air. Door seals spat free with mechanical clicks and vented steam, and like a flower in bloom the ramps opened, lowered, and slammed into the melted slush around the pod's whining engines.

Talos was the first from the pod, his red-stained vision scanning the mountain pass ahead. His helm's auto-senses muted the roaring wind to a tolerable background level.

The ground trembled, an earthquake's echo, as more drop-pods came down across the tundra. Already, the sky was darkened by landing craft and gunships fighting the vicious winds.

An identifier rune flashed white on the edge of Talos's retinal display. Mercutian's name glyph, though the vox gave all their voices a similar crackling cadence.

'We could do this alone. The five of us. But look

up, brothers. The sky is black with Stormbirds and Thunderhawks. How many of the Legion muster with us? Nine thousand? Ten? We have no need of them to prosecute this war.'

Now Xarl's name-rune flashed, bold and urgent as the squad moved across the snow.

'He may be a miserable bastard, but he's right. This was our glory. We did the work. We sweated for weeks on that wretched world, living amongst that pathetic cult, waiting for the Callidus Temple to open their eyes and fall into our claws.'

Talos grunted his disagreement. Mercutian was morose at the best of times, and could always be trusted to see the darkest edge of any event. As for Xarl… He trusted no soul outside their own warband, and relatively few within it.

'This is not some personal glory to be etched onto our armour,' said Talos. 'This is the Legion's vindication. The others deserve to be here. Let them redden their claws alongside us.'

No name glyphs chimed in response. He was surprised the others were letting it slide so easily. Surprised, but grateful. Talos stalked on, his armoured boots crunching through the snow to crush the rocks beneath. Other squads fell into rough formation behind First Claw, but Talos and his brothers were allowed the honour of leading the advance.

The trek through the mountains would have killed a mortal in moments. Talos felt nothing, protected from even the void of space in his Mark 5 war plate. Even so, to prevent his joints from freezing, his power-pack's active hum had risen in pitch. The vox-network came alive with technical servitors reporting that the oil pipes and fuel tanks in the landed gunships were already icing up.

The temperature gauge on the edge of Talos's visor display remained unmercifully hostile. After only half an hour of trekking uphill, his power pack was humming with almost distracting intensity. He kept wiping frost from his faceplate when it threatened to form a crust.

The next warrior to speak was Cyrion. Despite the vox stealing all tone and humanity from his voice, his irritation bled through easily enough.

'I could have lived with annihilating this fortress from orbit. That would satisfy my honour, and spare us this tedious trudge.'

No one replied. Every one of them knew this mission required visual confirmation before it could be considered complete. Laying waste to the Callidus stronghold from orbit would achieve nothing.

'Don't everyone agree at once,' said Cyrion dryly.

Talos scowled behind his visor, but said nothing even as Cyrion continued.

'What if the Callidus bitch lied? What if we're marching half the Legion in neat formation through these mountain passes and a host of ambushes await? This is the most foolish advance in history.'

Now Talos replied, his own temper rising to the fore.

'*Enough*, Cyrion. Humans cannot survive outside shelter here. How will they ambush us? With thermal suits and hurled rocks from the cliff edges? If that were even a threat worth considering, orbital imagery would have caught it by now. This is a hidden temple. Defending it with a host of cannons upon the walls would require serious generation of power, and attract easy attention from orbital scanning.'

'I still do not like this march upland,' Cyrion grumbled.

'The march is symbolic, brother. The Legion commanders wished it, and so it shall be. Let the Callidus stare down from their fortress battlements, and bear witness to the doom that comes for them.'

Cyrion sighed. 'You have more faith in our leaders than I, Talos.'

Once more, the others fell silent. Above them, the looming fortress, hewn from the mountain rock, drew ever closer.

THE SIEGE OF Uriah III would enter the annals of the Night Lords Legion for its significance, if not its duration. The fortress rising from the side of the mountains was shielded against orbital bombardment, with multi-layered void fields offering dense resistance to any assault from the skies. As with many such defensive grids, the overlapping shields were considerably more vulnerable to attack from the ground.

Behind the marching warriors came entire battalions of Legion war machines: massive Land Raiders leading the way for the more compact Vindicator siege tanks, along with their Predator counterparts. Arrayed across ridges, nestled atop outcroppings and landed by Thunderhawk carriers along cliff edges, the Legion's armour battalions aimed cannons and turrets at the fortress's walls.

There was no heroic speech. No inspirational mantra. With a single word of order, the tanks opened fire as one, lighting the night with the brilliant flare of lascannon beams, and the incendiary bursts from Demolisher turrets.

In the shadows cast by the flickering shield and the storm of assaulting fire, Talos watched the siege begin in earnest. Cyrion approached where he knelt on the lip of a cliff.

'How long do you think they can keep us out?' he asked.

Talos lowered his bolter, no longer looking through the gunsight. The fortress itself was blurred behind a mirage of wavering air – a haze that gave off no heat. The void shield distorted the view of what lay behind it, reducing the battlements to uneven silhouettes.

'With over five hundred tanks at the walls? This firepower would cripple an Imperator in a heartbeat. Blood of the Father, Cyrion… We've not gathered this much armour in one place since the Siege of Terra. The walls will fall, and we'll be inside before dawn.'

The prediction was true enough. The sky was not yet lightening when, four hours later, the void shield shimmered, fluttering like an ailing heartbeat, before disintegrating with a thunderclap of displaced air pressure. The Night Lords closest to the shield's edge were thrown from their feet, dozens of squads sent crashing across the icy landscape in the powerful rush of air, adding to the snowstorm's gale.

Without pause, without respite, the tanks turned their cannons upon the fortress's lower walls.

The first breach was torn exactly thirteen seconds later, a section of rock wall blasted inwards under a Demolisher shell. Squads broke into loping runs, moving around the still-firing tanks. They entered with the freezing wind, chainswords revving into life.

The defences were broken, and the slaughter could begin.

TALOS LED FIRST Claw through the catacombs, his boots crunching on the layer of ice already coating the stone. With the fortress breached, its innards were at the mercy of the blizzards tearing across the surface of Uriah III. Many of the Imperial servants dwelling within the temple died from exposure within minutes of the walls coming down, and those that survived deeper within the complex soon fell victim to the grinding bite of Legion chainblades.

The Night Lords purged the fortress, chamber by chamber, level by level. In the combat arenas, where the Callidus agents were put through their rigorous training, banks of esoteric machinery lined the walls. Bolters made short work of the priceless biomanipulation technology, explosive shells ripping apart the machines responsible for shaping generations of assassins.

First Claw moved through the catacombs, laying waste to the subterranean surgeries, their blades tearing medical equipment into ruin.

'These are the apothecarions where they implant muscle enhancers and the polymorphic compound that allow the Callidus to shapeshift,' said Talos. He reloaded his bolter, slamming a fresh magazine home and taking aim at an automated surgery table. 'Brothers. Leave nothing intact.'

Their bolters opened up with harsh chatters, detonating priceless, irreplaceable Imperial machines as the Night Lords left naught but scrap in their wake.

Yet, something was wrong. Cyrion voxed the others, lowering his bolter as they entered another underground apothecarion.

'As thrilling as this worthless vandalism is proving to be, I've been paying attention to the general channels. No squad has crossed paths with any assassins yet. Talos, brother, you were lied to. There are no Callidus here. It's an abandoned temple. This place is a tomb.'

Talos cursed, swinging his golden blade and splitting a surgical table in two. Both halves clattered to the tiled floor.

'She was *not* lying,' he said angrily. 'I have seen it in my visions. I heard the truth in her voice, after seventeen days of excruciation. The hololithic is *here.*'

The two warriors faced each other, edging closer to open argument. It was Cyrion that backed down, offering a salute, fist over his breastplate.

'As you say, brother.'

Talos cursed in Nostraman, a flowing sentence of bitter expletives leaving his lips and emerging harsh over the ragged vox-link. Just as he drew breath to order the squad onwards, the general channel sparked into life.

'Brothers, this is the Exalted. My honour guard has reached the thirtieth sub-level. It is a Hall of Archives. First Claw, come to me at once. Talos… You were right.'

TALOS ENTERED THE chamber, and confusion took hold before anything else. The librarium had clearly been swept clean long before the Legion had arrived in orbit, leaving empty bookshelves, blank display cases, and bare plinths.

Warriors from the Legion lined the walls – Night Lords from squads and warbands that First Claw didn't recognise. In the heart of the room stood the Exalted, its twisted bulk overshadowing the warriors nearby. The daemon in its heart was forever reshaping the Exalted's outer flesh, and the Legion lord hadn't been human – or even a transhuman – in many hundreds of years. A spined monstrosity of clawed hands and hulking armour breathed in a deep thunder rumble. It inclined its malformed head, grimacing through black fangs because it struggled to form any other facial expression through the mutations of its skull structure.

'Talos,' it said. 'The temple has been abandoned. The slaves left here were nothing more than custodians, remaining in the event of the Callidus's return.'

Talos stepped closer, his ceramite boots disturbing the dust of ages on the dark stone floor. Other footsteps tracked hither and thither across the ground. The tread of his Legion brothers. None were human. Humans had not walked these halls in years.

'I do not understand. You said I was right.'

The Exalted held out its claw, each bladed finger possessing too many joints. In the daemon creature's palm was a fist-sized sphere of discoloured bronze. A single lens peered from the sphere's side – a glaring eye of green glass.

A hololithic recorder.

'You *were* right. This remained, when all else was taken.'

'They wanted us to find it,' said Talos.

'It is not the original. Our hunt to destroy the original recording remains unfulfilled. But this… this is enough, for now. The Legion will thank you.'

Talos bit back his disgust at what the Exalted had

become, taking the bronze sphere without comment. A simple twist of the top hemisphere caused a series of clicks from within, and the soft whirring of the lens brought itself into focus.

A grainy image beamed from the lens, monochrome green like watered-down jade. It showed...

'The Lord of the Night...' breathed Talos reverently.

It showed a hunched figure, its posture and musculature somewhere between human perfection and bestial corruption. The distortion stole too much clarity to make any true details, but the figure's face – his narrow eyes and fanged maw – smote the hearts of all bearing witness to it.

Primarch. Konrad Curze, the Night Haunter, Commander of the VIII Legion. Their father. The genetic forebear and biological template of every living Night Lord.

The flickering hololithic primarch rose from a throne stolen by distortion. He advanced in a silence that spoke of faulty recording, his movements jerky and interrupted by static interference.

None of that mattered. After centuries, the Lord of the Night's loyal sons were seeing him once again. Their father's ghost, here in this tomb of a temple.

If the Callidus had left the hololithic record to mock the Legion that would one day find it, they had severely misjudged the closure it offered, and the resurgence of purpose felt by every warrior present. Gauntlets clutched at bolters with inspired strength. Several warriors wept behind their skulled faceplates.

'*Ave Dominus Nox.*' They chanted the words in worshipful, thankful monotone. '*Ave Dominus Nox.* Hail the Lord of the Night.'

The primarch's last moments of life unfolded before their eyes. The towering demigod laughed, still locked in eerie silence, and then leapt forwards. A burst of visual static scratched the image into oblivion, only for it to reset and restart a moment later.

A wraith doomed to repeat its actions into eternity: the Night Lords primarch rose from his throne again, spoke words that went unheard, laughed without sound, and raced forwards, only to vanish again.

'I remember seeing it in the flesh,' whispered the Exalted. 'I recall watching him rise from the throne, so many years ago, and obeying his order to watch as the assassin approached. I remember how he laughed before he leapt at her.'

Talos cancelled the archival playback, staring down at the metal orb in his hand. It had several settings, each one activated by turning the top hemisphere by a few degrees to the next frequency.

He lowered his hand, keeping the orb in his fist.

'We will ensure every Legion ship is granted a copy of the images contained here,' he said. 'Some things must be kept fresh in our memories. Come, brothers. We should return to orbit. There's nothing more for us to find here.'

THE DECK SHUDDERED beneath Talos's feet as the *Covenant of Blood* pulled out of orbit. He had stood with his brothers of First Claw on the command deck, as the Legion fleet bombarded the temple site from orbit. The lances cut down into the planet below, a tectonic barrage that levelled the entire mountain range.

Then, one by one, the Night Lords warships broke away.

Alone in his meditation chamber, Talos regarded the hololithic recorder orb once more. He turned the device to its first setting, and watched his father laugh in the seconds before his death.

He watched this seven more times, before twisting the recorder to its next setting. Nothing happened. He tried the next, and received the same result.

Only the last setting contained another archive. A vox-recording.

Talos recognised the voice immediately. It was the assassin who had slain his father in the age before the Long War. More than that, it was the woman he had disembowelled and torn apart himself, in pursuit of vengeance.

She spoke from the grave, ten thousand years dead, repeating the same words just as the primarch's spirit was caged into repeating the same actions.

This is M'Shen, daughter of the Callidus. I've found Commander Curze of the Night Lords Legion. I–

The recording broke into static.

This is M'Shen, daughter of the Callidus. I've found Commander Curze of the Night Lords Legion. I–

More static.

This is M'Shen, daughter of the Callidus. I've found Commander Curze of the Night Lords Legion. I–

Static.

BITTER END

by Sarah Cawkwell

FOR MANY YEARS, he had made bargains, accords and dark pacts, both with powers he could name and several more that he dared not. He could not remember the last time he had merely requested something and the Imperium had provided it. In the days of his hated and enforced servitude to the Corpse-Emperor, he had but to requisition something and it was his.

Now, whenever he wanted something, Huron Blackheart simply reached out with the might of his loyal Red Corsairs and he took it. His greedy, grasping claws closed around objects, people and entire star systems and stole them away. He looted and plundered, he stole and he murdered. Occasionally, though, he would come upon a treasure that he could not simply claim.

When this happened, he would be roused from the

shadows in which he now existed and he would hunt down his quarry in an entirely different manner. He would sit down with agents of the most powerful and most influential, and he would talk. He would barter and negotiate, bringing his considerable charisma and cunning to the fore, and he would make more deals.

His reputation preceded him wherever he went, and many wisely shied away from reaching any sort of arrangement with the Tyrant of Badab, fearing for their lives. But there were many more who boldly sealed their agreements with him in blood.

Sometimes, Huron Blackheart even kept his word.

IT HAD BEEN an agri-world once, before an exterminatus had rendered it an uninhabitable wasteland. Its given name was lost to memory, leaving it only with the identifier bestowed upon it during the halcyon days of the Great Crusade: Eighty-Three Fourteen. Nothing grew here any more, and the only things that lived upon its surface were the most tenacious of bacteria. Its seas had boiled away, leaving vast expanses of arid ground that was cracked and blistered. The ferocity of the bombardment had broken open the crust and disturbed something deep in the planet's core. Now, volcanic lava bubbled up through the wounds in the earth and spilled across its ruined surface like blood. There was a constant smouldering heat haze that loaned everything a slightly distorted, unreal appearance.

It was a prime example of an inhospitable environment, but the gigantic figures making their steady way across its broken surface were not in the slightest bit bothered by the poisoned air or the excruciating heat. They walked without tiring, keeping up a pace they could sustain for many days if they so desired. They had marched to war in this way many times. But on this day, there was no war to be had. This was a deputation sent to accompany their lord and master to a summit.

Huron Blackheart walked in the midst of half a dozen of his Red Corsairs, his face alone exposed to the hostile environment. The countless implants and prosthetics that held his brain within what remained of his skull meant that wearing a helm caused him great discomfort, and it was such a laborious and time-consuming process to rewire his cranium to accept one that he viewed it more as a hindrance than a benefit. The complex, wheezing workings of his replacement lungs and respiratory system filtered the atmosphere in much the same way as a helmet anyway, and thus the choking, sulphuric air had no effect on him at all.

He could have made this journey alone but had elected to field a show of strength. He was wily and astute, blessed with cunning and guile like no other. But he did not trust the individual with whom he was dealing.

It had been a tedious process setting up this meeting. Dengesha had not been prepared to travel to Huron Blackheart's stronghold deep in the heart of the Maelstrom, and neither did the Blood Reaver care to board a ship almost entirely populated by warp-witches. (He had used sorcerers for his own ends before, of course. Indeed, it had been his own cabal that had suggested Dengesha as the best possible candidate for the task at hand.) Increasingly heated exchanges had taken place until an impasse had been reached. Neutral ground was the only solution.

Before a rocky outcrop overlooking the volcanic plains of a world that had once teemed with life, the Red Corsairs stopped. Above them, the shape of another giant could be made out. A baroque silhouette, picked out by the weak rays of the sickly yellow sun, stood alone. One of Huron's retinue pointed upwards with the muzzle of a bolter, indicating the other's presence.

'I see him,' Huron said, simply. 'I told you he would come.' A deep chuckle came from his ravaged throat. 'He could not help himself.'

DENGESHA TOOK NO sobriquet in order to convey his greatness; it was not in his nature to embrace an honorific that extolled his deeds to the outside world. He was no Despoiler or Betrayer. He chose instead to let his actions speak for themselves. For centuries he had stood at the head of the Heterodox, a cabal of sorcerers who, it was rumoured, had splintered centuries earlier from the Word Bearers. Dengesha was said to have studied the heart of Chaos Undivided for more than five thousand years and, as a result, his well of knowledge ran deep.

There was nothing about Dengesha that suggested such great age. His visage was timeless and its individual features unimpressive. He bore several scars on his face, but more numerous were the countless runes and brands that had been seared into his skin. They writhed and twisted now under Huron's scrutiny, living things that spoke of a true disciple of the Dark

Powers. He felt no discomfort in the sorcerer's presence. He was confident and fully at ease.

The two Space Marines, the warrior and the psyker, had moved to meet one another within a cave in the rock face. Neither's attendant retinues were with them as per the terms of their agreement.

The cave had once been a natural wonder, the source of a wellspring that had kept the local agricultural workers provided with water. As high as a refinery tower within, it was studded with broken, jagged stalagmites and stalactites that glittered with seams of semi-precious rock. Here, high above the shattered plains, was the only moisture remaining anywhere on the planet.

Now, the underground spring that had once nourished crops and quenched the thirst of thousands of Imperial workers was a toxic sinkhole, steaming and roiling gently. Periodically, air would escape from a fissure and expand with a rush, spraying boiling water in all directions. It spattered against the armour of the two giants, who stood face-to-face. Neither gave ground or spoke for some time, and then the psyker broke the stalemate with a bitter greeting.

'Blood Reaver.'

Huron greeted the sorcerer in kind and they considered each other in silence a while longer. As their eyes locked, the sorcerer's head tipped slightly to one side. The master of the Red Corsairs felt the faintest brush on his mind as the other attempted a psychic evaluation. Dengesha's resultant sharp intake of breath brought a smile to Huron's lips.

'Difficulties, Dengesha?'

'You are no psyker and yet you are warded... What

is it that shields your mind from my sight?'

'Should you not be wary of admitting that you seek to invade my thoughts without permission?' Huron's voice was grating and harsh, dragged from replacement vocal cords and a vox-unit that had been tuned and retuned until it sounded as close to human as could be achieved. Which was not very close.

'You know my nature, Lord Huron. It is, after all, why you sought me out. Now answer my question.' Dengesha's words were demanding, yet his tone remained deferential. Huron approved of the approach. 'What is it that grants you this protection?'

'Perhaps you should tell me what you have heard?' The question was thrown back at the sorcerer, who folded his arms across his chest.

'I have heard,' he said, choosing his words carefully, 'in rumours whispered throughout the Eye, that the Four favour you. You carry a boon they have gifted you. I have heard that something walks at your side and grants you certain... benefits.'

'You are very well informed.' Dengesha took another sharp intake of breath and Huron continued. 'Does that surprise you, sorcerer? Do you taste envy? Are you curious as to why it is that the Dark Powers see fit to grant me such a gift? Look closely, Dengesha. Tell me what you see.'

The sorcerer considered the Red Corsair for a few moments. He looked the warrior up and down. A giant clad in desecrated red armour with so many augmetics and implants that he looked more like a blighted tech-priest or enginseer than the scourge of the Imperium. The metal-plated head shook slightly and a quirk of amusement twitched the lipless mouth.

'No, Dengesha. Look *properly*. Use your witch-sight.'
The sorcerer *looked*. And he *saw*.

THE WORD *hamadrya* had never been a part of Huron
Blackheart's vocabulary until the day he had been
reborn. There had been many deals made in those
few days when he had hovered in the grey mists that
lingered between life and death. His body had been
left all but useless in the wake of the Star Phantoms'
assault on the Palace of Thorns, and without the
anchor of its corporeal weight, his soul had been free
to wander at will.

Nobody knew who – or what – he had consorted
with in those days. But if the thought was never
expressed aloud, all of the Red Corsairs knew that
their lord and master had made *some* pact. He could
not have survived otherwise, despite the ceaseless
labours of his most faithful Apothecaries. They could
repair the physical damage to their Chapter Master's
body, but that was all.

But no one ever asked of the events that had transpired, and Huron Blackheart never volunteered the
information.

The hamadrya had begun its life as a *thought*. A
potentiality. A tendril of insubstantial warp-stuff that
draped itself invisibly across Huron's mantle. Over
weeks, months and years it had become something
more tangible. In its earliest stages, it was nothing
more than a wisp. A curl of smoky air that lingered
around the warrior's shoulder like a mist snake wrapping itself protectively around him. Huron himself
seemed either oblivious or indifferent to its presence, but over time he began to notice that he was

developing a sensitivity, and then a resistance, to psychic intrusions.

The more he realised this, the stronger the warding became, until eventually the ethereal presence at his shoulder took on a more corporeal form. Sometimes it was reptilian, sometimes avian, other times simian – but always animalistic and never larger than the breadth of the warrior's shoulder span. Others could see it, but never for long. Most of the time it could only be glimpsed briefly out of the corner of the eye, leaving the viewer wondering if they had seen it at all.

It granted Huron Blackheart an extra layer of power, one that boosted his already overinflated sense of ego. But it had limitations. It was a creature of the warp, after all.

THE SORCERER LOOKED. And he *saw*.

'I confess, my lord, that I did not believe the rumours to be true,' Dengesha confessed. He had considered the tale of the familiar to be nothing more than a figment of the mad Tyrant's overwrought imagination. Yet his witch-sight gave him a unique view. 'I have never seen its like before. Is this what they call the hamadrya?'

'Indeed it is. And you would do well not to concern yourself further with its origins, or its purpose. Consider instead the question my agent put to you.' Always quick to the point, Huron Blackheart did not care to linger on matters past.

'Yes, Lord Huron.' Dengesha bowed from the waist. 'I consider it a great honour that you seek my assistance in this matter. I understand that your... blessing loses power, that it becomes weaker the further from the heart of the Maelstrom you travel. In conjunction with your own *cabal*,' there was unmistakable superiority in Dengesha's tone as he said the word, 'I have determined what you need to overcome this limitation.'

'The hamadrya is a thing of the warp,' Huron said. He drummed his fingers idly against his armour-plated thigh. The noise reverberated through the cavernous chamber, the acoustics oddly distorted. 'It draws its strength from the powers therein. And the further from its source I travel…' He broke off and raised his head to study Dengesha. 'My cabal have told me what I need. A potent soul, shackled by arcane powers. The hamadrya can feed from its torment for all eternity. But my sorcerers, strong as they are, cannot do this one thing.'

Huron's red, artificial eye whirred softly as it focused upon the sorcerer. 'Give me my solution, Dengesha, and we will share the spoils of war.'

'You need a potent soul.'

'I have found such a thing. Sister Brigitta of the Order of the Iron Rose.'

'I have heard of this Order, and of this woman. The self-proclaimed saviour of her people. She who bears the sins of a generation upon her shoulders.'

'Aye. One of the faithful. A powerful symbol.'

'You need a suitable vessel. Such a thing will not be easy to locate, my lord. It could take many long months of searching…'

'You underestimate my resources, Dengesha.' Huron's twisted face distorted in a smile again and he twisted a loop on his belt, bringing an object slowly into view.

It was exquisite. Deep emerald green in colour, it was a fusion of bottle and vial, with a wide lip tapering to a long, slim neck that fed into a small oval bowl. It was encased within beautiful fretwork, wrought from copper or brass or some other burnished metal that snaked around its delicate surface.

'My cabal attached this vessel to my belt,' said Huron. 'They told me that only another sorcerer could remove it, that if I were to touch it myself the power would be tainted.' He shifted his hip slightly so that it was facing Dengesha, who snapped open the belt loop, taking the bottle in his hands. He could feel its imbued power; a thrum of psychic energy that made his hands vibrate gently as he held it. Huron studied him.

'On the understanding that you will give me what I ask for, I make a gift of this vessel to you so that you may work whatever fell deeds necessary. Do you accept?'

'Gladly, my lord. Such an arcane item... such a *relic* must have cost you dearly. Where did you locate it?'

'My sources are many and varied. Do not bother yourself with detail. Is it adequate for its purpose?'

'More than adequate.' Dengesha studied the bottle in admiration for a while, then with a series of hand movements, caused it to disappear. It was little more than cheap theatrics, and it did nothing to change the expression on Huron Blackheart's artificial face. 'This Sister Brigitta of yours will be heavily guarded, of course. I will need absolutely no distractions whilst I perform the binding.'

'Leave that side of the bargain to me, master sorcerer. My Red Corsairs will distract whatever pitiful forces guard her and you will take your coterie and perform your rituals. You will present me with what I want, and in return I shall give the Heterodox the world in her charge for your chapels, and its people for...' He gave a creaking shrug, 'whatever you see fit.' His augmetic eye darkened briefly as though he blinked – a slow, thoughtful thing that was somehow unsettling. 'Do we have an agreement?'

'A world and its subjects? My lord, that is... very generous of you.'

Huron shrugged again. 'My Corsairs and I will still take what spoils we desire, but it is not beyond me to show gratitude and generosity. Now tell me, Dengesha of the Heterodox, do we have an agreement?'

'We do.'

There were many who boldly sealed their agreements in blood. Dengesha of the Heterodox was one such individual.

Sometimes, Huron Blackheart even kept his word.

THE TEMPLE BURNED.

Since time immemorial, the Order of the Iron Rose had been cloistered within their monument to the Emperor of Mankind. A building of dizzyingly beautiful aesthetics, the temple had stood proudly within well-guarded walls for countless generations. The Sisters of Battle lived their studious lives there quietly, only leaving at times of war when their fierce battle skills were most needed. Then, their comparative gentleness could easily be forgotten in the face of their roaring battle madness.

Sister Brigitta was the incumbent canoness, but had always eschewed the title, preferring to remain on the same level as her sisters. She was dearly beloved by all who knew her. Intelligent and insightful, her words of wisdom on any number of subjects were treated as precious jewels to be collected and admired.

She stood now, clad in her copper-coloured battle armour, her silver-flecked black hair streaming in the breeze. The armour forced her to stand upright with a grace and dignity that added weight to her command. Her jaw was tightened and her face bore an implacable expression as she stared down from the highest chamber of the steeple at the slaughter taking place far below.

Tears ran down her face – not of fear, but of rage and regret that the sanctity of the temple had been violated. At either side, her two most trusted lieutenants also wept at the wanton destruction that rampaged below.

They had come without warning. They had struck fast and without mercy. The loyal Palatine Guard who protected the sacred grounds had done an admirable job of holding the enemy at bay, but ultimately they were only human. What hope did they have against the Adeptus Astartes?

Sister Brigitta surveyed the carnage. Seemingly endless forces of the giant Space Marines pitted against a pitiable wall of humanity. Delicate mortal flesh was the only thing standing between the Chaos forces and the Sisters.

From here, she could not see the faces of the brave Guardsmen dying in their futile efforts to protect the Order, but she imagined that each shared the same look of zealous ferocity. The Order of the Iron Rose preached that fear made one weak and had no place on the battlefield.

The barking report of bolter-fire filled the air, and the murderous whine of chainblades was all-pervading. The screams of the dying were agony to listen to, and the ground below was already running scarlet with the blood of the fallen. Some of the Chaos warriors fell upon their victims, hacking and dismembering. The sight sickened Sister Brigitta. Beside her, Sister Anastasia murmured a soft litany, commending the souls of the departed to the Emperor.

'We must meet in the central chamber,' the canoness said finally, tearing her eyes from the slaughter. 'Gather the Order, Sister Anastasia.'

'Yes, sister.' Anastasia left immediately to carry out her superior's command. Brigitta stood for several moments longer, salt-tears running down her weather-tanned face.

'The Order of the Iron Rose will stand to the last, traitors,' she promised, raising her voice to be heard above the growing wind.

THE RED CORSAIRS had dealt with the pathetic human threat in short order. Even as the last Guardsman died, pierced on the end of a chainblade, Huron Blackheart's warriors had turned their weapons on the temple walls and gates. They had been erected over the course of many years by master craftsmen and artisans, but what had taken humanity years to perfect and construct was levelled in minutes by four Traitor Marines and their multi-meltas. The irony of that equation amused Huron Blackheart enough that he laughed out loud.

He had accompanied his forces to the surface of this world but had taken no part in the battle. He stood to one side with Dengesha and his cabal of sorcerers, watching with displaced indifference as his Corsairs butchered their way forwards.

Another direct hit on the wall finally reduced it to molten slag, a huge cloud of pale steam billowing outwards from the destruction and coating the armour of the warriors in a fine film of grit. The Red Corsairs did not wait for their master's order to proceed. They crossed the threshold of the sacred temple and met the second wave of defensive forces with renewed vigour.

Dengesha walked forwards dispassionately, his cabal moving with him like a flock of birds flittering around their mother. Fighting independently, each warrior-psyker was capable of incalculable destruction; fighting as a unit, they were imbued with such power that no mortal man could look upon the forces of the warp flowing from them and hope to survive.

Dark lightning flickered from fingertips, fire burst from the palms of their hands and the very earth itself trembled where they trod. The sheer, raw power they exuded was tremendous, and Huron Blackheart watched their performance with something akin to hunger on his face.

Three Guardsmen were incinerated with a blast from Dengesha's fingers, their bodies catching fire as though they were nothing more than dead wood. They died in terrible agony, screaming and begging for mercy. Huron watched as their ravaged faces slowly melted, like candles burning down to the taper.

Another unfortunate soldier was caught in the mesmerising stare of one of the Heterodox and found himself unable to move. With a press of psychic power, the sorcerer burst the Guardsman's brain like a ripe fruit. The man fell to his knees, blood and grey matter dribbling from his ears before he pitched over, face first into the dust.

The wind had whipped up into a frenzy now, but this was no natural weather condition. This was the work of the Heterodox, and the gusts carried maddening whispers, half-heard promises and dire threats. They blew from the very heart of the warp itself and plucked at the souls of men with ethereal claws. Some who were caught in their path went mad in an instant, hacking and slashing at phantasms only they could see or hear. Others stood their ground more firmly, litanies of warding on their lips.

But each was slain. Each pitiful stalk was reaped, and the more death and destruction there was, the more powerful the cabal seemed to grow, until with a feverish cry to the dark gods of Chaos Undivided, the Heterodox unleashed the true horror of their collective.

FROM WITHOUT, THE sounds of battle echoed. From within, the Sisters of the Order radiated a calm composure. A small order, barely one hundred Sisters of Battle had gathered together in the central chamber. They were all clad in armour similar to Sister Brigitta's, although where hers was a burnished copper hue, theirs was a deep reddish bronze that glinted in the light cast by the candles on the walls.

'Our time here is short, sisters,' the canoness began when she had Anastasia's assurance that all were present. 'Our enemy has breached the gate and they will soon dare to desecrate the most sacred inner sanctum of our beloved Order.' Brigitta reached up as she spoke and braided her thick hair into a plait that hung like a rope down her back. None of the Order would go into battle with their hair loose. It was an affectation, but an important one. Brigitta's visual reminder of the very physical pre-battle preparation instilled focus amongst the gathered Sisters. In the ensemble, others mirrored her action.

'We will not stand by and allow that to happen. We will hold out against these intruders for as long as the Emperor gives us the strength to prevail. We will stand our ground until the bitter end. We fight the gravest of traitors, my sisters. We battle against fallen angels. Traitor Space Marines. And they bring witch-kin with them.'

A palpable ripple of dismay ran through the Sisters. They had stood proud against countless enemies. Aliens, cultists, even a preceptory of Sisters of Battle who had lost their way, and they had always triumphed. They had fought alongside Space Marines many times, too. But the Order of the Iron Rose had never fought *against* them.

Brigitta raised a hand for silence and she got it immediately. From outside the fortified walls of the temple, the muffled sounds of gunfire and terrible, bloody death could be heard, filling in the pauses in her impassioned speech.

'We are the beloved of the Emperor. We are the Sisters of the Iron Rose. We stand as a reminder that the flower of that name is protected by thorns. We will not allow these foul traitors to reach out and pluck us from existence without exacting our payment in blood first.'

She raised her bolter to her shoulder and cast her eyes around the assembled warriors. 'We will make our stand in the rear courtyard. If we draw the traitor filth out into the open, they may exact less damage on our temple.' It was likely a futile gesture, and most of the Order knew it, but they were words that encouraged her sisters. Brigitta was under no illusions; the battle that was coming towards them would likely be the last thing any of them saw. But they would die as they had lived, defending the Emperor's legacy.

THE CLOUDS ABOVE the temple boiled, swirling together in a dark mass of intangible horror. The wind was now a gale, screaming its unnatural, elemental fury across the surface of the planet and whipping up the detritus from the fallen walls into plumed, choking columns. Lightning coruscated within the cloud, and as it moved, it picked up dust and debris, including the corpses of the fallen.

The Chaos-driven maelstrom moved with almost agonising slowness across the battlefield. Beneath it, the earth split and wept streams of tar and sulphur. Those who still stood were either knocked from their feet by the quaking of the ground beneath them, or they were caught up in the storm's passage and sucked, screaming, into its abyssal depths.

From what remained of the temple walls, valiant surviving forces turned the defence guns on the cabal who stood as a pack, their hands raised, palms upwards, to the skies that bubbled overhead. Each of the twelve was a perfect mirror image of the others. All wore horned helms, and their stance was arrogance itself.

The armoured turrets around the temple roared defiance and one of the sorcerers was destroyed, his torso chewed apart by the stream of high-velocity shells. The cabal did not change position but, as one, their heads turned towards the weapons mounted on the wall.

Dengesha made a slicing motion with his hand, and the wind changed direction and increased speed, moving with impossible haste towards its new target.

SISTER BRIGITTA STOOD defiant amidst her battle-sisters. She was a woman who had lived a life filled with devotion to the Emperor, who she loved every bit as much as she cared for every woman who stood around her. Their honour and courage now, in the face of overwhelming odds, was a reward unlike any other.

From the youngest novice to Sister Anastasia, with whom she had fought in many engagements, she knew each one of them. She knew their life histories. She knew their hopes and she knew their fears. She was no psyker, but you could not live your whole life within an order and not gain an insight into the souls of those around you.

She loved her sisters and though she knew she might die here today, she knew that love would strengthen her faith and her resolve to stand her ground.

Her thoughts were wrenched back to the present as she heard the echo of a crashing thump in the distance. The sound of weapons being brought to bear against the gate.

'They come,' she said, her voice low and soft, yet carrying such authority that every one of the Order stood straighter. There was the sound of weapons being readied, of magazines being slammed into place, of swords being drawn from sheaths. There were over-laying voices murmuring litanies and prayers.

Another sickening *crump* against the gate.

'We will stand defiant,' Brigitta said, raising her bolter above her head. '*Ave Imperator!*'

The battle-cry was echoed, but it was drowned out by the sound of an explosion that blew in the ancient, stained crystal windows as the enemy breached the gates.

'Be ready! Hold firm! Do not doubt in yourself for one moment. Trust to your sisters and trust to your blessed weapons. *A morte perpetua. Domine, libra nos!*'

Battle-cries were torn from their throats and one hundred Sisters of Battle took up arms and prepared to make their stand.

THE MAELSTROM RIPPED the guns from their mountings as though they were plants placed in dry soil. The Guardsmen who had manned them were pulverised by the shrapnel from the destruction as the howling, unholy winds ripped the turrets into nothing more than scrap metal. Mangled pieces of weaponry tore through their bodies, cutting them to ribbons and, in one young soldier's case, decapitating them. The spiralling morass of metal and ruined flesh added its mass to the storm, and above the temple the skies began to rain droplets of blood.

At the final gate, Huron Blackheart's traitors had set melta-charges against the armoured portal. The blocky devices clamped to the towering hinges with a metallic *clang* and the Corsairs withdrew. The bombs detonated with a wash of heat and an earth-shattering explosion that rocked the ground.

Slowly, Dengesha's cabal ceased the link with their powers and the violent, raging winds began to subside. The first obstacle had been overcome. The second – and their objective – lay behind the devastated walls.

The Chaos sorcerer turned his helmeted head towards Huron. 'You must not kill her,' he said through the vox-bead in the Tyrant's ear. 'If she dies, her soul will be as good as useless to us. Do not let your barbarian horde rip the Order apart without first isolating the mark.'

A twitch of irritation showed on Huron's face. 'I am not completely without intellect, Dengesha.' The fingers that were wrapped around his massive battle-axe tightened visibly. The sorcerer's face could not be seen, but Huron could *sense* his smirk. 'I will be taking care of dear Sister Brigitta myself.'

'My *sincerest* apologies. I did not mean to imply you were anything but knowledgeable in the ways of warp, my lord.' Dengesha's sarcasm was biting, and Huron turned away from the sorcerer cursing the necessity of their temporary association. It would be over soon. The Order of the Iron Rose would be obliterated and he would take his prize.

He comforted himself with the thought. In due course, his familiar would feast from a soul most worthy of its hunger.

Striding across the courtyard, Huron surveyed the damage with an approving expression. What remained of the gate was barely recognisable as any sort of portal. Broken spurs of plasteel jutted in all directions, and the metal composite that had been mixed into the gate for reinforcement was little more than dust. Occasionally, more dust would fall in a pathetic clump from the walls either side of the entrance way.

The Red Corsairs strode forwards, warriors with a clear objective and purpose. In the eyes of the Imperium, they were renegades. But they were still Space Marines and the regimental mindset came easily to them. Until the fighting started, at least.

'Listen to me, my Corsairs,' said Huron across the vox. 'When we locate the Sisters, do not touch their leader. She belongs to me.' He addressed the entire group, but knew that not all of them would truly hear him. 'The toys we have despatched thus far have been an easy enemy and they will have sent out the word for aid. By the time that aid arrives, there will be nothing left but a smoking ruin.'

A few scattered roars of approval drew a nod from Huron. 'What we will come up against in there will be more challenging, but do not falter. We come to take a prize that will make us even greater than we are. The Imperium of Mankind and their pathetic Corpse-Emperor will rue the day they ever named us traitor.'

There were grunts of acknowledgement across the board, some coherent, others less so. Just as his band of renegades was drawn from a vast number of different Chapters, so their levels of sanity varied. Huron cared little for the butchers amongst his followers. They served a purpose in war, but when it came to more delicate matters they were an encumbrance.

Fortunately, he had enough sane followers to keep the borderline berserkers in check.

'Then we move with all haste to the final stage of our action here. Find the Sisters. Kill those you must, but leave the canoness alive.'

Without further hesitation, the Red Corsairs streamed into the sacred Temple of the Blessed Dawn.

THEY RAMPAGED THROUGH the temple without thought for preservation. Marble floors cracked and split beneath their heavy tread. Chainblades chewed through statuary and carvings alike, making firewood of huge portraits of Sisters and saints. Some riches were left intact. Over the years, the Red Corsairs had all developed an eye for goods that would please their lord and master, for it was said his collection of Imperial relics was beyond compare. They would retrace their steps before they departed and gather up such treasures, along with the weapons of the fallen. For them, that was the most valuable reward.

Their plundering steps ultimately took them through the central chamber where the Sisters of the Order had recently gathered. Dengesha nodded approvingly.

'This will be a good place for the ritual,' he said.

'Then you remain here, sorcerer, and make whatever preparation is necessary. We will seek out Sister Brigitta and I will bring her to you personally.' Huron ran his tongue over his metal teeth in a parody of hunger. He swung his battle-axe easily and it chewed its way through a beautifully painted rendition of some long-ago battle at which the Sisters had been victorious. Its shredded remnants dangled to the ground and the memory of the great war was lost to no more than a single stroke.

The first two Red Corsairs to throw open the heavy door that led out to the courtyard were torn apart by incoming bolter-fire. The Sisters of Battle had kept their weapons trained on the exit and the moment it opened they had pulled their triggers. The explosive rounds buried themselves in the armoured hides of the traitors and burst them apart in a storm of gore and ceramite shards. The bodies disintegrated messily, but their sacrifice bought those who followed enough time to bring their weapons to bear and return fire. Four Sisters were thrown backwards, unbalancing several more. Before they were back on their feet, the Red Corsairs had flooded into the courtyard and the fight began in earnest.

The Sisters of Battle were greater in number than the Red Corsairs and their armour afforded them a degree of protection. But they were facing an undisciplined rabble whose tactics were unpredictable at best and unfathomable at worst. The Sisters held their position, clustered around the canoness like a sea of bronze with a copper island at their centre. They formed a circle around where she stood on the rim of a fountain, crying out orders to her warriors.

The initial firefight did not last long. At a word from the Tyrant, the Red Corsairs pressed forwards, chainblades whining, and began to cut their way through the serried ranks of women. The ring surrounding the canoness grew tighter and smaller.

The stink of ruined flesh and spent bolter-rounds was strong in the air, and so much smoke rose from the detonations that it choked the courtyard with a fog of bloody vapour and fyceline.

'Courage, sisters!' Brigitta's voice was clear, like

a bell sounding through the uproar. 'Remember your teachings! You tread the path of righteousness. Though it be paved with broken glass, you will walk it barefoot…'

Brigitta paused in the recital as she watched Sister Anastasia's broken body fall to the ground. A grief unlike any she had ever known before passed through her with a shudder. She summoned up every ounce of her considerable inner strength and brought her bolter to bear on the hated enemy. Her voice rose through the noise once again.

'Though it crosses rivers of fire, we will pass over them…'

Her voice was strong and did not waver, but the strength of her armed guard was failing. Not through lack of zeal or fire – if she were to take any reward from this abysmal horror before her, it was that her beloved sisters died honourably and bravely – but through dwindling numbers. What had once been a ring several bodies deep now presented a barrier of barely a dozen of her Sisters.

A number of the traitor Red Corsairs had been felled, but their armour, stronger and more finely wrought than that of the Sisters of Battle, deflected more and protected them for longer. Brigitta realised with a sinking heart that they were probably not even dead; that their enhanced physiology would aid their recovery and that they might rise to fight another day. She *despised* them for it. She loathed their continued existence. To her mind, they represented the worst kind of faithless traitors the Imperium could have conceived.

She abhorred them for tearing apart the temple, her

home, the place where she had grown from a teenage girl to womanhood.

She…

…was bleeding.

Brigitta tasted, for the first time in her life, a tremor of fear. It was seasoned with the coppery taste of her own blood as she bit her lip hard enough to put her teeth through the delicate skin. The flavour of her own mortality gave her enough strength to complete her fervent prayer.

'Though it wanders wide, the light of the Emperor guides my – our – step.' She slammed a fresh magazine into her bolter and, letting out a screaming roar of battle rage, unleashed her full fury at the encroaching enemy.

At her feet, dead and dying Sisters spilled blood and viscera across the courtyard stones. The image of their defeat burned itself onto her retinas and branded hatred on her heart. Tears of anger and terrible, terrible grief blurred her vision, but she did not – she *would* not – falter. Not now.

She continued to fire her bolter into the enemy no longer caring whether she hit them or not. It became an act of sheer venomous loathing.

After a few short moments, she became aware that outside her immediate sphere of awareness the sounds of battle had ceased. Only one weapon continued to fire and that was hers. It did not detract from her focus, however, and she poured ammunition at the enemy until the last bolter-shell clattered to the floor.

One of the enemy, bareheaded and terrible, moved from the pack to stand before her.

'You are Sister Brigitta of the Order of the Iron Rose,' he stated. It was not a question. She looked up into his inhuman face and drew in a rasping breath. She had seen unhelmed Space Marines before and was used to their exaggerated features. But this... *creature*... who stood before her was so far removed from anything even remotely human that she felt, against her will, the urge to scream in incoherent contempt. A poisonous air of evil came from him and she felt sick to her stomach.

She began to quietly recite litanies of faith to herself, never once taking her gaze from this augmetic monstrosity. She neither confirmed nor denied the accusation of her identity but instead ripped the combat blade from its sheath at her side and struck at the traitor's throat. Blackheart sighed wearily before catching her wild lunge on the back of his claw. Then, with excruciating care, not wanting to kill her outright, he backhanded her into unconsciousness.

SHE WAS LIKE a rag doll in his arms, limp and lifeless, and as he carried Sister Brigitta into the chamber, Huron Blackheart marvelled as he always did at the papery inefficacy of the human body. He wondered how it was they had *any* resilience without the enhancements that he shared with all his gene-bred brothers. Brigitta's face where he had struck her was distorted. He had fractured her cheekbone at the very least, and purple bruising was swelling up around her jaw. Her braided hair had come loose and hung freely down.

Dengesha turned to study them. He had removed his helm, and Huron was struck once again by the wriggling sigils that marked the sorcerer's face. 'You did not kill her?'

'She is merely unconscious. Allow me a little credit.'

'Then lay her next to the vessel and I can begin the ritual.' Already Dengesha had made the preparations for the rite that would bind the potent soul to the cursed vial. The green bottle lay on its side, an innocuous and inanimate object. Around the chamber, Dengesha had marked out a number of unreadable symbols, each one drawn at the point of what formed the eight-pronged star of Chaos. Members of his cabal stood at seven of the points, the top-most remaining free and evidently awaiting Dengesha's leisure.

Huron moved forwards and dumped Brigitta's body without any ceremony on the ground where the sorcerer indicated. He noted as he did so that the sigils drawn on the floor were marked in blood, most likely that of the dead soldiers.

'You should step outside the borders of the mark, my lord. Once we channel the powers necessary to perform the binding, they will be potent.'

From beyond the broken walls of the temple, the distant sounds of shouting could be heard. The assistance that the temple guards had called for was finally arriving. Huron nodded to several of his warriors who moved wordlessly out of the chamber.

'They cannot be allowed to enter this place whilst I am working. The balance of this work is delicate.'

'My men will keep them away.' Huron took several steps back. 'Trust to their abilities to do that. I, however, will remain.'

'As you wish.'

Huron Blackheart had witnessed many rituals of

this kind in his life, but he had never seen one driven with such determination and single-minded focus. He watched Dengesha closely as the sorcerer moved back to take his point at the tip of the star, and listened intently to the words that he recited. It did him little good, as the sorcerer spoke in some arcane tongue that Huron did not understand, though the inflection was clear.

The seven other members of the Heterodox echoed his words, one at a time until the chant was being repeated with a discordant, impossible to follow rhythm. The sound grew and swelled, and all the while there was the underscore of the battle taking place beyond the temple walls.

A thick black substance, like tar from a pit, began to bubble up in the space marked out by the points of the star. It rose upwards, never spilling over the edge of its limits, and coated first the bottle and then the unconscious Sister Brigitta in a film of inky blackness. Dengesha's chant became almost musical, as though he were singing. His eyes were fevered and his expression one of pure ecstasy.

As the thick, gelatinous substance became more and more viscous, Brigitta stirred from her unconsciousness. Realising that she was being smothered, she opened her mouth to cry out. The fluid rushed into her mouth and she began to choke on it, writhing desperately on the floor as she struggled to breathe.

Dengesha stepped forwards from his position and moved to stand above her. Huron watched, leaning forwards ever so slightly. This was it. This was the moment. He had made countless pacts and agreements to reach this point, and so had his followers.

This was the point at which it would all pay off. Or the point at which it would fail.

Outside, the sounds of gunfire had stopped, but the Chaos sorcerer paid no heed.

Dengesha looked down at the wriggling human woman with a look of total contempt, then reached to take her arm firmly in his grip. He guided it to the glass vial and placed her hand upon it, wrapping his gauntlets around her tiny hands. He then spoke the only words that Huron could understand.

'Be forever bound.'

The oily liquid began to slowly ebb away, draining until all that remained was the faintest slick on the ground. Brigitta, who was in tremendous pain and almost frozen with terror, stared at the green vial, then up at the sorcerer.

Summoning every ounce of strength and fortitude she possessed, she spat in his face. Dengesha began to laugh, a hateful, booming sound that bounced around the walls of the chamber and resonated across the vox-network.

Then, abruptly, the laughter stopped. A look of utmost dread crept slowly over Dengesha's face. His fist, which had been ready to crush Brigitta's skull, suddenly opened out flat. His face slackened, his posture changed and he slouched suddenly as though wearied.

Huron smiled at him.

'What is this treachery?' The sorcerer spun around to face the Tyrant of Badab, who stood watching him with an air of amusement. 'What have you done, Blackheart?'

'Ah, Dengesha. Your fate was sealed the moment

you took the vial from me. You were quite right. I needed a potent soul. And my sorcerers found me one. *Yours*, in fact. And now, with the ritual of binding complete, your soul and the vial are united. You quite literally belong to me.'

'This is not possible! There is no way you could have... Your sorcerers are nothing compared to the glory of the Heterodox!'

'Arrogance has been the downfall of many a warrior of the Adeptus Astartes over the millennia, brother. My sorcerers may not be as powerful as you and your former cabal, but they are far more cunning.'

Seemingly bored of the conversation, Huron began to move around the chamber, occasionally turning over the body of a fallen soldier with his booted foot. He picked up a boltgun, empty of ammunition and dropped it back down with a clang.

Dengesha's face was fury itself, and he reached out to the powers of the warp. But none of them answered him. His black, tainted soul was no longer his to command. He looked to each of his cabal in turn and for their part, they turned from him.

'You all *knew* of this,' he stated flatly. 'You betrayed me to this *cur*...'

'Come now, Dengesha. If you seek to wound my feelings, you will have to try a lot harder than that.' Huron stooped and picked up a meltagun. 'My agents have been dealing with your cabal for months. They agree that their prospects with me and my Corsairs are more interesting than a lifetime of servitude under your leadership. It has been vexing, true – but I think you will agree that the ultimate reward is well worth it.'

On the ground, Sister Brigitta was listening to the exchange without understanding it. All she knew was that these two traitors were speaking such heresy as was almost unbearable to be party to.

Dengesha stared at Huron's back with a look that could have killed and perhaps once, before his soul had been plucked from his body, could have done.

'So you see, Dengesha. In a way, my promise to you is truth. Now that your Heterodox are part of my Corsairs, they will help themselves to the spoils of this world. You, however…'

The Tyrant of Badab crossed the distance between them with uncanny speed and fired the meltagun at the sorcerer. His head was vaporised, and seconds later what remained of his body crashed to the ground. Brigitta gazed up at Huron and there was a look of serene understanding on her face. Her doom had come and it was clad in the desecrated armour of the Imperium of Man.

'My faith is my shield,' she said, softly. The words rang hollow in her ears.

'No,' said Huron, equally softly, as one of the claws of his hand tore through her breast and skewered her. He raised her to eye level. 'It is not. And it never was.'

She let out a sigh as she died and slid free from his claw to the floor below. Without looking at the two corpses at his feet, Huron reached up and plucked the vial from the ground, reattaching it to his belt.

Sometimes, Huron Blackheart kept his word. But this was not one of those times. He did not care who he betrayed to reach his goals. Loyal servants of the Imperium or those who served the dark gods of Chaos. It made little difference to him. The end *always* justified the means.

'Take what we need,' he said. 'And then we leave.'

'IT WORKED PERFECTLY.'

'Surely you did not doubt that it would, my lord?' Valthex turned the vial over in his hand before handing it back to Huron.

'The curse worked exactly as you said it would. Thanks to your efforts, my familiar now has the strength it needs to grant me the blessing of the Four beyond the Maelstrom. Well done, Armenneus.'

'I live to serve, Blood Reaver.' Valthex dropped a low, respectful bow and Huron stalked away. Straightening himself up, the Alchemancer absently rubbed at a sigil branded into the skin of his hand.

It was not just the Tyrant who made pacts. The Patriarch would have to wait to see when he would be called upon to deliver his side of the bargain.

WE ARE ONE

by John French

Victory and defeat are a matter of definition.

– from the *Axioms of War*, Tactica Imperialis

I HAVE GROWN tired in this war. It has eaten me, consuming everything I might have done or been. I have chased my enemy across the stars and through the decades of my failing life. We are one, the enemy and I, the hunter and the hunted. The end is close now. My enemy will die, and at that moment I will become something less, a shadow fading in the brightness of the past. This is the price of victory.

My fist hits the iron door with a crack of thunder. The impact shatters the emerald scales of the hydra that rears across their width. Inside my Terminator armour, enfolded in adamantium and ceramite, I feel the blow jolt through my thin flesh. Lightning

271

crackles around my fist as I pull it back, the armour giving me strength. I bring my fist down and the metre-thick doors fall in a shower of splintered metal. I walk through their shattered remains, my feet crushing the scattered ruby eyes of the hydra to red dust on the stone floor.

The light glints from my armour, staining its pearl-white surface with fire and glinting from eagle feathers and laurels. The chamber beyond the doors is silent and creeps with shifting shadows. Burning torches flicker from brackets on jade pillars, the domed ceiling above coiling with smoke. Targeting runes and threat augurs swarm across my vision, sniffing for threats, finding only one. The shackled power in my fist twitches like a thunderbolt grasped in a god's hand.

He sits at the centre of the chamber on a throne of beaten copper. Void-blue armour mottled with the ghost pattern of scales, swathed in spilling cloaks of shimmering silk; features hidden behind the blank faceplate and glowing green eyes of a horned helm. He sits still, one hand resting on the pommel of a silver-bladed sword, head turning slowly to follow me as I advance.

'Phocron of the Alpha Legion,' I shout, my voice echoing through the shadow-filled silence. 'I call you to justice at the hands of the Imperium you betrayed.' The formulaic phrase of accusation fades to silence as Phocron stands, his sword in his hand. This will be no simple duel. To fight the Alpha Legion is to fight on a shifting layer of deception and trickery, where every weakness can hide strength and every apparent advantage may be revealed as a trap. Lies are their weapons and they are their masters. I am old, but time has armoured me against those weapons.

He moves and cuts, his blow so quick and sudden that I have no chance to dodge. I raise my fist, feeling the armour synchronise with the movements of my ageing muscles, and meet the first strike of this last battle in a blaze of light.

Ninety-eight years ago –
The Year of the Ephisian Atrocity

KNOWLEDGE CAN MAKE you blind, some say, but ignorance is simply an invitation to be deceived. I can still remember the times when I knew little of the Alpha Legion beside a few dry facts and half-understood fears. I look back at those times and I shudder at what was to come.

The death of my ignorance began on the mustering fields of Ephisia.

Millions of troops stood on the dust plains in the shadow of soot-covered hives, rank upon rank of men and women in uniforms from dozens of worlds. Battle tanks and ground transporters coughed exhaust fumes into the cold air. Munitorum officers moved through the throng shouting orders above the noise, their breath forming brief, white clouds. Above it all transport barges hung in the clear sky, their void-pitted hulls glinting in the sunlight, waiting to swallow the gathering mass of human flesh and war machines. It was the mustering of an army to break the cluster of renegade worlds that had declared their secession from the Imperium. It was a gathering of might intended to break that act of folly into splinters and return billions to the domain of the God-Emperor. That was the intention, though perhaps ours was the folly.

'Move!' I bellowed as I charged through the crowd, shoving aside men and women in newly issued battle gear. Helena came with me, pushing people out of our way with her will. Grunts and oaths followed us, dying to silence as they saw the tri-barred 'I' engraved on my breastplate and the hissing muzzle of the inferno pistol in my hand. My storm cloak flapped behind me as I ran, the burnished adamantium of my segmented armour bright under the sun. Anyone looking at me knew that they were looking at an inquisitor, the left hand of the God-Emperor, one who had the power to judge and execute any beneath the Golden Throne. The crowd parted before me like cattle scattering in front of a wolf.

'There!' shouted Helena from a metre to my left. I twisted my head to see the dun colour of our quarry's uniform vanish into a knot of troops. She was already moving before I had changed direction, confused-looking Guardsmen twitching out of her path as she ran through the parting crowd. I could feel the back eddies of the telepathic bow wave that she projected in front of her as she ran, hard muscles flowing under flexing armour plates, dark hair spilling behind.

I saw our quarry a second after Helena. A thin man in the ill-fitting uniform of an Ephisian trooper, his skin pale from poor nutrition and lack of daylight. He looked like so many of the rest gathered on that day, another coin of flesh for the Imperium to spend. But this man was no raw recruit for the Imperial Guard; he was an agent of rebellion sent to seed destruction at this gathering. We had been tracking him for days, knowing that there were more and that our only chance to stop them all was to let one run until he led us to the others. That had been the plan – my plan. But there was no more time. Whatever atrocity they intended was so close I could feel the cold fear of it in my guts.

'Take him down!' I shouted. Helena was raising her needle pistol when the man jerked to one side with the agility of a predator. He rolled and came up into a shooting crouch, lasgun at his shoulder. Helena dived to the ground as the lasgun spat bursts of energy in a wide arc across the space she had occupied. People dropped in the crowd around us, shouts of pain spreading like a tide. Dead and dying troops lay on the ground while their comrades formed a blind herd, scattering without direction or order.

Our man was already up and moving, weaving amongst the panicked troops, using the tide of confusion he had created as cover. I felt a twinge of admiration at the man's ingenuity. He was good, I had to give him that: determined, ruthless and well trained.

I came level with Helena as she pulled herself off the ground.

'Wait,' she said. 'We will not outrun him. I will handle this, master.' She bit off the last word. I looked at her. She had a face that was too thin and pale to be pretty, and a Scholastica Psykana brand surrounded her left eye with a blunt letter 'I' and a halo of wings. She gave me a humourless smile. Helena was my interrogator, my apprentice in the duties of the Inquisition. We did not like each other. In fact, I was sure she hated me on some level. But she was a fine interrogator and a devoted servant of the Imperium. She was also a psyker, and a lethally powerful one at that.

I nodded in reply. She looked away, closing her eyes, and I felt the air around us take on a heavy, burned-sugar texture as she drew power to her. Our quarry had already vanished into the shifting forest of human bodies around us. Hundreds of troops jostled like frightened cattle, and I heard officers shouting for order and situation reports in the distance. There was a frozen moment, a sliver of time that for an instant was quiet and still. I saw a young trooper no more than a pace from me, his face expressing puzzlement, his tan-coloured uniform still creased from storage. I whispered a prayer for forgiveness in that moment.

An invisible shockwave tore out from Helena, ripping bodies from the ground and tossing them into the air like debris in a cyclone's path. Bodies fell, broken, screaming as the telekinetic storm followed our quarry. It reached him, fifty paces from us, and flicked him off his feet. He hit the ground with a crack of bones. When I got to him he was sucking in air in wet gasps, his mashed fingers scrabbling at the lasgun just beyond his reach. I raised my inferno pistol and burned his reaching hand to a charred and blistered stump.

I did not bother to ask him how many other saboteurs were hidden in the mustering, or what their target was. I knew he would not give me an answer. It did not matter. He would tell me what I wanted to know anyway.

'Take it from him.' I flicked my pistol at the broken man on the ground. 'We need to know how many of them there are and what targets they are intending to bomb.' Helena took a deep breath, closing her eyes for a second before looking down at the man who twitched and gurgled at our feet. He went still, and I could feel the cold witch-touch on my skin. Helena's eyes were closed, but as I looked at her she spoke.

'I have him, but…' her voice quivered and I saw she was trembling. 'There is something wrong.'

'Get the information,' I snarled. 'We are running out of time. How many have infiltrated the muster? Where are the bombs?'

'They–' she began, but was cut off by a laugh that bubbled up from the man on the ground. I looked down. He was staring back at me with corpse-white eyes. In that moment I knew I had made a mistake. We are cautioned that assumptions are worse than ignorance, and looking at the man I knew that my assumptions would see me dead. This was no saboteur ring bent on a mundane atrocity. This was something more, something far more. Icy fear ran through me.

'We are many, inquisitor,' he said, his voice a racking gurgle of blood and shattered ribs. Beside me Helena began to spasm, blood running from her mouth and eyes. Her mouth was working, trying to form words.

'Witches. They are witches…' she gasped, her hand reaching to grip my arm, as the psychic storm built around us. 'I can feel their minds. There are more, many more.' I felt a greasy charge lick my skin and detected a stink of burned blood on the air. The broken man laughed again, his skin crawling with lurid warp light.

'We are many,' he screamed, and he was still screaming as I vaporised his head. The sound did not end, but filled my head, getting louder and louder. I looked up from the dead man and saw the extent of my mistake.

Across the plain, figures rose into the air on pillars of ghost light, their limbs pinned to the air, arcs of lightning whipping from one to another, connecting them in a growing web. Dark clouds the colour of bile and dried blood spilled into the sky. Across the mustering fields, hundreds of thousands fell to their knees, moaning, clawing at their skin, blood dribbling from their eyes. Some, with stronger will, had been able to arm their weapons and fire at the witch-chorus. Some found their mark and sent psykers to their death. But there were many, and the witch-storm rose in power with every heartbeat. I could feel the unclean power crawling over me like insects and the witches' voices pulling my thoughts apart. All I could hold on to was anger, anger that I had failed, that an enemy had fooled me. All the while their voices grew louder and louder, spiralling around each other as a single word emerged from the telepathic cacophony.

Phocron.

Dozens of minds screamed the name and the storm broke in an inferno that washed across the mustering fields. It turned flesh to ash and scattered it on a superheated wind. Hundreds of thousands died in a single instant, an army to conquer worlds reduced to twisted metal and dust. I watched the fire come for me, and felt something enfold me like a cloak of ice. I realised that Helena still gripped my arm as I fell into darkness.

I woke on a plain covered in ashes. Helena was next to me, her exposed skin burned and blistered, her breathing so shallow I thought she was dead until I saw her eyes twitch open. The energy needed to shield me still lingered on my skin as a cold shroud. I know now that she had saved us both, but at a price. The power she had channelled to shield us had almost burned her psychic talent out. She lived, but she was a shadow of what she had been and never became an inquisitor. Amongst an overwhelming tragedy, her sacrifice still lives in my memory like the ghost touch of a lost life.

Around us there was nothing but a landscape of desolation beneath a bruised sky. It was quiet, but in my mind echoed the name of he who had perpetrated this atrocity.

Eighty-four years ago

WE CAME OUT of the iron-grey sky on streaks of blood-red fire. Staccato lines of flak and the bright blooms of defence lasers rose from the fallen city like the claws of a dying god raking the sky. Landing craft and assault carriers were punched from the air. Burning wreckage fell in oily cascades of smoke amongst the city's glittering domes and spires. The air rang with shells fired from orbit and the howl of attack craft engines. The wrath and might of the Imperium fell on the city, and it screamed as it burned.

In the gloom of my Valkyrie's crew compartment, we felt the ferocity of the invasion as shuddering blows that shook the frame around us. It was close inside the assault carrier, the air tinted red by the compartment's tactical lights and spiced with the smell of sweat. Even in such a confined space, my storm trooper detail kept their distance, even if that distance was only centimetres. I knew each of them by name, had fought beside all of them and personally selected them as my guard during this invasion. We had bled and struggled side by side, but I stood apart from them. To feel the power of the Emperor in your hand is to know what it is to be alone. It is a fact that I had long ago accepted.

'Lord?' The voice was raised against the thunderous sound of the battle outside. I looked up from the holographic map to see Sergeant Draeg looking down at me, his face framed by oil-black armour. 'Theatre command wishes to know where you intend to make your landing.'

I smiled, letting careless humour wash over my face. 'Do they indeed?' I asked.

Draeg grinned back at me. 'Yes, lord. They say it is so that they can coordinate to properly support your operations.'

I nodded, pursing my lips in mock consideration. I am not given to humour, but to lead people to death, you must wear many masks. Something exploded close by and the Valkyrie bucked. I felt my back pressed against the hard metal of the flight bench as the pilot banked hard.

'Little late in the day for a coordinated strike, don't you think, Draeg?' I gave a small shake of my head. 'Tell them I will update them shortly.'

'Yes, lord,' nodded Draeg. 'And our actual target?'

I looked back to the holo-display, coloured runes winking in clusters over a plan view of the city, shifting with objectives and tactical intelligence. The city was called Hespacia, a glittering jewel that had fallen to greed and lies and pulled the rest of its planet with it. The ruling guilds had overthrown the Imperial government and given their souls, and those of their people, to the dark gods. This, though, was not why I had come to see it fall beneath the hammer of Imperial retribution. I had come not because of Hespacia's heresy but because of its cause.

'The Onyx Palace.' I handed the sergeant my holo-slate. 'Assault position marked.' I watched the thinnest cloud of fear pass over the sergeant's blunt features. We were heading into the heart of the corruption, and we were doing it alone, without support.

'Very good, my lord,' said Draeg and began to bark a briefing to the other storm troopers. I checked my own weapons: a blunt-nosed plasma pistol, holstered on the thigh of my burnished battle plate, and an eagle-headed hammer, which lay across my knees.

The Valkyrie bucked again, shaking from invisible blows. We were close. I did not need to see the tactical data to know it; I could feel it in the shuddering metal around me. In the decade after the burning of the Ephisian mustering I had changed much and learnt more. Suspicion is the armour of the Inquisition, and I had come to appreciate its value. Rebellion had spread, pulling a dozen worlds into heresy and corruption, and with it had come a name, a name I already knew: Phocron. Arch-heretic and puppet master of betrayal, his agents and traitors spread through our own forces like a contagion. Even with the might of a crusade at our backs, we bought every victory with blood. Ambushes, sabotage and assassination ate our strength even as we advanced step by bleeding step. So I came to this damned city to cut off the rebellion's head, to kill the enemy I had never seen. I came to kill Phocron.

The side doors of the Valkyrie peeled back, and the burning stink and howl of battle flooded over us. Beneath us buildings flicked past, aflame and so close that I could see the patternwork on the blue-green tiles that covered so many of their domed roofs. In the streets, figures moved from cover to cover, the sound of their small battles lost amongst the roar as fire fell from the sky in an unending rain.

Above the burning city sat a tiered mountain of pale stone the colour of dirty ice. A series of ascending domes and balconies, it glowed under the luminous haze of void shields, which flickered and sparked with the impact of munitions and energy blasts. This was the Onyx Palace, seat of governorship on this world and the heart of its betrayal. Phocron was there; it was his bastion. The layered shields sheltered him from the bombardment, but they would not deny us.

The Valkyrie hit the void shield envelope, sparks arcing across its fuselage and an electric tang filling the air. The tiered balconies of the palace rose before us, studded with dark weapon turrets that spat glowing lines of fire. We banked and tipped, rounds hammering into the armoured airframe. The engines howled as they thrust us towards the palace's summit. Others came behind us, delta-shaped wings of Vulture gunships and more assault craft. The air shuddered with the rolling scream of launching rockets and the bellow of explosions. Domes and statue-lined bridges flicked past. I could see figures, some crouched behind sandbags, others already running from the detonations that walked up the flank of the palace in our wake.

As we crested the highest dome I saw Phocron for the first time, a figure in dark armour with a single,

black-clad companion and a cluster of cowering figures in billowing silk robes. He stood close to the
edge of the balcony as if he had been watching the
ruin that he had forced the Imperium to bring to this
world.

The Valkyrie pivoted, its engines screaming as it
skimmed the stone slabs of the platform. My storm
troopers were already dropping out of the door, hitting the ground one after another. Draeg gave me a
grin, hurled himself out, and then it was me tumbling
the few metres to hit the tiled platform. The world
spun for a second, then I was up on my feet, training
and instincts doing the work of thought. My armour
responded to my movements, thrusting me forwards
faster than muscle could. Behind me, more storm
troopers spilled onto the platform.

The robed figures clustered around Phocron died,
hellgun blasts burning through their silk finery. A few
ran, swathes of coloured fabric spilling behind them,
their bare feet slapping on the marble. Phocron stood
impassively, his hands empty, the sword at his waist
undrawn. Behind him, a figure in a black storm coat
and silver domino mask stood equally unmoved. I
fired, plasma hissing from my pistol. Others were firing too. Bolts of energy converged on the two figures,
but splashed against a shimmering dome of energy.

Draeg and his squad were in front of me, sprinting
towards Phocron and his aide.

'Try and keep up in that armour, lord.' I heard the
sergeant's grin over the vox. I spat back a very unlordly
oath.

As the first shots hit Phocron's energy field, Draeg
drew his sword. Lightning sheathed it with a crackle.

'Close assault, get inside the shield dome,' the sergeant spat over the vox. The hammer in my hand sprang to life, its generator making it vibrate with straining power.

Draeg was the first through the shield dome, raising his sword for a backhanded cut, muscles ready to unfold the momentum of his charge into an armour-cracking blow. But Phocron moved at the last instant before the blow struck.

I have fought a lifetime of wars and met many enemies blade to blade. I have studied the business of killing, the workmanlike cut, the parry and riposte of a duel, the nicety of a perfectly timed blow. I have watched men kill each other in countless ways. The art of death holds no mystery to me. Yet I swear, I never saw death dealt with more malign genius than at that moment.

Phocron's sword was in his hand. It was long, its double-edged blade damasked in a scale pattern. A saurian head snarled from its crossguard. It met Draeg's sword in a thunder crack of converging power fields. Draeg was fast and conditioned from years of war to react to such a counter, but in this moment those instincts killed him. He shifted his weight to let the Space Marine's blow flow past and open his enemy to another cut. He did not expect Phocron to drop his sword.

With no resistance, Draeg's sword sliced down and cut air. Phocron turned around the sergeant's sword, so close their armour brushed. The gauntleted hand slammed into Draeg's armour at the throat. I saw the sergeant's head snap back, his body rag-loose as he fell to the ground.

The rest of Draeg's squad had not been far behind him and they opened up as they came through the shield dome. Phocron was already moving towards them at a flat run. The first died as he squeezed his trigger. Phocron's hand closed over the hellgun, crushing the storm trooper's fingers into the trigger guard. The man screamed. Phocron pivoted, the gun still spewing a stitched line of energy. The hellgun's fire hit the next two storm troopers at point-blank range, burning through flesh and armour. With swift delicacy, the Space Marine looped an arm around the screaming man and gripped the webbing belt of grenades across his chest.

I was a pace from the edge of the shield dome when I realised what was about to happen. Phocron turned and threw the screaming man at the rest of the storm trooper squad. The force of the throw broke the man's back with a sharp crack. I could see the pins of the grenades glinting in Phocron's fingers. The dead man hit the platform in front of his comrades and exploded.

The blast sheared through the rest of the squad in an expanding sphere of shrapnel. Fragments of metal, flesh and bone pattered off my armour. I could see Phocron and his storm-coated henchman through the pall of smoke and dust. They were running.

'Target is moving,' I shouted across the vox. 'Close and eliminate.'

I fired, plasma burning ionised trails through the dust cloud. I ran after the two figures. Behind me, the rest of the strike force advanced. I reached the edge of the dust cloud. The fleeing pair were at the edge of the platform. Behind them, the city burned. They turned and looked back at the force running past the bloody remains of Draeg and his squad. They ran without looking at Phocron's sword, left forgotten on the ground.

The plasma charge concealed in the blade detonated, unfolding into a glowing sphere of sun-hot energy. I felt the heat through the skin of my armour as the blast tossed me into the air and slammed me into the paving. Warning chimes sounded in my ears as my armour's systems sensed damage. Something wet moved in my chest as I sucked in a breath and found I was alive. For a few seconds, I could see nothing. I tried to raise my head and found that my vision was smeared with blood. I blinked until I could see. Bright light shone from behind me where the sphere of plasma still burned. Phocron stood, his blue armour black in the glare of the plasma bloom.

I pulled myself to my feet with a flare of pain and a grind of servos from inside my armour. My hammer was gone, scattered across the platform by the explosion. Two storm troopers who had been close beside me began to haul themselves up. Phocron shot them before they could stand, the guttural bark of the bolt pistol almost lost in the sound of the battle raging in the city. I was standing, my plasma pistol whining in my hand as it focused its power. The muzzle of Phocron's pistol pointed directly at me, a dark circle ready to breathe fire.

A Valkyrie crested the edge of the platform with a wash of downdraft. Its hull was painted in the storm-grey of Battlefleet Hecuba. I could see the worn kill marks and unit tags under the cockpit. For an instant, I expected it to open up with its chin weapon, for it to rake Phocron and his companion with fire. Then it spun, drifting down until its open side doors were

level with the platform. A crewman in an Imperial
Navy uniform reached down to help the storm-coated
figure into the side door. Phocron vaulted after and
the Valkyrie swooped away. I fancied that the Alpha
Legionnaire was looking at me with his emerald eyes
until the craft was lost amongst the hundreds of others that swarmed above the dying city.

I breathed, letting pain and frustrated anger spill
out. Something did not fit. It had seemed as if Phocron
had anticipated our attack, that he had waited for it
to come so that he could slaughter us. No, it was not
just a slaughter. It was a demonstration of superiority.
I can defeat you in a thousand ways, I can kill you
as I choose, it had said. Then this sudden retreat. It
did not fit. His forces were being overwhelmed, the
city filling with thousands of Imperial troops – but
then why not withdraw as soon as this became clear.
Unless…

I suddenly felt cold, as if ice had formed inside my
armour. I thumbed my vox-link, breaking through
clearance ciphers until the voice of the invasion's
commanding officer spoke into my ear. General Berrikade had a thick voice that spoke of his ample waist
and heavy jowls. He was no fool, though.

'Lord inquisitor,' he said, his voice chopped by static.

'General, all troops are to be withdrawn from the
city immediately.' There was a pause, and I could imagine Berrikade staring incredulously at the vox-speaker
in the strategium aboard an orbiting battleship.

'Lord,' he began, speaking carefully. 'If I may
ask…' He never finished because at that moment
Phocron answered the unspoken question. As the
words left Berrikade's lips, the city's plasma reactors,

promethium stores and chemical refineries exploded.

Across the city, glowing clouds rose into the sky, their tops broadening and flattening as they met the upper air currents. The shockwaves broke buildings into razor-sharp fragments and clouds of dust. An instant later, concentric waves of fire and burning gas swept through the streets. The sound and shockwave reached me in seconds, flipping me through the air with a bellow of noise. I must have hit the ground, but I never felt it. The blast wave had already pulled me down into darkness.

Later, while I healed, I was told that tens of thousands of Imperial troops had been killed, and hundreds of thousands more renegades and millions of civilians burned to nothing or crushed under rubble. The rebellion died, but the Imperium had taken a great wound and nothing was left but charred ruins. Only the Onyx Palace had survived. Its plasma reactors had not been overloaded, and that had saved my life. When I was told this, my first thought was that Phocron had wanted someone to survive to witness him rip another bloody chunk from the flesh of the Imperium. Then I thought again of the dark mouth of Phocron's bolt pistol and the death that he had withheld. No, I thought, he did not want just anyone to witness his victory; he had chosen *me* to witness it. To this day I do not know why.

A year ago

THE SHIP DRIFTED closer. Through the polished armourglass of the viewport, I could see its crippled engines bleed glowing vapour into the vacuum. It was a small vessel, barely large enough to be warp-capable, and typical of the cutters used by traders and smugglers who existed on the fringes of the Imperium. The ship I stood on was massive by comparison, layered with armour and weapons bastions. It was a predator levi-athan closing on a minnow. The *Unbreakable Might* was an Armageddon-class battle cruiser and mounted enough firepower to break other warships into glow-ing debris. Against the nameless clipper, it had barely needed to use a fraction of its might. A single, precise lance strike had burned the smaller ship's plasma engines to ruin and left it to coast on unpowered.

I turned from the view with a clicking purr of aug-metics. My eyes focused on Admiral Velkarrin from beneath the cowl of my crimson robe. He was rake-thin, the metal flexes of command augmentation hanging from his grey-skinned skull in a tangled spill down the back of his gold-frogged uniform.

'Launch a boarding party, admiral,' I said. Velkarrin pursed his colourless lips but nodded.

'As you wish, my lord.' He turned to give an order to a hovering officer.

'And, admiral…' He turned back. 'They are to observe maximum caution.'

'Yes, my lord.' He gave a short bow. I could tell he resented my commandeering his command and his fleet. Hunting smuggler vessels and pirates while war washed across star systems must have galled him. Part of me was faintly amused by watching his pride war with fear of the Inquisition. The rest of me cared nothing for what he felt.

'I will meet the boarding team personally upon their return,' I told him.

Velkarrin gave another curt bow in acknowledgement and stalked away, hissing orders at subordinates.

I turned back to watch our latest prey draw closer, my eyes whirring as they focused. They had rebuilt me after Hespacia. My eyes and face were gone, replaced by blue-lensed augmetics and a mask of twisted scar tissue fused onto a ceramic woven skull. My left leg and a portion of my torso had been so mangled that they had been replaced. Ceramite plating, organ grafting and a leg of mechanised brass meant that I still lived and walked, even if it was with a bent back and the stutter of gears and pistons. For a while after the disaster of the Hespacia attack, I thought of my injuries as a penance for my lack of foresight, a price for ignorance written forever into my body.

Since that lesson I had done much to address my failing. The war against the rebel worlds had grown many times over, sucking in armies and resources from across many star systems. The Imperium was no longer fighting a war of containment but a crusade of retribution. Under my authority, and that of the Adeptus Terra, it was named the Ephisian Persecution. I had watched our forces struggle for decades as more and more worlds had fallen to rebellion and the influence of the dark gods. It was a war we were losing because we were fighting an enemy for whom lies were both a weapon and a shield. Understanding that enemy had been my work in the decades since Hespacia burned.

I had expended great energy in tracking down information on the Alpha Legion. From the sealed reports of Inquisitor Girreaux to half-understood accounts from the dawn of the Imperium, I had reviewed them all. I knew my enemy. I knew their nature, their preferred forms of warfare, and their weaknesses. Sometimes, I thought I knew them better than I knew myself.

Their symbol was the hydra, a many-headed beast from legends born in mankind's earliest days. It was both a mark of their warrior brotherhood and a statement of methodology. To fight the Alpha Legion was to fight a many-headed beast that would twist in your grasp. As soon as you thought you had a part pinned, another unseen part would strike. Should you cut off one head, two would grow to replace it. They wove secrets and lies about themselves, hoping to baffle and confuse their enemies. Subterfuge, espionage, ambush and the untameable tangle of guerrilla warfare were their specialities: wielded through networks of corrupted followers, infiltrators, spies and, on occasion, their own martial skill. They were wrapped in the corruption of Chaos, steeped in betrayal and bitterness ever since their primarch and Legion had betrayed mankind ten millennia before.

The enemy I faced now was but a single scion of that heretic brood, but no less formidable for that. Phocron was a name that had infiltrated every theatre of the Ephisian Persecution like a silent, coiling serpent. I knew that even before we had learnt his name he had seeded a dozen worlds with insurgent ideologies and built up control over witch-cults and heretic sects. Now he moved from warzone to warzone, plunging worlds into rebellion, corrupting our forces and punishing the Imperium for every victory. The Ephisian Atrocity and the Burning of Hespacia were just two amongst the subtle and devastating attacks he had made on the Imperium. Throughout his coiling dance of destruction, he had stayed out of my grasp, a shadow opponent locked in a dual with me across dozens of worlds.

Beyond the reflective layer of armourglass a shuttle boosted towards the crippled ship on trails of orange flame. Rather than follow Phocron's trail I had decided to attack him where he was most vulnerable: his transportation. He had no fleet of warships for he did not take planets by orbital invasion or the threat of bombardment. He took worlds from within, moving from one to another unseen. That implied that he moved using pirate and smuggler craft; small ships that could pass unnoticed and unremarked through the wild borderland of the subsector. A scattered task force of Imperial ships had tracked and boarded nineteen vessels so far with no result. The ship I watched would be the twentieth.

TWO HOURS LATER, I stood amidst the promethium stink and the semi-ordered chaos of one of the *Unbreakable Might*'s main landing bays. Bright light flooded the cathedral-like space, gleaming off the hulls of lighters, shuttles and landing craft. Figures moved over them, working on the mechanical guts exposed under servicing plates.

I stood with Velkarrin and a guard of twenty armsmen, their bronzed void armour reflecting the bright light. The admiral stood a few paces away, consulting with two of his attending officers. The away team had reported that the vessel appeared to be nothing but a smuggler, crewed by deserters and outlanders. They had found a cargo of illegal ore destined for some pirate haven out in the Halo Margins. The lex-mechanic who had accompanied them had drained the smuggler ship's data reservoirs for later analysis. As on the nineteen previous occasions no connection with Phocron or his shadow network appeared to exist. Still, I wanted to meet the boarding party on their return, to search their accounts for details that they might have failed to report. Once that was done, the smuggler ship would be blasted into molten slag.

The armoured shuttle glided into the dock, its passive antigravity field filling the air with an ionised tang. It settled onto the deck with a hiss of hydraulics and a creak of ice-cold metal. The shuttle was a blunt block of grey armour the size of a mass ground hauler, its surface pitted and scored by atmospheric translation. Blast shields covered the armourglass of its cockpit. I heard the echoes of vox-chatter between the pilots and the deck crew as they moved in to attach power lines and data cables. The ramp under the chin of the shuttle hinged open, revealing a dark space inside. Velkarrin and the armsmen looked towards it, expecting the boarding team to appear from the gloom.

Something was wrong. I reached for the plasma pistol at my waist, my hand closing on the worn metal of the grip at the same moment that the docking bay went dark. Complete blackness enfolded us. For an instant, there was silence, and then voices rose in confusion. The pistol was in my hand, its charge coils glowing as it built power with a piercing whine. In the direction of the shuttle, two eyes glowed suddenly green. There was a motorised growl as a chain weapon gunned to life, and then the shooting started.

Our armsmen guard opened up, shotgun muzzles

flaring as they fired into the dark. The noise was like a ragged, rolling bellow. In the jagged light of muzzle flare I saw my enemy standing on the ramp of the shuttle. His armour was dark, mottled by patterns of scales. In one hand he held a toothed axe, in the other a bolt pistol. He stood still for an instant as the shot rattled from his warplate, looking at us with glowing green eyes. Behind him stood a figure in a silver mask and storm coat. In that brief moment I thought that the empty eyes in the silver face were looking into mine.

The armsmen had closed ranks around Velkarrin and I, forming a deep circle of bronze armour. I aimed and fired, but Phocron was already gone, moving through muzzle flash, a whirlwind of slaughter caught through blinked instants.

He hit the first armsmen with a downward blow. I heard the scream of motorised teeth meeting metal and flesh.

He was two strides nearer, an arc of dismembered dead at his feet. I heard a yelp of fear close by, recognising the admiral's voice by its tone.

The bolt pistol flared and roared, three armsmen dying in an oily flash of light. He was three strides away. There was a smell of offal and meat in my nose. Beside me, I heard Velkarrin turn to run and thud to the deck as his feet slipped on something slick and soft. The plasma pistol whined in my hand.

I raised my pistol, lightning dancing across its charge coils. Phocron was above me, chainaxe raised, scale-patterned armour glistering with blood. He brought the axe down in a diagonal cut. I pulled the trigger and plasma flared from the barrel of my pistol.

I missed, but the shot saved my life. Jerking aside to avoid my shot, Phocron missed his target. The teeth of the chainaxe met my gun arm just below the elbow, the back-swing slicing through Velkarrin as he tried to stand.

The lights came on as shock hit me. Blood was spilling from the chewed stump of my arm. I staggered a step before my legs gave way, and I collapsed to the floor in a clicking whir of gears. People moved, shouting. I was aware of a lot of weapons surrounding me very quickly.

I looked around, trying to focus through a pale fog that seemed to be floating across my vision. Blood glistened under the bright lights. The ramp of the shuttle was still open. Later, I would find out that none of its crew or the boarding party had returned from the smuggler ship; the voices in the vox-chatter and reports had been perfect mimicry. Of Phocron and the man in the silver mask, there was no sign.

One month ago

THE WAR COUNCIL overseeing the Ephisian Persecution gathered on board the *Unbreakable Might*. Generals, war savants, vice-admirals, magi, bishops militant, palatines, commissar lords and captains of the Adeptus Astartes; all came to my call. The strategium of the battle cruiser was a two-hundred-paces-wide circular chamber of raked seats carved from granite. I waited at the centre, under the eyes of the gathering worthies, and watched.

They came in small groups, looking for faces they knew, judging where it was their right to sit, who they had to avoid and who they had to greet. It was like watching the shifting gears of Imperial politics and power play out in miniature. There a Sparcin war chief in burnished half-plate and white fur cloak, trailed by a clutch of tactical advisers. Here a psykana lord, a withered white face within a hood of cables, sat next to a spindle-limbed woman in carmine robes, the cog-skull of the Adeptus Mechanicus etched on the brass of her domino mask. Servo-skulls moved above the assembling throng, scanning, recording, sniffing the air for threats and spreading incense in thick breaths.

Amongst the crowd I saw some of my own kind, inquisitors or their representatives, moving amongst the rest like imperious masters, or remaining still and silent on the edges. I had invited none of them but they came anyway, my reputation enough to bring them. Some even called me 'lord inquisitor'. Rank within the Inquisition is a complex matter. No formal structure exists amongst this shadow hand of the Imperium that answers to none but the will of the Emperor. Lordship is a matter of respect, a title of acknowledgement granted by peers to one who has earned it by the power of their deeds. My war against Phocron had pulled respect and renown to me like a flame gathers insects. As the greatest masters of war in this volume of space gathered at my call, I could see why some might call me lord.

I sat on a high-backed chair at the centre of the chamber. A symbolic hammer rested beneath my left hand, my right on the black iron of the chair's arm, fingers of polished chrome clicking softly on the dark metal. It had been a year since I had lost my right arm in the ambush that had killed Admiral Velkarrin and nearly claimed my life. The bionic replacement still ached with phantom pain.

In that year, I had not been idle. Following his attempt on my life, Phocron had simply vanished. No trace of him could be found on the ship or on the smuggler vessel. This, and the sudden loss of light at the moment of attack, could only mean that his network of traitors extended deeper and higher in our forces than I had considered possible. Trusted acolytes and agents of my own had gone to work, and now I gathered together the leaders of the Persecution to share what I had found. A few knew what was about to happen, most did not.

I watched as black-visored troopers sealed the doors to the chamber and waited for the grumble of conversation to fade. When it had, I stood.

'There is much to speak of,' I said, my voice carrying up the tiered seats. I saw some shift at the lack of formal greeting or acknowledgement of the honour and position of those gathered here. I let myself smile at the thought. 'But first there is a matter that must be dealt with.' I gave a slight nod as if to emphasise the point, and those waiting for that signal acted as one.

Even though I was prepared for it, the psychic shockwave made me stagger. On the tiered seats, a dozen figures convulsed as the telepathic and telekinetic power enfolded them in a vice-like grip. I felt an oily static charge play over my skin. There was a sound like wind rustling through high grass. The needle slivers hit the convulsing men and women, and one by one they went still as the sedatives overrode nerve impulses. There was an instant of shocked silence.

'Do not move,' I shouted as the black-visored

troopers moved through the crowd. They clustered around each of the stricken figures. Null collars and monowire bindings were slipped over necks and limbs, and the bound figures were dragged across the stone floor like sacks of grain. The shock in the rest of the crowd was palpable; they had just seen a dozen of their senior peers, men and women of power and distinction, overcome and dragged away. You could almost feel the thought forming in all their minds; *traitors in our midst*. The pale-faced psykana lord nodded to me and I favoured him with a low bow of thanks. A murmur of anger and fear began to build in the chamber.

'Our enemy is among us.' I raised my hammer up and brought its adamantine head down on the granite floor. Silence gathered in the wake of the fading blow. 'It walks amongst us, wearing faces of loyalty.' My voice was soft but it carried in the still air. 'Our enemy has used our strength against us, directed us into traps, mired us in blood and shackled our strength with lies. A year ago, on this ship, that enemy came close to ending my life with his own hand. That such a thing was possible is a testament to his ability and audacity.' I paused, looking around at the faces watching me, waiting to see what would come next. 'But I survived, and in that attempt he exposed the extent of the treachery within our forces.' I pointed to the dozen spaces on the tiered seats. 'Today I have removed the heads of the hydra from among us.' I paused as murmurs ran through the audience.

The traitors had been difficult to find without arousing their suspicion. It had been delicate work to find them, and more delicate still to prepare to remove them in a single instant. The twelve taken in the chamber had been the most senior, the most highly placed of Phocron's agents and puppets. Some, no doubt, had not known what end they served; others, I was sure, were willing traitors. There had been generals amongst them, senior Munitorum staff, an astropath, a confessor and even an interrogator. At the moment they had been taken, parallel operations had gone into action throughout the Persecution's forces, cutting the corruption out from among us. Most of the infiltrators would be killed, but many would be taken and broken until their secrets flowed from them like blood from a vein.

'The enemy has blinded us and led us by the hand like children. But at this moment he has also handed us weapons with which to destroy him. Knowledge is our weapon, and from the traitors who walked among us we will gain knowledge.' I stood and picked the hammer up, its head at my feet, the pommel resting under my hands. 'And with that knowledge, this Persecution will cut the ground from under the feet of our enemy. We will wound and hound him until he crawls to his last refuge. And when he is crippled and bleeding, I shall take the last head of this hydra.'

Twelve hours ago

A HUNDRED WARSHIPS came to bear witness to our victory. They ringed the jagged space fortress, their guns flaring as they hammered it with fire. The *Hydra's Eye* turned in its orbit around the dead world like a prize fighter too dazed to avoid the blows mashing his face to bloody pulp and splintered bone.

In the end, it had been the words of a traitor that had betrayed Phocron's refuge. One of those taken from the strategium of the *Unbreakable Might* had known of another agent in Naval command. That agent had been taken in turn, and his secrets ripped from his mind by a psyker. That information had been added to fragments gleaned from others, winding together to make a thread that had led to the system of dead planets in which the *Hydra's Eye* hid. That it was the current refuge for Phocron was implied and confirmed by many sources once we knew where to look. Once I had the location of Phocron's base, I ordered an immediate attack.

The *Hydra's Eye* was truly vast, an irregular star of fused void debris over fifteen kilometres across at its widest point. Its hull was a patchwork skin of metal that wept glowing fluid as macro shells and lance strikes reduced its defences to molten slag. There had been enemy ships clustering around the irregular mass of the space fortress like lesser fish beside a deep-sea leviathan. Most had been pirate vessels, wolf packs of small lightly armed craft. All died within minutes, their deaths scattering light across the jagged bulk of the *Hydra's Eye*. Our guns went silent as a cloud of assault boats and attack craft swarmed towards the wounded fortress. I had not watched as Phocron's last means of escape died in fire. This was the end of my war and I was ready to strike its last blow myself. When the first wave of attack craft swarmed towards the space fortress I was there, my old body wrapped in armour forged by the finest artisans of Mars.

An animal is at its most dangerous when wounded and cornered. Phocron's followers did not fail to hammer this lesson home. The forces on the *Hydra's Eye* were a mixture of piratical scum and renegades inducted into Phocron's inner circle. They spent their lives without thought, their only care being to make us pay many times over for each of them that we killed. I could see Phocron's vile genius in their every tactic. Some hid in ceiling ducting or side passages, waiting for our forces to pass before attacking from behind. Others pulled Guardsmen quietly into the dark, strangling them before taking their uniforms and equipment. Dressed as friends, the renegades would join our forces, waiting until the most advantageous moment to turn on the men beside them.

The structure of the fortress itself spoke of a twisted foresight. Dead ends and hidden passages riddled the structure. Passages and junctions seemed to split and channel us, portioning our forces so that they became divided. We had bodies enough to choke every passage. We would win, that was without doubt, but every inch cost blood. Those bloody steps had led me here to this chamber and this final battle.

Yes, every step had cost blood; every step for a hundred years, from the mustering fields of Ephisia, through the Burning of Hespacia to here, where I will face my enemy for the last time. I am alone, the rest of the Imperial force lost behind me in the bloody tangle of the *Hydra's Eye*. So I will face my enemy alone, but perhaps that is as it should be.

PHOCRON MOVES AND cuts, his blow so quick and sudden that I have no chance to dodge. I raise my arm, feeling the armour synchronise with the movements of my ageing muscles. My fist meets his strike in a blaze of light. For a second, it is his strength against mine, the energies of weapons grinding against each other. I am looking into his face, so close that I can see the pattern of finer and finer scales on his face-plate. The deadlock lasts an eye blink. I fire my storm bolter a fraction of a second before he moves. The burst hits him in the chest at point-blank range and spins him onto the floor with the sound of cracking ceramite. I spray his struggling form with explosive rounds as he tries to rise.

I take a step closer – a mistake. He is on his feet faster than I can blink, spinning past me. The tip of his sword glides over my left elbow as he moves. The energy field sheathing my fist vanishes, the power feeds severed with surgical care. I turn to follow him. His sword flicks out again, low and snake-strike fast. The tip stabs through the back of my left knee. Pain shoots up my leg an instant before it collapses under me. Tiles shatter under the impact. He is gone, moving into blind space behind me. I try to twist around, my targeting systems searching. He is going to kill me, one cut at a time. Despite the pain, I smile to myself. The Alpha Legion do not simply kill, they bleed you bite by bite until you have no doubt of their superiority. But that pride is their weakness.

A cut splits the elbow of my right arm. I do not even see where it comes from. Blood is running down my alabaster-white armour and dribbling across the crushed tiles. My right arm is hanging loose at my side, but I hold on to my storm bolter through the pain.

He walks into my view. There is a casual slowness to his movements. He has stripped me of my strength, crippled me and now wants to look into my eyes as he kills me. He stops two paces from me and stares down at me with green eyes. The tip of the blade rises level with my face. His weight shifts as he prepares to ram the sword into my eye.

This is the death stroke, and it is the chance I have been waiting for.

I bring my left arm around in a swing that hits him behind the right knee. The fist has no power field, but it is still a gauntlet of armour propelled by a layer of artificial muscles. It hits with a dry crack of fractured armour and bone.

Phocron falls, the hand gripping the knife splayed out to the side. I pull myself to my feet, gripping my storm bolter with the last of my strength. It does not take much. All I need to do is squeeze the trigger. Fired at point-blank range, the explosive rounds shred his arm. Before he can react, I move and squeeze the remainder of the storm bolter's clip into his left arm.

He flounders in a pool of blood and armour fragments. I put my knee on his chest and grip the horns of his helmet with my left fist. Seals squeal and snap as I wrench the helmet from his head. For an instant, I expect to see the face of a monster, a monster that created me, that drove me to become what I am. But the face under the helm is that of a Space Marine; unscarred, dark eyes looking up at me from sharp features. He has a small tattoo of an eagle under his left eye, the ink faded to a dull green.

I reach up and take my own helmet off. The air smells of weapons-fire and blood.

'Phocron,' I say. 'For your crimes and heresies against the Imperium of Mankind, I sentence you to death.'

He smiles.

'Yes, you have won. Phocron will die this day.' There is movement at the edge of my vision.

I look up. There are figures watching me from the edges of the room. They wear blue armour, some blank and unadorned, some etched with serpentine symbols, others hung with the sigils of false gods. They look at me with green glowing eyes. Amongst them is a normal-sized man wrapped in a storm cloak, his face hidden by a silver mask. The image of a figure in a mask stood against the burning backdrop of Hespacia, and caught in muzzle flash on the *Unbreakable Might* flicks through my memory.

The man steps forwards. His right hand is augmetic and holds a slender-barrelled needle pistol. There is a clicking purr of gears and pneumatics as the masked man walks towards me. I start to rise. The masked man reaches up with his left hand and pulls the silver mask away. I look at him.

He has my face.

THE NEEDLE DART hits the inquisitor in his left eye and the toxin kills him before he can gasp. He collapses slowly, the bulk of his armour hitting the tiled floor with a crash.

We move quickly. We have only a few moments to secure our objective, and we can make no mistakes. The inquisitor's armour is stripped from his body, piece by piece, the injuries he sustained noted as they are revealed. As the dead man is peeled from the armour I remove my own gear and equipment, stripping down until there are two near identical men, one dead and bleeding on the floor, the other standing while his half-brothers finish their work.

My augmetics and every detail of my re-sculpted flesh match the man who lies dead before me. Years of subtle flesh-craft and conditioning mean that my voice is his voice, my every habit and movement are his. There is only the matter of the wounds that were carefully inflicted to injure, but not kill. I do not cry out as my Legion brothers cut me, though the pain is nothing less than it was for him, the dead man whose face I wear. The wounds are the last details, and as the blood-slick Terminator armour covers my skin, all differences between the dead inquisitor and I end. We are one, he and I.

They take the inquisitor's body away. It will burn in a plasma furnace to erase the last trace of this victory. For it is a victory. They take away our crippled brother who was the last to play the role of Phocron. A corpse is brought to take his place, its blue armour chewed by bolter-rounds and crumpled by the blows of a power fist. A horned helmet hides his face and a shimmering cloak hangs from his shoulders. This corpse is the final proof that the Imperium will require to believe they have won this day: Phocron, dead, killed by his nemesis. Killed by me. The Imperium will see this day as their victory, but it is a lie.

Phocron never existed, his name and legend only extant in the mind of the Imperium and the obsession of the man whose place I take. Phocron existed only to create this last meeting. Many of the Legion were Phocron, playing the role to create a legend that was a falsehood. I will walk from this chamber in victory and my legend will grow; my influence and power will spread further. Decades of cultivation and provocation have led to this one moment of transformation, the moment we give the Imperium a victory and transform it into a lie. This is our truth, the core of our soul, the essence of our craft. We are warriors unbound by the constraints of truth, assumption, or dogma. We are the reflection in the eternal mirror of war, ever-changing, unfixed, and invincible. We serve lies and are their masters. We are their slaves and they are our weapons, weapons which can defeat any foe, break any fortress and grant one warrior victory against ten thousand. I am the one who stands against many. I am Alpha Legion, and we are one.

TORTURER'S THIRST

by Andy Smillie

'I must know. I must know what lies beneath the flesh, what powers a man to draw breath when death is so much easier. I must inflict pain to level you, to strip away your falsehoods and pretences. I must show you yourself, so that I may know your secrets.'

– Torturer's saying

APPOLLUS ECHOED HIS jump pack's roar as it drove him downwards. He landed hard, scattering a mortar formation and crushing their spotter beneath his ceramite boots. The enemy's ribs cracked, the bone fragments spearing his innards while his organs drowned in blood. Appollus grinned. The other six members of his Death Company slammed to the earth in ordered formation around him. The backwash of their jump packs scoured the flesh from a slew of enemy warriors, filling the air with the rancid tang of burned flesh.

'Bring them death!'

Appollus opened fire with his bolt pistol, dispatching a trio of the enemy in a burst of mass-reactive rounds. The Brotherhood of Change were everywhere. A teeming mass of mauve robes and onyx masks, they pressed towards him with unrelenting fervour. Appollus thumbed the fire selector to full-auto and fired again. A swathe of Brotherhood cultists died, their bodies blown apart, pulped by the explosive rounds. Yet they did not falter. Heedless of the losses inflicted upon them, the Brotherhood lashed out at Appollus like men possessed. The tip of a barbed pole-arm cracked against his shoulder guard. He side-stepped a thrust meant to disembowel him and jammed the muzzle of his bolt pistol into his attacker's torso. A shower of limbs and flesh-chunks rained over his armour as he pressed forwards, spattering his black battle plate crimson.

The sharp tang of blood was suffocating. It was a siren's call to the killer inside him, beckoning him onwards into the press of flesh. Another blade flashed towards him. He parried the downwards stroke with his crozius, and smashed his bolt pistol into the faceplate of another of the Brotherhood. The blow caved in the side of the cultist's skull. Lines of brain-viscera clung to Appollus's bolt pistol as he swung it round and opened fire on the endless mauve horde.

The Brotherhood had been human once. Scholars from the librarium world of Onuris Siti, their counsel was sought by all who could afford it, from cardinals to Planetary Governors. But the Sitilites had turned their back on the Emperor and his Imperium. They had sworn dark oaths to darker gods, burned their librariums to the ground and denounced the teaching of the Ecclesiarchy.

Appollus snarled as he gunned down another group of attackers. He could smell the taint of the warp upon them; it saturated them, drifting from their pores like a foul poison. A warning sigil flashed on his helmet display. He was down to his last round. He blinked it away with a snarl, and blew the head from a bulbous assailant whose torso was at odds with his rawboned legs – only a raw aspirant was unable to discern his ammo count by the weight of his weapon. Appollus mag-locked the pistol to his armour, and buried his combat knife into the distended neck of the nearest cultist.

Behind them, the guns of the Cadian Eighth continued to fire in a desperate attempt to hold the line against the Brotherhood's advance. The *snap* of a hundred thousand lasguns crackled in the air like lightning, as a thousand heavy bolters continued their thunderous chatter.

Ahead of him, the Death Company were pushing forwards. Wielding their chainswords two-handed, they hacked a path through the Brotherhood's ranks. Orphaned limbs tumbled through the air like morbid hail, ripped from ruined torsos by the adamantium teeth of the Death Company's weapons. Still the enemy came, clawing and grabbing at their arms and legs. For all their rage-fuelled vigour, Appollus knew his brothers would eventually be pulled to the ground, drowned beneath the tide of flesh assailing them.

Appollus threw his arms out, his ceramite-clad limbs smashing ribs and shattering jaws. They needed to regain the initiative, to maintain momentum.

'With me!' Appollus growled over the vox.

He bent his knees, angling his jump pack towards the enemy at his rear. With a thought, he activated the booster. The cultist behind him died in a flash, incinerated in a gout of flame. Dozens more flailed around screaming, their flesh running from their bodies in a thick soup.

The raging thrusters threw Appollus forwards into a wall of enemy. He tucked his chin into his pauldron, using the shoulder guard as a battering ram. Bone broke, and necks snapped as he battered through the press of Brotherhood. A red status sigil blinked on his display – fuel zero. He pressed the release clasp and the booster fell away. Momentum carried him onwards another ten paces. He rolled, knocking over a handful of assailants, before rising to his feet to begin the slaughter anew.

'Chaplain Appollus.' Colonel Morholt's voice crackled in his ear.

He ignored it and pushed onwards. His weapons blurred around him as he hacked off limbs on instinct. His blood hummed in his veins, his twin-hearts bellowing, choirmasters propelling him through a chorus of death. This was what is was to be a Flesh Tearer. To lose oneself in the joy of slaughter. To maim. To kill. He eviscerated an enemy and tore the midriff out of another, stamping his boot down to crack the skull of a cultist whose leg he'd removed a heartbeat before. Thick gore splattered his armour, blood pooled around his gorget.

He felt lighter without the jump pack, and his progress through the forest of bodies quickened. But the Death Company were already ahead of him, churning the Brotherhood into fleshy gobbets that slid from their armour like crimson sleet.

'Chaplain, you've extended the cordon. Pull back to your sector.'

Appollus barely registered the colonel's pleas, his attention fixed on the lumbering brute that was trying to bludgeon him to death with a pair of crackling warhammers. Hemmed in on all sides by the press of enemy warriors, Appollus had no room to manoeuvre. He blocked his attacker's opening swing with his crozius, the weapons sparking off one another in a haze of blistering energy. Appollus felt his feet slide back under the force of the blow. The earth beneath his feet was slick, churned into a thick paste by constant bombardment and the hundred score warriors who had charged across it. He growled, sinking his weight through his knees to steady himself. The brute advanced on him, swinging again. Appollus stepped inside its guard and brought his head up into its jaw, grinning as he heard the sickening snap of bone. He reversed the strike, driving his forehead down into the brute's face. The blow cracked the creature's faceplate, and it cried out in pain as the obsidian fragments embedded themselves in its skin. The brute dropped its weapons, reaching up to pull the shards from its flesh.

'Die now!'

Appollus threw an uppercut into his foe's chest. It spasmed hard, blood pouring from its broken mouth as the Chaplain wrapped his fingers around its heart.

Appollus squeezed the organ, grinning as it burst in his grasp. He tore his hand free, beheading another of the Brotherhood before the brute had even collapsed to the ground.

'Hold position! Emperor damn you, hold the line!'

Colonel Morholt's voice became like a persistent whine in Appollus's ear. He growled in response, deactivating his comm-feed even as he tore his crozius from another of the arch-enemy's pawns. His duty was to lead the Death Company in battle, to direct their fury to the heart of the enemy. Their rage was beyond his means to restrain, it could be sated only by blood. They had no place anywhere but at the enemy's throat. Brother Luciferus had made that plain before dispatching them to this accursed planet. Appollus grinned, never had the Flesh Tearers' Chief Librarian spoken a greater truism. To pull back now would be to invite the Death Company's wrath upon Morholt and the rest of his regiment.

A persistent warning sigil flashed on Appollus's retinal display as his armour's auspex detected incoming artillery.

'Morholt,' Appollus snarled.

Locking his crozius to his armour, he grabbed the nearest brute by its head. The hulking traitor voiced a throttled scream as Appollus threw himself to the ground, dragging the unfortunate down on top of him. His helmet's audio dampeners activated to preserve his hearing a heartbeat before a staccato of explosions burst around him.

'I am his weapon, he is my shield!' Appollus bellowed the mantra through gritted teeth as the ground shuddered under multiple detonations.

The siege shells exploded in coarse bellows that threw dirt and malformed bodies into the air like sparks burning away from a firecracker. Flame washed over him, incinerating the screaming brute sheltering him and burning the litany parchments from his armour.

The heat liquefied the ground beneath him, his armoured bulk sinking further into the muddied earth. Biometric data scrolled across his retinal display as the bombardment ended. The concussive force of the blasts had strained his organs, but his armour had held and he was already healing.

A pair of faded ident-tags told him Urim and Rashnu had taken direct hits, blown into fleshy rain by the artillery barrage.

'Rest well, brothers.'

When the battle was over, Appollus would gather whatever fragments of their armour remained and take them to the Basilica of Remembrance. They would be mourned, as would the loss of their gene-seed.

'Cease fire!' Appollus growled into the vox.

A burst of static shot back in answer.

Snarling, he pushed himself up out of the dirt, cursing as his gauntlets slid into the earthy soup.

'Hold your fire, Morholt, or by the blood I will kill you myself!'

Appollus surveyed the destruction. The enemy dead carpeted the landscape, like purple reeds flattened by the wind. The remaining four members of his Death Company were scattered among a line of shallow craters to his left flank.

Las-fire flickered from the edge of the blast zone. The Brotherhood were starting to rally. An autocannon shell glanced his pauldron, spinning him down into the mud.

'Forwards!' Appollus roared as he regained his footing.

But the Death Company were already charging towards the Brotherhood, bolters barking in their hands as they advanced into a hail of las-fire.

'We are anger. We are death.'

Fire burned in Appollus's limbs as his legs pumped him towards the foe. Ignorant of the las-fire that licked his armour and the solid-state rounds that threw up dirt in his path, he charged towards the wall of enemy.

'Our wrath knows no succour.'

Ten more paces and he would be among them. His gauntlets would drip in entrails as he ripped apart their blasphemous forms.

'Our blades know no–'

Something unseen struck Appollus in the chest, flipping him to the ground. He landed hard, a crack snaking along his breastplate. He groaned as he lifted his head, blinking hard to clear his vision. Pain suppressors flooded his system but did nothing to quell the searing pain in his skull.

The enemy stopped firing.

Grunting with effort, Appollus got to his feet. He stumbled forwards, but the ground swung up to meet him. Blood filled his mouth as his head struck the ground. Roaring with frustration, he pushed himself onto all fours. He would crawl if he had to. Only death would stay his wrath.

Ahead the ranks of the Brotherhood stood immobile, taunting him.

Behind his skull helm, Appollus's face was set in a

snarl of pure hate. He cast his eyes over the traitors, searching for sign of his Death Company. A flash of mirror-black armour among the mauve robes caught his eye. He made to look again, but in the same instant was yanked from the ground, tossed into the air and slammed back down with bone-breaking force.

Pain burned through him, as though a molten needle was being threaded into his very marrow. He couldn't move, his limbs pinned to the earth, trapped beneath a huge, invisible weight. Patches of hoarfrost rimed his armour, spitting as they cracked and reformed. The stench of sulphur choked the air around him.

Psyker.

The thought formed in Appollus's mind the briefest of instants before he glimpsed the mirror-black armour once more and darkness took him.

FILMY WATER DRIPPED onto Appollus's face, stirring him. His head ached in a way he'd not felt since Seth had struck him in the duelling cages. Easing his eyes open, he saw thick iron chains looped around his ankles. He was naked, strung up like butchered cattle, his head a metre from the ground. His wrists were shackled too, fixed beneath him by a chain that ran through a loop set into the bare rock of the floor. Appollus strained at his bonds, his muscles rippling with effort as he tried in vain to break the irons from the floor.

'The blood grant me my vengeance,' he spat, growling with frustration.

The light in the chamber was poor, uneven. The faint smell of promethium hung in the air, drifting from oil burners. Appollus strained his eyes, snatching glimpses of his surroundings in the flickering lamplight. The chamber was perhaps five metres across, its walls pocked and irregular, hewn from solid rock by axe and pick. The air was damp, and algae and moss clung to the walls in thick patches.

There was no sign of an exit. Appollus closed his eyes, his Lyman's ear filtering out the noise of the water as it continued to drip from the ceiling. Slowing his breathing, he quietened his heart, the drumming of his warrior-pulse dropping to a whisper.

The door was to his rear. His skin tingled at the light wisps of air that pushed into the chamber through the gaps at its edges. Someone stood just beyond it. He could hear the regular exhaling and changeless heartbeat of a bored sentry. There were…

Footsteps.

Appollus focused on their steady rhythm as they grew closer. Judging by the gait, his visitors were human. Two men, one with a limp.

The guard's pulse quickened. Appollus smiled at his gaoler's discomfort.

The footsteps stopped outside the door, and Appollus listened as the two men spoke to the fearful sentry. The blasphemous curs spoke in the tongue of the arch-enemy. Appollus clenched his jaw. Though he couldn't discern what they were saying, he recognised the tone well enough. The visitors were the guard's superiors, his deference to them unmistakable.

The door opened inwards, the sound of its heavy latch sliding free a welcome relief from the ravaged consonants that ground from the men's throats.

Appollus tasted the familiar tang of recycled air as

the door opened. The chamber was underground; a ventilation system fed air in through the corridor. He concentrated on the air as it brushed against his skin and decided that the nearest circulation shaft was perhaps ten paces beyond his cell. The door clunked as it swung closed. It was thick, but with a sufficient run-up he was confident he could fell it.

'Welcome, Chaplain.'

The speaker's voice brought Appollus's attention back into the room. The man stank of sulphur and day-old blood.

Appollus opened his eyes but remained silent. As a Chaplain, it was his duty to listen. To hear the sins of his brothers and distil their lies before they had even formed on their tongues. He had taken confession from the best of men, men of power and great strength. He had listened to the broken voices of terrible men, men whose twisted machinations had seen the end of civilisations, as they lay on his interrogation rack.

His visitor was neither.

'You hold secrets, Chaplain.' This time it was the second visitor who spoke. His voice was deeper than that of the first, and he struggled over the words as though unused to making their sounds. He bent down as he spoke, holding a long blade so that Appollus could see its blood-encrusted barbs. 'Secrets that our master would know.'

The man wore the mauve robes of the Brotherhood, though he wore no mask. Instead, the skin of his face had been dyed oil-black. Gleaming slivers of glass sat where his eyes should have been, sparkling even in the low-light of the chamber.

Fratris Crucio.

Appollus recognised his visitor from the numerous engagement reports and after-action accounts he'd studied. The Brotherhood's master interrogators were infamous throughout the Khandax warzone. Tales of their atrocities drifted from foxhole to foxhole, hushed whispers that crept along the trench line. Fratris Crucio, a byword for terror. Storm-coated officers of the Commissariat had adopted the stories as their own. It kept the men of the Imperial Guard fearful, alert. Vigilance along the watch-line absolute. To be captured by them was to suffer a fate far worse than simple death.

Appollus spat in the torturer's face.

The man tumbled back screaming, clawing at his face as the acid-saliva burned away his flesh. His companion knelt down over him but did nothing to ease his torment, simply inclining his head and watching as the acid ate into his brethren's eyes.

'Your strength will not serve you.' The torturer said finally, picking up the fallen blade and pushing it into Appollus's ribs. 'It will not last.'

The pain was excruciating but Appollus did not cry out.

It was the least of his worries. Pain was temporary, ended by absolution or death; a slight inflicted upon his body and no more. But what the pain stirred in him – the anger, the bloodlust – that was terror. It thundered in his veins, threatening to drown his organs in a tide of red and rage. He would not allow himself to succumb to the curse; such a fate had no end.

Appollus closed off his mind from the pain. He

pictured the High Basilica back on Cretecia, his Chapter's fortress home world. Tens of thousands of candles burned along the stone edges of the basilica's aisles. One flickering memorial for each Flesh Tearer who had donned the black armour of death. The red of the candle wax was used to seal the saltires and affix the litany parchments to the armour of every new Death Company Space Marine. As a novitiate in the Chaplaincy, Appollus had spent years tending to the candles as he recited the catechism of observance; a decade-long mass that armoured his mind and allowed him to walk among the damned of his Chapter, untouched by their madness.

He lost himself in the memory, beginning anew the observance as his torturers continued to violate his flesh.

'HE HAS SAID nothing, lord. He will not speak.' The Crucio bowed as he entered the chamber, keeping his eyes fixed on the black curvature of his master's armoured feet.

Abasi Amun, encased in full battle plate, sat on an immense throne wrought from the ore-rich stone of the cavern around him. He was still, unmoving, like a sculpture stolen from the grand halls of a monarch.

'Nothing?' Abasi Amun's voice rumbled around the cavern. The metallic resonance of his helmet's vox-caster sounding machine-harsh in the enclosed space.

'He does not scream, lord.'

'Then you have failed me.' Amun said, standing.

'No, no. Perhaps...' the Crucio stammered, his mouth dry with fear.. 'Perhaps he knows nothing.'

Amun shot forwards in a heartbeat, flowing like

black water across the chamber's expanse to lift the torturer by his neck. The Crucio gasped, his hands grasping in vain at Amun's gauntlet.

'He hides something, a truth.' With a flick of his wrist, Amun snapped the Crucio's neck. 'I sensed it on the battlefield, he keeps something from us,' Amun continued, talking to the limp corpse in his hand. 'I will know his secret.'

Amun brought the corpse closer and whispered. 'I will know.'

PAIN. APPOLLUS AWOKE with a start, expecting the sharp kiss of a blade or the cruel attentions of a neural flail. There was no trace of either. A lone figure stood before him, cloaked in shadow. The jagged light from the oil burners seemed to avoid the figure, flickering around the edges of his form but never quite illuminating him.

Appollus bared his teeth in a growl. He needn't see his enemy to know him. He could hear the figure's twin hearts thump like an indomitable engine in his chest. The shadow before him was an Adeptus Astartes. Greatest among traitors, a true pawn of the arch-enemy. A Chaos Space Marine.

Blood rushed to Appollus's muscles as he tensed against his restraints. The hatred locked into his genetic code willed him to rend the figure apart, to strike him dead. He bit down a growl. There was something else, something more. It clawed at his mind like a burrowing rodent. He could smell it. Hiding among the pungent, oleaginous balms the Traitor Marine used to maintain his armour was the foul, corrupting stench of the warp.

'Psyker,' Appollus snarled.

'You are observant, for a puppet of a false god.' The Chaos Space Marine paced forwards, throwing off the shadows the way a man might remove a cowl. 'Where you look only to the blood of your crippled father for strength, I have embraced the power of the great Changer.' The Traitor Marine flexed his arms. 'His limitless majesty feeds my veins.'

The warrior's power armour was mirror-black, its edges rounded and its surface polished to an impossible sheen. Yet it reflected nothing of the chamber. Its smooth plates were devoid of Chapter insignia and symbols of loyalty. Appollus averted his gaze. The armour was hard to look upon. It was at once dark and formless, yet as solid as the rock walls surrounding them.

Appollus looked again; he had seen its like before. 'You were there, in battle.'

The Traitor Marine dipped his head in mock deference. 'I am Abasi Amun. How should I address you, Chaplain?'

Appollus looked up at Amun's breastplate, surprised to now see his reflection staring back at him, though the tortured figure he looked upon bared little resemblance to how he had last seen himself.

The Crucio had been studious in their work.

The master torturers had administered a potent mix of toxins that had retarded his Larraman's organ and prevented his body from healing as it otherwise might. Hundreds of deep lacerations and patches of dark bruises covered his body. Several layers of skin had been shaved away from his abdomen, exposing the dermis. His face was gaunt, sapped of its chiselled sternness. Appollus met his own gaze, looked deep into his own eyes. They burned back at him with fierce intensity, reminding him of what he already knew – he would never break.

Appollus focused on the darkness of Amun's helm. 'Have you come seeking repentance, traitor?'

Amun laughed, a booming sound, incongruous with his subtle, insubstantial presence.

'My Crucio have broken many of your kind. But you, you defy me still. So close to death and yet you will part with none of your secrets.' Amun moved behind Appollus. The pressure seals around his gorget gave a popping hiss as he unclasped his helm.

'If your body will not give me the truths I seek, then I shall take them from your mind.'

Appollus snarled, his eyes fixed on the wall opposite him. 'I warn you, traitor. To know my secret, is to forfeit your life.'

Amun grabbed Appollus, his gauntleted fingers a vice around the Chaplain's throat.

'You are in no position to make threats, Chaplain.' Amun relaxed his grip. 'Save your piety. These are the final moments of your existence.' Amun removed his gauntlets as he spoke. 'I will find my answers. I will offer up your soul to my master and leave your body to rot, like the kingdom of your father.'

Amun's eyes crackled with eldritch lightning that leapt to his outstretched palms. He curled his fingers back. The energy coalesced into a flickering ball of white fire. The temperature dropped below zero as Amun muttered a prayer in an inhuman tongue. Blood ran from Appollus's orifices as frost began to rime his limbs.

'I know... no fear.' Appollus muttered, forcing his tongue to work through the viscous fluid filling his mouth.

The fireball drifted from Amun into Appollus's torso, breaking into a fulgurant web that coursed over his flesh then vanished beneath it.

Appollus screamed.

Amun ripped into Appollus's mind. In an agonising instant, the mental barriers that had taken the Chaplain decades to erect were torn asunder. His way unbarred, Amun proceeded with more care. Haste or disregard would leave Appollus a dribbling husk, his mind ruined and his secrets lost forever.

The chains binding Appollus rattled like weapons-fire as his body jerked. His skin rippled like water as half-clotted blood slid in thick clumps from his nostrils.

Amun cut deeper. He peeled away the surface thoughts that floated in Appollus's conscious mind and prized apart the lies of memory. Blood ran from the Chaplain's lips as they gave voice to a near constant stream.

Alone in the inner reaches of Appollus's mind, Amun snarled. The Flesh Tearer was close to death, but the truth still eluded him. Abandoning his earlier care, Amun burned to the Chaplain's essence. He would know, he must.

'There...' Amun's mortal body mouthed the word as his psychic tendrils found the truth he had been searching for.

Even as he touched upon it, Amun knew he had made a mistake. The Chaplain had no knowledge of the wider Imperial forces, he knew nothing of troop dispersments or defence plans. His secret was far more potent, far deadlier. He concealed a rage, wrath in its purest form. A burning halo fire that wrapped around his soul like a serpent. Amun tried to run to withdraw his mind back to the safety of his body. But it was too late. The rage had found a new home, a new vessel to enact its bloody will, and it would not be denied its prize.

Abasi Amun screamed.

The door swung open. Two of the Brotherhood burst in, their lasguns trained on Appollus.

'Lord Amun…'

Abasi roared and ran at the guards, knocking them to the floor. A panicked lasgun-round scored Appollus's thigh. Another clipped his bonds, burning a deep score in the metal links.

The guards screamed in desperate horror as Amun set about them. He was a starved creature, a cornered beast hunched on all fours. He growled, low and feral as he ripped the two cultists apart with his bare hands and sank his teeth into their flesh.

'While I breathe, I am wrath.' Appollus snarled with effort as he snapped the bonds holding his wrists and swung up to break the chains around his ankles. His shoulder crunched like split kindling as he hit the ground.

Amun rounded on him, saliva and bloodied flesh-chunks dripping from his mouth.

In full battle plate, the sorcerer was more than a match for the naked and battered Appollus. But under the rage's thrall, the Traitor Marine was frenzied, uncoordinated. Appollus had fought among such warriors for longer than most men lived. He could read Amun's strikes before the warrior threw them.

Slipping a right hook, Appollus spun the lengths of loose chain dangling from his wrists around his fists, and punched Amun in the face. Blood fountained from his ruined nose, spraying Appollus's face crimson.

The Chaos Space Marine struck back with a flurry of reaching swipes. Appollus rode their momentum, absorbing their impact on his arms, though a shooting pain told of a fractured humerus. He snarled, stepping inside Amun's guard to deliver an uppercut. The sorcerer's head jerked backwards. Appollus followed it, landing two consecutive blows, before grabbing the back of Amun's head and pulling him into a headbutt.

Amun roared as he staggered backwards, lashing out with his foot at Appollus's legs.

The ceramite boot cracked Appollus's shin and knocked him to the floor. The Chaplain rolled to his feet, limping to keep the weight from his damaged leg and cursing himself for getting too close. He couldn't afford to be careless, he had to keep his own bloodlust in check.

Amun growled as he regained his footing, a stream of saliva washing from his mouth to hiss on the chamber floor. The smell of Appollus's blood was like a knife in his brain. He needed to taste it, to devour the marrow in the Chaplain's bones, to savour every last scrap of his flesh. Roaring, Amun charged.

Pain ran like molten steel in Appollus's veins as he darted forwards, turning around Amun to loop his shackles over the Chaos Space Marine's throat. The movement brought him around and onto Amun's back. He forced the chains tight, his arms burning with the effort as Amun fought to buck him.

Amun dropped to one knee, a gurgling roar dying in his throat as his wind-pipe collapsed. He thrashed at Appollus in a mix of panic and rage as the beast within him struggled against death.

'Die, traitor.' The words ground from between Appollus's bloodied teeth as he wrenched Amun's head from his shoulders.

Even in death, Amun's body continued to fight, his adrenaline-soaked limbs twitching in denial as his corpse shivered on the ground.

'Your place is at our enemy's throat.'

Luciferus's words resurfaced in Appollus's mind as he watched Amun grind against the stone of the floor in the last spasms of his death throes.

'Your blood be cursed,' Appollus snarled, bending to retrieve Amun's blade. He would speak with the vulpine Librarian when next they crossed paths.

Coated in blood, both the traitor's and his own, Appollus was reminded of the crimson armour he'd donned before his ordination. 'In blood we are one. Immortal, while one remains to bleed.' Using his teeth to scrape a finger clean, Appollus guided a bead of saliva around his chest, burning the toothed-blade symbol of his Chapter into his breast.

THE IRON LIFT rattled to a stop with a sharp grinding of gears. Appollus threw open the mesh door and stepped into the corridor, leaving the crumpled bodies of two Brotherhood to bleed out behind him. He felt his pulse quicken as he thought of the moment his fingers had closed around the first's aorta, and remembered the satisfying snap of the second's neck.

They were the third patrol he'd come across since his escape. He hoped they would not be the last.

'His blood is strength.' Appollus mouthed the axiom as he stalked, a little unsteady on his feet, along the corridor. The exertion of his escape had forced the bulk of the Crucio's toxins from his system, adrenaline washing through him like a cleansing fire, and dark scabs of crusted blood covered his torso where his flesh had begun knitting itself back together. But he still ached to his bones, a pungent sweat clothing his body.

Appollus touched a hand to his head, rubbing his skin-starved knuckles into his temples. The psyker's touch still lingered in that pain. But pain wasn't the only thing Amun had left him with. As he fought to stave off the rage, the Chaos Space Marine had been careless. In his panic, he had let his surface thoughts spill out; a tumultuous wave of half-formed images that had bombarded Appollus's untrained mind. The psychic noise had been like harsh bursts of static filtered through a howling gale. Yet Appollus had done more than hold on to his sanity. With iron-willed devotion and unyielding resolve, he had focused on his duty, on his brothers.

Appollus stopped as he reached a bend in the corridor, recognising every glint of ore in the wall ahead. Zakiel, Xaphan, Herchel and Ziel; the four Death Company were alive. If what he'd gleaned from Amun's mind was true then they were languishing in a cell at the end of the corridor. He pressed his back against the wall, feeling his muscles tense as the sharp rock tore into his skin, and listened.

There were two of the Brotherhood patrolling the

corridor. Appollus ground his teeth, feeling his anger grow with every thump of their traitorous hearts. He listened to the fall of their booted feet, to the clack of their weapons as they swung loose on straps. His pulse raced as the stink of their unwashed flesh drifted to his nostrils. A red mist mustered behind his eyes. A tremor passed through his hands, forcing his fists into balls of sinew. The urge to kill was great. He looked down at the Chapter symbol on his breast as he waited and let out a slow breath of calm. Rage was not yet his master.

He waited. He counted. Focusing on the guards' footsteps, he waited until the distance was right.

'I am death!' Appollus rounded the corner and threw his knife into the chest of the nearest of them. Running, he caught the body on his shoulder before it fell, and charged towards the second. The man spun round, startled, sweeping up his lasgun and opening fire. Appollus felt his corpse-shield shudder as a half dozen rounds cut into it, and snarled as a round sliced the flesh from his bicep. A second later he barrelled into the guard, tackling him to the ground. Appollus recovered first, pinning the cultist beneath him and thundering a fist into his face. He hit him again and again, deaf to the cracking of bone and ignorant of the visceral lumps of brain matter that dripped from under the cultist's mask. Only when his fist struck rock, did Appollus stop.

The reek of torture greeted Appollus as he entered the cell, hitting him as surely as any blow. He snarled in disgust, craving the air-filtering properties of his battle helm. The four Death Company hung from the ceiling, chained in the same manner as he had been. He growled, angered by the extent the Crucio had violated their bodies. Ziel was in the worst state, the skin of his left forearm peeled back to reveal bone. Their eyes widened as he approached. They wanted to kill. Even over the stench he could smell their bloodlust. He wouldn't keep them waiting. Raising the lasgun he'd stripped from the Brotherhood guards, he shot through their bonds.

'Brothers.' Appollus spread his arms. 'I feel your thirst.' He thrust an arm out, jabbing his blade towards the door, 'The enemy are many, but they are flesh. We, are immortal lords of battle. We are wrath. We are death.'

The Death Company growled, shaking their limbs loose, their fists opening and closing as they sought to rend.

'Kill until killed. Leave none alive.'

Appollus watched them go, surprised by how much effort it took not to follow them. He ached to join the Death Company in slaughter. The Brotherhood had wrought a terrible injustice upon him, and he vowed he would see it drowned from his memory by a river of their blood. But he had gleaned more than his brothers' location from Amun's mind, and he had another task to attend to first.

THE CAVERN WAS immense. The largest by far that Appollus had encountered. Banks of luminators hung on racks of chain, suspended from the ore-rich rock of the ceiling. Plasteel panels had been bolted down over the rock of the floor to create something resembling a functioning hangar. Rusted supply crates were heaped in small clusters around the walls.

At the far end of the chamber, an antiquated Storm-bird drop-ship sat locked to the deck. Its oil-black flanks were polished clean of insignia. The armour on one of its wings had been peeled back, exposing the plasteel frame beneath. Fuel cables and pressure hoses hugged its sides like creeper-vines. Beyond it, a flickering energy shield kept out the infinite void.

Appollus stared through the electro-haze of the shield. The surface of the asteroid stretched as far as he could see, a pitted landscape of undulating rock and trenched gullies. If what he'd learned from Amun was correct, the damaged Stormbird was the only transport off this rock.

Shouldering his stolen lasgun, he moved towards the drop-ship. The weapon was lighter than he was used to, like a child's toy compared to the reassuring weight of his bolter. The lasgun followed his eyes as he scanned for targets. A trio of Brotherhood cultists rounded the Stormbird. Appollus fired, killing them without breaking stride. He ground his teeth. He missed the reassuring bark of his boltgun; the clinical snap of the lasgun was far removed from the visceral booming of mass-reactive rounds.

Klaxons screamed from what sounded like every surface. Strobing red light filled the cavern and cast wicked shadows among the rock. The resounding thud of booted feet warned Appollus of threats to his left and rear. The Brotherhood were spilling into the chamber from every angle.

He snarled as weapons-fire began competing with the klaxons, las-rounds cutting the air around him. Firing in blazing streams on full-auto, Appollus cut down the forerunners. He grinned darkly as the familiar tang of blood filled the air, and continued moving towards the drop-ship. The remaining Brotherhood approached with more caution, ducking back behind what little cover they could find. He counted at least sixty of them as he panned his weapon around, slamming in a spare powercell as the charge counter flashed empty.

To his left, an arm reached up to throw a grenade. He shot it off at the elbow. Its owner cried out an instant before the explosive detonated. Gobbets of flesh and bloodied robe fountained into the air. *Fifty-seven.* Appollus updated his mental tally as he ducked under the tangle of fuel feeds.

The Brotherhood stopped firing.

Appollus used the moment's respite to assess his options. The Brotherhood had formed a firing perimeter. A few had unsheathed blades and were edging towards him. He smiled. They were waiting for him to break for the Stormbird, but he had never had any intention of boarding the vessel.

Appollus opened the intake valve in the nearest fuel hose and lifted the locking catch. Choking promethium vapour wafted out, forcing a cough from his lungs. Appollus ejected the powercell from his lasgun and struck it hard with the hilt of his knife.

'He is my shield.'

Appollus dropped the sparking energy cell into the fuel pipe and ran. He ran with all the speed his enhanced physiology could muster. He ran like a man racing to the side of imperilled loved ones. He ran in the only direction the Brotherhood hadn't refused him. He ran towards the energy barrier.

Shutting his eyes to protect them from the shield's

glare, Appollus threw himself through the barrier and out into the void.

Less than a heartbeat later, the Stormbird detonated, the promethium in its fuel tanks exploding outwards in a halo of fire.

Too late, the Brotherhood realised what Appollus had done.

The nearest of them were incinerated in the initial blast, vaporised where they stood. The others fled as best they could. Flaming shrapnel chased them across the chamber, tearing through flesh and bone with all the care of a maddened butcher.

Appollus watched as the rolling carpet of flame pushed out through the energy shield and vanished, its ire stolen by the airless void. He followed the fire's retreat, diving back through the barrier and rolling to his feet.

Shards of burning metal littered the chamber. The broken and torn corpses of dozens of Brotherhood cultists were strewn about like discarded dolls. Some of the traitors were still screaming, thrashing around as their faceplates seared their skin, the thin metal super-heated by the blast. The smell of cooked blood hung in the air, as tangible as the ground beneath Appollus's feet.

Fire and the flickering, red light conspired to recreate the Hell described in ancient Terran myth. Appollus smiled as he strode through the carnage: that made him the Daevil.

The remaining Brotherhood staggered from cover, their robes singed and ragged. They moved without purpose, staring at the smouldering wreck of the drop-ship, gripped by disbelief at what had transpired.

Appollus paced towards them. Smoke drifted in wistful columns from his limbs, his void-frozen skin singed by the heat of the energy shield.

A bleeding Crucio, his face knotted in confusion, glared at Appollus. 'Fool. That was the only ship.' The Crucio indicated a smouldering crater filled with tangled ceramite and plasteel plating. 'You are trapped here with us.' He spread his arms to indicate the rest of the Brotherhood who had recovered enough to ready their weapons. 'When I'm done with you, all the pain you have suffered thus far in your miserable life will seem like an eternity of ecstasy. On your flesh I shall redefine the art of my sect. I will hear you beg for death, *Chaplain*.'

'No, heretic.' Appollus stopped ten paces from the nearest cultist. He took a breath and looked down at the knife in his hand. Pulling back his broad shoulders, he straightened to his full height and raised his knife towards the Crucio. 'You are mistaken.'

At the rear of the chamber, a lift rattled and bucked to a stop, its iron grate swinging open.

'It is you who are trapped here with us.'

The Crucio looked over his shoulder.

Behind him, Zakiel, Xaphan, Herchel and Ziel paced into the cavern, bloodied blades grasped white-knuckle tight in their murderous hands.

Appollus smelled the torturer's fear and smiled.

'Fear not, *torturer*,' Appollus snarled. 'You will not have time to beg.'

VOX DOMINUS

by Anthony Reynolds

PART ONE

She had no face.

Or at least, not a face that he could discern.

Whenever he tried to focus on her, her features became blurred and smudged, like an over-developed pict image. Indeed, even to try made his eyes hurt. If he looked at her askance, focusing past her, he could see something of her features. They were unremarkable, it seemed. Air tubes fed into her nostrils, and her expression was blank. But whenever his gaze was drawn closer again, trying to discern more, her face would fade into obscurity.

He was as a ghost, floating weightless and insubstantial, unconstrained by his physical flesh-prison. He had cloaked himself in protective wards and enacted the letting-rituals that would hide his presence. But still *she turned her blurred child's face up towards him.*

She saw him. Her power was astonishing. She pierced his aegis without effort.

'Daal'ak'ath mel caengr'aal,' she said, in a long-dead tongue that he nevertheless understood. 'The blightwood grows.'

A convulsion wracked his earth-bound body back on the **Infidus Diabolus.** For a moment he was in both places at once. He could smell the powerful incense coiling around him, could hear the chant of his Host and feel the vibration of the ship's engines. Yet he was also in the fathomless ocean of unreality, where the vision had brought him, surrounded by nebulous darkness and the powerful psychic void-presence of this girl.

The vision began to shatter like a flawed crystal, threatening to send him crashing back to his body. It cracked and splintered, leaving just the girl's blurred face, looming close in to his own. He could not look away.

He could see her eyes now. She allowed him to see them. Galaxies shone in their fathomless black depths. She looked through him.

He tried to retreat, willing himself back to his body, but she held him, ensnaring him with her will. Her face was close now, filling his vision. It shivered, violently, shaking and shimmering before him.

A bewildering array of images, sensations and feelings flashed through his mind then, an overwhelming display. She was showing him these things. She wanted him to see them.

Later, when he returned to his flesh, he would be unable to recall exactly what he saw. Vague impressions and sensations would be all that he was left with: skies of burning yellow, an oppressive drone of a billion melancholy *daemonic voices; a slender woman's face, shining like milk and moonlight, tears running down her face. She was in a place of darkness, surrounded by movement. He saw a single blue eye, so clear and so perfect, with three pupils that jutted together to form one.*

Devoid of context he could not understand them, nor perceive their purpose.

Lastly, he would remember that phrase. 'Daal'ak'ath mel caengr'aal'. The blightwood grows.

The child – whatever she was – had seen the face of gods, and she had not baulked before them.

Then she pushed him away with her tiny child's hands, sending his spirit hurtling through the void, spinning out of control, and the lightning flash of images and sensations was severed.

Back on the *Infidus Diabolus*, Marduk smiled.

THE BLACK-EYED CHERUBS exhaled a heady smoke and he breathed it in, letting it coil within his lungs as he rose from the waking dream. To a lesser being, the incense would have been fatal. To the Dark Apostle it was merely an aid in communing with the Dwellers Beyond. The poisons it contained helped open his soul, the better for the gods to speak their will through his flesh. Still, their message was often confused and difficult to discern.

Who was the faceless girl? What message did she have for him? One thing he was sure of was that he must possess her. He must have her knowledge. He must have her power.

The Host was gathered in prayer in the expansive cavaedium at the heart of the *Infidus Diabolus*, but the Dark Apostle was alone, unobserved and hidden from view, away from his congregation. He knelt before a shrine covered in candles and braziers. Fire and faith danced in his eyes. Shadows writhed in the darkness beyond the candlelight.

The martyry he prayed within was dedicated to his former master, Jarulek. He liked to come here to worship – it made him feel close to his gods. It had been he who had ended Jarulek's life, after all, an action that had clearly been ordained by the Ruinous Ones.

No one within the Host knew the dark secret of Jarulek's death, of course, though many no doubt suspected, Marduk's Coryphaus among them. This pleased him. Jarulek was a fearsome warrior-priest and beloved of both Council and gods. Any warrior able to best him would be rightly feared.

Besides, Marduk himself sat on the Council now. His power and reach had surpassed that of Jarulek. Truly, the gods had blessed him.

The morbid chanting of the Host surrounded Marduk, embracing him and echoing around the enclosed space of the martyry. Behind it, barely audible, other sounds could be discerned. Hisses, groans, muffled screams. Those beyond the veil of existence were making themselves heard. The denizens of the living ether were joining the Host in prayer. It was a good sign.

The service had entered its final movement. The droning reaffirmation of faith was led, as ever, by the Coryphaus. The Host's newly appointed First Acolyte had completed his ritual sermon and gloriatus, and the doxastika was now nearing its conclusion.

Enusat. The new First Acolyte. Marduk had personally

chosen him, picking him from among a wide field of aspirants. Though there had been many more likely candidates presented to him on Sicarus, postulants handpicked for larger things from among the Hosts of other Dark Apostles, he had chosen Enusat from within his own ranks – never again would he allow an outsider to hold a position of influence within the Thirty-Fourth, not after his last Acolyte's treachery.

What Enusat lacked in formal teachings and religious indoctrination, he made up for in other ways, ways that could not be learnt by rote or by any amount of studying the Urizen's holy scriptures. He was highly regarded within the Host and respected by all. What's more, Marduk trusted him, utterly and implicitly, as he trusted few others. Such loyalty was to be valued. Everything else could be learned.

Most First Acolytes harboured dreams of power, always looking for their moment to overthrow their master. Such was the accepted way of things in the Legion, and Marduk himself had certainly fallen into that camp. He had no such fears with Enusat, however. He was a wardog, fierce and utterly loyal; a devout killer with an unwavering sense of duty. Tell him to saw off his own arm and he would, without question or hesitation.

Marduk felt the presence of an attendant hovering at the martyry's entrance. He could smell the foetid odour of its decaying flesh, and could hear the uneven rasp of its breath. It had been lurking there for some time, but it knew better than to disturb his meditations.

The final, doleful verses of the doxastika were intoned, and a deep, resounding bell tolled. Silence filled the void.

Marduk rose to his feet, servos in his revered battle plate purring softly. His armour had been with him since he had been first embraced into the Legion, and was as much a part of him as his own flesh.

For a time after the Boros Gate campaign, he had worn the ancient Terminator armour that had once belonged to the Warmonger, but the bond had not been the same. To not wear his own engraved plate felt akin to missing a limb, and while the Terminator armour was powerful, he had disliked the sensation of restriction it brought to his movement.

His own armour itched beneath his skin now, fusing to him, joining with his flesh and bone. Perhaps it was jealous and sought to ensure it was never removed from him again. The notion did not concern him. What need had he to remove it?

He turned. His face was hidden in shadow, backlit as he was by the braziers and candlelight. Only his left eye could be seen, burning with lurid witch-fire.

He towered over the hunched servant cowering before him.

'Speak,' he said.

'We near our destination, revered one,' hissed the robed creature, keeping its gaze obediently downcast. 'The time of translation is near.'

'Good,' said Marduk. 'See that the Coryphaus and First Acolyte join me on the bridge.'

'As you will it, revered one.'

The pitiful creature backed away, bowing as it retreated, but Marduk gave it no mind. His mind was already occupied, projecting forth to the battle ahead. Too long had he been cloistered in the halls of Sicarus.

His left hand closed around the haft of his crozius,

and he felt a thrill rush through his enhanced system. He longed to kill. He ached for it.

It was time to praise the dark gods in the manner that pleased them most – by killing in their name. It was time to worship in the purifying fires of battle.

FROM NOTHINGNESS THE *Infidus Diabolus* burst into reality, trailing etheric afterbirth. Kilometres in length, its powerful form was protected by thick adamantium plating and shimmering void shields. Weapon banks bristled along its flanks, raised like the hackles of a threatened beast. Crenellations, domed templum roofs and skeletal cathedral spires ran down its spine.

The veil was thin here on the edge of the Eye, and the void was stained with swirls of colour. Dark shades of red and orange were cut through with ribbons of purple and blue, coiling and running together like oils atop a film of water. A trio of dying suns lit the Word Bearers strike cruiser from different angles, casting it in shades of deepest crimson.

A second ship flashed into existence alongside the *Infidus Diabolus*. Thousands of kilometres separated them, but in the emptiness such distances were as nothing. Indeed, most naval battles fought in the void were conducted at a range well beyond human sight, slow moving ballets that ended in the silent deaths of tens of thousands at a time.

These two ships, however, were not engaged in void war. They were not foes. Nevertheless, neither were they unguarded in each other's presence. They kept a respectful, wary distance from each other, like predators that chose to hunt together for mutual benefit, while knowing they would turn on each other as soon as prey became scarce.

The second ship was the *Vox Dominus*, and it dwarfed the *Infidus Diabolus*. It was a hulking battleship, Carrion-class, and though it was lacking in speed and grace, it was utterly brutal in short-ranged engagements, able to cripple and tear apart all but the most heavily armoured of capital ships.

It was the pride of the Third Host, a mighty vessel that had spread the word of Lorgar from one end of the galaxy to the other for millennia. Once it had been called the *Vox Domina*, but that had changed along with the focus of the Legion's worship long before the nature of the Dwellers Beyond had even been fathomed by the other Legions.

Rippling waves of the living warp shimmered across the ships' forms for a moment, like a parting caress from the gods themselves, before the last vestiges of the ether were shed.

A flare of light lit one of the *Vox Dominus*'s shadowed launch bays and an escort shuttle designated *Lux Aeterna* spat forth, hurtling across the void between the two ships. It appeared tiny and insignificant as it closed the gap between the two battleships, a tiny mote of dust in the unfathomable, empty expanse.

'Shuttle inbound,' croaked a servitor hard-wired into the command console of the *Infidus Diabolus*. 'Do we engage?'

A wry smile curled at Marduk's lips.

'I'm not sure that the Third Host would appreciate it if we turned our guns upon their revered Dark Apostle,' he said.

'Do we engage?' repeated the slaved creature, its putrefying flesh twitching spasmodically.

Marduk sighed. 'Do not,' he said.

'Open embarkation deck thirteen-four,' said Kol Badar. 'Disengage automated defence turrets.'

'Acknowledged,' drooled another half-mechanical wretch.

'Should we not go to meet him, master?' said First Acolyte Enusat.

His gaze was utterly without guile, but nor was it weak. Indeed, no one could ever accuse Enusat of weakness, for it was not a fault he possessed. Quite the opposite. He had a reputation for stubbornness and tenacity, and had depths of endurance that put the rest of the Host to shame. His faith was stronger than steel.

Marduk knew that if he ordered it, Enusat would unsheathe his ceremonial kantanka knife and draw it across his own throat. He'd do it willingly if that was his Dark Apostle's wish, and if the hyper-coagulants in his demi-god's blood sealed the wound before it claimed his life, he would open his veins a second time.

Uncomplaining, uncompromising and fanatically devout, Enusat was the embodiment of what it was to be a Word Bearer. He was a truly ugly whoreson, however.

He had a face that looked like it had been immersed in acid. It looked that way because it had, in fact, been immersed in acid. It had also been shot, repeatedly beaten, burned and cut, so much that it now resembled little more than a roughly head-shaped lump of tortured flesh, from which two pale eyes peered at the world. His nose was swollen and shapeless, and his mouth was an angry slash. His teeth were made from dark steel, his own having long ago been smashed from his jaw.

Prayer beads and rosaries hung from his wrists and at his belt, and selected holy epistles from the *Book of Lorgar* had been scrimshawed across the plates of his armour. A tattered, blood-stained wolf skin, ripped from the corpse of a defeated priest of Russ, hung across his shoulders, and a scroll case carved from the thigh bone of the Hex-Deacon Hannaknut hung from his waist, containing an illuminated page from the holy *Lamentations of Betrayal*, a gift that Marduk had given him on the day he had been ordained as the Host's new First Acolyte.

His armour was of an old mark, and heavily-modified. His greaves were bulky with the additional plating and stabilisers that marked him as a heavy weapons specialist. A powerfully built warrior, he stood Marduk's equal in height, though his wide shoulders made him seem larger. Both, however, were overshadowed by the Terminator-armoured Coryphaus.

'Let him wait,' said Marduk.

'He will not like it,' said Enusat.

'And that is exactly the point,' said Marduk. 'I am of the Council now. Nahren must learn his place in the order of things.'

'I understand, master,' said Enusat, bowing his head.

'Petty games and politics,' growled Kol Badar. 'It achieves nothing but to spread the seed of resentment.'

'A necessary evil,' said Marduk. 'What the esteemed Coryphaus fails to understand is–'

The Dark Apostle's words were forgotten as a warning light began to throb, accompanied by a grating alarm.

'What is it?' demanded Kol Badar.

'Unidentified etheric surge,' replied a slaved servitor. 'Quadrant X.P. Ninety-nine point three point two.'

'Another ship making transference?' said Marduk.

'I don't think so,' said Kol Badar, scanning the stream of data feeding across the curved black monitors above the bridge's command console. 'It doesn't read like that kind of signature. Warp anomaly, more likely.'

'Master,' said First Acolyte Enusat. He had moved closer to the broad viewing oculus and was staring out into the void. Marduk joined him. 'There,' said Enusat, pointing.

Beyond the *Vox Dominus*, the void was churning. The garish green and purple swirls smeared across the emptiness were coiling towards a point beyond the hulking battleship.

'That does not look good,' said Marduk.

The bleeding colours of the void were being drawn in behind the holy *Vox Dominus* with increasing vigour, spinning faster, creating a kaleidoscopic whirlpool to the vessel's aft.

Its engines were flaring as it attempted to extricate itself from the danger, but it was a cumbersome ship and not built for rapid manoeuvring. Having only just emerged from the warp, its plasma engines were not even close to operating at full power.

'How close is it?' asked Marduk.

'Too close,' replied Kol Badar. 'All power to primary thrusters. Get us away from that thing.'

The void rippled. A rent in the fabric of reality tore open in the centre of the swirling maelstrom behind the *Vox Dominus*, sucking matter and anti-matter into it like a siphon. For a brief moment, a place distinctly *other* could be glimpsed through that gaping window, a place of noxious yellow skies and dying worlds. Immense tentacle things coiled within sulphuric clouds, things the size of planets.

'Gods above,' breathed Enusat.

'Yellow skies,' murmured Marduk.

Enusat could feel something – it gnawed at the back of his mind, scratching inside his skull. It was disturbing but not an altogether unpleasant sensation, like a host of unintelligible voices whispering in his head, the sounds blurring together into one sonorous babble.

Despite the power being re-routed to its engines, the *Infidus Diabolus* was being drawn inexorably backwards. The ship groaned in protest, the drag of the warp anomaly fighting against the impetus of its engines. Straining metal shuddered and screeched as the ship gave voice to its torment.

It was not the only vessel being affected.

The *Vox Dominus*, so much closer to the warp anomaly, had no hope of pulling away. It was being inexorably drawn into the gaping rent in unreality.

Enusat grabbed on to a spiked railing for balance as the ship was hauled off centre, still staring out into the vacuum beyond the oculus. Almost half of the *Vox Dominus* had been pulled through the rift now, its back section existing in that daemonic otherworld. Then, with one final surge, it gave up its fight, and was sucked fully through. The rift slammed shut behind it, sending a ripple through the void that shook the *Infidus Diabolus* to its core.

Warning alarms blared. Viewscreens flickered, and the lights on the bridge dimmed. Every Word Bearer aboard the strike cruiser felt an uncomfortable wrench in their forsaken soul as the wave passed through them, a nauseating imbalance that made them reel.

Marduk suffered more than most, for his link to the warp was the strongest. His world spun, and he dropped to one knee, clutching at the command console for balance. He clenched his eyes tightly shut as intense pain lanced through his mind. Black bile rose in his throat, and he spat it onto the deck. Its acidic touch made the floor-grill steam and hiss.

Then the moment passed and power was restored to the bridge. Enusat reached instinctively to help the Dark Apostle, but he stayed his hand at the last moment.

'Very wise,' snarled Marduk, having seen the movement, as he hauled himself to his feet unaided.

The Coryphaus was staring out into the void, and Marduk moved to his side.

Of the *Vox Dominus*, nothing could be seen. The anomaly too was gone, leaving just a patch of disturbed colour in its wake, still slowly spinning, before it became once again inert, as if nothing had happened.

'Inbound shuttle has touched down on deck thirteen-four,' said a servitor, breaking the silence.

Marduk swore. He had forgotten the Dark Apostle.

'Thank the gods he was not aboard the *Vox Dominus*,' said Enusat.

'A small mercy,' said Marduk. 'Now it just remains for us to tell him that his entire Host is missing.'

'We should move,' said Kol Badar. 'This area of the Eye is unstable.'

As if his words had been prophetic, another alarm began shrieking.

'Perfect,' said Marduk.

THE HOLE IN the universe tore open once more, precisely where it had been less than a minute earlier. Once again the *Infidus Diabolus* fought against its surging pull. But it was not the *Infidus Diabolus* the warp had come for. This time, the rift came bearing a gift.

A snub-nosed tug emerged from the swirling colour, an ugly vessel that appeared barely void-worthy. It was small, no larger than escort-sized, but its engines were immense for its size, and it was powerful enough to advance against the whirling pull of the warp rift. A massive chain was affixed beneath its aft.

It was dragging something into reality. Something huge.

'Well that's… unexpected,' said Kol Badar, staring at the unlikely sight.

Behind the tug, the *Vox Dominus* listed lifelessly as it was dragged from the spinning rent. Its engines were dead, and its plasma core cold. It was being hauled along like a carcass – the prize of a successful hunt. As it cleared the warp, the rift snapped shut behind it.

'Have Dark Apostle Nahren escorted here immediately,' said Marduk. 'He might like to see this.'

He stared at the tug vessel, as if his eyes might bore through its hull. There was something there… Something that called to him.

A previously inert servitor slaved into the control deck began to convulse.

'We are being hailed,' said Kol Badar.

'Bring it up on screen,' ordered Marduk.

A whitewash of static and crackling interference filled the oculus before resolving itself into a face that might once have been human but was now so warped and diseased that it was barely recognisable. Enusat's eyes widened.

'Death Guard,' spat Marduk.

HIS LEAN, IMPERIOUS face was as emotionless as stone. He did not speak. He did not move. Even the cold black points that were his eyes gave away little of the true fury burning within.

Dark Apostle Nahren had seen more wars than every other Word Bearer present on the bridge put together. He had fought alongside the Urizen, and was counted among the most loyal warrior priests in the holy order. Marduk himself had trained under Nahren as an acolyte, and knew him as an uncompromising, fierce and highly respected Dark Apostle.

The hyper-observant may have noticed he breathed slightly faster and shallower than was normal, or that a tinge of blood-shot colour had stained his otherwise colourless, hieretic-inscribed cheeks. Few would register such telltale signs, but Enusat read them as clearly as a tome laid bare before him. The Dark Apostle's rage was incandescent, and threatened to explode at any moment.

Enusat's enhanced biology interpreted that anger as the threat of violence and responded in kind, flooding his system with adrenaline and combat stimulants. Every Word Bearer present could taste the aggression in the air, and their nerves were on a knife-edge – every one of them was ready to kill, their gene-enhanced bodies primed for battle.

Nahren stared unblinking at the distorted face on the vid-screen.

'What. Did. It. Say?' he said, the muscles of his jaw twitching.

'Salvage,' said Kol Badar. 'They say they claimed the *Vox Dominus* as salvage.'

'Salvage,' said Nahren, his voice measured, yet barely held in check. '*Salvage?*'

Enusat watched, fascinated, as the Dark Apostle struggled to maintain his control. Nahren's armoured hands balled into fists, accompanied by the whine of servos and fibre-bundles flexing.

It was an unforgiveable insult to see the *Vox Dominus* treated in such a way, and their first instinct had been to annihilate the stocky tug vessel. Had its crew been simple pirates, the wreckage of their ship would already have been scattered to the four winds of Chaos.

No contact had yet been established with Nahren's Host. The *Vox Dominus* appeared completely lifeless.

Dark Apostle Nahren was accompanied by an honour guard of five mute Word Bearers, a tight-knit cabal of warriors known as the Bloodsworn. Enusat knew them by reputation. Veterans of Calth, they were the elite of the Third Host, its most favoured sons. The plates of their armour were archaic and ornate, stylised to resemble snarling daemons and gargoyles, and they were liberally hung with trophies, chains and religious icons. Their mouths had been ritually sutured shut with thick consecrated wires. Enusat was no psyker, and his connection to the warp was weaker than many within the Host, yet even so he could feel the presence of fettered daemons lurking within the souls of the Bloodsworn. They were potent warriors, indeed – and they were only five.

Five veterans, perhaps all that remained of the Third Host. Enusat could well understand Nahren's simmering rage.

Contact had been made, however, with the snub-nosed tug vessel. It had identified itself as the *Death's Head*, using old, pre-Isstvan Legion codes. In truth, it had only been those codes that had forestalled his master's hand. The Dark Apostle had been intrigued.

'Explain yourself, Death Guard,' said Kol Badar, speaking into the vox-link. 'The *Vox Dominus* is a holy vessel of the Seventeenth Legion. Explain to us how you justify claiming it as *salvage*.'

The reply was slow in coming, delayed by distance and warp interference. The distorted face on screen crackled and blurred, but the grimace it displayed might once have been classed as a smile, back when the malformed face had been capable of such an expression. Its shoulders rose and fell, and a horrible croak bubbled from the vox-unit.

Hor hor hor.

'Do I hear this wretched creature right?' asked Dark Apostle Nahren. 'Is it laughing at us? Truly?'

'Our patience wears thin, Death Guard,' said Kol Badar. 'Explain yourself. Why is it that we cannot make contact with the *Vox Dominus*? And how is it that you dare claim a holy vessel of the Seventeenth Legion as salvage?'

The creature's mouth – or what was left of it – began to move. Its rasping voice rattled through the vox-unit a moment later, completely out of synch with the movement.

'Most esteemed brethren of the... Seventeenth,' croaked the voice, 'I fear you must be... mistaken.' The words were slow and drawn out, deep and wet. It reminded Marduk of a corpse's death rattle. 'My soul-brothers and I... came upon this vessel, that which.... which you declaim as the... *Vox Dominus*... adrift, lost. Lifeless...'

'Lifeless?' erupted Nahren. 'What do you mean by that?'

'I can... perceive that our... brethren of the Seventeenth appear vexed by this revelation,' spoke the Death Guard legionary. It was difficult to judge if his voice was being affected by the poor communication link, or if he actually spoke in this drawn-out, painful manner. Somehow, Marduk suspected the latter. 'Nevertheless, it is... with... urgh... assurances most sincere that I present unto you the... truth of the matter.'

'We waste our time communing with this rotting fool,' said Nahren under his breath. 'Let us be done with it, and quickly.'

Marduk bowed his head in appeasement. 'Of course, Dark Apostle,' he said, soothingly. 'Once we have established under what circumstances these scavengers came upon the *Vox Dominus*, we will, of course, ensure you are quickly reunited with your Host.'

The Death Guard legionary continued on, unaware or uncaring of the interruption.

'...came upon the ship, adrift in the warp – unclaimed... moribund. Flotsam, nought but flotsam. Jetsam drifting... on the tides of the god-sea. All attempts... urgh... were made to contact any remaining crew... gnrrrr.... No response forth came.'

'This creature is insufferable,' said Kol Badar, muting his words so that they were not relayed. 'And to think we once called them brothers.'

'They are still our brothers,' said Marduk. 'They are the blessed children of Grandfather Nurgle, living embodiments of His favour. They are worthy of our respect, though they are clearly misguided in attempting to claim that which is not theirs to claim.'

'What does he mean, *adrift in the warp*?' asked Enusat. 'The *Vox Dominus* was only gone for a matter of minutes.'

'One minute and twenty-seven seconds, adjusted,' said Kol Badar.

'Re-open the vox,' said Nahren. Kol Badar's gaze flicked to Marduk, who nodded almost imperceptibly. A slight smile tinged his lips as he saw Nahren bristle. No Dark Apostle liked having his orders questioned.

'Why is it,' Nahren said, addressing the pixelated, distorted image of the XIV Legion warrior, 'that you claim the *Vox Dominus* was lifeless and floating adrift when we all know that is a lie?'

The Death Guard continued to chuckle. It was a horrible wet sound akin to some monstrous amphibian croaking. Or dying. Enusat could not decide.

Hor hor hor.

'It mocks us,' said Nahren. 'Bring your broadsides to bear. They have no void shields. They will soon change their tone.'

'Do not seek to give me orders,' said Marduk. 'You are a guest upon my bridge, Nahren, nothing more.'

Nahren's dark eyes locked on to Marduk's. Across the vox, the Death Guard's chuckle deepened, before descending into a hacking wet cough.

Hor hor urgh.

'Why is it that you laugh, Death Guard?' snarled Kol Badar.

'The *Vox Dominus* has been gone... urgh... far longer than you seem to understand,' drawled the foul figure filling the viewscreen.

'How long?' said Marduk, turning away from Nahren's wrathful gaze.

The Death Guard's answer silenced the bridge.

'In excess of... three thousand years.'

The *Invisus* was an ugly brute of a gunship, considerably smaller than a Stormbird. The Host had salvaged it a century earlier during a fire-fight with Red Corsair renegades on the fringe of the Maelstrom. Its paintwork was blistered, peeling and blackened by fire. Hooks and barbs protruded in rows down its body, like the spines of some feral world beast.

Once, perhaps, it had been nothing more than a cargo-transport, most probably designed to transport mining goods from worlds located precariously close to the borders of reality. In the years since, however, it had undergone considerable modification. The Corsairs had outfitted it with heavy armour plates and shield banks, though it was unarmed but for a pair of forward-mounted lascannons jutting from beneath its nose. It was more a shuttle than a warship.

Though far from the most elegant or powerful of

vessels, it had served the Host well since its capture. It had been honoured with the name *Invisus* and infused with a daemonic entity of a lesser pantheon, giving it a limited, belligerent sentience.

Marduk had a certain affection for it, though he knew it well enough not to fully trust it. It had learned to fear him, but he had no doubt that it would turn on him if it was ever presented with the opportunity. The trick was not to give it that chance. The notion did not overly concern him. It kept things interesting.

The *Invisus*'s engines gave a throaty growl as fresh blood was smeared across the underside of its fuselage. The wretched attendants undertaking this task hissed and jabbered under their breath as they worked, their repulsive bodies hidden beneath coarse black cloaks and cowls.

Several of the Host's warriors were moving around the exterior of the *Invisus*, chanting monotonously as they swung heavy censers back and forth. Thick clouds of incense infused with mind-altering herbs and bone dust billowed out in their wake, curling around the gunship like living tendrils, caressing it and infusing its being.

Marduk cut a jagged gash across his left palm, clenching and unclenching his hand into a fist to get the blood flowing. Intoning a benediction, he placed his bloody handprint upon the face of each of the Host's warriors who had been chosen to board the *Vox Dominus*. What they would find was anybody's guess.

Nahren had already boarded his own shuttle, the *Lux Aeterna*, impatient to be away, but Marduk would not be hurried.

Eighteen warrior brothers received the Dark Apostle's blessing, kneeling before him in turn. Enusat was not present, though the Host's new First Acolyte was accompanying the boarding party. He had already received Marduk's blessing, and was hooked into the pilot's throne on the *Invisus*, joining with it and preparing for launch.

Last to receive Marduk's bloody handprint was Kol Badar. The Coryphaus stepped forwards to receive his blessing, his thick features set in his customary snarl.

Earlier, Marduk had announced his intention to join the boarding party himself.

'You cannot,' the Coryphaus had said with typical bluntness. 'You are the Host's Dark Apostle and you are of the Council. We have already lost the Third. The Legion can ill afford to lose two of its Apostles as well.'

'I appreciate your intent, Marduk,' said Nahren. 'But I agree with your Coryphaus.'

'I would not wish it said that I would not aid a fellow Apostle,' said Marduk.

'Your aid is appreciated,' said Nahren. 'Let your First Acolyte go in your stead. It would do your Host good to see your faith in him.'

Marduk had bowed his head in respect.

'It shall be as you suggest, old master,' he said. *The old fool*, he thought. That had been easier that he could ever have predicted.

Kol Badar closed his eyes to receive Marduk's blessing. The Dark Apostle placed his hand upon the Coryphaus's face, murmuring an orison of blessing. The bloody handprint dried almost instantly upon his flesh, the hyper-coagulants within doing their work.

'I say again, this is folly,' said Kol Badar, as Marduk

pulled his bloody hand away from the towering warrior's face.

'I agree,' said Marduk. 'This is a mummer's farce. But I must be seen to make an effort. And there are relics on board. Weapons. Armour. Ammunition. We cannot simply abandon the ship to the Death Guard.'

'No good will come of it,' Kol Badar had said. 'Mark my words. But I will do as you order, Apostle.'

'If it is as the Death Guard suggested, salvage what you can. If the ship is still in working order we will give Nahren a skeleton crew and he can limp back to Sicarus with his tail between his legs,' said Marduk. 'We will continue on without him.'

'You think the Death Guard will stand by idly while we do this?' asked Kol Badar. 'The Fourteenth Legion are stubborn. They will not relinquish their prize easily.'

'Then you must *convince* them,' Marduk said. He wiped his hand upon his tabard. Already the wound was sealed. He accepted his spike-knuckled gauntlet, held out to him by a hunched, black-robed attendant, and secured it back over his hand. He felt it join with his flesh, and felt once again complete.

'There is something you are not telling me,' said Kol Badar, his voice low.

'You know me too well,' said Marduk.

'I am starting to. Well? What is it you are scheming?'

'Something that will bring the Thirty-Fourth great power.'

'The Thirty-Fourth, or you?'

'They are one and the same, are they not?' Marduk said with a smile. 'A Host is only as strong as its Apostle.'

Kol Badar grunted noncommittally.

'It is best that you do not know,' said Marduk, dropping his smile. 'But be ready. It may come to pass that there will be the need to spill our brothers' blood.'

'The Fourteenth's? Or Nahren's?'

'It would be wise to be ready for any eventuality.'

Kol Badar bowed his head in ascent. 'As you will it,' he said.

'Go with the gods, bearer of the word,' said Marduk. Kol Badar bowed his head again, then turned and strode away. The *Invisus*'s assault ramp sealed behind him with a resounding crash, and the gunship's engine whine rose to an ear-splitting scream.

The *Lux Aeterna* was the first to leave, launching into the void without further delay. Flames roared as the *Invisus* rose from the deck and rotated slowly to face the gaping aperture of the launch bay. A glistening, nigh invisible skin was all that kept the roiling madness beyond at bay.

With a braying roar, the shuttle jolted forwards. It slipped effortlessly through the insubstantial barrier, sending ripples across its surface. Half a dozen nimble fighters followed, darting out to act as escort. Within moments, they were gone, swallowed by the void.

Once they were gone, Marduk signalled to Sabtec, the most senior warrior-brother of the Host that had not left with Nahren.

'It is time,' said Marduk.

'Are you sure she will be on board?' asked Sabtec.

'She is,' answered Marduk. 'And she is waiting for me.'

* * *

THE *Vox Dominus* filled their vision as the shuttle approached. It was easy to believe, looking upon it up close, that the ship had weathered three thousand years adrift in the warp as the Death Guard claimed.

Easy for the First Acolyte to believe, at any rate – Dark Apostle Nahren steadfastly refused to countenance the Death Guard's claim.

The thick armoured plating of the *Vox Dominus* was heavily corroded, to such a degree in places that the exterior of the ship had been completely eaten away, exposing its dark interior. Rust and verdigris covered those cannon batteries that could be seen; most were completely obscured by strange orange-hued growths. If the ship had lain upon an ocean bed for hundreds of years and dredged up, Enusat imagined it would resemble something like this. It was a decrepit and pitiful shadow of its former glory.

The First Acolyte peered at it through the metre-thick armourglass as he piloted the *Invisus*. The curved window distorted the *Vox Dominus* strangely.

'No evidence of battle damage,' he noted.

'No evidence of any life, either,' said Kol Badar from behind him.

'That does not mean the Third Host is dead,' said Enusat. 'The Dark Apostle believes we may yet find survivors.'

'I would not hold my breath,' said Kol Badar.

'Nor I,' said Enusat.

The battleship was in a serious state of decay, but there were none of the tell-tale las-burns, nor the gaping rents that void-torpedoes or cannon broadsides would inflict, to indicate conflict. The only wounds that the immense ship seemed to have were those caused by the passage of time.

Just ahead of the *Invisus*, Dark Apostle Nahren's shuttle tracked to starboard, stabiliser jets firing. Target locks flashed in front of Enusat's retinas, and there was an angry buzzing in the back of his head. The dark soul of the shuttle was urging him to squeeze off a burst of fire at the other ship. He blinked the targeting reticule away, reasserting his dominance. It was always this way with the *Invisus*. It delighted in testing him.

The two ships were running along the ventral embarkation decks of the *Vox Dominus* now, checking each in turn. Some onboard systems seemed to remain in operation, and Dark Apostle Nahren believed it might be possible to lift one of the hangar bay shields remotely. Enusat pulled the *Invisus* in behind the other shuttle, following its lead.

Enusat did not feel it likely that they would find an operational hangar, but he was proven wrong. After manoeuvring beneath the rotting carcass of the *Vox Dominus* to check the lower aft launch bays, they found what they sought.

The two shuttles drew level beyond the shield of a launch deck on the lower aft side. Its surface was pitted and scarred. Limpet-like growths clung to it.

'They look organic,' said Kol Badar, and Enusat was forced to agree. Few living things could withstand lengthy exposure to the void, but it was not unheard of, especially on the shore of the Ocean of Souls.

At a remote impulse from the *Lux Aeterna*, the immense docking bay began to open. The void rendered the movement perfectly silent, but Enusat could imagine the groan of tortured metal as it lifted for the first time in the gods alone knew how long. Millennia, it seemed.

To Enusat's surprise, the deck's shimmering integrity field remained intact. It held the vacuum of space at bay, glistening like quicksilver. The *Lux Aeterna* passed through, causing it to ripple like the surface of a lake.

Enusat turned in his pilot throne, his movement tugging at the ribbed cables connecting him to the shuttle's controls. Kol Badar stood behind him, his lupine face up-lit by the red internal glow of his revered Terminator armour. The Coryphaus gave a slow nod.

'Follow them in,' he said.

'By your command,' said Enusat. He turned and settled back into the embrace of the shuttle's worn, human-leather seat. He eased the shuttle's controls forwards, feeling the ship's dark soul buzzing in his mind. The *Invisus* was uneasy. Did it sense something that their sensors could not, Enusat wondered? The thought departed as quickly as it had come. To linger on doubt was not in his character.

The *Invisus* slipped through the shimmering field. The embarkation deck was cavernous and as dark as the pits of Hades. That was not some empty metaphor, either. Enusat had been to Hades, and it was indeed rather dark.

The shuttle's runner-lights panned left and right. The air was thick with particles. Dust perhaps.

'And lo, the Faithful entered the Cimmerian gloom, seeking the Light of Truth,' quoted Enusat.

Kol Badar grunted. 'Where is that from?'

'The *Fifty-Seventh epistle of Mahnarhek the Infested*,' said Enusat.

'Remind me. What happened to the "Faithful" at the end of that passage?' asked Kol Badar.

'They were devoured alive,' said Enusat, 'yet in being devoured, they attained true enlightenment.'

'How comforting,' said Kol Badar.

'CLEAR,' SAID KOL Badar, his voice crackling across the vox-network.

With a grunt, Enusat relaxed his grip on his autocannon. Holding it one-handed, he leant it against his shoulder, the long barrel pointing vertically. With his other hand he removed his grilled Mark Three helmet, accompanied by the hiss of equalising pressure.

He breathed in deeply. There was air aboard the *Vox Dominus*, which he had not expected. It was hot and tasted foul, but it was air nonetheless. The oxygen content was low, low enough that an unaugmented human would have lasted no more than a few minutes at best, but the atmosphere was perfectly survivable for one of the Legiones Astartes.

It was also uncomfortably humid. Rivulets of moisture already ran down the plates of his armour, and he blinked sweat from his eyes.

The Coryphaus had been wrong in his earlier prediction. There *was* life on the ship. Abundant and verdant life. It just was not the life that they were seeking.

It clung to the walls and hung low from the ceilings. The ground underfoot was soft, spongy and uneven. It was a veritable forest of fungus, lichen and moss, and it transformed the interior of the *Vox Dominus* into an otherworldy jungle, more akin to a death world than the belly of a battleship.

It was bewildering in its diversity. Pallid stalks rose from the ground in dense clusters, reaching towards the ceiling like saplings seeking sunlight. Stinking polyps the colour of diseased liver protruded from between fan-like fronds as delicate as lace. Bulging brain-like sponges covered in fuzz grew atop spotted stems. Coral-like clusters grew alongside oddly shaped stinkhorns and earth-tongues, each one more wildly coloured than the last. Puddles of water collected in hollows, filled with brightly coloured algal blooms – likely the source of the oxygen that Enusat now breathed.

The only light on the deck came from the void, a diffuse orange-red glow, and from pockets of glowing phosphorescent fungi. These clusters resembled undersea anemones, with tiny finger-like protuberances waving gently in the air.

Even now the deck had been declared clear, the warriors of the Thirty-Fourth Host moved warily through the transformed embarkation deck, bolters and chainswords at the ready.

'This has the air of the plague god about it,' said Kol Badar. His voice was a harsh growl, distorted by his quad-tusked helmet, giving it a crackling, mechanical quality.

Enusat glanced across the deck to Nahren. The Dark Apostle stood motionless, staring around him, his face a mask of controlled fury. He held his immense crozius in a tight, two-handed grip, its spiked head crackling, as if it embodied his hatred. He looked ready to brain someone.

'It would seem the Dark Apostle of the Third Host has come to the same conclusion,' said Enusat.

Nahren's bodyguard, the Bloodsworn, stood in a rough circle around their master. Each wore a horned helmet with the skin of a human face grotesquely stretched over its faceplate, and they were armed with an eclectic mix of weapons: chainaxes, power blades, bolters and plasma weaponry. Some of those veterans, Marduk had told him, were possessed by more than a single entity – even unarmed they would be dangerous foes.

'If there were survivors on board, they would have come to meet us,' said Kol Badar. 'We'll find nothing here but death.'

Enusat was inclined to agree.

'Come, First Acolyte,' Kol Badar continued. 'Let's see what the Apostle has in mind now that he's seen this desolation with his own eyes.'

The Bloodsworn bristled as they approached, feral growls rumbling forth from the vocalisers of their helmets. It was probably the only sound they could make with their mouths sewn shut, Enusat thought.

'Their conversational skills must make the months of warp-transit just fly by,' he said in a low voice, eliciting a snort from the Terminator-armoured Coryphaus. His helmet transformed it into a harsh blurt of distortion.

The Bloodsworn stepped protectively in front of their Dark Apostle, weapons raised. Enusat, his helmet secured at his hip, resisted the urge to turn his autocannon on them. It would not be wise to antagonise the Dark Apostle or his bodyguard when they were already close to snapping. A single spark, and they would erupt. Nevertheless, he refused to be intimidated.

An ugly smile split his mangled face, exposing his gleaming black-steel teeth. He couldn't help it. Part of him longed to test himself against these veterans.

He and Kol Badar stopped a few steps back from the Bloodsworn, staring down the barrels of their live weapons. If Enusat had been wearing his helmet, warning runes would have been flashing before his eyes, keying him into the targeters locked on him.

'Call your pups off, Apostle,' growled the Coryphaus, 'or I'll be forced to put them on a leash.'

Nahren stared up at Kol Badar. He looked ready to strike the Coryphaus, but after a moment, with an oppugnant lack of urgency, he gave the command for his Bloodsworn to stand down. Enusat was almost disappointed.

The Dark Apostle spoke the order in the tongue of daemons. The harsh, unnatural sound was like a punch in the face. The Bloodsworn responded instantly, easing back and turning their weapons away from the two warriors of the Thirty-Fourth Host.

'What now, Apostle? I have no wish to risk my warriors here any longer than necessary.'

'Cowardice,' snarled Nahren.

Enusat saw a vein at Kol Badar's temple twitch, and his expression hardened.

'The anomaly could reappear at any moment and claim us, as it has already claimed your Host,' said Kol Badar.

''We do not leave until I have answers.'

'You command the Third Host, Apostle. What is left of it. You do not command the Thirty-Fourth.'

'I know where I stand in the Legion,' snapped Nahren, 'and it is on a far higher step than the place of any Coryphaus. Even the great Kol Badar. Marduk lent me your strength in good faith. Do not dishonour your Apostle, Coryphaus.'

The silence was punctuated by the sounds of water dripping somewhere.

Do not antagonise Nahren, Marduk had said to him before he had left the *Infidus Diabolus*. *Even without a Host, he is dangerous.*

'There are certainly questions to be answered,' said Enusat, seeking to deflect the rising tension.

'I would hear how the Death Guard can explain all this,' said Nahren, gesturing around them. 'I would like to see if they dare speak their lies to my face. Let's ask them, shall we?'

Kol Badar's expression was dark but, somewhat grudgingly, he opened up a vox-link to the sleek fighters that had escorted them across the expanse separating the *Vox Dominus* and the *Infidus Diabolus*.

'Bring them in,' he said.

'THERE THEY GO,' said Sabtec, gesturing to the glowing map before them. 'It is just as you predicted.'

He was stood with Marduk overlooking the small, portable strategic display. Behind them, his squad made ready for battle, checking weapons and ammunition as they filed onto the small shuttle, once a smuggler's vessel, small and discreet. Heavy machinery was being loaded on board, along with a floating casket guided by robed attendants.

A small, ruby-red icon had appeared alongside the larger three-dimensional representation of the Death Guard vessel on the glass tablet. The small icon flashed as it moved away from its larger parent ship.

'Good,' said Marduk. 'Prep the engines. I want us launched the moment the Death Guard set foot aboard the *Vox Dominus*.'

'It will be as you wish,' said Sabtec.

'I want the *Death's Head* silenced,' said Marduk. 'I do not want the Death Guard knowing what we are doing until the deed is done.'

'They will not know we are upon them until the last moment,' said Sabtec. 'And by then it will be too late.'

'Inbound,' said Kol Badar. 'Be ready.'

Enusat planted himself behind a rockcrete barrier designed to protect against engine blast. The position was located centrally, allowing him to cover virtually the entirety of the embarkation deck. His legs were set wide in a braced position, and the stabilisers in his greaves hummed softly, working to keep him locked in place, ready to compensate for the weapon's monstrous recoil.

His wore his helmet once more, having tired of the heady stink and heat of the ship's interior. A flood of information was presented before his eyes. He blink-clicked through external diagnostics displaying temperature, humidity and the chemical breakdown of the air, and on through logistical data including heat-sink readouts, ammunition updates and energy-strain. Tactical readouts presented themselves to him, analysing the heart-rate and life-functions of his warrior-brothers. A crosshair matrix followed where his eyes focused, eagerly seeking a target.

The barrel of his beloved high-calibre weapon was almost two metres in length, most of which was encased in a perforated barrel ventilation shroud. An underslung chainblade bayonet protruded a further half-metre beyond the snarling daemon that formed the weapon's wide-bore muzzle.

The autocannon was hung with fetishes and religious icons, and its bulky casing was inscribed with holy passages from the *Book of Lorgar*. A heavy chain shoulder-strap locked over Enusat's shoulder, taking the weapon's considerable weight, aided by internal servos.

His right hand clasped the weapon's grip, thumb resting lightly on its firing mechanism. He guided the autocannon's direction with his left hand, grasping the handle atop the weapon's casing. Suspensors lightened the load, and the servo-bundles built into his armour made him able to heft the immense weapon as easily as an unaugmented mortal would a rifle.

The autocannon was belt-fed from Enusat's oversized backpack, which acted as an ammunition reservoir as well as the power source for his armour. The ammunition feed was protected by a flexible casing. While not capable of such a high rate of fire as a heavy bolter, his weapon was far more powerful, able to rip through rockcrete and vehicle plating like paper.

The other warriors of the Thirty-Fourth and the Third Hosts had taken up defensive positions, hugging the *Invisus* and the *Lux Aeterna*, and taking advantage of the cover provided by the overgrown embarkation deck. Bolters were held at the ready, and warriors knelt at the corners of armoured bulwarks half hidden by fungal overgrowth.

Dark Apostle Nahren stood out in the open,

awaiting the arrival of the inbound Death Guard shuttle. The Bloodsworn stood with them, as did Kol Badar, an implacable bulwark of heavy armour and belligerence. The bladed lengths of his power talons clicked against each other as he waited.

Enusat revved his autocannon's underslung chainblade, and black smoke rose from its engine.

The Death Guard shuttle resembled some kind of repulsive insect, bloated to gigantic proportions, as it passed through the embarkation deck's shimmering integrity field.

Every panel of the ship was heavily worn, pitted, and dented. Rust and corrosion encrusted its armour plates, and in places it looked like the rot had eaten completely through the hull. Enusat was surprised it was even void-worthy.

The dilapidated ship's weapons looked very serviceable, however, and they rotated freely in their turrets, sweeping across the Word Bearers arrayed to greet it. Each time they swept over him, a host of warning runes flashed up before Enusat's eyes. He heard the *Invisus* growl like an angry beast. Its weapons were trained upon this newcomer, this rival, and it longed to assert its dominance.

'Hold your fire,' said Enusat, both to the Word Bearers of the Thirty-Fourth and the gunship. He could not speak for Nahren or the Bloodsworn, of course.

The hull of the Death Guard's shuttle was bulbous, and it was held aloft upon a large pair of circular jets. Those jets were rotated downwards now, making the air shimmer with their heat as it hovered slowly forwards, inching its way into the embarkation deck.

The windows of its dual cockpit were convex and bulging. They seemed to be made up of thousands of tiny octagonal segments, making them resemble the compound eyes of an arthropod. While the hull of the shuttle was the grey-green colour of a bloated, water-logged corpse, and covered in sections of scabrous rust and corrosion, those eyes were a deep and iridescent amber.

The corroded ship settled to the deck in the space between the *Invisus* and the *Lux Aeterna*, seven insectile legs unfolding to take its weight. They looked far too slender to support its bulk, and the metal was rusted and befouled, but they held, keeping the ship's hull some three metres off the deck.

There was a shuddering groan, and a crack appeared in the bloated underside of the ship. Sickening yellow smoke poured from within. It hit the ground and spread outwards, concealing the deck in low fog.

The noxious vapour lapped around the legs of Nahren, Kol Badar and the Bloodsworn. Even fifteen metres away, the high levels of toxicity and acidity of the fog registered on Enusat's auto-sensors.

The crack in the ship's underside continued to expand like a gaping wound, gradually resolving itself into a slowly descending boarding ramp. Thick, saliva-like strands stretched out between the separating sections and dripped to the deck like thick syrup.

The ramp settled with an audible groan. There was a sharp hiss as an internal airlock was released, and the air was suddenly filled with the buzzing of insects. A dense cloud spewed from within the shuttle.

Most of the insects were small, but some of the revolting creatures were the size of a man's fist. Their bloated abdomens hung low beneath glistening carapaces and foulness dripped from their engorged probosces.

The cloud expanded like a dark shadow to engulf the warrior-brothers of the XVIIth Legion. Enusat was suddenly very glad he was wearing his helmet. Of the Word Bearers, only Dark Apostle Nahren was bare-headed. Fat, crawling flies with gleaming, multi-faceted eyes settled upon his face, but the Dark Apostle paid them no mind. The Plague Father was a part of the Ruinous pantheon, and the Word Bearers honoured him as they honoured all the Greater Powers.

The cloud of flies continued to expand, dissipating somewhat as they spread out, though a thick mass of them remained buzzing around the shuttle's now lowered boarding ramp. That was where Enusat focused. Crosshair reticules followed the movement of his iris as he searched for a target through the cloying smoke and buzzing insects.

Then he saw them.

A host of red targeting icons lit up before him.

'Contact,' he growled.

'I see them,' said Kol Badar.

The threat-registers resolved into bulky, power-armoured silhouettes advancing slowly down the embarkation ramp. Enusat's finger tensed on the trigger.

The Death Guard stepped onto the deck of the *Vox Dominus*.

'Launch,' ordered Sabtec, and the sleek, black-sided shuttle eased itself from the embarkation deck.

Its cogitators had been working frantically. Three servitors slaved to the devices had been burned out, their organic systems failing with massive subdural haemorrhaging, but the calculations had been completed successfully – Marduk hoped – and had been input into the shuttle's nav-cortex. Both the *Infidus Diabolus* and the *Death's Head* were moving; the trajectory calculation had to be perfect.

After three short bursts of stabilising jets to set them on the right course, the shuttle went dead, all of its systems shut down. It became nothing more than a lifeless piece of flotsam, like so many others floating in the void, though one that was moving on a perfect collision course with the *Death's Head*.

Their progress through the vacant, orange-hued expanse was slow – they did not want to warn the *Death's Head* of their approach – and would not make contact for several hours.

The Word Bearers settled themselves and calmed their breathing as the oxygen cut off and the temperature began to plummet.

A hint of a smile curled the corner of Marduk's lips.

NARGALAX. THAT WAS the name he gave them. It was not the moniker he had borne upon his home world of Barbarus, nor the cult name he had been given upon indoctrination into the Death Guard. Rather, it was the name that the Plague Father had gifted him; the name he had taken on after his infestation.

While Enusat acknowledged that he was not exactly pleasing on the eye, he was nevertheless a vision of classical grace and nobility next to the bloated living corpse that called itself leader of this piratical band of diseased legionaries.

His appearance, however, was not repugnant to Enusat. It was, after all, the blessings of the Plague Father that had wrought this change upon the Death Guard's physical body. In truth, he was more fascinated than repulsed. It was amazing to him that anything could be this riddled with disease and corruption and yet still live. Truly, Nargalax wore the blessings of the gods upon his flesh.

His armour would once have been bone-white, but now it was slick with filth and discoloured an unhealthy shade the colour of a rotting cadaver. His body was grossly swollen, and his armour was cracked and split, unable to fully contain his foetid bulk. Pustules and sores had ruptured across its surfaces, weeping foul-smelling blood and pus. Segmented cables, filth-encrusted and wet, protruded from his body like ropes of intestines, and bony spines protruded along the edges of his armour. It was difficult to say where his plate truly finished and flesh began. Enusat guessed that they had become as one.

An array of rotten heads hung at his waist, their eyes, mouths, nostrils and neck stumps stitched and waxed shut. They hung alongside a mace, a barbaric weapon that had a corroded, curved blade protruding from its heavy weighted head. A double-barrelled combi-bolter was mag-locked at his side.

It was only when the Death Guard reached for his helmet that Enusat noticed his mutation. A thick, segmented tentacle had sprouted from his left tricep, growing from a rupture in his armour. It was the colour of dead flesh and covered in a thick layer of mucus.

With the aid of this grotesque tentacle, and accompanied by a sickly sucking sound of protest, Nargalax had removed his single-horned helmet to reveal his bloated corpse-face.

On the Imperial mausoleum planet of Cerberus IV, the river Acherus had been choked with the bodies of dead Guardsmen. By the end of the siege there had been so many bodies there that it had been possible for the Host's Rhinos and Land Raiders to cross the river and enter the prime city even though the bone-bridge had been destroyed. Nargalax's face reminded Enusat of those drowned Guardsmen, both in colour and the manner in which it was bloated.

His flesh was pallid and sickly, and the dark purple bruising of congealed blood spread like stains beneath his leprous skin. Most of his mouth and jaw were missing, replaced by a mass of tubes and pipes. His left eye was swollen and misshapen, filled with styes, milky, and leaking. As soon as he had removed his helmet, a cluster of tiny flies had settled there to feed upon that fluid. Movement rippled beneath his necrotised flesh. As Enusat watched, several wriggling maggots emerged from the corner of that eye, like pallid tears.

More feeder pipes and cables were crudely drilled into his temples and at the back of his skull, and the flesh around their entry points was dead and foul. Patches of wispy grey hair still clung to the left side of his rotting scalp, hanging past his shoulders, perhaps a last concession to vanity. The Death Guard's skin rippled with movement from within – maggots and worms fed upon his rotten flesh.

Yet perhaps the most off-putting of Nargalax's features was his right eye. It was the stark blue of flawless glacial ice, completely untouched by disease or taint. It was clear and bold, and offered an indication as to what he might have looked like before the touch of the Plague Father had claimed him

It was not so much the eye itself that was disturbing, for it was perfect, but rather the contrast it represented, staring out from its sunken socket in the face of a bloated cadaver. Its perfection seemed to make everything else that much more foul.

The only strange thing about it was its pupil, which looked more like three overlapping pupils joined as one. For all the misery that had afflicted Nargalax's flesh, his one clear eye was always laughing, even if what was left of his mouth could not. Creases formed readily at its corner.

There were seven legionaries of the Death Guard accompanying their foetid captain, rotting flesh in the shape of warriors of the Legiones Astartes. Enusat was certain that if their armour could be pried loose, they would collapse into a formless, rotting mass. Sores upon their rotten, fleshy armoured plates wept with pus, blood and oil. Their foul secretions pooled beneath their cloven-toed boots, spreading out onto the algae-slick floor. Insects and plant life fed upon the foulness they deposited.

Each of them held a corroded bolter across his chest. Enusat was amazed the weapons still worked.

Even before the Death Guard had given themselves over to Nurgle, they had a reputation as implacable warriors, able to endure punishment far beyond that of the other Legions. Relentless, unbreakable and as unstoppable as an incoming tide – that had been the defining characteristics of the Legion before they had thrown in their lot with the Plague Father, and his touch upon them had exaggerated these qualities even further.

The seven were not alone. Mortals accompanied the Death Guard, creeping out from their shuttle in the wake of their immense masters. They were wretched, repulsive creatures, all of them in various stages of decomposition. The Word Bearers were shocked and disgusted that they did not appear to be slaves and servants, and that Nargalax spoke of them in fatherly tones. *His flock*, he called them; the *afflicted*. Dark Apostle Nahren made no attempt to hide his disdain. It was the way of the Word Bearers to look upon mortals as cattle, to be used and dominated, not to be treated as anything even close to approaching equal, which was how Nargalax seemed to regard these worthless meat sacks.

There were a score of them, a ragged militia that bore a range of crude weapons. Most carried autoguns and lasguns in various states of repair, while others cradled little more than stub guns and cudgels. Many of them wore what were clearly Imperial-issue flak vests and helmets. Deserters, no doubt. All wore breathing apparatus, mostly full-faced black masks with circular goggles filled with a glowing green fog. They stared out through that mire with pallid, corrupted eyes filled with cataracts and cancers.

All were human or a close approximation, but for one brute that stood taller than even the legionaries. It was a hulking mass of vat-grown muscle and brutality, bedecked with an oversized gasmask pulled over its disproportionately small head. One of its arms had been replaced with an immense rotator drill. The weight of the heavy machinery gave the creature an awkward, lopsided posture. Kol Badar stared at that one with narrowed eyes, and he flexed his power talons.

Hor hor hor.

It was a horrid wet sound akin to a death rattle, and Nahren's grip on his holy crozius tightened at the sound. Enusat tensed, half expecting, half hoping that the Dark Apostle would lash out. He was a little disappointed when he did not.

'Tell me where my Host is, Death Guard,' said Nahren.

Nargalax was still chuckling as he answered.

'If it did not leave the ship,' he drawled, his voice slow and ponderous, 'then it is still here.'

'You know more than you are offering, creature.'

'The Chaplain does not listen, no,' said Nargalax, still chuckling. His voice was hollow and painfully slow, croaking forth from a rusted vox-grille set into his throat. 'This is not our work, I pray and confirm. Neither I, nor any of my brethren have stepped aboard this hallowed vessel, not until now. I can confirm that... urgh... and pledge my honour against the claim.'

'Yet this is your patron's work. You would not deny that, would you?'

'So it would seem, so it would seem,' drawled Nargalax, his good eye laughing. 'The Grandfather's pestilential touch is here, yes. But it is so wherever there is rot and decay. My brethren and I cannot... be held accountable for all His great works, no?

We found your vessel abandoned, lifeless, drifting. It did not respond to our vox-hails. Hence... we merely sought to tow it to a safer location before we investigated further. There was a disturbance in the warp, and we were drawn through. And here we are, accused of piracy and worse.' He laughed again, deep and slow, making his whole body shake. 'I wish it were not so... but I have no more knowledge of the whereabouts of your kin than you.'

'You lie,' said Nahren.

Nargalax shrugged. 'You see what you choose to see, little Chaplain,' he said. 'But I do not lie.'

Enusat believed him. He also believed that the Death Guard knew more than he was offering.

'I must get to the bridge,' Nahren said, turning away from Nargalax to speak to Kol Badar.

'Why?' asked Kol Badar.

'I must know the truth. This creature,' said Nahren, gesturing contemptuously towards Nargalax, 'will accompany me. It will be the first to die if it has spoken any falsehoods.'

The Death Guard merely laughed.

'The First Acolyte of the Thirty-Fourth will join me as well,' added Nahren.

'Me, Apostle?' asked Enusat.

'I would not have the Thirty-Fourth leave without me,' said Nahren, still addressing Kol Badar, ignoring Enusat completely. 'I trust that Marduk would not wish to have to find yet another First Acolyte...'

THEY PRESSED FORWARDS through corridors so filled with fungal life that it was easy to forget they were on a ship at all. They were completely cut off, and lost contact with those on the embarkation deck within minutes.

Only a small group was pressing on into the infested interior of the *Vox Dominus*: Dark Apostle Nahren, his five mute Bloodsworn and Enusat, providing them with support in the form of his heavy autocannon. Lastly, the Death Guard captain Nargalax marched with them. Seven they were, in all.

'An auspicious number,' said Nargalax. 'Grandfather Nurgle... would be pleased.'

He was a hostage, little more, and Nahren had promised him a painful death if any evidence came to light of his involvement in the disappearance of his Host and the defilement of the *Vox Dominus* itself.

The Death Guard captain had only laughed, deep and long – *hor hor hor* – and told him that there was no pain that could be inflicted upon his flesh that would cause him any discomfort.

'You'd scratch an itch, and I'd thank you for it,' he had said. Nevertheless, the Death Guard acquiesced to the Dark Apostle's demand, willingly it seemed to Enusat.

They walked single file, yet even so, the going was difficult and slow. In places their route was so overgrown that they had to cut a path, and soon their blades dripped with milky ichor and burning sap. Elsewhere they cleared their way with controlled bursts of promethium fire. Enusat had wondered if that would provoke a reaction from Nargalax, but it hadn't. The Death Guard captain appeared unmoved, even as huge centipedes and crawling insects squealed and writhed in their death throes, flames boiling their innards.

Their advance was all the slower for the presence of Nargalax. He would not be hurried. Enusat doubted he *could* be hurried. Each step was heavy and laboured. It reminded Enusat of the way the immense machines of the Collegia Titanica moved – slow yet powerful and unstoppable. Nargalax *was* heavy, ungodly heavy. Anything beneath his tread was crushed. His movement was as inexorable as an incoming tide. Fungus browned and withered wherever he trod, and Enusat was careful not to step upon any of the toxic secretions that he left in his wake.

Enusat walked behind him, and was glad once again for his helmet. Bloated flies and biting insects hung around the Death Guard captain in a dense swarm, and he was certain that his stink would have been repellent. How Nahren and the Bloodsworn stood it was beyond him. Already the Bloodsworn sported a florid array of bites and sores upon their flesh.

The minutes dragged into hours, and still they pushed on into the darkness, trudging through the overgrown corridors to reach their destination. It got hotter and more humid as they continued deeper into the interior of the *Vox Dominus*. It was obvious that Nahren's patience was wearing thin at their ponderous pace, but there was little the Dark Apostle could do to hasten their advance.

At last they reached their destination: the ship's bridge. The immense blast doors leading inside were sealed.

'That could be a good sign,' said Enusat, though he didn't believe his own words. The doors were almost completely concealed beneath moss and hanging lichen. Clumps of bulbous fungi protruded from their surface like tumours. The doors had been designed to withstand considerable attack from without in the event of a boarding action, and lacking las-cutters and seismic hammers, it would take some time for the party to gain access.

They would have to make do with what they had. Thankfully, Enusat knew that these blast doors were nowhere near as thick as those of the vessels of the Imperial Navy, or xenos species. This was a ship that had been designed for use by the Legiones Astartes. Few would dare launch a boarding party against the Word Bearers, and if they did – and were successful enough to fight their way to the bridge – then the battle was already lost. The XVIIth put their trust in their bolters and blades, and their faith – not barriers of plasteel and adamantium.

'Melta-charges,' ordered Nahren. Several of his Bloodsworn began cleaning off the overgrowth of fungus and plant life from the blast doors' surface, working to make crevices and joins visible. Others readied and primed the heavy melta-charges they wore at their hips.

They fired in concert. Each had been carefully placed to knock out the locking mechanisms of the blast doors. Super-heated metal ran like lava. Even so, the doors remained shut. Though the locks had been blown, the portal still needed to be physically pried open.

With an inclination of his head, Nahren set the Bloodsworn to work. Their forms suddenly shifted, their bodies blurring and flickering. For a fraction of a second, two beings seemed to inhabit the space where each of the Bloodsworn stood. In some cases, three or more stood as one, their images superimposed over each other. Mighty horns rose from their heads, and eyes filled with burning witch-fire stared forth from shadowy, daemonic faces as the human-skin drawn across their helmets came to life.

Like wax figures before a flame, their bodies softened and changed. Toothy maws tore open upon breastplates, and burning eyes formed, blinking and staring out balefully, in the centre of the Bloodsworn's foreheads. Bony spurs and spines pushed from shoulder plates, kneepads and elbows, curving and jagged. Arms bulged with newly formed musculature, and fingers fused together to form talons and claws, or elongated into whipping tendrils, studded with spikes.

'Impressive,' said Nargalax.

'If I find any evidence in the ship's log of your involvement in this, I will set them on you, Death Guard,' promised Nahren. Nargalax merely laughed.

Slender blade arms were thrust into the molten gap at the centre of the blast doors. Hooked claws appeared on either side, gripping tightly, piercing the solid metal skin. Unnatural musculature bulged as the possessed Bloodsworn hauled at the unsecured doors, straining with all their warp-given strength. Clawed talons that had grown from boots gripped the gridded plasteel flooring beneath the bed of lichen and algae underfoot, veins straining fit to rupture as the pack hauled the doors open.

Enusat lowered his autocannon from his shoulder, holding it at the ready, covering the door. The gods alone knew what they would find within.

With a grinding sound of protesting metal, the

doors began to move. Shuddering and squealing, they were pulled back, the four-way aperture parting to reveal a glimpse of the bridge beyond. Yanking and pulling violently, the Bloodsworn managed to open the doors wide enough that they might enter.

'Most impressive,' said Nargalax.

LIKE AN ASSASSIN'S blade, the black-hulled shuttle closed in on the brutish *Death's Head*, which was still attached to the *Vox Dominus* by an immense chain.

Marduk rose from his meditative trance instantly, alert and ready. Sabtec and the others roused themselves also, running final diagnostics and weapons checks. It was almost time.

The Dark Apostle released the restraints that kept him locked in place, and pushed himself gently from his seat. The artificial gravity had been suspended along with all other systems, and he propelled himself to the front of the ship, using hand-holds to guide his progress.

Sabtec joined him in the cockpit. The *Death's Head* loomed before them, growing larger with every passing second.

'The calculations were correct, it seems,' said Sabtec. 'Thank the gods they did not change their course. They have not registered us yet.'

As if on cue, the *Death's Head* made a slight adjustment, turning almost imperceptibly as it began to shift its position. No doubt its crew saw them as some fragment of wreckage or an asteroid, and they were shifting to avoid a collision.

'They have now,' said Marduk. 'Let's move.'

They were less than a kilometre away when the

Death's Head finally realised what was happening. By then, they were far too close for anything to be done. All the *Death's Head* could do was sit and wait to be boarded.

ANY HOPE THAT had remained that the bridge of the *Vox Dominus* might somehow have been spared the fate of the rest of the ship was shattered as the group clambered through the half-opened blast doors.

'The spores must have spread through the air ducts before the bridge was sealed,' said Enusat.

Spindly mushrooms that glowed with pale, phosphorescent light lit the room. Vividly coloured mould and fungus covered every surface, and hairy strings of lichen hung down in great cascades, linking ceiling to floor. Enusat tracked his autocannon back and forth, seeking a target, but the only movement and life within came from the myriad of disturbed insect-life seething around the fungal growths. He eased his finger off the trigger. The bridge was as dead as the rest of the ship.

Nahren moved straight for the command pulpit. Enusat moved cautiously, ducking beneath an outcrop of fungus the colour of congealed blood. He stepped over thick, rope-like roots, and moved to an overgrown lump that he judged to be a terminal. He brushed aside a metre-long, brightly coloured centipede with a sweep of his arm, and tore at the thick matting of moss. Brushing it away easily, he revealed a small, circular screen. More scraping revealed a control panel, and he began to flick switches and dials. It came as no surprise to him that the screen did not awake.

Nahren was having similar results, it seemed. He swore, and pounded his fist into an oculus viewscreen, cracking it beneath his fury.

'This is hopeless, Apostle,' Enusat said.

That was when the dead Word Bearer grabbed him.

'The blightwood grows,' it said.

Daal'ak'ath mel caengr'aal.

PART TWO

The darkness was absolute. All but the barest of life support systems had been shut down on the Infidus Diabolus *months earlier. The over-recycled air was low in oxygen and stale. Without the hum of engines or the chanting of the Host, the halls were silent, haunted only by the groan of the ship's hull.*

'We should never have stepped foot aboard the Vox Dominus,' *said Marduk, a voice in the darkness. 'You advised me against it. Would that I had listened.'*

There came no reply. Indeed, the Dark Apostle had expected none.

'Nahren would have insisted he go aboard regardless, to see the truth of the Death Guard's claim for himself. That was his right. It was not for me to dissuade him. But we should not have followed. The warning signs were there. I was just too blind to see them.'

He let out a slow, hissing breath. His hands turned to fists in the darkness.

'We should have rained fire upon the rotting hulk of the Vox Dominus, *and sent the Death Guard to damnation along with it. They will suffer for this. This is not our fate.'*

The words sounded hollow and empty.

'This is not our fate,' he said again, more quietly this time.

Silence was his only answer.

ENUSAT HADN'T SEEN the figure slumped in the control seat, for it was so covered in fungal growth and moss that it had become one with its surroundings. Nevertheless, he saw it now.

It had no eyes – those had long since decomposed – but its head turned, and it stared up at him nonetheless, empty sockets boring into him like drills. Its face was wasted and shrunken, the skull clearly visible beneath waxy, pallid skin. Its lips had drawn back, giving it a corpse-grin.

It had hold of his arm. Beneath the covering of moss and a cluster of limpet-like fungus, he could see that that hand was encased in gore-red plate. This was a brother of the Third Host.

Enusat tried to jerk away, but its grip was cold and deathly strong. It held him like a vice. Its brown, rotten teeth parted, jaw moving, and it spoke.

'The blightwood grows, thew-clod, weirwood, horedew, noth.'

Daal'ak'ath mel caengr'aal, gol'akath, mor'dhka, jakaeh'esh.

The first voice emerged from the throat of the creature that had once been a Word Bearer, and a cluster of beetles scrabbled from its mouth, disturbed by the creaking vocal cords. That voice was low-pitched and hoarse, like a heavy creaking door. The other voice was something far more disturbing; it was the voice of a daemon, something older and more powerful than anything Enusat had ever encountered. It made his flesh creep and his stomach coil.

It grinned at him then, and began dragging him towards it.

'Copse and corpse, corpse and copse.'

Grink'ah'tok mal daeth'ma'gol, daeth'ma'gol mal grink'ah'tok.

MARDUK SMILED. THE head of his holy crozius was embedded in the head of a mortal, and he pulled it free with a wet sucking sound. He gave it a shake, dislodging the worst of the blood and brain matter.

He surveyed the carnage around him. The ambush had been perfectly executed.

The ship had been drastically undermanned, crewed mostly by mortals that had either been picked up off-world or bred on board. Only three of the Death Guard had been left behind – doubtless their captain had taken most of his warriors with him in a pathetic attempt to impress or intimidate.

They had boarded the ship within a minute of discovery, and were killing moments later.

Sabtec pushed a corpse off his blade with a boot, and it slumped lifeless to the floor with the others.

'How many?' asked Marduk.

'Thirty-two kills,' answered Sabtec, kneeling to clean his blade on his last victim's shirt.

'Any injuries of our own?'

'Nothing of note,' said Sabtec.

'I sense her nearby,' said Marduk. 'With me.' Sabtec rose instantly, moving with the Dark Apostle deeper into the ship. There was not much to it, and it did not take them long.

The strode into a darkened storage deck, and Marduk halted, listening. Lengths of chain hung from plasteel crossbeams overhead, and they swung languorously, clinking musically. Water dripped from somewhere. Marduk turned around on the spot for a moment, then dropped his gaze to the grilled flooring.

'There,' he said, nodding towards a handle set into the floor.

Sabtec hauled the hatch open. It slammed to the floor with a resounding crash, revealing stairs that descended into darkness.

Marduk made his way down into the gloom. It was a pit, wide and deep, with no exit but the hatch. In a corner of the metal-sided pit cowered a cluster of robed mortals. They were females, a dozen or more of them, and each of them was truly ancient, with withered, frail hands more akin to talons, and matted long white hair. They were blind, their eyes milky, and they whimpered and shook, shielding their hideous crone faces.

A tingling sensation at the back of Marduk's head told him he had found the one he sought. Sabtec hissed, and he knew that the warrior could feel it too.

'Come out, sweetling,' he said, grinning wolfishly. 'I'll not eat you up.'

The harpy flock wailed but parted, leaving just one small figure standing alone.

It was a human child, a girl, no more than four years of age. The tingling became an uncomfortable itch, an insubstantial scratching in the back of Marduk's skull. He gritted his teeth, and blood leaked from his eyes, the only tears he could weep. The girl's power was more than he had anticipated.

She wore a dusty grey robe that hid much of her tiny frame. It trailed across the ground behind her. Her hands were hidden in overlarge sleeves, and around her head and shoulders she wore a tightly wound headdress, charcoal grey, leaving just the pale oval circle of her face visible.

Or at least, that was where her face should have been.

ENUSAT SLAMMED HIS brick-like fist into the deathly creature's grinning mouth, rocking its head backwards and shattering teeth. Still it did not release its grip. Its head rolled forwards again, grinning toothlessly. He slammed his fist into its face once more, and felt bones shatter beneath the blow. The command throne turned, groaning, and the creature fell to the floor, torn loose from its seat. It left a man-shaped impression behind. Still, it held on to him, like death itself.

Enusat stamped down hard on its arm, finally breaking its grip. From the floor it stared up at him.

'Copse and corpse, corpse and copse.'

Grink'ah'tok mal daeth'ma'gol, daeth'ma'gol mal grink'ah'tok.

It began to rise. Enusat backed away, lowering his autocannon.

The bridge was alive with movement and shouts of warning as more of the corrupted Word Bearers rose from their overgrown surroundings, rising from thrones and stepping from the walls. They were covered in fungus, perfectly camouflaged until they began to move.

Enusat had his autocannon levelled at the one

that had grabbed him as it staggered towards him, grinning manically.

Unseen, another creature emerged behind him, seeming to step right from the wall. The left half of its face was completely obscured by fungal growth. It grabbed him from behind, hands closing on his neck. The one before him was closing in. He squeezed his autocannon's trigger, hurling it backwards and splattering gobbets of flesh and skull shards out in a fine cloud behind it. Then the other one dropped him to his knees. The strength in its limbs was incredible.

Nahren was before him then, charging forwards, his face twisted in hatred. His crozius was almost as tall as him, and he drew it back in a powerful, swinging blow. There was a sharp crack of discharging energy as the spiked head of the holy weapon connected, and the creature was hurled away. Nahren offered a hand, helping Enusat to his feet. The foe that Enusat had gunned down was rising to its feet once more, despite missing half its head. Sickly brain matter, porridge-like and foetid, was dripping down its side. Where half its head should have been there was a ghostly monotone afterimage, showing the Word Bearer's face as it had appeared in life, untouched by disease or decomposition. This spectral ghost-image was transparent, and it fixed Enusat with a look of pure hatred.

One of the Bloodsworn leaped upon it, tackling it to the ground. The possessed Word Bearer's huge, crab-like claw encircled the creature's neck, shearing its head from its shoulders, leaving just the transparent face of an apparition in its place. Still, it was not slowed.

It rolled atop the possessed Bloodsworn warrior, and brought its fists together on either side of his head, once, twice, crushing his helmet. The daemonic entity that had inhabited the warrior departed instantly, returning his body to its previous, unaltered – and now very dead – state.

He heard Nargalax's booming laughter – *hor hor hor* – and threw a sidewards glance towards the Death Guard legionary. Was this his doing? It seemed not; the bloated warrior ripped apart one of their corrupt attackers with a controlled burst from his twin-barrelled combi-bolter, laughing as it was sent dancing away from him under the weight of his fire. He wielded the weapon one-handed, the weapon steadied by his bulbous tentacle. In his other hand he held his short, thick-bladed sword. Its edge was heavily notched and chipped, and noxious slime dripped from its tip.

Another of the Bloodsworn was down, dragged to the ground by three of the corrupted Word Bearers. The other Bloodsworn were laying about them with talon and claw, dismembering and hacking into dead flesh, but their enemies would not stay down. On they came, ghostly power-armoured limbs replacing those that had been ripped away. One of them was more spirit than flesh, now, but still it refused to fall. It could, however, still kill.

One of the apparitions thrust an incorporeal hand into the side of the head of one of the Bloodsworn, fingertips pushing through skin and bone as if it were not there. The Bloodsworn felt its touch, though, that much was plain. Blood welled in the warrior's eyes and ran from his nose, and he fell to the ground, twitching and jerking violently.

'We have to go!' shouted Enusat.

One of the unholy creatures came at him, clutching at his face, and he thrust the whirling chainblade slung beneath his autocannon into its chest. The whirring blades tore open its armour, which came apart like sodden wood, and ripped through its fused ribcage, splattering filth in all directions. Still the creature clung on. A squeeze of the trigger sent it flying.

'Back! Back!' roared Nahren, smashing another foe into the ground.

Enusat was walking backwards, swinging his heavy autocannon from one side to the other, pumping shots into the enemy. At the entrance to the bridge he halted, planting his feet in a wide brace position, providing covering fire for the Dark Apostle and the remaining Bloodsworn. Nargalax joined him there, his twin-barrelled combi-bolter coughing staccato bursts of fire.

At another barked order from the Dark Apostle, this time his voice tinged with a daemonic command, the Bloodsworn disengaged from the fight, blood and ichor dripping from their wounds, witch-fire flaring in their eyes.

One by one, the battered Word Bearers extricated themselves from the bridge, clambering back through the half-opened blast doors, until only Nargalax and Enusat remained. None of their ambushers now were whole. Most were lacking one limb or more, and many sported gaping holes and rents punched through their bodies – large craters formed by Enusat's autocannon, smaller detonations from bolters, and liquefied, gaping rents from melta and plasma weaponry. All exposed pellucid grey ghost-flesh and armour, showing the Word Bearers as they were in their prime. There were more than a dozen of them, all told, and they closed in without hurry, walking forwards slowly.

'You go,' said Enusat, urging the Death Guard to make his exit.

'We'll go together,' said Nargalax, snapping off another burst of fire, detonating another assailant's head.

The enemy were closer now, and Enusat depressed his thumb-trigger, letting loose a salvo of fire on full auto. He swung the barrel of his weapon in a wide, sweeping arc, pumping shot after shot into the implacable advance, and empty shell casings tumbled around him, tinkling like so many tiny bells. Muzzle-flare lit up the room like an orange-tinged strobe. The sound was deafening, even through the aural dampeners of his helmet.

In the corner of his eye, Enusat saw a rapidly decreasing number clicking down as he tore through his ammunition store. It was accompanied by a small icon, a bar that was rapidly filling as his weapon's temperature began to soar, even as the barrel began to glow red-hot.

The weight of his fire, combined with Nargalax's and that of the Bloodsworn, who were snapping off shots from outside the bridge, ripped through the enemy, jerking them backwards and half-spinning others as shots clipped them. But the shots had no effect on their spectral forms, the storm of gunfire passing through them without effect.

The legs of one of the corrupted Word Bearers were cut out beneath him by a surging melta-blast, and the creature fell to the ground. With a jerk, the spirit pulled free of the now legless flesh body, leaving it completely behind, and commenced its advance.

With a last torrent of fire, Enusat barked 'Now!' and the Word Bearer and the Death Guard as one put up their smoking weapons and stepped back through the half-open blast doors, covered by the fire of the Bloodsworn.

They backed away, still snapping off shots. The enemy stopped at the edge of the bridge, staring after them. They did not attempt to pursue them. Perhaps they were unable to cross that boundary, for whatever reason, Enusat thought.

In their centre was the warrior that had torn fully loose from his fleshy body. A fan of blades framed his bald head, rendered in monochrome tones of grey. His hands were at his sides. He stared after them. His face was devoid of emotion, but his eyes seemed to hold an accusation. *You left us here*, they seemed to say.

'That was Dol Vaedel,' said Nahren. 'Coryphaus of the Third Host.'

As one, the dead Word Bearers spoke.

'The blightwood grows,' they croaked.

Daal'ak'ath mel caengr'aal.

'Let us leave this place,' said Nahren, bitterly. 'There is nothing here for us. The Third Host is dead.'

WHENEVER MARDUK TRIED to focus on her features, they became blurred and smudged, making them impossible to discern. It was as if they were hidden by a psychic shroud. Indeed, even to try made Marduk's eyes hurt. If he looked at her sideways, focusing past her, he could see that she had normal, unremarkable human features, but whenever his gaze drifted back to her face, it became once more an obscured blur.

'What is this abomination?' breathed Sabtec. There was a tremor in his voice.

'She is an augur, and she is marvellous,' said Marduk. 'Her name is Antigane.'

'How do you know the... *child's*... name, my lord?' asked Sabtec.

'She is telling me,' said Marduk, a smile lighting his features. 'She is a child in body only, this one. The souls of other augurs and skalds dwell within her. So many! Seers, witches, mystics, crones. The line is strong and pure. Before her was one named... Chattor? No, Chattox,' Marduk corrected. 'She was slain by bolt and fire by the gene-kin of the Imperial Fists, though they wore black, not yellow.'

'Templars,' said Sabtec. 'The bastard get of Dorn.'

'Templars, yes,' agreed Marduk. 'I can see them. She is showing me her deaths. Before Chattox was Demedike, and before her was Arabis of Davin. Do I understand that right?'

Marduk laughed softly in wonder.

'Davin?' said Sabtec.

'Oh yes,' said Marduk. 'She is of the true blood.'

I have been waiting for you, she pulsed.

NARGALAX STOPPED IN his tracks, forcing Enusat to halt so that he didn't bump into him.

'No!' said the Death Guard captain. 'She is mine!'

'What is wrong?' said Enusat.

'Treachery,' said the Death Guard captain, still staring straight ahead. All of his humour had evaporated, like a lake under a rising sun, and his right hand reached towards the hilt of his corroded blade. 'She belongs to me!'

'Of what do you speak?' said Enusat. 'Whose treachery?'

Nahren and the two of his Bloodsworn that remained had become aware that something was taking place now, and were turning back. Sensing something amiss, they began to fan out around the lone Death Guard. The Bloodsworn's weapons were not raised – not yet – but Enusat could feel their tension.

'What is this?' growled Nahren, turning and stamping back over the uneven ground.

'I did not lie,' said Nargalax. 'This vessel was as it is now when we found it.'

'I believe you, Nargalax,' said Enusat. 'But what is this treachery you speak of?'

The Death Guard captain turned his head towards Enusat.

'You seek to take that which is not yours to claim,' he said. His blue eye was not smiling now. All that was there was a cold, burning anger. 'Fools. You have damned yourselves with your greed and lust for power.'

'I like not your tone, Death Guard,' said Nahren. 'You are the ones that took something that did not belong to you – this ship.'

'I did not lie,' Nargalax said again. 'Your precious Host was gone by the time I found this ship, claimed by the Garden. The Plague Father's strength waxes strong... His borders expand. I was enacting my duty. A world beyond the veil has been chosen. I *will* send this ship into this world, furthering the spread of

Grandfather Nurgle's domain. I bore you no ill will, nor those whom the Garden has already claimed. But now you will join them.'

'The Garden... of Nurgle?' asked Nahren. 'You speak of it as a sentient thing.'

'And so it is,' said Nargalax. 'For all your books and chanting... you know nothing, little man.'

'There has been no treachery,' said Enusat. 'You are mistaken.'

'I am not,' said Nargalax. 'The treachery... is being enacted even now.'

'Marduk,' snarled Nahren. 'What has the fool done?'

'Killed you all,' said Nargalax, and everything changed.

THERE HAD BEEN a disconcerting lurch, something akin to the dislocation felt during warp transit. A wave of nausea crashed over Enusat, and he felt his gorge rise, acid burning the back of his throat. Then it was past, and the First Acolyte saw that they were no longer standing within the hold of a ship.

'What in the names of the gods?' he said, staring around him.

They were in the depths of a rotting jungle – a *true* jungle. Twisted boughs of decaying trees, of a size and design that defied rationality, curled around each other overhead, forming a nigh impenetrable canopy, hanging with an overabundance of lichen, vines and fungus. In the few gaps in that impossible canopy, sulphuric yellow skies could be glimpsed.

The air was thick with flies, many bloated to gigantic proportions, and the ground was deep in rotting mulch, worms and crawling insects. A foetid river filled with drowned corpses could be glimpsed through the undergrowth, and doleful bells tolled in the distance, as if summoning the devout to a requiem mass.

A spray of blood splattered across Enusat's faceplate, blurring his vision as combi-bolter fire took one of the Bloodsworn in the side of the head. He went down, the bolter in his now dead hands firing wildly. Enusat grunted as a bolt ricocheted off his chestplate and detonated in beneath his left pauldron. Warning icons indicating the extent of the damage to his armour and body flashed before his eyes, but he blinked them away angrily.

Nahren turned, bringing his heavy crozius around in a lethal two-handed arc, but Nargalax met the blow with his left arm. It would have had as much effect had the Dark Apostle struck stone – the weapon was stopped dead.

Nargalax's tentacle curled around the haft of Nahren's holy weapon, trapping it. The Death Guard pulled the Dark Apostle in close with a violent jerk, and rammed his wide-bladed sword into the Dark Apostle's side.

'No!' roared Enusat, levelling his autocannon on the pair of combatants. He did not fire, however, as Nargalax had turned Nahren, shielding himself from the First Acolyte. Enusat could see the tip of the powered blade protruding from Nahren's lower back. It dripped with noxious poisons.

Nargalax twisted the blade, and Nahren hissed in pain, still fighting for control over his crozius. The last remaining sworn brother of the Bloodsworn was circling left, his plasma gun raised to his shoulder.

'You brought this on yourself, Word Bearers,' Nargalax said in a loud voice, his blue eye burning coldly. 'You seek to take that which was not yours. And now you will never leave the Garden.'

The Dark Apostle spat in his face. The acidic saliva dripped down the Death Guard's face, and steam rose from the welts it formed in its passage. The Dark Apostle released the grip of his right hand from the haft of his crozius, and in the blink of an eye he had his bolt pistol drawn. He pressed the barrel up underneath the foetid rolls of Nargalax's chin.

'You are not walking away from here, Death Guard,' said Nahren.

'You are right, Word Bearer,' said the Death Guard captain with a gargling laugh. 'I am not.'

Nahren squeezed the trigger of his bolt pistol, firing up into the Death Guard's rotten brainpan.

The bolt should have blown the Death Guard captain's skull to fragments, but even as the shot was fired, Nargalax's body was transformed into a million crawling, writhing bugs, worms and beetles. They held the shape of the Death Guard captain for the briefest of moments before they collapsed to the forest floor, a seething pile of foulness that dissipated into the undergrowth and was gone.

Nahren slumped to his knees, clutching at his stomach.

'Damn,' said Enusat.

SOMETHING SCRATCHED AT the back of Kol Badar's mind, and his eyes narrowed as he sought its source. There was something very wrong here.

'Coryphaus!' came a warning shout, and he turned

to see a vast pile of foulness made up of millions of worms, beetles, bugs and roaches resolving into the shape of a heavy-set, plate-armoured warrior. Nargalax. Blood dripped from the tip of his plague sword. Word Bearers blood.

'Take them!' he bellowed.

He claimed the first kill, a bolt from his combi-bolter detonating one of the corrupted Guardsmen's heads. Other mortals were ripped apart as the Word Bearers unleashed their firepower on the move, heading for cover, but the enemy were firing now too.

Eschewing any form of cover, the Death Guard planted their feet and began pumping shots at the Word Bearers. Three shots pummelled one warrior-brother backwards, cratering his chestplate, before a fourth took him in the throat. Another dropped to the ground, a stray shot taking him in the side of his knee and almost tearing his leg off. Returning fire, the Word Bearer struck one of the Death Guard, blowing chunks from his chest, but the legionary hardly even rocked backwards, and his return fire dropped another Word Bearer. Truly these were Mortarion's sons.

Another warrior-brother was cut down by Nargalax, his corroded power blade hacking from collar bone to sternum. The wound festered in seconds, turning rotten and foul, and the Word Bearer died with a scream on his lips.

Kol Badar moved towards the Death Guard captain, determined to avenge his brethren. A bolt struck him in the left shoulder, and he growled, more in irritation than pain. He snapped off a burst of shots, killing two of the gasmask-wearing mortals.

He saw two of his Word Bearers round on a single

Death Guard warrior, flanking him. They pounded him with bolt-rounds, but he took it all, even as gobbets of flesh and chunks of his armour were blown from his body. The legionary killed the first of the Word Bearers, pumping him with shells, then turned on the second. The Word Bearer ducked into cover to reload, and the Death Guard walked steadily after him, sliding a fresh drum of ammunition into his own bolter.

Kol Badar ripped the Plague Marine's head off, and at last it slumped to the ground, liquefying as it did so. He snarled in frustration as he saw that he'd lost sight of Nargalax.

He heard a mechanical roar, and glanced across the embarkation deck to see one of his warriors pinned against a wall by his throat, held aloft by the three-metre tall abhuman. The roar he heard was the immense rock-drill that had replaced the creature's right arm, and it turned to a screaming whine as it was thrust up into the Word Bearer's body, shearing through armour, bone and flesh with frenzied ease, as well as drilling half a metre into the adamantium wall behind him.

A targeting matrix locked on to the abhuman, and Kol Badar let the Death Guard's severed head slip from his talons. Snarling, he strode towards the towering ogryn brute, unleashing a torrent of fire as he went.

His bolts embedded themselves no more than a centimetre into the hulking abhuman's flesh before they detonated, spraying plenty of blood but doing only circumstantial damage. Armour plates had been inserted into its body, the Coryphaus realised.

The wounds got the brute's attention, however, and

it swung towards him, the thick, ribbed pipe of its mask swinging around like a grotesque proboscis. Kol Badar stalked directly towards it, still firing, ignoring the bolt-rounds that streaked by him. He unloaded a full clip into the huge abhuman, halving his rate of fire. The idiot creature swatted at his shells as if they were flies, its roars of pain and rage muffled by the thick black rubber mask it wore strapped over its head. Its beady eyes stared out through green-tinged glass goggles, and he saw them narrow to points, realising at last the source of its pain.

With a muffled roar, it broke into a lumbering run towards him, its drill-arm spinning. It lowered its shoulder, intending to slam him off his feet. That suited him just fine.

Using all the power in his gene-enhanced frame, augmented by the strength of the servo-muscles and fibre-bundles of his armour, he struck the charging brute a backhanded blow with his power-taloned fist, sending it crashing to the ground. Its momentum gouged a deep furrow through the deck before it came to rest against a bulkhead, which crumpled inwards against its weight.

Kol Badar closed in, stamping after it. It tried to rise, staggered and fell again. Its gasmask had been half ripped away and hung limp from one side, and its brutish jaw was hanging loose, broken in a dozen places. Its maw was a repulsive, toothless cavity, and it had no nose to speak off, just a pair of slits from which protruded a cluster of mucus-slick cables and pipes. Its eyes were wet and dribbling.

It tried to rise again, this time succeeding, but Kol Badar was on it then, clamping his power talons around its neck. With a savage yank he tore out its throat. The creature tried to bellow, but nothing came from its mouth but a splatter of blood. It stubbornly refused to fall, though; too inured to pain or too stupid to realise that it was already dead.

It rammed its rock-drill into Kol Badar's thigh, whirring madly. His ornate Terminator armour resisted for a moment, then gave way, and the rotating drill ripped through fibre-bundles and flesh, tearing at muscles and churning through bone.

Closing his talons around the abhuman's mechanised arm, Kol Badar forcibly withdrew the drill from his leg, and dark blood gushed from the wound. He fired his combi-bolter into the beast's face, pounding its adamantium-like skull, blinding it and pulping the flesh there; but still it fought on.

Balling its massive hand – a hand that could enclose a mortal man's body in its grasp – into a giant fist, the brute struck Kol Badar in the side of his helmet. The blow dented his helm and snapped two of its tusks, and he reeled back a step, staggering. It was like being hit by a solid artillery shell.

It was on its knees now. Kol Badar mag-locked his combi-bolter to his thigh and limped forwards. He grasped the huge monster's head in his hands and gave a brutal twist, eliciting a sickening crack, and it slumped, finally, to the ground.

Calmly, ignoring the pain of his leg and the gunfire spattering around him, Kol Badar reloaded his combi-bolter.

Marduk's voice came to him then, crackling through the vox-network.

'I have what I came for,' he said. 'It is time to leave.'

'Nahren is still within the ship,' said Kol Badar.

'Leave him,' came the crackling reply. 'He is of no consequence.'

'Enusat is with him.'

This time there was a delay before Marduk answered.

'How far away are they?'

'I don't know – we've had no contact with them.'

'Go,' said Marduk. 'His is a noble sacrifice. He will be remembered.'

Kol Badar was about to argue, but the battle was faring poorly. It had only been under way for minutes, but bodies were strewn across the deck floor. Their spilled blood had attracted the attention of flying insects, which were busy feeding and laying eggs in ravaged flesh. Six of his Word Bearers were already down, as opposed to only two of the Death Guard. The number of human mortals was inconsequential.

'Word Bearers,' he roared. 'We are leaving!'

THOUSANDS OF ROTTING, flyblown heads hung by their hair from the lower branches above them, like so much rotting fruit. They looked down upon these new arrivals, eyes dripping with mucus and pus, and their mouths gaped open.

'The blightwood grows,' they said, as one.

Daal'ak'ath mel caengr'aal.

Already, foetid vines and crawling ropes of roots and stranglethorns had grown over the body of the fallen Bloodsworn. Tiny mushrooms burst from the flesh of his face, and insects and maggots already filled his mouth and eyes. Within moments, he was subsumed into the undergrowth, feeding the decay.

Enusat moved to the Dark Apostle's side, and helped him to his feet.

'I'll be fine,' Nahren said.

Something grotesque fell from on high suddenly, crashing down through rotten branches to fall before Enusat, Nahren and the last of the Bloodsworn. It was a foul, membranous birth sac, and it hit the ground with a wet thump. Something squirmed and writhed within. Enusat lowered his autocannon, but Nahren pushed the barrel of his weapon aside.

'No,' said the Dark Apostle. 'It would not to do raise the ire of the Plague Father, not here in His realm.'

'Did the tainted one speak the truth, then?' he replied. 'Are we truly within the Garden of Nurgle?'

'Look around you,' said Nahren. 'We stand in the presence of greatness.'

A single, curving horn pierced the birth sac flopping around before them, and amniotic fluid, blood and mucus spilled out in a flood. A swarm of insects flocked to the disgusting feast, but Enusat's eyes were locked on the creature rising before them.

The single horn rose from its forehead, and it clawed its way free of the clinging membrane, its spindly limbs slick with birth fluids. It was a gangrel creature. If it stood straight, it would be fully two heads taller than any of the Word Bearers, yet its back was twisted and stooped, its spine clearly visible, protruding through its drowned-man flesh. It had the bloated stomach of a plague victim and the open sores of the diseased. A single great cyclopean eye blinked in its head, filled with cataracts and oozing styes, and its chest heaved as it took in its first, heaving breath.

It saw them, and blinked. Its fleshy, worm-like lips

parted, exposing rotten tusks and gravestone teeth, and worms writhed in its throat.

'Onetwothreefourfivesixseven,' it groaned. It took a lumbering step towards them, legs wobbling like jelly. 'Onetwothreefourfivesixseven, seven, seven, seven.'

It took another step, this one more stable as it got used to the notion of walking. It lifted a hand towards them. Its nails were incrusted with filth.

A second birth sac thudded to the ground behind them, and a third fell nearby. Others crashed through the branches, bringing with them a tumble of rotting leaves and maggots.

'I think it best we leave this place,' said Enusat.

'I am not certain that is going to be a simple task,' said Nahren.

TOO LATE, KOL Badar noticed the worms and millipedes writhing underfoot. Too late he realised that something was taking shape behind him. He turned with a snarl, talons lashing out, but he could not stop the sword thrust in time.

Nargalax's blade took him in the shoulder, the jagged, evil weapon grinding against bone as it spitted him. His flesh burned as toxins and poisons entered his system.

'She's mine,' said Nargalax. 'You have no right.'

He twisted the blade, made Kol Badar hiss.

'This will kill you... you know,' said the Death Guard, almost as an afterthought. 'But it will not be a fast death.'

Kol Badar's vision wavered. There were shouts, and bolts whickered by him to strike Nargalax, but the Coryphaus hardly registered the cries, and the

Death Guard captain merely laughed as he retracted his blade. The Coryphaus was half dragged aboard the *Invisus*, which was adding its own supporting fire, and the shuttle's assault ramp slammed shut. Still the Death Guard's laugh could be heard.

Hor hor hor.

MARDUK WAS WAITING for them as they disembarked, bloodied and battered.

Kol Badar's face was wan and slick with sweat, and he leaned on Sabtec as he hobbled onto the deck.

A child with no face stood by Marduk, and Kol Badar glanced down at her, struggling to focus.

'I hope it was worth it,' he said between clenched teeth.

'Oh, it most certainly was,' said Marduk.

Then the klaxons began to sound, and the smile dropped from Marduk's face.

'GOODBYE,' SAID NARGALAX.

The Death Guard stood on the deck of the *Vox Dominus*, surrounded by fecund growth and the last remnants of his warband. His blue eye was cold with hatred as he stared out at the *Infidus Diabolus* in the distance.

He did not blink as the roiling anomaly dragged the Word Bearers ship through its surging portal, nor when it snapped shut behind them.

It was done.

ENUSAT SUPPORTED THE weight of the Dark Apostle. The lone Bloodsworn remaining of Nahren's entourage ranged out in front, scouting the way. They had been travelling for what – weeks? Months? It was impossible to gauge. The unfathomable jungle spread out before them, immense and immeasurable, and on they tracked.

They had seen such sights as to make Enusat weep in despair and wonder. But none of that mattered now.

Nahren's wound would not close, and while they patched it frequently with the crude poultices they made, held in place with mud and leaves, it was foetid and stinking with foulness whenever Enusat inspected it. The Dark Apostle's skin was waxy and grey, and his veins were black and throbbing.

They saw ships hanging low in orbit from time to time, inert and apparently lifeless. There were dozens of them, of all sizes and shapes. Some Enusat recognised as battleships and cruisers of human design, while others were strange and unnatural – xenos vessels. In places they were so low that the canopy had enveloped them. They looked like ancient ruins, suspended above the noxious plague world, encrusted with filth and hanging with coiling vines. Spindly branches, like reaching skeletal hands, clutched towards those ships that had not yet been claimed.

Some time earlier they had seen a pair of smaller vessels hauling one of the hulks away, dragging it free of the clinging trees and twisting sky-roots. They had not tarried to watch for long, however. A spawn-cluster of tiny, bulbous daemons had burst from an overgrown pitcher plant nearby, spilling out upon the jungle floor, giggling and gnashing their teeth. In a tumble, they had waddled and rolled towards the

Word Bearers. While they were hardly threatening, they were attracting larger beings, things as large as mountains that crushed the jungle beneath their bulk, and so they had hurriedly moved on.

Looking up now through a gap in the canopy, Enusat saw a new ship arrive, blinking into existence. The poor fools, he thought. Do they yet understand their fate?

For a moment, he thought that the ship might be the *Infidus Diabolus*, but then it was obscured once more as the writhing canopy closed over.

'What... is it?' said Nahren, his voice weak.

Enusat shook his head. He must have been mistaken.

'It is nothing,' he said, and they continued trudging deeper into the Garden of Nurgle.

ABOUT THE AUTHORS

DAVID ANNANDALE

By day, David Annandale dons an academic disguise and lectures at a Canadian university on subjects ranging from English literature to horror films and video games, shaping his students into an army of servitors awaiting his signal to rise. He is the author of several thriller and horror novels and the acclaimed short story 'Carrion Anthem' for Black Library. He lives with his wife and family and a daemon in the shape of a cat, and is working on several new projects set in the grim darkness of the far future. Visit him at www.davidannandale.com.

SARAH CAWKWELL

Sarah is a north-east England-based freelance writer. Old enough to know better, she's still young enough not to care. Married, with a son (who is the grown-up in the house) and two intellectually challenged cats, she's been a determined and prolific writer for many years. She hasn't yet found anything to equal the visceral delights of the Warhammer universe and is thrilled that her first piece of published work is within its grim, dark borders. When not slaving away over a hot keyboard, Sarah's hobbies include reading, running around in fields with swords screaming incomprehensibly and having her soul slowly sucked dry by online games.

AARON DEMBSKI-BOWDEN

Aaron Dembski-Bowden is a British author with his beginnings in the videogame and RPG industries. He's written several novels for the Black Library, including the Night Lords series, the Space Marine Battles book *Helsreach* and the New York Times bestselling *The First Heretic* for the Horus Heresy. He lives and works in Northern Ireland with his wife Katie, hiding from the world in the middle of nowhere. His hobbies generally revolve around reading anything within reach, and helping people spell his surname.

JOHN FRENCH

John French is a writer and freelance games designer from Nottingham. His work can be seen in the *Dark Heresy, Rogue Trader* and *Deathwatch* roleplay games and scattered through a number of other books including the award-nominated *Disciples of the Dark Gods*. When he is not thinking of ways that dark and corrupting beings can destroy reality and space, John enjoys talking about why it would be a good idea, and making it so with his own Traitor Legions on the gaming table... that and drinking good wine.

JONATHAN GREEN

Jonathan Green is a freelance writer well known for his contributions to the Fighting Fantasy range of adventure gamebooks, as well as his novels set within Games Workshop's worlds of Warhammer and Warhammer 40,000, which include *Iron Hands* and *The Armageddon Omnibus*. He has written for such diverse properties as *Sonic the Hedgehog, Doctor Who, Star Wars The Clone Wars* and *Teenage Mutant Ninja Turtles*. He is also the creator of the popular Pax Britannia series of steampunk novels, published by Abaddon Books, and has an ever-increasing number of non-fiction books to his name. To keep up with what he is doing, go to *www.jonathangreenauthor.com*

ANDY HOARE

Andy Hoare worked for eight years in Games Workshop's design studio, producing and developing new game rules and background material. Now working freelance writing novels, roleplaying game material and gaming-related magazine articles, Andy lives in Nottingham with his partner Sarah.

ANTHONY REYNOLDS

After finishing university Anthony Reynolds set sail from his homeland Australia and ventured forth to foreign climes. He ended up settling in the UK, and managed to blag his way into Games Workshop's hallowed design studio. There he worked for four years as a games developer and two years as part of the management team. He now resides back in his hometown of Sydney, overlooking the beach and enjoying the sun and the surf, though he finds that to capture the true darkness and horror of Warhammer and Warhammer 40,000 he has taken to writing in what could be described as a darkened cave. His online blog can be found at *http://anthonyreynolds.wordpress.com/* or you can follow him on Twitter @_AntReynolds_

ANDY SMILLIE

Forged from beef and brawn, Andy Smillie emerged from the blacksmith's fire like a slab of Scottish iron. Hailing from the northern reaches of Glasgow, he crossed the border into England intent on conquest, but instead found gainful employment at Games Workshop. Leaving a trail of carnage in his wake, he eventually settled in the Black Library where he works in marketing by day and as a literary superhero by night. His writing credits include a swathe of articles for various sci-fi, fantasy and hobby magazines. His debut work of fiction, 'Mountain Eater', was released in 2011 in the digital publication *Hammer and Bolter*. You can read his blog at *http://asmileylife.wordpress.com/*

CHRIS WRAIGHT

Chris Wraight is a writer of fantasy and science fiction, whose first novel was published in 2008. Since then, he's published books set in the Warhammer Fantasy, Warhammer 40,000 and Stargate: Atlantis universes. He doesn't own a cat, dog, or augmented hamster (which technically disqualifies him from writing for Black Library), but would quite like to own a tortoise one day.

He's based in a leafy bit of south-west England, and when not struggling to meet deadlines enjoys running through scenic parts of it. Read more about his upcoming projects at *www.chriswraight.worldpress.com*

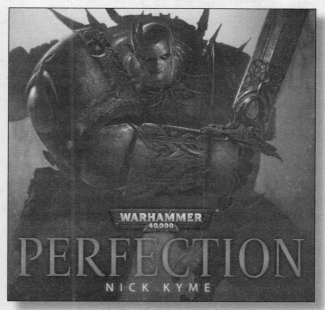

The champions of the Blood God battle for supremacy in the Arena of Blood

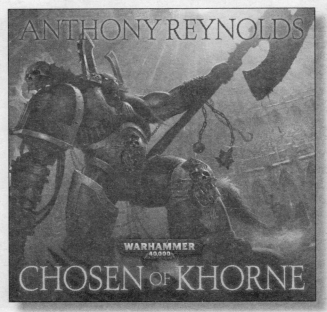

ANTHONY REYNOLDS

WARHAMMER 40,000

CHOSEN OF KHORNE

Download the MP3 from blacklibrary.com
Listen to an extract